SPARE OF THE ALPHA

THE ALPHA KING'S BREEDER
BOOK TEN

BELLA MOONDRAGON

For Joe

CONTENTS

1

THAT'S NOT A BEAR

Aviva

THE WIND HASN'T YET SWEPT LAST AUTUMN'S LEAVES OFF THE FOREST floor. Soft, pale green tufts of spring grass poke out in heaps as I crouch behind a large bramble bush, the earthy scent of the early blooms all around us momentarily stealing my senses.

But only briefly. Ten year old Shoshannah smells like adrenaline and the pancakes with blueberry syrup she had for breakfast as her soft red hair whips across my cheeks, her body rigid and bright green eyes focused on the sparse trees ahead of us.

Lora, six, fidgets on my other side. "Aviva," she hisses, tugging on the sleeve of my tunic. "I have to pee!"

"Shut up, Lora," Shosh whispers, her arm flexed as she draws back her arrow, which looks massive against the child-sized bow I whittled for her as a Solstice gift.

"Breathe in," I whisper against the rim of my little sister's ear. She does, holding her breath. "Line up. Release–"

The arrow whizzes past our hideout and spins through the air. A squeak echoes through the forest before it falls silent again.

"What'd she get!?" Lora bounces upright, squirming from foot to foot as she tries to peer over the bush.

"A squirrel," Shosh frowns, her eyes meeting mine. "This is boring, Aviva. I want to shoot an elk."

I haul her to her feet by the collar of her sweater–which used to be mine as a child and has seen better days. "You can't bring down an elk with a bow that small. When you can shift, you can go on the big hunts with me. This is just practice anyway." I motion to the three rabbits hanging from my belt. "It's enough for supper already."

"Aviva!" Lora whines as she dances around. "I'm going to pee my pants again–"

"Okay, okay, okay." I gently clip a disappointed Shosh on the underside of her chin before guiding Lora to a thicket of alder trees, collecting the squirrel along the way.

Shosh follows behind, lazily swinging her bow. "But you got to hunt deer and elk and all kinds of things at my age."

"Times were different back then," I grunt, holding Lora upright as she attempts to do her business in the cover of the bushes. She gets distracted by a shiny beetle on one of the trees and nearly sends us both toppling over. "Lora, pay attention. You're going to pee on your shoes."

"Times weren't *that* different," Shosh argues, sighing dramatically.

"I assure you that they were. There, see? It wasn't that much of an emergency, was it?" I yank Lora's leggings up and dust the leaves and dirt from her homespun dress and wool jacket.

"But when you were my age–"

"When I was your age," I cut in, giving my sister a sharp look. She frowns at me, but her cheeks go pink as I continue, "I had to hunt to put food on the table for the whole tribe. Everyone who could walk was out in the woods scavenging for anything they could find. You're lucky you get to spend the summer learning to hunt instead of wasting all of your arrows and blistering your fingers just to come home with a fledgling missing its hind quarters because you shot them off."

"Did you do that?" Lora giggles, and I nod, playfully sticking out my tongue at her.

"It's all I had to eat for days, too."

"I wanna play with the bow now!" Lora grabs for the bow, but Shosh yanks it out of her tiny hands.

"It's not a toy, Lora. And it's mine!"

I rise to my knees and plant my hands on my hips, watching the two girls tussle over the shitty little bow I made from thin, roping alder branches. Shosh gives Lora a look that rattles me to my core, however.

"Wipe that scowl off your face," I tell her, and not in the least bit kindly. "You look like Mercy right now."

Shosh sees red at the mention of our eldest, and least fun, sister. "I do not look like Mercy."

"Well, you're acting like her." I peer up at the sky, at the sun starting to creep back toward the horizon. "We've got an hour until we need to head back to the village. We're going to head back now."

Both girls pout and fuss about it but I'm used to it. Ever since the last of the snow melted, I've been taking Shoshannah and Lora out in the woods to learn how to hunt. Lora is mostly here for moral support, even if she's a bit loud and slows us down with her pockets full of rocks and twigs, but in a few years she'll be in Shoshannah's shoes, out here with a bow that looks like it belongs to one of her dolls.

Shosh takes hunting very seriously. She's keenly aware of her surroundings and has sharp senses that will blossom into something deadly over the next decade until she comes into her wolf powers.

But she wants more. And more, and more. Unhappy with the three rabbits and the squirrel she nabbed today, she continues to pout and hiss under her breath as I try to keep the girls on track toward our village.

"One day," she mumbles, sniffling, "I'm going to get a golden elk, and I'll be the best hunter in all of the land. Better than you, Aviva."

"Well, you'd be the first hunter in over a hundred years to snare a golden elk." I give her a little nudge, smiling down at her. "You'd better keep–"

The wind changes course, and I smell… something foreign. Sweet, dark, heavy and hard to describe.

Except I know that scent. Musk and leather. Fire and parchment. Whiskey.

A wolf.

A male.

I grab the girls and toss them in the shelter of two large cottonwood trees. "Do not move," I whisper, but Lora teeters to the side, her rocks falling out of her pockets. I lunge for her, losing my grip on Shosh's collar, and the little devil jumps out from behind the tree with her bow outstretched and an arrow primed and ready.

The word, "No," doesn't even have time to leave my lips before the arrow darts through the air, sure and straight.

A sharp yelp echoes through the forest, bouncing from tree to tree, followed by a low, rattling growl.

"Fuck, fuck, fuck!" I hiss, shoving the girls behind me as a rustling sound fills my ears. There's a small clearing only a few yards from us, down a hill where the spring grass bleeds into a swiftly moving creek. The creek bed is lined with bushes, all tangled and covered in bright green leaves. How Shoshannah saw the impossibly large, dark brown wolf stopping to take a drink from the creek before I did is beyond me.

"I got a bear!" she gasps.

"That's not a fucking bear," I reply under my breath, and push both girls behind me. I shift. My clothing and weapons are fashioned to fit my body in both forms. My knife belt becomes a halter that fits securely over one shoulder, looping over my back and belly. My bow still rests on my back despite it being totally useless without thumbs, but I digress. It doesn't matter now, not when the wolf is lumbering out of the bushes, gasping and snarling in pain.

What was once my dress–secured by loops and string, covers a good portion of my bright red fur, the same color as my hair, and just as thick, curly, and untamable–now falls over my back and billows in the wind. I'm a smaller wolf, for sure, but compared to the beast starting to charge me, I'm honestly just fucking toast at this point.

I lunge forward, stomping on my front legs, baring my teeth and growling like I've gone completely feral. Lora screams. I doubt she's seen the wolf charging up the hill toward us yet. I know I look scary as hell right now, though.

But her scream stops the wolf. He skids to a halt, his ears pinned to the top of his head, Shosh's arrow sticking from his shoulder. Blue eyes meet mine before he peers over my shoulders at the two young girls I'm guarding with my life.

I'll fight to the death for them. I will paint this clearing with his blood before he gets within a foot of them. That's a promise.

I snarl again, edging a step closer, all of my fur standing on end.

He steps back.

"Aviva?" Shosh whimpers. Lora chokes on hiccups somewhere behind me.

I take another step, and the wolf continues to retreat until I've pushed him back down the hill toward the bushes and the creek bed. It's a stalemate now. I'm not going to move or stop snarling until he leaves. He lowers his head in submission–a slight bob to show me he isn't going to harm us–but I'm not anywhere close to believing that. I watch, teeth bared, as he turns his massive head and bites down on the arrow with a grunt, ripping it free of his shoulder. Blood splatters, and behind me, the girls are still trying to muffle their fear.

I keep my eyes on the wolf, on the stranger. He smells so unfamiliar. He's not from our pack, Endova. I know that for sure. He's not from Navvan, either, and definitely not from Teshka, which is over a hundred miles south of here, on the sea.

He starts to turn back to us. I lunge, snarling and growling loudly, and his ears prick forward, then slowly fold back to lay flat once again.

"Aviva!" Lora cries.

The wolf turns from us after another long once over of my face, of my eyes, and hobbles away, splashing through the creek and eventually out of sight.

I shift back to my human form and tie my dress back in place, my hands shaking as I adjust my knife belt and draw an arrow from my quiver, slinging my bow over my front. "Go, now," I tell the girls, stepping into the boots I'd leapt out of moments ago. I pick up my socks, stuffing them in my belt. "Shosh, move it."

"I'm sorry!" she bellows, tears running down her pink stained cheeks.

My heart quakes as I roughly grab both girls and haul them against me, holding them tight. Lora and Shosh wrap their tiny arms around me as I look over my shoulder at the creek, at the woods beyond, everything caught in the glare of the setting sun.

* * *

"Where have you been?" Mercy scowls as I brush past her into the narrow kitchen of our hovel built into the side of a hill, like most of the buildings in Endova. The earthen walls keep the house warm in the winter and cool in the summer and protect us from the biting wind and torrential rains, as well.

I set the dead animals on the butcher block, ignoring her. She grabs my arm.

"I'm talking to you!"

"I took Shoshannah hunting."

"Bah!" She gives me a little shove, knocking my hip bones into the wooden table that houses the butcher block. "It's useless, you know. She's a girl, Aviva."

"So am I." I start skinning the rabbits. Three, and perfectly white. Shosh and Lora will have new mittens for when the weather starts to turn again.

"You'd be better off staying here instead of running off into the woods every chance you get. Your husband isn't going to allow you to shift all day and ignore your duties at home."

"I'm not married yet, Mercy."

She crosses her arms over her breasts, scowling at me. Her dark brown, glossy hair is swept back away from her impossibly beautiful face. She's tall and lithe. Graceful. Lovely. But her soul is rotten, and she's the biggest bitch I've ever met in my life. "You will be after this year's Harvest Festival. Hardan of Navvan is going to give father six goats for you."

I wipe my bloody hands on my dress, turning to her. "And to think I'm only worth four. He must really like me."

She scoffs, looking down her nose at me. "You're not worth the filthy clothes on your back." She snatches the rabbits off the block before I can stop her.

"Hey!"

"Get cleaned up. We're supposed to be in the meeting hall in twenty minutes."

I whirl toward her as she walks away with the rabbits. "Why?"

"Because we have guests." She smirks at me over her shoulder. "From Silverhide. The Alpha has come to call, and he brought gifts." Her smirk turns rancid as her beautiful smile cracks. "Do not get in my way."

2

A GIFT FOR A KING

Ryan

"WHAT HAPPENED TO YOU?" ANDREW ASKS AS I WALK BACK TO WHERE he's waiting with a few wolves and men in their human forms, all of them carrying goods or pulling carts with our tents and what I hope are peace offerings for our new neighbors.

Andrew's light brown hair nearly touches his shoulders now compared to the short cropped hairstyle he used to wear in Crescent Falls. His dark eyes, the color of coal, are brighter, though. Happier. More at ease.

I look my lead warrior, my meager forces commander, up and down as I walk up to the group. The left sleeve of my long sleeve shirt–handmade from linen spun and sewn by hand–is stained with blood. I look down at it and shrug. "I met some friends."

"Friends?" Jacob, who used to run my garage, chuckles.

I smirk as I rest my hands on my hips and scan the small caravan of men and wolves who've been traveling with me for the better part of the day. We left the new territory of Silverhide this morning, before dawn, hoping to reach Endova by dusk.

9

"We're nearly there," I tell the group, tilting my head toward the muddy, not-so-well-beaten trail. "It's clear."

"I dunno," Andrew teases, looking me up and down. "You sure we're not going to run into these new friends of yours?"

I don't pay him any mind as the group starts walking again, the carts bumping over puddles of mud and rocks.

I fall into step behind them, nursing the sharp ache in my shoulder. It's just a muscle wound, thank the Goddess. Whoever put an arrow through my shoulder is a terrible shot.

But judging by the wolf I'd encountered, it was likely one of the girls in her company.

My pack left for Eastonia two years ago. We made it in one piece. The journey hadn't been easy for the second wave of mostly women and young children once we left the Roguelands and the packed, dirt roads we'd traveled on, and the numerous villages we'd been able to stay in on our way.

But once my pack set foot in the valley we now call home... well, it's been the best thing I've ever done.

We miss the modern conveniences from time to time. Television isn't a thing here, obviously. My Uncle Ryatt's impressive powers somehow fuel the lights we picked up in the Roguelands and installed through the small village we constructed over the last two years and somehow allow us things like hot, running water.

But it hasn't been totally comfortable. We nearly starved that first winter. I had to return to the Roguelands to buy cattle, seeds, and extra supplies that next spring. My pack spread out, starting farms, raising animals and planting gardens, but we didn't have anything to trade or use to barter with our only neighbors when their only communal event–The Harvest Festival–came around.

They also wanted absolutely nothing to do with us. All but Jerrod, the patriarch of the Endova pack, and the closest tribe to our village at only thirty miles away.

He sent some of his tribe to help when an illness swept through our village. His hunters showed us the best hunting spots in our little sliver of the Deadland, and what creatures to avoid.

Because there are creatures out here. Stuff out of nightmares, honestly. Stuff that even the fanatic movie directors back in Crescent Falls couldn't cook up in their wildest dreams.

Andrew falls into step with me as the first lights of the village of Endova glisten over the softly rolling hills at the base of the forest. "Are you still going to Moonrise next month?"

"I have to," I reply dryly, rolling my aching shoulder with a wince. "My parents are visiting. My brother, too, with his sons. James will be in charge while I'm gone."

Andrew nods. "Sydney will want to see the village. What you've done is pretty impressive—"

"What we've all done," I correct, glancing at him. Like James, I've known Andrew since I was a kid. His dad is one of my dad's generals, but he broke with our born pack to join Silverhide when I started it. Most of my pack members came to me in that way. Warrior training buddies. College friends. Guys I met during drunken, riotous nights at the bars. Eventually, people started finding their mates, bringing women into the mix. More people started showing up at the gates to meet me, to gauge whether they wanted to join. Soon, I had a hundred members, all sharing a common desire.

Live freely. Be outside in nature. Get back to our roots.

What better way to do that than by nearly starving to death or being eaten by not-so-mythical creatures in some far off land?

Jacob motions for the wolves pulling the carts with our supplies for what will be a three day stay to pull off to the side in a grassy clearing surrounded by trees just outside of the village. "We'll set up camp here," he shouts to me. "You go ahead!"

I nod, stepping out of the way of another passing cart.

Andrew, who I've tasked with learning the customs of the strange tribes who've inhabited the Deadlands since what I assume must be the dawn of time, falls into step beside me. They've lived in relative peace here, fending for themselves against all odds. When Ryatt offered me this opportunity, I expected there to be nothing here. No grass. No trees. Just miles and miles of rolling, barren… nothing. It had been like that during our first days traveling to the center of the

Deadlands, well past the ancient settlements of what was once a great, thriving metropolis. Ella told me the Firestone Witches used to have cities all over the place, but the Deadlands fell to some great blight way back in history I've failed to study.

The barren land eventually gave way to thick forests that surrounded rich valleys of grass and wheat. Bushes covered with berries grow all over the higher hills, and the woods are full of elk, deer, and other small creatures.

The hunting has been my favorite aspect of this move so far. Everyone enjoys it. We can spend our entire days hunting or out working with our hands, building whatever we need, farming, and gathering at night to eat the spoils of our hunts and hard work in the fields.

It's almost enough to blur the memories that still haunt me at night.

Andrew and I follow the group who didn't stay to set up camp into the village, walking between what looks like two small hills.

But they're not hills. All of the buildings in Endova are either built into hillsides, or completely covered in dirt. You can walk on top of them and not know an entire house lies beneath. A fire that never seems to go out even in the worst weather burns at the center of the village. People dressed in homespun in bright, rich colors stop to look at us as we pass into the center of the village where laundry still hangs on lines roping from house to house, and a few shops are shutting down for the night.

The villagers give us our space as Andrew pulls me aside, the rest of our group continuing toward the largest building of them all, the only one not covered by earth. It's two stories tall and made with thick, dark stone. The meeting hall. Not the pack house. There is no Alpha here.

In the shadow of one of the hill houses, he hands me a fresh shirt. "You're bleeding all over the place."

"Will the elders really care that much? They know what we're up against out there in the forest." I shrug out of my shirt regardless, wincing as blood trickles down my arm through a bandage roughly and hastily wrapped around my shoulder. It'll heal–slowly. I possess none of Sydney's gifts. While I'm able to heal more quickly than a human, all this moving around isn't helping.

"They care about a lot more than you realize."

"Which is why I brought gifts, right?"

Andrew nods. "They will barter with you, offering you gifts in return. You have to accept everything. It's an affront if you don't."

"Everything?" I chuckle.

"Everything, seriously." He wads up my bloody shirt and tosses it in the cart loaded with gifts for the tribe. Meat from a recent hunt. Spring berries. Some of our stash of last year's grain harvest. And a half barrel of the strawberry-rhubarb wine Dahlia, James's mate, made.

But the most precious gift is the incredible pelt that catches the light of the fire as the cart passes us. It shines like liquid gold as the men near the entrance of the meeting hall. "Let's get this over with, then," I grumble, shaking out my arm.

Andrew follows me into the meeting hall, which is swarming with bodies and music. A hush falls over the crowd, some of which are standing, and others are seated at several long tables toward the walls. The scent of wine and mead fill the air as people part to allow us to enter, and soon the only sound to be heard over my steady heartbeat are the cart wheels bumping over the uneven stone tiles.

A group of elderly men stands toward the head of the room. Jerrod, their patriarch, is impossible to miss. Tall, broad, with a long, black beard and small green eyes, he turns to me, his mouth stretching into a warm, welcoming smile. "Alpha Ryan," he says in a thick accent, bowing his head. "It's an honor."

"The honor is mine," I tell him, bowing in return. Sure, I'm techni-cally the Alpha King... of my own people. A hundred of them. These people don't care. "I've brought gifts to thank you for your hospitality and allowing us to join your spring hunt." I motion for the cart to be brought closer. The wolf pulling it comes to stop, panting slightly.

"Poor boy. Hurry, unfasten him." Jerrod snaps his pudgy fingers, and two men come running up to his side. "Have this pup brought round some clothes, food, and wine."

"He's fine," I assure him, but Andrew elbows me hard in the arm. I grunt in pain as my wound aches. The wolf is led away, and I glare at Andrew as I motion toward the cart. "Meat, grain, berries, and wine–"

Someone gasps, then shouts ring out in their rough, hard to understand accents.

"Is that…?"

I notice a woman pointing a finger at the cart, at the pelt rolled up and sitting in the back.

"Oh," I smile, walking around to fetch it. I'm rather proud of this pelt, honestly. I've never seen a more beautiful creature in my life, and honestly, it almost felt like a sin to hunt and kill it, but after three weeks tracking it, I had to come back with something. I lift the pelt into my arms. "An elk hide, I believe. I've never seen one this color–"

"My Goddess," Jerrod says, his eyes going wide. "A golden elk?"

A commotion erupts as people jostle toward us, trying to get a better view. I look at Andrew in confusion, but he shrugs, scratching his head as I'm surrounded. Several hands reach out to stroke the pelt, followed by murmurs of shock and awe.

For a moment, I wonder if I've done something wrong.

But Jerrod steps forward.

"Uh, here," I say, shoving the pelt into his arms. He nearly drops it.

The crowd goes quiet as Jerrod runs his meaty hand over the pelt. Is he… crying?

A glimmer of red catches my attention in the far corner of the room. Red, thick, curly hair inlaid with… seashells?

Dark brown eyes meet mine in a glare. I glare back, the wound on my arm singing in pain.

Well, well, well. If it isn't the little red wolf who looked like she was ready to rip my head off earlier today.

"This is for us?" Jerrod asks, stealing my attention away from the beautiful, furious looking young woman trying to melt into the wall.

"It's for you, Jerrod," I tell him.

His eyes go even wider, if that's even possible.

"For this, I give you my daughter." He snaps his fingers, and people start moving.

"I.... *What?*"

3

THE CURSED ALPHA

Aviva

THE MEETING HALL IS CROWDED FROM WALL TO WALL. I HUG ONE OF the walls, my back pressed flat against it as I try to blend in with the dark stone. Everyone is merry as they walk between tables laden with food and drink. Everyone in attendance has worn their finest fabrics and beads. Many of the single, of age, young women have truly gone all out, in fact.

I cross my arms under my less-than-ample breasts and tap my nails against the long gold chains looping around my neck, inlaid with multicolored beads of turquoise and amethyst.

The necklace is one of the few things I have left of my mother except for Shoshannah and Lora. Mercy didn't want the necklace because turquoise is a stone rather than a gleaming gem, and amethyst "washes her out," or so she says. In fact, she didn't want much of mother's things at all when she died six years ago, a few days after Lora came into the world. Her dresses were taken apart and refashioned. Her knickknacks were gone in a matter of hours. She simply… disappeared, like mist into the ether.

I run my fingertips over the necklace and continue scanning the crowd at the thought of my mother. Mercy and Lora look like her with their dark brown hair that never seems to tangle, and her big, green eyes. Where Shosh and I got our dark eyes and insanely temperamental red hair, I have no idea, but we stick out like sore thumbs.

A young blonde woman wearing a pale yellow woven dress and golden bangles on each wrist bumps into me. "Gods, there you are!" She shoves a goblet of wine into my hand and kisses me roughly on each cheek. "I didn't think you'd come tonight, but I heard Matilda tell Rochel that she heard Miriam saying that she saw Mercy basically dragging you here by your hair!"

I roll my eyes to the ceiling and laugh. "Mercy didn't drag me anywhere, I assure you, but I was forced to come, yes."

"Did she dress you?" Freya is her name, and she's my closest friend. My only friend, if I'm being honest. Her glacier blue eyes sweep over the frumpy red dress tied at the waist with a leather belt. "It's huge on you!"

"I'm pretty sure it's a bed sheet," I grumble into my wine before taking a huge drink. The wine is sweet and full, landing like aged honey on my tongue. Freya picks at the short hem of her own dress. Compared to her, I'm dressed like one of the elders who is long past their prime hunting days and has settled into a life of sitting around and bickering with the younger folk. Showing skin isn't considered crass by any means. Hell, there's several men walking around with their shirts off right now despite the slight early spring chill in the air outside. Freya's legs are on full display as she steps beside me and rests her back against the wall.

Most of the clothes we wear are made to be functional while shifting to prevent tearing. Everything is made by hand, of course, woven on looms. Shredding dresses apart every time I left the house would be entirely wasteful.

But if I were to shift now, I'd get tangled in this beast of a dress. I'd suffocate, likely, strangling myself in the fabric.

"You're awfully quiet," Freya smirks, nudging my shoulder.

"Cannon is looking over here, you know. I think he's hoping you'll look back at him."

"Cannon is looking at you," I correct, giving her a nudge back. "Anyway, Mercy reminded me that my father means to sell me to the highest bidder a few months from now when the tribes meet for the Harvest Festival. So far, I'm worth roughly… six goats. I'm practically off the market. I'm not sure anyone can compete with that kind of bride price."

Freya snorts a laugh. "Speaking of Mercy." Her eyes slide to mine as she tilts her head toward my graceful sister, who is laughing prettily as she entertains a group of our warriors. Her coy smile and fluttering eyelashes hide the sour glint to every word that leaves her lips.

"Her dress is beautiful," Freya sighs, and she's right. She's right, because I was the one who made it… for myself. "She's hoping to catch the attention of the Alpha of Silverhide, isn't she?"

"She's stretching it out with her massive–"

The main door to the meeting hall opens, sending a rush of night air into the space. I can't see over the crowd, but I know the Alpha has arrived based on the excited and curious murmurs drifting through the air.

I settle back against the wall with a sigh.

Freya stops trying to catch a glimpse of him and turns back to me. "I'm shocked your father allowed him to come here after all the rumors swirling about him."

I arch my brow. "What rumors?"

Freya beams with excitement at the notion that she has gossip to spread to me. "You didn't hear? He went to Navvan to try to introduce himself, and their elders wouldn't allow him into the village, claiming he was cursed."

"Cursed?" I tip back my wine, shaking my head. "Cursed, how?" I don't know much about this Alpha other than that he's related to Alpha King Ryatt in some way and comes from a far off land called Crescent… *something*. I don't know, and I don't really care. We're far enough removed from the Roguelands that word about the happenings in Eastonia reaches us weeks, if not months, after things happen.

This Alpha simply showed up deciding he was going to settle here.

"I heard," Freya hisses over a rush of fresh murmurs, "from my grandmother, who heard this directly from our priestess's mouth, mind you, that the priestesses in Navvan said the Alpha has a stone heart."

"A stone heart? That seems bothersome and inconvenient–"

Freya grabs my arm. "I heard that he has a stone heart because he *murdered* his own mate! That's why he's here in the Deadlands. He got thrown out of his old territory by the king himself."

I frown at her. "Freya, do you know how ridiculous that sounds?"

She shrugs. "It's what I heard. Grandma said he reeks of a wolf who's fallen out of the Goddess's favor, and therefore the Navvan wouldn't allow him to even speak to their patriarch." She shakes her head. "Can you imagine, Aviva? Killing your own mate?"

"I can't." I can't because the idea of finding a mate is so far from my mind that it feels foreign and strange. I don't know anyone who's ever found their supposed fated mate. A bond destined in the stars by the Goddess. I don't think it's real. In fact, I think it's a fairy tale. We don't mate for love. Not in the tribal lands, at least. Women come of age and are married off, sought for their skills and physical attributes, and are married to members of other tribes to prevent inbreeding.

There's so few of us in the Deadlands. I'm pretty much related to everyone in Endova in some way, shape, or form.

So, my fate is marrying Hardan, who I'm hopefully not related to, and living in his tribe for the rest of my life.

I haven't put much thought into marrying. I've done all I can to prevent it from happening, actually, but as the daughter of the patriarch, I'm pretty much a princess without a fancy dress and crown of jewels on my head.

But because of Mercy, I'm generally overlooked. I'm okay with that.

"Look, there he is!" Freya says with a nudge, pointing her finger through the crowd.

I look out over the crowd and spot…. *No.* I blink, then glare at the impossibly tall, broad man towering over my father. His stormy blue eyes meet mine in a glare as well and I find them... too fucking familiar.

Then I see the blood soaking through his fresh, light gray shirt. A wound, I realize with a twisting sensation in my stomach, that's on his *shoulder*.

"That's him!" Freya hisses excitedly, shaking me so hard I nearly drop my wine. The freshwater clam shell beads woven throughout the two small braids framing my face clink together, but I haven't dropped my gaze from the Alpha, and he hasn't even blinked.

The crowd rushes toward him again and then all I can see is the top of his head.

"What are they freaking out about?" Freya stands on her toes to try to see over the crowd. Her eyes go wide and she gasps.

"What?" I ask, standing on my toes now.

A glint of gold. The Alpha is handing my father a pelt of pure–*gold*. "This is for you," he says in a low, steady voice. My stomach twists as I watch the Alpha thrust a golden elk pelt into my father's arms like it's nothing. *Like it means nothing*.

"For this," Father chokes, "I give you my daughter–"

Another excited gasp ripples through the crowd. Out of the corner of my eye I see Mercy start making her way through the crowd looking smug, her cat-like eyes creased as she passes a group of young women who look particularly disappointed.

How did he get a golden elk? How the fuck–

"Aviva?" Father booms. "Where is Aviva?"

My blood runs cold. I back into the wall again, praying to meet a doorway by some miracle, but I'm met with hard stone instead.

Mercy stops in her tracks, her eyes narrowing into slits. "Aviva?" she hisses, her cheeks turning red with sudden fury.

Then I'm being grabbed. An older man yanks on my arm, and I make the mistake of yelping in surprise. Father looks right at me, smiling widely. "There she is. Alpha Ryan, my daughter–"

"No!" I shout, yanking my arm back.

The entire room goes so silent I can hear my own heartbeat.

I look up at Alpha *Ryan*. What an odd name. It sounds unfinished.

And he–he doesn't look like any of us. I've never seen anyone as tall or as broad. I know beneath the fabric of his shirt he's wholly, utterly built. Built like a stone temple, able to withstand wind and rain and foes coming to collect. Solid muscle.

He stares at my father in disbelief. "I'm sorry, I think I didn't understand–"

"My daughter, Aviva," Father takes my arm and pulls me toward them. Digging in my heels doesn't stop my body from moving over the uneven stone. "For the pelt. You have given me a gift worth more than I have to offer in return–"

"I don't need anything–" Alpha Ryan grunts as the blond man standing at his side elbows him sharply in the side. It's a movement that doesn't go unnoticed, at least to me.

"My daughter, Aviva. She is older, yes, at twenty-two, but she is able to bear children. She is strong, fit, and a skilled hunter. She will help fill your tables and carry on your lineage."

"Father, let me go," I hiss.

He ignores me, continuing, "A wife from my tribe is my gift to you, Alpha." And with that, he practically throws me against Alpha Ryan, and cheers from the crowd around us split the air into pieces.

Alpha Ryan catches me, steadying me with a hand on my shoulder before quickly letting me go.

He's warm. Heat radiates from him like I'm standing beside a fire. The Alpha looks down at me in shock, then frowns, but the man beside him whispers in his ear in their strange dialect. They speak our language but faster, with a heavy, lifted accent. I hear the stranger say, "You can't refuse," and I know my fate is sealed when Alpha Ryan sighs and tears his gaze from mine.

He turns back to my father, who shakes his hand.

And I am betrothed to the Alpha of... whatever pack he comes from. Silverhide. That's it.

"A toast," Father exclaims as my heart beats out of rhythm. A new goblet of wine is thrust into my hand, the deep red liquid spilling over the rim. "To Alpha Ryan, of the pack Silverhide, and my daughter, Aviva. May your union be fruitful."

"May your union be fruitful," the crowd echoes.

Standing side by side with Alpha Ryan, I scan the crowd, my face flushed and pale. I catch Freya's gaze. She gapes at me, her eyes nearly popping out of her head. A few young women our age crowd her, whispering enthusiastically. Word will spread in minutes about this, I'm sure. Anyone who missed this moment will know the details of how I was traded for... well, I can admit being given away in marriage in exchange for a golden elk pelt is the highest of compliments. Despite everything, I feel more than a little smug when my gaze lands on Mercy, who's simmering with fury at the edge of the crowd, leaning her hip against one of the tables laden with food.

"We'll hold the ceremony in four nights, on the full moon," Father says to us even though I'm trying to find the quickest, easiest route out of here. "Can you stay the extra day? It's just a hand-fasting, since our traditions dictate binding ceremonies take place on the Harvest Moon, during the festival this fall."

"Oh, uh, sure," Alpha Ryan grunts, then drains his wine.

Father squints, then gasps, grabbing the Alpha's arm. "Alpha, you're injured? Who did this to you?"

Panic catches in my lungs, making it impossible to breathe. I hold the Alpha's gaze as his eyes slide to meet mine. Father will have Mercy whip the breath out of Shosh, I already know it.

But Alpha Ryan holds my gaze, one of his dark brows lifting ever so slightly as he... smirks.

"It might be a good thing your daughter is a skilled hunter," he says in his low, steady voice that sends a shiver of warmth licking down my spine. "I'm accident prone, apparently."

4

I DON'T LIKE YOU

Ryan

"You're sure there's no way out of this?" Jacob asks Andrew two hours later. We're sitting around a campfire roughly a half mile outside of the village.

Andrew nods, glancing at me before hugging his knees. "These tribes are steeped in tradition, guys. I don't know what else to say. If Alpha Ryan refused the girl, he would have been offered another, and another, and if he'd refused to marry outright, she would have been given as a… concubine, perhaps."

I close my eyes for a moment and sigh around the rim of my water jug. The sweet, heavy wine and mead I'd been served over and over again, my cup never empty, has my head pounding already.

But the second I close my eyes, I see her. Aviva. What a name. It dances over my tongue like a song, and it seems fitting for her.

She's a very strange woman, and I mean that in the nicest way. She has a glare that could slice through glass and make mountains tremble in fear. And those eyes? The darkest shade of brown I've ever seen. They seem depthless, unending.

25

It was easy to spot her in the crowd when I arrived. Her wolf had been a sight to see earlier in the day with its bright red, curly fur. Her hair matches that fur perfectly, falling over her shoulders and back in thick, tangled curls with little braids throughout. Aviva seems untamed, wild, and sharp.

But I'm not looking for a wife.

And she certainly didn't seem happy with the arraignment, either.

"Did anyone know the significance of the pelt we gave Jerrod?" I ask the group of men sitting around the fire. No one speaks. I let out my breath. "Andrew, what is hand-fasting?"

"Uh, I believe it's like… an engagement, maybe. Or a less formal approach to marriage." He looks around, and I feel utterly out of place, not for the first time.

We know so little about these people. The terrain in the Deadlands has been one thing. Learning the culture and customs of those who call this place home has been tricky to navigate, more challenging, in my opinion, than setting up a new territory and trying to survive our first few hard winters.

"It might not be a bad thing," Jacob says with a shrug. "We could use someone like her in our pack. She knows the tribes. She grew up here in the Deadlands."

He's not wrong. "I'm being forced to take a woman away from her family because her father traded her for a pelt I meant to give as a gift."

"These people don't trade and barter like we're used to. And… It's obvious Jerrod has wanted an alliance with us since we arrived. They have bride prices for their women, and the pelt… Well, it was worth a whole hell of a lot more than a few bags of grain and a keg of mead in return." Andrew blows out his breath. "We do need access to the Harvest Festival," Andrew says slowly, meeting my gaze. "This is the alliance we were lacking."

"He's right," Jacob breathes. "We need to be able to trade with the other tribes and barter our own wares, otherwise we risk another winter with minimal supplies."

"We can trade in the Roguelands," another man, Turner, cuts in.

He's young, single, and headstrong. He was also in attendance when the patriarch of Navvan basically chased us off their territory with a spear.

"It would take us over a month to reach the Roguelands with carts laden with wares to trade. It's not a feasible option."

Another man on the other side of the fire adds, "We need to be more careful about what we trade, otherwise all of us will end up with wives."

A ripple of laughter echoes around the fire but it's not enough to break through the tension in the air.

Me marrying this perfect stranger is a solution to our problems. That's the unfortunate truth. They're right about her being our way in, our way to get comfortable with the three tribes of the Deadlands. In the future, I'm hoping more Alphas will bring their people here to spread out and pave their own territories, and I want the tribes on my side when that happens.

Aviva is from Endova, the largest tribe. "I do have to marry her," I tell them. "For more than one reason. We need to stay allies with Jerrod and the Endovians. We need her help back home, if I'm being honest."

"Then you're doing it?" Jacob asks.

"I don't see that I have much of a choice. Plus, you're right about the Harvest Festival. That's our only opportunity to mingle with other people. For trade, of course. But also to beef up our own numbers. We have several single men who need to find wives and start families of their own. We need to integrate ourselves, and my *wife* is how that'll happen." The words taste strange on my tongue.

The men confer quietly as I rise and dust off my pants. It's night. The stars are out and thick overhead, and the moon is nearly full. I should be going to bed to prepare for the upcoming hunt, but I walk past my tent and out into the cool night air.

The forest around the village is sparse and open. I wanted to explore it before we settled in at our camp, but the night took a turn. Several of my men are drunk, most of them against their will. Food and drink had been flowing freely and those who came to the meeting hall couldn't leave without trying a glass of each of the numerous wines and meads.

We'd been fed like kings. I step over a few of my men in their wolf forms as they sleep on the cold, hard ground; totally full of food and wine.

Eventually, the soft murmuring of conversation fades, and I'm alone in the woods, my hands stuffed in my pockets as I pick my way along a dry creek bed.

I need to clear my head enough to think this through. I had no intention of marrying. Having a child? Well, perhaps. I do need an heir, but they're ways to do that that keep me separated from the woman bearing said child. I could use a breeder like my grandfather, and just... not fall in love with her like he did. I could adopt, sure. I could say fuck it and let my pack fall to James and whatever sons he has with Dahlia.

The thought of James sends a pang of guilt ringing through my chest.

Hadley pops into my mind. The memory of that night in the car when I drove her away from Sydney's house comes rushing back, flooding my senses. She unbuckled her seatbelt and kissed me while I was sitting at a stoplight. I'd been so surprised I didn't know how to act, but it didn't feel... right.

Everything from that moment forward was confusion. I wanted her, but I didn't. I felt the bond but it was all wrong, upside down and twisted. Now I know why. She was working with the enemy, right under my nose. It was like our bond was trying to show me that so I could *help her* get out of the mess she made.

Instead, I killed her.

I felt our bond snap when I took her life. I felt like I was being torn to pieces when she took her last breath while my jaws were still closed around her throat.

I left Crescent Falls hoping to leave her ghost behind, but I can still feel her here, right now, watching me through the shadowed woods. It's like she's tugging me along, luring me deeper into the woods where the creatures from my wildest nightmares reside.

I turn to the left and follow the creek again. The water is calm and shallow enough that I can see the rocks beneath glimmering in the moonlight. A structure comes into view. An old, toppled stone building rises between the trees. In the moonlight, I catch glints of silver littered throughout, or metal, or something of the like.

I take another step toward the building, which is missing its roof and nothing more than a stone outline of what once stood there, when a soft wisp of movement catches my eye.

* * *

AVIVA

ALPHA RYAN SLOWLY TURNS HIS EYES UP TO MEET MINE. HE DOESN'T relax when he sees me standing on the remnants of a stone archway. "Are you going to shoot me?" he asks, crossing his arms over his broad chest.

I hold my arrow in place, my muscles locked and tight. I don't say a word to him as he lowers his gaze and attempts to peer inside the structure.

"What are you guarding?" he asks. "I was wondering where you ran off to during the feast."

"You shouldn't be this far from your camp." I adjust the arrow so it's aimed directly at his heart as he moves closer to the building. "There's all kinds of dangerous things out here."

"I think you might be the most dangerous of them all," he says dryly, grunting a bit as he crouches to peer through the gaps in the stone wall.

I keep my arrow locked even though he seems unfazed by it. "I'm actually glad I ran into you again tonight. Third time's the charm, I guess." He rises, his eyes meeting mine.

This is the third time we've encountered each other in the last day but the first time we've spoken. The first time, we'd been in wolf form. The second, I'd been handed off to him in the promise of marriage and ran away the second my father had his back turned.

I went home and changed out of the bed sheet dress and into something more comfortable. It's a pale cream wool that I wove specifically for shifting. A high slit shows off my hip bone as I turn to follow him with my arrow. "What do you want? Are you here to take what you think is already yours?"

He chuckles–a deep, rolling sound. "No. I'm not."

"Then why did you follow my scent here?"

"I can't even pick up your scent, Aviva." My name rolls off his tongue in his accent and it sounds… beautiful. I turn my spine to steel, my arm beginning to tremble from the strain of holding my arrow back and poised to strike. "How do you keep it covered so well?"

"If you were a better hunter, maybe you'd know."

His eyes meet mine, a soft, dark blue in the moonlight. I can readily admit he's handsome. He has chiseled features that make him look like some kind of god of old. His beard is neatly trimmed but thick, covering a jawline that could cut glass.

No wonder I ran off against the whispers of disappointment and awe that hugged the meeting hall. Every young woman in that room had been watching his every move while praying he was watching theirs.

"You can ask for my sister instead, you know," I tell him.

He tucks his hands in his pockets and looks up at me. "The one who shot me through the shoulder? She's rather young, don't you think?"

I scowl down at him. "Not Shoshannah. Mercy is my elder sister. She's single and of marrying age. She's better looking than I am. You'd be happier with her."

He rolls his lower lip between his teeth and chuckles again. "What? You don't want to marry me? Even though we've known each other for so long? What has it been now… seven hours?"

"You're a sarcastic prick," I shout, and his answering smile works its way up my spine, leaving me slightly dizzy.

"I've been called worse." He paces directly below me, unfazed by the arrow pointed at the top of his head. "You should come down before you break your neck."

"Then we'd both be out of this marriage."

"I don't like this either," he tells me, leaning casually against the column of the archway. "But I think we both know we don't have a choice."

"You're an Alpha, aren't you? Don't your people have different customs? Isn't that way you're here? To try to overpower and change us? Simply throw my father off a cliff and take over the tribe like you intend to."

He frowns at me. "No." He picks a piece of lint from his shirt and looks up at me. "I'm here because I wanted to be. I'm here, in your neck of the woods, because I need your father as an ally, and he's been kind to my pack so far. I understand that refusing his gift, his payment for the pelt–"

"The golden elk," I remind him.

He rolls his eyes. "For the pelt," he continues dryly, "it would be considered rude to deny him what he offered in exchange. So, you're to be my wife unless you call it off."

"I can't."

"Why not?"

"Because that's not up to me."

"You'd be the one marrying. You don't have a say?"

"Of course I don't."

He furrows his brows. Gods, this man knows nothing about our kind, does he?

I scoff and relax my arms, sliding my arrow back in the quiver. "Did you really come here blind, with no notion of our culture and how you would be welcomed by the tribes who inhabit this land?"

With practiced grace, I jump down ten feet to the forest floor and rise, looking up at him with my hands planted on my hips. He gapes at me for a moment as he looks up at the stone archway, then down at where I now stand.

I dust off my dress even though it's immaculate. "What? You've never seen someone jump before?"

"What are you?" he asks, taking a single step in my direction.

I let myself feel smug for a split second. "Just a hunter."

His gaze sweeps over me in a way that makes every downy hair on my body stand on end. "You seem like a lot more than that."

It's the first time anyone has ever said anything like that to me. I bury the warmth rising in my chest, banishing it. "Ask for Mercy instead. I'm doing you a favor."

"And would me taking your sister over you be doing you a favor?" His eyes light on mine and hold. "Do you have ties here, a lover–"

"I don't cook."

"I don't need a cook."

"I don't like sewing unless it's for myself."

"All right–"

"I don't like you," I say pointedly, and he smiles.

"I don't like you either."

We stare at each other knowing this is pointless. Alpha Ryan doesn't understand why it's impossible for me to call this off myself. I'm just a woman. The tribes are patriarchal. I have no standing. What my father and the elders say goes.

But he does understand one thing about the tribes. When you're given a gift, you keep it. When you're given a blessing, you cherish it. When you're given something you don't like, you suck it up and accept it.

Because it's the only way to survive in a world that's dead set on killing us.

A low growl echoes in the distant forest in emphasis. "Go back to your camp, Alpha Ryan. It's not safe out here." I shift before he can reply and run off in search of the noise.

5

IMPRINT

Aviva

RAIN PATTERS ACROSS THE WOODEN ROOF COVERING ONE CORNER OF the old temple. I roll off the makeshift bed of hay and wool blankets I keep here. I stretch, rolling my neck. My hands are still bloody from the rogue I encountered last night as I gather my weapons and head down to the creek.

I sleep out here sometimes, especially when the weather is nice. The old temple is just far enough from the village where I don't have to worry about running into anyone during my nightly hunts but also close enough to keep me out of harm's way from the beasts that linger in the thick forest beyond the village.

I'm washing my hands when I catch Alpha Ryan's lingering scent. I forgot he'd come here last night, encountering me by accident, I believe. I try not to think about it as I walk back to the village, but it's hard not to imagine every facial expression, especially the wry twist of his lips whenever I spoke.

Something about Alpha Ryan grates on my nerves. Maybe it's just because he's a male. Maybe it's because he talks back as much as I do, each remark more cutting than the last. If we are to wed, it's not going to be an easy marriage. Maybe he'll understand that and leave, taking Mercy with him.

I hike the six rabbits I snared over the course of the night over my shoulder as I walk into the village which is already up and bustling like usual. No one even looks in my direction as I cross the main square. No one ever notices me. No one but Alpha Ryan, who is standing beside one of his supply carts divvying out bags of grain to a small circle of villagers. He watches me walk by. I don't look at him until I pass, then throw a glare over my shoulder.

He chuckles and looks back at his cart, but I catch him looking at me again, one final time, before I cross between two hill houses and step down into mine.

I've barely crossed the threshold before Mercy's hands are at my throat. She shoves me against the snug, earthen wall of the entry. "Where have you been?"

"Hunting," I snarl, shoving her back.

"Do you realize what happened last night and how embarrassing it was when you ran off? Father gave you to an Alpha, Aviva."

"I guess I'm worth more than six goats, huh?"

She snarls at me. "I should have been the one Father chose. I'm the oldest, and I mean, look at you, Aviva. Covered in blood and dirt, twigs stuck in your hair. What was father thinking?"

"There was a rogue ten miles north of the village. I had to take care of it."

"You're meant to be here weaving and sewing like the rest of us! Not running through the woods showing off–"

"I'm not showing off," I growl.

Mercy looks me up and down, her eyes lingering on the slit in my dress. "Sure, Aviva. I saw you walk past the Alpha just a few moments ago." She reaches down and tugs on the hem of my dress. "Do you think you can tempt that man? Have you looked in the mirror lately?"

"I'm sorry I was given to him instead of you. It wasn't up to me, Mercy. You know that as much as I do. I doubt the Alpha even knew what he was doing when he gave father that pelt."

"Don't act so smug," she growls. "Father just wanted to be rid of you."

I doubt our father remembers I exist unless he needs me for something. "Let me go. I need to dress these rabbits."

"I'm not done!"

"What do you want, Mercy? Do you want me to fall on my knees and beg your forgiveness for being thrown at the Alpha you had your eye on? This wasn't up to me."

"If it were up to you, you'd live in the woods like the beast that you are!"

"I might be a beast, but at least I'm not a sniveling, jealous bitch! Let me pass!"

Mercy's hand meets my cheek in a vicious slap that knocks me slightly off kilter. I gasp, my vision going red, and lunge for her. This wouldn't be the first time we've gone at it like this.

But a squeak in a doorway down the hall stops me before I catch Mercy by the throat and slam her to the ground like she deserves.

Lora and Shoshannah are standing side-by-side, owl eyed and worried. Mercy chuckles slyly when she notices them standing there. "Oh, don't look so glum, Shoshannah. It does nothing for your features."

Shoshannah's full lower lip quivers before she turns her expression to steel and glares at Mercy. "You need to say sorry for hitting Aviva."

Mercy rolls her eyes, planting her hands on her ample hips. "Oh, Shoshannah. Now that Aviva's being married off and leaving us, you'll have to start acting like a woman. You're not going to go hunting anymore, do you understand? You'd be lucky to be married off to someone half as wealthy with a quarter of the territory our dear sister now has, for some fucking reason." She throws a glare at me and continues, "Actually, you look so much like Aviva that I doubt anyone would want you, anyway."

"What the fuck is your problem?" I snarl, giving Mercy a shove.

Shoshannah fumes, but Lora is teary eyed as she clutches the teddy bear I used to sleep with every night as a child. I look between the girls, hiking the rabbits back over my shoulder. I don't want them to see this. "Both of you, come with me."

Mercy opens her mouth to protest as both girls sprint toward me, but I open the door and trap her behind it. "Hey!"

"Hurry now, before the wicked witch catches us and turns us into toads," I taunt, and both girls giggle and run outside. I slam the door behind me, blocking out Mercy's curses and shouts, and walk behind the girls through the village.

"Where are we going?" Shoshannah asks as Lora grabs my hand, her other hand clutching her bear.

"To clean the rabbits in peace." We pass the meeting hall where Alpha Ryan and the blond man from last night, I assume his Beta, or whatever his second is called, are still standing with their cart.

I don't look at him as we walk by, but I can feel his gaze on the stinging, red side of my face where Mercy's hand left a welt.

His gaze lingers as we cut between two hills and begin walking back into the woods where I belong, according to Mercy.

* * *

"Are you really leaving?" Shosh asks, knee deep in the creek with a rabbit pelt in her hands. She washes it off in the calm water, her skin pink to the knees from the chill.

I glance at Lora, who's building a house for the fairies on the creek bank, before saying, "Yes, I am." It's the first time I've accepted my fate. It settles in my stomach like a large rock, weighing me down.

"Can I come too?"

"No, Shosh. You can't. You have to stay here and take care of Father and Mercy."

"I hate Mercy," she grumbles, shaking out the pelt before laying it on a flat rock with the others to dry in the sun.

"You don't hate her," I sigh.

"I do. She's so mean. She hit you. We're not supposed to hit."

I chew my lower lip, thankful my hands are busy skinning the remaining rabbits. Otherwise, I'd be tempted to cup the hand shaped welt on my cheek. "Mercy wants to get married and is jealous that I'm getting married first, is all. She'll calm down once I'm gone."

"Why is she so mean to you?"

I toss her another pelt, and she deftly starts rinsing it. "I don't know." I think I know, but I don't like thinking about Mama. Shosh was only four when she died. Mama was dead before she even got to hold Lora for the first time. But I was sixteen, and Mercy was seventeen. We'd been there when she took her last breath–and whispered her last word. Aviva.

She'd said my name, not Mercy's. She'd reached for my hand, not Mercy's.

I close my eyes at the memory and sigh.

"Hello," Lora says, giggling.

I open my eyes as Alpha Ryan's voice ripples through the clearing around us. "Hi there."

I stand abruptly, and Shosh, taken off guard by a stranger's voice nearby, drops the pelt in the water where the current starts carrying it away. She shrieks in panic, but the Alpha scoops it out of the water, shakes it off, and hands it back to her.

Shoshannah has no idea she's staring at the wolf she shot with her arrow yesterday, but I do. I clutch the handle of the blade I've been using to skin the rabbits as the Alpha's gaze turns from her to me.

Alpha Ryan motions to the rabbits. "Did you catch these yourself?" he asks Shosh.

"I'm Lora!" Lora shouts, bouncing up and down.

"Hello, Lora. I'm Ryan," he laughs.

Shoshannah, still standing in the creek, gives him a skeptical once over before edging through the water in my direction. "Aviva got these rabbits. I got a few yesterday, but Mercy gave them away."

I frown. I was wondering what happened to the three rabbits and the squirrel Shosh snared during our trip yesterday. My eyes stay on Alpha Ryan, however, as he stands on the opposite side of the creek from us. Shosh can tell I'm tense and is acting accordingly, squaring her little shoulders and turning her expression to something unreadable and slightly bored, but Lora is giggling, swinging her bear around, and enthusiastically talking about her fairy house.

Alpha Ryan nods along, his eyes occasionally flickering to mine.

"I'm going to be a hunter like Aviva when I grow up," Lora concludes. "Shoshannah is training with Aviva to be a hunter too. Oh, yesterday, did–did you know she shot a wolf with an arrow because she thought it was a bear?"

"Did she?" Ryan chuckles, his eyes sliding to mine again. "That's very impressive. What is she going to do with the pelt?"

Shoshannah tilts her chin. "I didn't kill it. But next time, I will–"

"We don't kill other wolves, Shoshannah," I say quietly, keeping my eyes on Alpha Ryan. My gaze grazes over his arm. If he's wearing a bandage beneath his shirt, I can't tell. "Unless they deserve it."

"Aviva chased it off," Lora says matter-of-factly, her round face shining with pride. "It was SO BIG. Like, THIS BIG!" She stretches her arms high above her head.

"That's a big wolf," Ryan nods, smiling softly.

I can feel tension settling between us as he turns back to me, his gaze sweeping over my face. I blush, knowing he's looking at the welt on my cheek. He can probably see each of Mercy's fingers outlined in crimson.

"Girls, take these back to the village for me. Shosh, after you put the meat away, start salting the pelts. I'll be there shortly to help you hang them to cure." Shoshannah, to my surprise, doesn't argue and quickly gathers the rabbits and Lora, leading her away. Lora sings a song about the fairies in the woods which she likely made up just now, but neither Alpha Ryan nor I speak until her voice fades completely.

"Is there a reason you're following me?" I ask, dropping my gaze as I crouch to clean my knife in the creek.

"I wanted to know if you're going on the hunt."

I nod. I wouldn't miss it. The spring hunt is a big deal. The pelts and furs gathered tonight will be traded at the Harvest Festival in a few months for the supplies we need from Navvan and Teshka.

Endova has the best hunting lands, therefore, our furs are the finest quality and the most coveted.

Alpha Ryan doesn't know any of that. To him, this is just recreation. I feel slightly bad for thinking so little of this man I barely know as I rise and meet his gaze.

"What happened to you?" he asks, motioning to his cheek, to the very place where mine still stings.

I reach up and cup my face, my cold hands a welcome relief. I can feel my heartbeat through my skin. Mercy got me good this time, that bitch. I'm kind of impressed. "It doesn't matter. I might have deserved it."

He arches a brow. "Why would you deserve getting hit so hard it leaves an imprint of someone's hand on your face?"

I lick my lips. "I called my sister a bitch."

"Was she being one?"

My mouth twitches into a smile despite my best efforts to keep it tamped down. "She was."

"Did you hit her back?" There's a teasing hint in his voice, and his eyes shimmer with warmth. I wonder if he has siblings and has experienced something similar.

"I wanted to," I admit.

"Let me guess," he chuckles, pacing across the creek bank. "This is the same sister you want me to take back to Silverhide instead of you?"

"She has other… fine attributes other than her personality."

He hums a laugh, his mouth slightly lifted in a wry smile. "The hunt then. I'll see you tonight?"

"That depends," I smile.

"On what?"

"If you can keep up."

6

A WAGER

Ryan

"I FEEL LIKE WE'RE IN COLLEGE AGAIN," JACOB MURMURS AS WE LEAN against the side of one of the earthen buildings on the outer ring of the village. He rolls his shoulders before crossing his arms over his chest, purposefully flexing.

Andrew leans forward to peer at him, snorting, "Yeah, and just like in college, the chances of you getting' any tail tonight is slim to nonexistent."

"I've put on like thirty pounds of muscle since then," Jacob hisses, flexing his biceps in emphasis.

I'm standing between them with my arms crossed as we watch the group of hunters—two dozen or so, by my estimation—prepare for the hunt. One group is entirely female and has my group's full, unwavering attention.

"Do you remember the night," Andrew laughs, pointing an accusatory finger at Jacob, "when you brought Gretchen Crosby to the fall formal afterparty?"

"I don't want to talk about that–"

"And her *boyfriend* showed up, and instead of kicking his ass and taking her back to our dorm room, you ended up playing flip the cup with *him* until three in the morning."

"I didn't know she had a boyfriend, first of all—"

"Who'd she end up going home with, anyway?" Andrew asks, chuckling.

Jacob furrows his brow and scratches his head, shrugging. "I don't remember."

"Well it wasn't you!"

"Obviously," Jacob growls, turning his attention back to the group of women tittering like little birds as they steal glances in our direction. He winks at one of them, and she blushes, whispering enthusiastically with her friends.

"Now I remember," Andrew teases, then nudges me hard. "Good ole' Ryan took her home, and her best friend, too, if I remember correctly."

I roll my eyes to the fading light of the sunset and say a soft prayer to the Goddess to strike me where I stand.

"What are you talking about?" Turner asks as he saddles up next to us. Andrew tilts his head toward the women, and Turner goes a little pink in the cheeks. Poor kid.

I tune Jacob and Andrew out as they continue to bicker about a life that feels so far in the past I can barely conjure the memory of it. Young, free, and wild.

I don't feel so young, or so free, right now. Not as I scan the groups diligently preparing for what I thought was going to be a night spent as wolves, hunting for deer and elk under the light of a nearly full moon. This is going to be a lot more than that based on the way the hunters are sharpening blades and examining spears before fixing them to halters worn across their chests and backs.

"Ryan could fucking *pull*," Jacob laughs, directing his words at an increasingly red Turner, who I doubt has ever talked to a girl without wanting to throw up. He's been twenty-one for a week, if that. Which is why we brought him. He needs the experience as a wolf, but Jacob and Andrew seem to be trying to bait him into going to talk to the

Endovian women still batting their eyelashes at us and giggling a few yards away.

"What does pull mean?" Turner asks innocently.

"He could just look at a woman, and she'd end up in his bed. He was a legend at Wellington."

"That's not necessarily true," I argue, which only adds fuel to the fire. Soon, Andrew and Jacob are filling Turner in on what our college days, and the early days of the Silverhide pack, looked like. Nights spent at bars. Mornings spent tangled with women I wouldn't remember again.

It was easy. I enjoyed partying. I loved the chase, and I knew I had a special knack for laying on the charm, but damn, it's been... years since then. I can't say I don't miss it. I liked who I was back then, before I ever felt the mate bond. Before the mate bond ruined my life, and I ended Hadley's.

I turn my attention back to the other hunters, taking in their strange clothes and assortment of weapons.

"Holy shit," Jacob swears.

"What?" I follow his gaze and find... Aviva.

"Who is that?" Turner asks, choking on the words.

"That's Ryan's soon-to-be wife."

"If she doesn't kill him in his sleep before then. That's why he has our guys pulling double shifts at night guarding the camp," Andrew murmurs, but his tone has dropped from its previous taunting tone.

We drop into stunned silence as she moves through the crowd of hunters looking like something out of a dream. Her thick red hair is braided down her back, still decorated with those shells that catch the last colors of the sunset, casting a halo around her face. She's smiling, which is... fuck... intoxicating in a way I hadn't expected.

She's wearing a leather skirt that hits her mid-thigh and a matching top that shows off her midriff. She's fucking jacked, honestly. She's a very small woman, maybe Kenna's height, but leanly muscled like she's in constant movement throughout the day, which I wholeheartedly believe.

"Her friend," Andrew says with a nudge to my ribs. "Who the hell is her friend?"

"That's Freya," Jacob whispers on my other side. "Don't get your hopes up, man. She's an elder's daughter too."

"Fuck," Andrew hisses.

Fuck is right. Now both women are looking in our direction. Aviva looks me up and down and smirks before turning to the other female hunters. She is the only one carrying a bow, however. The rest have a few blades each, all worn on nearly identical leather belts. Their outfits are all similar, too, with those weird loops and strings. I imagine they come apart when shifting, and then my dirty mind wanders to whether she's wearing anything underneath.

Her head whips around, her eyes meeting mine in a playful glare, but a glare nonetheless.

Jacob sucks in his breath and blows it out. Even Andrew stiffens.

She starts walking over.

"*Here we go*," I breathe, straightening up to meet her halfway. Her posse of women follow, hanging back by a few feet. Only the golden-haired Freya, who Andrew is simping over, steps up beside her with her arms crossed and a smirk on her daintily beautiful face.

"Aviva," I say by way of greeting.

"Alpha Ryan." She looks from me to my men, then rolls her eyes back to mine. "Are you not going on the hunt tonight?"

"I am. Why?"

She makes a show of looking around. "I see no weapons. In fact, I see four men standing around with their dicks in their hands while we do all the work."

Her group cackles. My men blow out their breaths and choke with surprise.

"If you need my help with something, all you have to do is ask." I edge a step closer to her. "Nicely."

"I don't know what that word means."

"I believe it."

She glares, I glare back. Why do I love this so much?

"What do you need weapons for? This is a hunt. We're wolves. Our teeth and claws are enough," Andrew chuckles.

The women ignore him completely, but Aviva turns slightly, throwing me a look over her shoulder. "You're going to want to change," she says, tilting her head as she inspects me.

"Why?" I ask, arching a brow.

Freya glances at Andrew with a sly smile, and I swear I can sense Andrew's heart just skipped a beat.

"You're going to shred your clothes apart, unless you're planning to harvest the meat and pelts naked after making a kill." Her smile cuts through me like a heated blade and awakens something primal I don't think I've ever felt before. "It still gets rather cold at night, and it's a long walk back to the village from the hunting grounds. I'd hate for you to catch a chill only a few days before our wedding."

The women behind her send soft peals of giggles rippling through the air between us.

I shift my weight, firmly planting my feet further apart as I cross my arms over my chest and hold her gaze. "I'm sure you'd enjoy the show."

She arches her brows as Jacob and Andrew snicker behind me.

Something is in the air right now. Whether it's adrenaline from the upcoming hunt, or possibly a touch of embarrassment that I'd caught her in a moment of vulnerability this morning, I'm not sure. But Aviva is out for blood, and she's targeting me.

I'm all right with it. I can play games too. I fucking love games. What Aviva doesn't realize is that *I always win*.

I step up to her, closing the distance between us. She isn't prepared for it and almost takes a step back on instinct.

"I'm curious about these skills your father said you possessed when he *gave* you to me," I say wryly, drawing out the word *gave* just to see how the color rushes to her cheeks. "I've only caught a glimpse of your talent when you had your arrow pointed at the top of my skull." I look down at her, giving her the cocky smile that used to get me any girl I wanted. I know for a fact Aviva is more likely to lodge one of her fine blades in my ribs than swoon. "I want to make a wager with you, little wolf."

Her group whispers excitedly, but Aviva is stone-cold. "What kind of wager?"

I run my tongue across my lower lip and eye the women gathered behind her before meeting her unwavering gaze. We haven't been this close before. Her eyes aren't a deep, dark brown. Not totally. Flakes of cherry and copper hug her pupils. Hundreds of freckles stretch across her cheeks and the bridge of her nose. Her eyelashes are thick and a darker red than her hair, the color of a rich, aged whiskey.

She's fucking beautiful.

"We're going to hunt together. If you get a clean kill first, I'll marry your sister instead." I lean down, smiling as I continue, "But if I get a kill first, you're going back to Silverhide with me without a fight and leaving your fucking attitude here in Endova."

She shoves me, but I catch her wrist. My thumb circles over her pulse, and her heart is beating rapidly, just like I expected.

"Do we have a deal?" I ask.

She rips out of my grasp but doesn't step away. She holds out her hand in silence. I take it, and she shakes my hand once but digs her sharp nails into my skin. Her eyes bore into mine before she tears away, turning and cutting through the crowd of women.

Freya scowls at me and Andrew before turning on her heel and following Aviva. The rest of the women follow, talking in hushed whispers, but then Aviva stops and turns back to face me.

"What are you doing, Ryan?" Jacob hisses. "You can't make a wager on this. I thought we agreed that we needed this alliance with her tribe–"

Aviva stalks back toward us, the sunset casting her in a halo of light just as the sun slips below the horizon and sends peels of shadows over her face. A horn blares, low and ominous, a signal that the hunt is about to begin.

"Alpha Ryan!" she shouts over the sudden movement of the hunters who begin to shift and dart out of the village.

"What?"

"You'd better start preparing to take Mercy back with you to Silverhide." She stops several feet away, ignoring the wolves darting between us.

"Why is that?"

"Because I'm taking you to Fell Valley."

The women gasp, and Freya grabs Aviva's arm, hissing something I can't hear over the horns and thundering wolves.

A chill works its way down my spine because of the feral look in her eyes.

"What's in Fell Valley?" I ask, and she smiles.

"It's not what's in it but what's above it. We're hunting for mountain goats." She shifts and darts away at the speed of light.

"Shit," I hiss, trying to get out of my shirt and pants. I have no idea where Fell Valley is, but I know for a fact that if I don't hurry up, she's going to get there first, and I really don't want to be leaving this Goddess forsaken village with her sister instead of her. I take off after her in a sprint, tearing out of my clothes as I shift.

Andrew and Jacob shout my name, but their voices fade into the distance as I weave through the wolves heading out for the hunt.

She's hiding her scent again, but it's hard to miss the red wolf as she breaks from the group before it reaches the forest.

I follow.

I'm not letting her win this.

This is also the most I've felt like myself in over two years, and I'm not ready to let that feeling go.

7

HUNTER BECOMES THE HUNTED

Aviva

ALPHA RYAN IS THE LARGEST WOLF I'VE EVER SEEN BY A LONG SHOT. While his overall mass is incredibly shocking, if not a little intimidating, he's much slower than me.

I can hear him lumbering through the woods behind me as I dart around trees and fly over creek beds, sprinting deeper and deeper into the outer ring of the ever dark, ever untamed forest that sits on the outskirts of Endovian territory.

The spring hunt is technically taking place in the sacred hunting grounds our tribe guards year round, but I've had my fill of deer. Plus, Alpha Ryan already snagged a golden elk, which up until two nights ago, had been my ultimate prize. Now that pelt is hanging in the meeting hall–a trophy–and a constant reminder of how my bride price was paid.

I shake the thought out of my head and pick my way down a sharp decline into a shadowed valley where the trees rather suddenly drop off, revealing nothing but dry, rocky earth.

I don't need to look behind me to know that Ryan is doing his best

49

to stay close. Rocks come loose beneath him as he growls and snarls his way down the side of the ravine. What a big idiot. Honestly, did he really think he was going to win this bet? *With me?*

I leap over rocks bigger than most of the earthen houses in Endova as I dart across a mile long field of boulders left behind by some ancient glacier. Eventually, I meet the other side of the valley and start leaping up again, careful not to let any loose rocks hit Ryan as he climbs behind me.

Not that I care. I don't, do I? No, I don't. I really don't. I still glance over my shoulder from time to time to make sure he's still there.

I stop at the top of the first rise where the mountains I've been running toward for the past hour come into full, startling view. They're massive, taking up most of the night sky as I rest at their base and gaze up at the rocky, uneven cliffs above my head. Ryan's scent-all male, all warm fragrances that make my senses go haywire, which is incredibly annoying-reaches me, and then he's spraying me with rocks as he skids to a stop at my side, panting.

I whip my head in his direction and snarl at him, hoping he'll take the hint and shut up, but he groans and sits back on his haunches, slouching his broad shoulders.

He's built like a barrel. Like a bear with long, muscled wolf legs. His head is twice the size of mine, and I could stand beneath him and my back wouldn't even brush the underside of his belly.

Mutant beast, that's what he is. I bare my teeth at him just because I feel like it then turn back to watch the mountain.

He sees what I see after a few minutes. Several white dots move along the rocky, uneven face of the cliff. I count six mountain goats. Mostly males, from what I can see from this distance, which is exactly what I'm here for. I couldn't care less about the meat, although it would be welcome if the Goddess sees it in Her heart to let me catch one. I want the pelt and the horns. I need them, actually, if I'm really going to be leaving my tribe and joining Alpha Ryan's pack.

A deer appears a few yards away from us, oblivious to us crouching in the rocks. I expect Ryan to leap into action. It wouldn't be hard for him to kill it. He'd win the wager.

But he doesn't move. He waits beside me, thrumming with nervous energy. I slowly move my front paw, knocking a rock loose from our hideout. It rolls away, bouncing down and slamming into boulder after boulder. The deer, spooked, runs away.

I slowly turn my head to look at Ryan. His eyes meet mine, a dark blue in the moonlight. He lowers his snout, teeth bared, as if to say, "Don't do it."

I jump from our hideout, my legs carrying me up over the remaining boulders and toward the rocky cliff. He's right behind me, slower, of course, but gaining ground as I dip into a pocket of trees where another deep, dark forest begins and hightail it toward the cliff base.

Hunting for goats is extremely dangerous, even as a wolf. Most hunters stumble upon them by chance rather than seeking them out. They like to stay high in the mountains, picking their way across the most treacherous territory to stay out of the reach of predators. But in the spring, they come down from their mountain top homes to graze on the newly thawed moss and alpine flowers that grow along the lower elevations.

That doesn't make it any easier, however. These goats are balanced on the face of the cliff, and I need a way to get up.

I break out of the trees and look up. The first goat is only a hundred or so feet above my head.

Ryan sends a low warning growl toward me, but it's swept away by the stiff, cool breeze coming off the mountain.

I leap, clawing my way up, picking my way across shallow ledges made of shale. I keep my body light and agile, never putting weight in my legs, and always moving. The goat has no idea I'm underneath it. Its companions higher up haven't noticed me, either. The wind is carrying my scent away from them.

Out of the corner of my eye, I see Ryan running along the base of the cliff, back toward the valley of boulders, looking for an easier way up. If he thinks he's getting a goat, he's delusional.

I'm running out of room to climb in my wolf form, however. The shale starts slipping beneath me, so I jump, shifting mid-flight, and pull out two of my daggers before my body collides with the cliff face. My blades sink into the soft, crumbling stone, sending sharp vibrations down my tired arms.

I grope for my footing while watching the goat, only twenty feet above me now, still munching on moss and oblivious to the threat directly below him. He's large, a pure, soft white. He's maybe a few years old judging by the horns that stretch in nearly straight lines from the top of his thick skull. I need him. I want him. I won't leave without him, even if I have to chase him up the mountain.

I send a quick prayer to the Goddess for Her blessing to take this life. I pray to the older, forgotten gods that She answers then make my move.

My bare toes find a ledge with only a few inches of space to spare, but it's enough to ease the growing strain in my arms. I release one blade and quickly sheath it, then grip the cliff face. I repeat the process with the other blade until both hands are free, and I can begin to climb again. The wind hurts, though. Bitter and fierce at this altitude, I have to close my eyes every time it blows, but I keep climbing. There's a wider ledge just below the ledge where the goat is standing, creating an overhang of rock. If I can get to that, I can use my bow to strike the goat. The goat will fall into the trees below without hitting me if I keep myself pressed to the cliff face.

It's a solid plan. Nothing can go wrong.

I reach for the ledge when a keening sound is carried through the wind, and the goat looks up, its thick, white coat rustling.

A screech like the sound of a person losing their life tears through my ears, cutting straight into my soul. Terror blinds me, and my hand slips. I yelp in panic as the wind rushes toward me again, nearly knocking me off the few inches of rock my toes are resting on.

Something thunders above me, and the goat and its companions startle, grunting and bleating as they begin to run along the cliff face, knocking rocks loose. I look up and shout in alarm as a huge rock, probably the size of Lora, hurtles toward me. It slams into the goat's head and bounces past me, but the goat is falling with it and—

White fur fills my vision. It's back brushes over my head. I lose my footing as it passes me.

'AVIVA!' Alpha Ryan's voice explodes through my head at the very moment I lose my footing, my fingers slipping from the rock.

His voice bouncing through my skull is almost as shocking as the fact I'm about to die. How is it possible? I can mind-link with my pack, not strangers. His voice is still echoing through me when something snaps across my back. Tree branches give way beneath me, filling my vision. I reach out instinctively, curling my hands around a branch. It slows me down, but it's not enough to break my fall completely.

With the branch in hand, I careen toward the forest floor where I land on top of the absolutely, most definitely dead goat and bounce off it, landing with a crunch. The air is knocked from my lungs as pain echoes through my body.

Moonlight streams from a hole in the treetops as I lay motionless, gasping for breath.

But it strikes me that I'm not alone. It's totally dark save for the ribbons of moonlight all around me, but there's something else here, for sure. Something that makes my skin crawl.

I wince in pain as I roll over onto my belly. My bow is smashed to bits, my arrows scattered and snapped all around me from the fall. I push up to all fours but rest on my knees, my back cracking vertebrae by vertebrae.

I can feel my whole body, which is a good thing. Nothing is broken save for my bow. My eyes adjust to the darkness, and an old campsite comes into view… but not that old, I realize with a start. It's recently been abandoned–and hastily. A tent is pitched nearby, flapping in the wind. The fire isn't smoking anymore, but I can smell the remnants of charred wood and the scents of what must have been a group of hunters from Navvan.

Not Endova. I'd recognize these scents if that were the case.

I look around the clearing, taking in the caches of clothing and an abandoned spit where a deer carcass is burnt to a crisp, totally forgotten.

Something happened here. Something happened recently, within the last twelve hours, I estimate.

A twig cracks nearby, then a rumbling sound like a rockslide tears toward me. Two massive shadows roll out of the woods in a blur of flesh, claws, and teeth.

It's Alpha Ryan and something… else.

He thrashes with the unfamiliar beast, closing his massive jaws around its short, bulky neck as they skid across the clearing, busting through the tent. The canvas fabric wraps around them both, momentarily blocking my view as I scramble for my blades like I can do anything about this right now.

I choke on a gasp, trying to fill my lungs with much needed air, as I grasp for the pieces of my bow and desperately try to make it work, all while Ryan is battling only a few yards away. His snarls sink into my soul. He's pretty fucking scary, I'm not going to lie.

I look back at him just as the moonlight spreads to the center of the clearing, illuminating the other creature for the first time, and I'm… frozen. Frozen in actual, bone-shaking fear.

It's a bear. At least, at one point in time it was. Now, it's mangled and mutated, its eyes swirling with dim, flickering power. The bloody taste in my mouth isn't from biting my lip as I fell. It's the metallic taste of magic.

It's a hellhound. I've never seen one. If I had, I wouldn't have been able to tell the tale. I'd be dead.

When the bear opens its mouth and roars, the sound is tangled with the pleading gasps of whoever's soul was used to tether the hellhound to a witch.

"ALPHA RYAN!" I scream as he sprints toward the hellhound and rolls with it toward the edge of the clearing. They fall out of view again, and all I can hear are their grunts and snarls.

But then it grows so silent I can hear the wind rustling through the new, spring leaves overheard. The sound of flesh tearing fills my ears, then grunting pants, and then a large, lumbering shadow is swaying through the darkness.

Swaying toward me.

8

WHO'S IT GOING TO BE?

Aviva

ALPHA RYAN SHIFTS BACK TO HIS HUMAN FORM, CLOAKED IN SHADOWS.
He's breathing heavily as he lumbers through the camp, crouching to
rip into a clothing cache.

I watch his shadow in silence, my heart beating out of rhythm. I
only look away when the wind parts the treetops and allows moonlight to spread over the clearing again, illuminating the hellhound
lying broken and in pieces at the very edge of the tree line.

It takes two shallow breaths before it starts to fall in on itself,
turning to ash that's carried away by the wind.

I slowly turn my gaze back to Alpha Ryan who is standing now,
wearing a pair of pants that don't fit him at all, the button holding
them in place undone. Moonlight ghosts over his frame. Instead of
tight, wiry muscles, he's just… huge. There's nothing lean about him. I
can see the outline of his abdominals as he turns slightly to face me.
The muscles in his chest and shoulders flex as he pulls on a shirt,
tugging it down over dark chest hair that trails down to his navel and
down… further.

I've never seen a man like him before. A man who can kill a hell-hound with his claws and fangs. I'm used to being both predator and prey while in these woods. I've killed rogues. I've fended off rival packs' people.

Alpha Ryan might be the most dangerous thing in this forest right now. I doubt he's ever been prey in his life.

My eyes slowly slide back to the swirling pile of ash.

"Are you hurt?"

"No," I whisper. I'm not sure he can hear the word. My throat aches, and my lungs burn.

He stalks toward me then stops, his eyes narrowed and nearly black in the moonlight. But his expression is fierce—furious. "That was impressively idiotic," he snaps, his voice dripping with malice. "I watched you fall a fucking hundred feet, Aviva. You could have died! You should be dead, actually. I can't believe you made it."

"I–"

"What the fuck were you thinking?" he roars, and every fine, downy hair on my body stands on end at his tone. Anger, yes. It's clear that he's fucking furious right now. But there's something else, something raw and broken that laces through his words and fills the empty space with questions, and I'm not sure I want the answers. "We could have been hunting deer, Aviva. That was the plan. Instead, I watched you scale a fucking mountain and then nearly fall to your death!"

"I was always planning on coming here and hunting a goat," I snap, but my voice trembles. "This had nothing to do with you."

"It has everything to do with me. You came at me before the hunt began. You taunted me. When I made our wager I thought–" He sucks in a breath, still standing several yards away. "This was *my* fault."

I clutch my broken arrows in my hands and squeeze. "What are you talking about? How is this your fault?"

"I pushed you–"

"I agreed to the wager!"

"You're a show off!"

"I wasn't showing off for you!"

"Then what was this about?" he growls, teeth bared, his hands curling into fists at his sides. Another blast of cold wind comes down the mountain and rushes over the camp, ruffling the thick wool of the dead goat separating us. "Do you even understand what it was like watching you fall, Aviva? Knowing that I'd find you here in pieces and have to take you home to your father with your blood staining my hands? I didn't shut you down like I should have. I should have dragged you back to the village the moment I realized what you were hunting. I let you do this. I made the wager knowing it would set you off because I–" He hesitates to finish, closing his eyes for a moment. Again, a raw, empty emotion fills his voice as he says with remarkable, heartbreaking calm, "I have enough blood on my hands already. I would have never forgiven myself if anything had happened to you."

I look down at the goat, saying, "It's customary in my culture, when a woman marries, to give her parents something as a parting gift." My throat nearly closes around the words. "When I was young and training as a hunter, I knew that one day I'd have to marry, and I promised myself that when that day came, I wouldn't give my father a new tapestry or berries I'd picked in the glen. I'd bring him a golden elk pelt, or I'd bring him a goat. You beat me to the golden elk, so I decided I'd go to Fell Valley, where our ancestors are from, and I'd bring him a goat so he could have the pure white pelt and horns, and every time he looked at them, he'd be reminded that his daughter trained for years, spent every night in the forest, just to bring him back a piece of our history before I left our pack forever. I was going to do this whether it was you, or some other man, standing beside me at the temple."

He holds my gaze, steady and unwavering.

I lick my lips, finding them dry, and say, "You won, Alpha Ryan."

He furrows his brows, his mouth ticking into an angry sort of smile. "I didn't win." He motions to the goat, but I shake my head.

"I didn't make a clean kill. That was one of your terms. The rock that fell struck the goat. I fell on top of him. You…" I look back at the ashy remains of the hellhound, still wondering if this is some sort of weird dream or uncanny vision from the Goddess Herself. "You killed a hellhound on your own. You made a clean kill. You win."

Silence falls between us—thick and heavy. So heavy I could cut through it with my blades if I had the strength to move my arms.

"It doesn't count. I have nothing to show for it."

"You have me. I'll go willingly." I barely recognize my own voice. It's a total, complete submission. It's a soft version of myself I don't understand, but it feels right, at least right now. Maybe it's because we both just stared death in the face, but Alpha Ryan also softens, his shoulders slumping, his eyes sweeping over me as he inspects me for injuries I haven't mentioned or noticed.

I wince and curl into myself as another gust of bitter wind bursts through the camp.

"Come on," he says steadily, closing the distance between us. "There's a small cave nearby. I saw it when I was trying to find a way up the cliff."

"You were going to try to stop me?"

"I wasn't sure what I was going to do." He bends to gather my scattered weapons. I move on unsteady feet. I watch him make his way through the camp, gathering supplies in a leather bag leftover from the hunters who got the hell out of here for obvious reasons. He steps through the pile of ash leftover from the hellhound and pulls two bedrolls from what used to be the tent then tilts his head toward the trees.

"I have to process the goat."

"I'll come back for it," he says quietly. Without a word, I follow him out of the clearing and through the trees, following the base of the cliff. I don't bother glancing up. I don't need to be reminded of how far I fell. I feel it in each step I take. My bare feet ache, and my toes are practically frozen.

I deserve it. It was stupid. What had he said? *Impressively idiotic.* That's a new one, but it's fitting. I refuse to admit I'd been showing off because I don't believe that was the case, but he'd said *impressively...* so.... he might have been impressed.

Actually, why do I care?

I huff a breath, and he looks over his shoulder at me. I refuse to meet his gaze, focusing instead on the cliff, watching the shadows play over its jagged gray surface.

Within a few minutes, we reach the cave he mentioned, which is little more than a cleft with a narrow open space within. It doesn't stretch into the cliff more than twelve feet, but it's enough space to work with. He dumps the bag and bedrolls inside, then leaves without a word. I also leave, gathering dry sticks and stones to build a fire ring at the entrance of the cave, and have a small warming fire started by the time he returns with the goat resting over his shoulders, carrying it like it weighs nothing.

"Thank you for starting the fire," he says by way of greeting as he sets the goat down. He tosses me a pair of rolled up socks he must have found at the camp.

I accept them, rolling them on as I continue to warm myself in front of the flames, working on one of my knives. "Aren't you going to say it's not safe to have a fire in case there's more danger lurking in the woods?"

"Like I said before, you're the most dangerous thing out here," he smirks, and I feel like a weight is being lifted off my chest. Whatever raw, icy emotion he's conveyed earlier is gone, replaced by his usual slightly aloof friendliness.

I meet his eyes and quickly look away, going back to sharpening one of my blades with a rock. The moon hangs overhead as we start to skin the goat. I wordlessly guide him through the process, and he follows my lead, neither of us speaking until the moon is starting to fade from view, and the sky is turning from inky black night to a deep violet, the stars beginning to dim.

The silence starts to become too much, so I finally speak, my voice raspy from lack of use. "How did you kill that hellhound? No one has ever done that before."

He shifts his weight as he rolls up the goat skin into a tight bundle. "Like a wolf would. I tore out its throat."

I shiver even though I've done the same thing to numerous rogues.

"But it was a hellhound. No one has ever killed one before. And the witches—"

"They're no witches left in the Deadlands, at least any witches that don't bend the knee to the queen in Moonrise. Any hellhounds left are just roaming aimlessly," he cuts in, moving on to packing up the meat.

I shift my weight. "How do you know that?"

"Because I didn't just come here to set up a new pack territory." He looks at me, his eyes shining like raw sapphires in the faint light of early morning. "What have you heard about me, Aviva?"

I frown, not liking the tone he just used. He arches a brow. I blow out my breath, leaning my head against the rock face at my back. "That you're cursed."

"Well, that's a new one. I was thinking you'd say who my family is—"

"I heard that you murdered your own mate, that you were cast out of your homeland by the king, and now your heart is made of stone." I look at him and instantly regret my words. His eyes are on the sunrise, his expression unreadable but set and cold.

A chill runs up the length of my spine as I straighten. "Did you do that?"

"It's complicated." He clears his throat and rises.

"Alpha—"

"My name is Ryan," he says coldly. "To you, it's Ryan."

"Okay...." I hop to my feet as he kicks dirt over the fire and starts shrugging out of his shirt. "Hey, you were the one who asked what I heard about you. I answered."

His eyes sweep over my face. "I know."

"Then why—"

"Nothing matters more to me than my pack and my family," he says, holding my gaze. "Nothing. I'll do what I need to do to keep them safe and secure. Even if that means hunting every rogue and ancient creature still plaguing the Deadlands." He pauses, his lips parting slightly as if he's rolling his next words over his tongue, debating. "Even if it means marrying a stranger because I need the alliance with her father and can't promise I'll ever be able to love her."

I don't know why this affects me so much. I've never looked at marriage as an act of love. It's survival. It's the act of carrying on our kind. Of aligning our packs.

But hearing Ryan say it… well, it doesn't feel good.

"I did kill my mate," he confirms without so much as blinking, and takes off his shirt. "So, now you know. The rumors are true, and I'm giving you the choice now. Am I marrying you, or your sister?"

I watch the way the sunrise plays over his features, illuminating him in gold. "Did she deserve it?" I ask in the very same way he asked me that question yesterday morning at the creek after Mercy slapped the hell out of me, when I'd told him I'd considered hitting her back.

He scans my face, and as the sunrise bathes us in gold, I swear I see one corner of his mouth tick into a smile despite the raw pain behind his eyes.

"You–or your sister?" he asks again, softer this time.

9

DAY OF CHANGE

Aviva

RYAN AND I WALKED IN OUR WOLF FORMS BACK TO THE VILLAGE BY sunset, each of us dragging makeshift sleds fashioned from items we found at the abandoned camp to carry the meat and pelt from the goat.

While I wondered if we could mind-link somehow after I'd heard him call my name when I'd fallen, neither of us spoke. We arrived at the village shortly before the sun set when the sky was painted gold, and the moon had just started to rise again. We weren't even the last hunters to arrive. The entire village was alight with music and dancing to celebrate a very successful hunt.

But I didn't partake in the celebration. I left the pelt with Ryan and immediately shifted back to my human form and walked out of the village again, to the creek, where I splashed frigid water over my dirty, aching skin until I was clean. I then returned home and sank into the hottest bath I could handle, brushing out my braids, picking out the beads, and sinking below the surface.

Now, I blink at the early morning sunlight peeking through the circular window above my head. It's another beautiful day. Warm and sunny. I shift my weight on the flat of thick furs and a few goose down mats that act as a mattress–a very common sleeping arraignment here in Endova–and Lora grumbles, snuggling closer to me. Shoshannah is at my other side, sleeping with her fist tucked under her chin, her wild red hair matted and covering half of her face.

The girls always end up in my bed. Even when I'm out hunting all night, I'll come home to find them curled in the furs with a spot between them left just for me.

My heart sinks as I gather Lora closer and rest my chin on the top of her head. She smells like the lavender soap Mercy makes. Our older sister makes the most luxurious soap out of the animal fat I bring back from hunts.

I close my eyes again and breathe in familiar air, but the sounds of the village waking up for a very important day begin to drift through the window, through the earthen walls, and I know I can't ignore this day forever.

I hope I made the right choice when Ryan asked me if he was taking me or Mercy back to Silverhide. I hope I don't come to regret my decision. I hope, years from now, I look back on this day with nothing but peace in my heart, and not, "What if?"

It's a full moon. I can feel the energy in the air as I rise and strip out of the cotton shift I slept in last night after my bath. I change into something comfortable and walk on bare feet down the snug hallway that every room in the house branches off from and turn into the kitchen to make a cup of tea. I notice Mercy's door is already open, and her room is empty.

She has a big day today, doesn't she?

I close my eyes and sip the tea slowly. I should eat, but I'm not hungry in the slightest. Nothing sounds good. Nothing will taste good, either, not when I feel like I'm going to throw up at any given second.

Eventually, the girls wake up and start whining for breakfast. I make pancakes, a favorite of both of them, and use the last of the blueberry syrup. "You'll have to pick more blueberries this fall," I tell

Shoshannah as I shake the bottle for the last drop. Shoshannah's lower lip quivers, but Lora is scarfing down her breakfast, gasping for breath between bites. "Chew your food, Lora. You're going to choke!" I pour her some more milk, which she gulps down. "Lora!"

"I have to go, Veev. Shosh, too. We're supposed to be practicing for the ceremony tonight."

Shoshannah takes a single bite of her breakfast before sliding off her stool and allowing Lora to bounce her out of the house. I follow them to the door and watch as they join a group of young girls who call out to them with giddy excitement.

Shoshannah looks over her shoulder at me as I lean in the doorway, her dark eyes wide and wet with unshed tears. She's old enough to understand this now. Women leave their packs and move on. We look forward to it, honestly. It's an adventure, but it's also a heartbreaking time for the family left behind. One day, it'll be her turn to leave the nest. I'll sit on the hill overlooking the ceremony grounds during her wedding at the Harvest Festival, watching her be bound to her husband under the light of the full, golden harvest moon. I'll probably want to cry then, too.

When the girls move out of sight, I watch the villagers dart about with armfuls of food and meat, preparing for the wedding feast. Some hunters are still working on their hides and processing meat from the hunt yesterday. I sip my tea as I watch a few of Ryan's men working on an elk carcass near the fire pit where several spits are roasting meat for tonight already. They laugh and joke with each other happily. Fulfilled. I don't mind his people, honestly. They're young and spirited. They're respectful, which I hadn't expected.

I'm not sure what I expected from Ryan, but it hadn't been *this*. This feeling in my chest like I have to know where he is all the time. Like I want to hear his voice and hear him say my name. I tell myself it's because he's new and interesting. We also almost saw each other die, which I'm sure binds people together in a way, but we're so... so alike. Hardheaded and bold, I'm shocked we worked so well together taking apart that goat rather than resorting to throwing punches.

I find him in the crowd as a flash of white catches my attention.

He's standing with my father as they examine the goat hide which is now hanging to cure. My father claps him on the shoulder and motions to Mercy, who is fluttering around helping out with the preparations. She smiles softly, shyly, at Ryan, and I immediately turn into the house and shut the door behind me.

I'm making the right decision. This is the right choice.

The only person who comes to call on me is Freya—two hours later. I'm picking at Shoshannah's cold pancakes in the kitchen when she arrives, bustling in with a basket of ribbons and other trinkets. "Good Goddess, did you brush out your curls?"

I reach up and try to pat the frizzy mass of red curls surrounding my head like a fiery halo. "I just washed my hair last night."

Freya groans, resting the basket on her hip. "We have some serious work to do. Come on." She disappears from the doorway, but I catch up to her in moments. There's one mirror in our house. It's small, handheld, and belonged to my father's mother. It's a bit rusted along the outer edges but Freya props it up on the windowsill in my room nonetheless then sits behind me to start weaving my hair into something manageable. It's going to take hours. Whatever. I have all damn day.

"Where's Mercy?" she asks around the fresh-water pearl pin clamped between her teeth. Her fingers move with expert skill as she pulls my hair away from my face, twisting the curls the way she wants them before pinning them in place.

"I'm not sure. She has a lot to do today."

Freya scooches closer to me, sitting crisscrossed behind me, her knees resting against my hips.

"Are you sure about this?" Freya asks.

I nod, watching my reflection in the mirror.

"What are you going to wear?"

"I haven't decided." I haven't put much thought into anything, actually. After my brief conversation with Ryan before we left Fell Valley, I've let my mind go blank and totally numb. It's the only way I can survive this day, I think. I'm not sure why it aches so badly to think about.

"Your blue dress with the deer fur along the hem is my favorite. I think you should wear that."

"Okay," I reply in a whisper, and we fall into silence for several minutes as she continues to decorate my hair with pearls and ribbons.

This is just a hand-fasting ceremony, but the entire village will be dressed in their traditional wear. After the ceremony, a huge feast will be held, and then dancing and singing around the fire will begin. I've only seen a hand-fast once, and I was thirteen at the time. A Teshkan hunter who'd come to visit his mother's family ended up falling in love with one of the women from our pack and paid her bride price after a three day hunt that nearly took his life and that of his companions. They were hand-fasted here in Endova and married officially during the Harvest Festival. It was such a beautiful ceremony. All of the children, me included, sang an ancient song while a length of white fabric was wrapped around their joined hands, and we'd led them around the fire three times, all of us holding lanterns while the rest of the village was shrouded in darkness, the only other light that of the full moon.

It was also the first time it resonated with me that I'd marry and leave one day. Mercy, too, had gone through the motions with me, wondering why anyone would ever want to leave their village, and their family, for a man.

Freya rises and settles in front of me as the sun peaks in the sky and starts to fall back toward the horizon. Time is moving swiftly but also ticking at a crawl. I've never felt so strange. All I want to do is run away, hide in the woods, but I can't.

"I have a feeling that once the Alpha and his people leave, the village won't feel the same," she says softly, rubbing a pale pink powder made of dried rose petals on my cheekbones. "There's just something different in the air now."

"Change," I agree, meeting her cornflower blue eyes. "Everything feels different."

She smiles sadly. "I guess we'll see, won't we?"

Freya takes her leave with a soft peck to my cheek, leaving me looking at my reflection in the mirror. I look the same but softer. My hair is still wild with curls poking out of the pins she spent hours sticking in place. But my cheeks are rosy, and my eyes are bright, and I look… ready. Ready for whatever comes next.

I hear the front door open and close with a snap, sending a soft rustle of outside voices drifting inside. Mercy's footsteps pause at her door before she sighs and begins walking toward my room, slowly, as if debating something.

I turn, resting on my knees, as she fills the doorway. My eyes widen as I realize what she's holding in her hands. "Mercy… where did you get that?"

She swallows hard and lifts the bundle of white and cream fabric. "Azalea kept it all this time. I had no idea until this morning. I've been cleaning it, mending it a little."

Azalea was our mother's best friend who lives with her family on the other side of the village.

I stand and walk toward Mercy as she carefully unravels the fabric, revealing a long dress made of woven white and cream wool. It has long, loose sleeves that taper at the wrists which are trimmed in white ermine fur. The off-the-shoulder neckline is trimmed in the same soft fur and decorated with pearls and moonstone beading that makes it look like raindrops are clinging to the fur.

It has a high slit on the side. I run my fingers over the fur trim along the slit, smiling to myself. "So she could still dance?"

"Yeah," Mercy whispers, her eyes misting over. "I guess Father gave this to Azalea for safe keeping. I didn't realize–I thought everything had been given away."

My sister and I stare at each other. It's been years since we could look at each other and not want to scratch each other's eyes out. Again, there's just an energy of change in the air today, so that has to be why we can suddenly be within a foot of each other. Memories of our mother sitting at the edge of her bed while Mercy and I played dress up with this very dress flutter to the forefront of my mind, nearly bringing me to tears.

"It's beautiful," I tell her. "It's perfect."

"I know. I have some alterations to make, I think." She tilts her head down the hallway. "Can you help?"

"Yeah, of course."

She smiles, hanging the dress over her forearm as she scans my face before turning on her heel and walking away, but her voice echoes toward me, lifted and sweet, "I'm going to fix whatever Freya did to your head, too. Grab some more pins and a bowl of water, we have work to do, Aviva."

10

JOINED BY BLOOD

Ryan

THE ENTIRE VILLAGE IS QUIET AND DARK, WHICH IS STRANGE. ALL OF the lights and fires have been put out in the individual homes, and even the main fire in the large, open pit at the center of the village has burned down to embers that glow like stars. Andrew, Jacob, and I walk side by side into the village after taking the afternoon to rest and prepare for tonight, unsure of what's to come.

I only managed to lie on my sleeping bag for a while staring at the roof of my tent, my mind whirling. Married. I'm getting married. And it doesn't mean anything but unity between my pack and my bride's people.

I have a lot of business to take care of tonight other than bind myself to a woman I barely know. I was able to talk to Jerrod briefly this morning while showing him Aviva's goat hide, but he's a busy man and promised he'd find me after the ceremony before he walked off with Mercy to discuss the feast and celebration to follow.

So, I've been sitting around our camp with my head in my hands wondering how the fuck I got here and what my future holds. I'm not

71

sure how I'm going to explain this to my family. Thankfully, after Sydney's royal mess with Sarah two years ago, I'm sure my parents will look at this situation and shrug. It could be worse. I don't think Aviva has powers. She's strong, yes, but so am I. We're alike in that way, but that might be the only way.

But she also doesn't have bad guys creeping through the shadows around her. She didn't wipe my memory. She isn't mated to an enemy.

The thought of her mate, a man she hasn't met yet and who likely doesn't know she yet exists, rocks me to my core, but I shove those emotions deep down where the rest reside, trying to keep my head clear.

Andrew and Jacob lead me along a path woven between the earthen structures and up a slight hill where the full moon, distant and pure silver, is casting long strings of light all over the rolling landscape and forests beyond.

No one speaks as we near the temple which is another building built into the hillside. Light pours from the circular windows cut into the side of the hill, and shadows move inside. Soft conversations and murmurs follow as we close in on the temple, and my heart is starting to beat erratically. I stop walking, tucking my hands in my pockets.

"What's up?" Jacob whispers, eyeing the people standing near the entrance of the temple. The whole village showed up for this cere-mony. Our guys, too, are standing around outside, mostly excited about the feast and party to follow. Not everyone can fit inside the temple, I guess. Dozens of people line the path leading to the entrance, watching us, as I turn to Jacob and Andrew. "I just didn't–I didn't see this for myself."

"You want me to take your place?" Jacob asks in all seriousness. He would. Not because he wants my soon-to-be-wife for himself but because he's loyal and willing to do what needs to be done for our pack, for his Alpha. For me.

"No, I just need a minute." I need a minute to scrub Hadley's memory from my mind. I don't know if I ever imagined myself marrying her, but after I realized we were mates, I did think about a future with her in it.

This wedding doesn't feel wrong. I know I'm doing the right thing for my pack. I know this is a sacrifice I have to make. My bride is making the biggest sacrifice of all, however. It's killing me that she can't marry her own mate, or even marry for love, but that doesn't seem to matter in her culture.

And, it's not like I can marry for love or as my mate because I gave that up to save Sarah and Dahlia, the mates of the two most important men in my life, other than my father and uncle.

I have nothing to lose. But my bride is losing everything and gaining me. That's not a fair trade off, in my opinion.

Andrew and Jacob start tugging on my shirt and adjusting my hair. I stand there and take it, my mind reeling over what's about to happen next. Mom's going to be heartbroken she missed this, regardless of the circumstances of how this wedding came to be. I scratch my naked, freshly shaved, jaw, feeling a little exposed without the beard I've let grow out over the past two years.

"He looks fine," Andrew rasps to Jacob. Both of them are equally as nervous. We all tried to get some information about what this ceremony entails, but none of us are totally sure what's about to happen next. I wouldn't be surprised if I had to strip naked, or walk over coals with bare feet or something else of the like.

"They're waiting for us to begin," Jacob says, squeezing my shoulder. "It's time. After this, we can all go home."

Home. I am looking forward to returning to Silverhide. I'm sure James is wondering where the hell we are, given that we were supposed to return tonight.

Before I know it, I'm inside the temple standing at the back of the singular room. Jerrod and two of the other elders stand behind me, and soft conversations ripple through the crowd standing along the walls and outside the temple. There isn't a priestess in attendance, which I find strange. It strikes me that this fall, during the festival, I'll have to do this all over again with everyone from all three packs in attendance.

That's the goal, at least.

I rock on my heels. If I was wearing a watch, I'd check it because I've been standing here for ten minutes, and my bride is nowhere to be seen. My gaze slides to the left where a group of children stand, poking each other and generally goofing off out of boredom. Shoshannah and Lora are with them, and while Lora is twirling around in what I assume is a new dress she's rather fond of, Shoshannah is giving me the same kind of glare her sister has given me on several different occasions. I smile at her. She promptly sticks her tongue out at me and crosses her arms over her chest, turning away.

I can't win over every sister in this family, I guess.

A hush suddenly falls over the crowd. Jerrod sighs with relief.

And then she's there. Mercy and Aviva walk down the aisle. Aviva's dark eyes shine in the light of the full moon illuminating the room through a hole in the ceiling overhead as I take her in.

Candles at my back cast shadows on Aviva's face as she keeps her head lowered. Her hair is intricately woven into an updo at the base of her slender neck, dusted with pearl beads that gleam in the moonlight, her curls unusually tame. Mercy steps up to me wearing a dress of blue, bowing her head slightly to her father as she hands him a length of white fabric. She says something in a language I'm not familiar with before turning to face me.

She bows her head and steps back, allowing my bride to take her place before me.

Aviva is wearing a dress of white wool with white fur accents. She looks like a moon beam as her eyes raise to meet mine. Her cheeks are flushed, and I have to admit I'm a little disappointed she's not the feral, untamed version of herself right now. Instead, she's quiet and unsure. She's radiant, however. The soft glow of her skin and the fiery red of her hair contrast with the white dress, like a warming fire dancing against a backdrop of silver-white snow. But her expression is withdrawn and nervous, which guts me.

I want to take her hand and tell her it's okay. I want to tell her we don't have to do this. But when I asked her who I'd be marrying tonight, whether I'd be taking her home to Silverhide, or Mercy, she made her choice.

"*You're stuck with me*," she said, giving me that devious smile that makes my blood simmer.

In reality, *she's* stuck with *me*, and I feel awful for it. She deserves so much more than I can give her. She deserves someone who can love her–because I can't.

"I look around this village and see the hurt in my people's eyes at the loss of our daughter, our sister, and our friend, Aviva," Jerrod says, his voice booming through the room and out into the night, where the rest of the villagers are straining for a view of the ceremony. "Our Aviva, who has trained our best hunters, protected our village from the rogues that plague these sacred lands of our ancestors. Tonight, she leaves our village to start a new journey within the pack Silverhide, to become the wife of an Alpha." Jerrod looks at me then, smiling softly. "No man has come to me thus far that has been more worthy of her than this Alpha. Together, they shall usher in a new era of peace and prosperity to our lands."

I barely know this man. He can't know whether or not I'm worthy of her. But I'm watching her face as he continues to rain compliments on her character and achievements, things I know she did without needing or wanting recognition and thanks in return. Her eyes are on my chest, blank and unseeing, like she's stuck in her head, processing everything her father is saying.

I steal at glance at the onlookers, watching as they nod along. Jerrod shifts into a different language, and soon he's asking us to join hands.

I haven't touched Aviva other than steadying her at the meeting hall when this betrothal was announced. Her hands are warm and so much smaller than mine. I run my thumbs along her calluses on impulse, imagining her holding her bow as I paced beneath her at those ruins in the forest.

I tighten my grip, curling my hands around hers, and her eyes lift to meet mine.

I hold her gaze. The rest of the room around us fades like it's just the two of us, and I'm... feeling a little lost. A little hot, all of the sudden. Her touch is not what I expected. I don't feel the way I expected.

I expected to feel... nothing.

I'm tempted to let go, but then another elder takes my left hand and slides an incredibly sharp blade across my palm. I don't even have time to process what's happening. I almost lunge at the elder when he takes Aviva's right hand and slices across it. I watch pain play across her face and it hurts *me*.

"Together, you are joined. Our people are now your people, and your people, our people," the elder says, clasping our hands together.

The sensation is like fireworks exploding through my chest. She feels it too but tamps down her surprise as the length of white fabric is wound around our aching hands, keeping them firmly clasped together.

I hold her gaze, shocked. Is this... I've heard of imprinting, but this is different. This feels...

Lora's soft voice cuts through my profound confusion, lifted in an off-key song in that same strange, ancient language half of the ceremony was in. My gaze is still on Aviva's face as more children join in, and the song is bright and joyous, cutting through the more serious notes weighing us down. Jerrod turns us to face the elated crowd, who are all singing now and clapping as he gives me a little shove, and I start leading my wife out of the temple and into the open, night air.

The children run ahead of us with lanterns swinging at the end of sticks longer than most of them are tall. The rest of the village follows behind, their song following us back into the village proper. The children run toward the fire pit, twirling around excitedly. I look at Aviva, and she's smiling, tears in her eyes as she watches her little sisters jump around with their lanterns.

I find myself squeezing my hand around hers and feeling... good. Good, for the first time in over two years.

Shoshannah is given a torch which she promptly throws into the fire pit, igniting the flames once again.

"What are we supposed to do?" I ask Aviva over the song, "Jump into the flames?"

Aviva laughs, and it's the most beautiful sound I've ever heard. She tugs on our joined hands and leads me around the fire once, then twice, then three times. It's a madhouse, everyone dancing and beating on drums. After the third rotation, she brings us to a stop, and Mercy comes to our side, carefully unwinding the fabric.

But I look at my wife–my *wife*–and wonder how the hell I got here and what I did to deserve this after everything that I've done.

Andrew saddles up to us carrying goblets of wine which he hands to us. "So," he says smoothly as the celebration begins with riotous enthusiasm all around us, "I guess a first kiss isn't part of your culture?"

Freya skips to a stop at Aviva's side. "No, it's not. That's between the couple and the Goddess, you uncultured heathen."

Andrew gasps at the insult, but Freya and Aviva are both snickering at his expense.

"What do we do instead?" I ask Aviva, my voice slightly raspy. Maybe it's from the shock or the strange sensations echoing through my body, through our... our bond, something forged by blood, I realize, curling my fingers into the palm of the hand that was joined with Aviva's.

She looks up at me, her eyes softer than usual, but playful and... happy. "We dance," she says, and takes my hand.

11

WEDDING NIGHT

Aviva

R YAN MOVES LIKE A LARGE, LUMBERING ANIMAL, BUT I KNEW THAT. HE'S
not light on his feet whatsoever, but I can't fault him for not knowing
any of the steps to numerous dances passed down from generation to
generation as I tug him around the fire, spinning in dizzying circles
while my right hand throbs as it heals from being sliced open and
slapped against his, our blood mingling.

It was, admittedly, a very odd sensation I still can't put into words.
Even now, two hours later, my hand feels all tingly, and those tingles
have worked their way up my arm and deep into my chest, blooming
into something new, heavy, and strange.

I've never danced so much in my life, but eventually Ryan and I
were parted by other celebrators who joined the dancing. I lost him in
the crowd an hour ago, but maybe that's for the best. I need this veil
of delusion to lift so I can think clearly and come to terms with what
has to happen next.

I look up at the stars and the full moon overhead as I lie on top of
a random earth house just outside the inner ring of the village. I roll

over to my side and watch several people dart into the rolling hills to shift beneath the full moon, called away from the celebration by the thick energy in the air.

I want to shift, too. I'm overwhelmed and itching to get out of this dress. Full from a delicious dinner and several glasses of sweet, brightly flavored mead, I'm also ready to fall into bed and close my eyes.

But I'm supposed to fall into bed with Ryan tonight, aren't I?

I groan and start to roll back over onto my back, but I spot Ryan moving through the crowded village center toward where my father is standing with three other elders. I sit up, squinting past the bonfire sending sprays of amber light all over the village, and watch as Ryan takes my father to the side.

Then I see Freya lingering nearby, standing on her toes to get a better look at Ryan and the elders. I rise, debating leaving my quiet perch, when my father turns from Ryan and starts speaking to the other elders again, who seem to be arguing about something.

What the hell is going on?

I hike up my dress and pick my way down the side of the hill just as Freya comes tearing in my direction, her face lit up in a delirious smile.

I drop the long skirt of the dress, still standing on the slight rise of the hill, while Freya claws her way up, squeaking a yelp as she slips on the grass and bangs her knees.

"What in Goddess's name are you doing?" I laugh as she pops up and runs in my direction.

"You won't believe," she pants, "what I just accomplished." Her blue eyes are wide and excited as she takes my hands, heaving a breath. "I'm going with you."

"Going with me… where?"

"To Silverhide, of course." She heaves another sharp breath. "Where else?"

I stare at her as she places her hands on my shoulders to steady herself. She pulls me to the ground where we sit side by side overlooking the party still going on below. "How?"

"How did I do it? Well, I ran into your husband a few minutes ago. He was looking for you."

I bite back a sigh as she meets my eyes, scanning my face. "Was he?"

"Well, yeah. You're his wife now. I think he and his men are about to go back to their camps. When he saw me, he asked where to find you, and we started talking about you—"

"What about me?"

She smirks, nudging me with her shoulder. "I just told him I hadn't seen you look so happy before. You rarely dance, you know. That was a treat."

"Wait—how—how're you coming to Silverhide with me?"

"Oh, yeah. Well, if you'd let me finish." She rolls her eyes to the stars, sighing happily. "Your husband seemed worried about you running off tonight, into the woods, and I said you wouldn't do that because you know how much this means to him."

I snort a laugh, and she rolls her eyes back to mine, smiling devilishly.

"And then I might have mentioned how hard it's going to be for you to adjust, especially without any friends in Silverhide since all your friends are here in Endova, to which he seemed shocked that you had any friends, besides me."

"Okay, get to the point!"

"That Andrew guy mentioned how their Beta's wife is having a baby soon, and how James, whoever that is, but I assume he's the Beta, or whatever…. Where was I? Oh, Andrew mentioned how this James guy and his wife might need a little extra help with the baby when it's born, any day now I guess, and I kept mentioning how lonely you'd be in Silverhide all on your own, and eventually Alpha Ryan wanted us to just shut up, and he asked if I'd be willing to travel with you and spend the summer with his pack to help you acclimate—"

"Are you serious?"

"Yeah. He's just a man, Aviva. It wasn't hard to put the idea in his head. He walked right up to our fathers and pled his case, to which my father agreed, as long I'm not housed with any single men, and he returns me to our tribe during the Harvest Festival."

My mouth drops open. "But–do you have any experience with babies?"

She shrugs, picking at the grass underneath us. "Of course, I do. I have more experience taking care of mothers, though. My older brothers are both married and have kids now, you know. Anyway, I'm going with you, Aviva."

The heavy burden weighing down my chest lifts a touch. I'm not even sure what to say. I'm happy, of course, and exceedingly relieved, but there's still an undertone of nerves running through my veins that makes me want to run into the night and disappear.

"What's on your mind?" Freya says after a heavy beat of silence.

"Nothing. I'm just tired."

"You're never tired. You're nervous for tonight, aren't you?"

"I don't know what you're talking about."

She hums a laugh and turns to face me, giving me a sharp, knowing look. "You know where... *it's* supposed to go, right?"

I grind my teeth and scowl at her. "I'm twenty-two, Freya."

"So?"

"So... I've seen men naked before."

"Well, we all have. We're wolves, after all. But do you know where it goes?"

"Yes." I growl, but my cheeks are burning.

"And you know how babies come to be?"

I swallow hard. I don't want to think about babies or the act of making them, but I'm a wife now. This is my divine purpose, according to our culture.

"You have to do the marital act," she says dramatically, then lifts her hands, making a little circle with her thumb and forefinger one hand, and pumping her forefinger on the opposite hand through it.

I lightly smack her hands away as she laughs. "It can't be that bad, you know. I've heard people like it."

"And what does your mother say?" I ask her, hugging my knees to my chest.

"I'm sure she'll tell me all about it when someone pays my bride price. Who knows? Maybe Andrew will finally grow some balls and flirt with me instead of just staring at me every chance he gets." She looks smug as she turns back toward the bonfire. "Maybe I'll marry into the Silverhide pack, just like you, and we can grow old together like we planned. But, until then, I just want to know that you're prepared for tonight."

I lick my lips as nerves bloom through my body, making my skin prickle. I've seen Ryan naked but only his outline. He's huge, and I'm sure he's that big all over. He could crush me and suffocate me to death just by rolling over in his sleep, I'm sure.

But there's a part of me that's a little excited, even though I hate to admit it. Ryan makes me slightly dizzy when he's around. And tonight, when he'd held my hand, and the length of cloth was wrapped around our joined hands to signify our unity, his touch had burned into me like fire that ignited something new in my blood.

Something, I admit, that has me incredibly curious about how it would feel if he touched me... elsewhere.

But another thought plagues my heart, cutting through every other feeling. I look down at the bonfire and spot Mercy carrying Lora back to our house. Lora is slumped over her shoulder, limp and asleep. I wonder where Shoshannah is, then spot her sitting with a group of girls close to her own age and smile to myself as Shosh laughs.

I'm not ready to leave them. I raised those girls like they were my own. Mercy and I were all they had when it came to a mother's love, and it kills me knowing I won't wake up with them in my arms anymore.

"They're going to be okay," Freya says quietly, resting her hand on my knee. "You know they are."

"They're just so young still. I thought I had more time before this happened."

"They're old enough to know what to expect. Women leave the village every year to marry."

My throat aches as I watch Shosh hop up as Mercy calls out her name and runs to our house to be tucked into bed.

I rise, dusting off my dress. "I need to go home and pack–"

"You're already packed up."

Freya and I turn to find Ryan standing at the bottom of the hill, his white shirt unbuttoned down his chest and his hair ruffled. He looks slightly off kilter, likely from the drinks being shoved in his direction all night and the fact I made him dance for over an hour before reality slapped me in the face, and I ran away from him.

His eyes meet mine in the moonlight, steady and unreadable. "I could have done that myself," I tell him hotly.

"Well, we're leaving in a few hours, just before dawn. You should rest before then."

Freya stands as I begin walking down the hill, meaning to brush past him and walk home, but he catches me by the arm.

I know I'm being mean. I know I shouldn't be glaring at him, my own husband. I know he had no idea what he was doing when he gave my father that golden elk pelt. I know he didn't want this just as much as I didn't, but we did it anyway.

Because we had to.

This isn't about love. He will sleep with me tonight, taking my innocence, not because he wants me or feels anything for me, but because I am his wife now.

"You're coming back to my camp," he says, his voice low and soft, like the words hurt.

It would look odd if I didn't go with him tonight, wouldn't it? We share the same sentiment, obviously, because he looks like he would do anything to allow me to walk away and disappear into my own house.

I look up at Freya, who's watching us with a curious expression on her face. When Ryan turns his head to start walking me away, Freya repeats the crude motion with her hands, and I smile despite the chill licking down my spine.

I'll be okay. I doubt Ryan will be aggressive with me. I doubt he'll

hurt me on purpose. He wouldn't, right? He's not like that. I haven't–
he hasn't ever made me feel like I should be scared of him....

We walk in silence to his camp. A few tents are still up, but his
men are actively packing their belongings and items they acquired
during trade with my village.

Ryan leads me into one tent, which isn't big enough for more than
two people. There's nothing but a mat to sleep on, a few blankets, and
a bag of my things. The few dresses and clothing items I own are
neatly packed away, my mother's golden necklace sitting on top.
Everything I own in one little bag. Mercy must have done this today
while she took care of everything else for my wedding.

My heart sinks.

I turn to Ryan, my chest aching. I open my mouth, but the words
I'm looking for are lost when I notice the pain in his eyes as he looks
at me, his gaze sweeping over my face, then my body, and back up
again. "You'll be able to see your sisters to say goodbye in the morning. We're leaving in four hours. Get some sleep."

He leaves the tent.

He doesn't come back.

12

SWOLLEN RIVER

Ryan

JERROD STANDS BESIDE ME IN THE GLARE OF EARLY MORNING. BOTH OF us are pretending like we're watching the dark, angry storm clouds barreling toward us, directly in the path I'm supposed to be traveling today, and not the heart wrenching scene taking place only a few feet away.

Aviva is doing her best to explain to a fitful Lora that they'll see each other again. Lora is shaking her head and shoving her teddy bear against a desperate Aviva's chest, telling her to take it to keep her safe at night. What's worse is that Shoshannah is nowhere to be found. She didn't come here, to the edge of the village, to say goodbye to Aviva, and I can tell by the forlorn look on Aviva's face that this is one of the most painful things she's ever had to do.

I'm gutted. Absolutely gutted. This feels so incredibly unfair.

Jerrod sighs beside me, cursing under his breath. I glance at him, noticing the wetness in his eyes. He catches me looking at him and smiles sadly, shaking his head. "I know you think me a cruel man for

87

giving away my daughter like this, but I assure you, this is the best thing for her."

"How?" I'm not dumb enough to say what I really feel. That he boxed me into this. That he knew I couldn't refuse because I needed this alliance for my pack. That I'd take her with me even though I think it's wrong.

"My wife, Gemma, was from the Roguelands. She came here during the Great War two decades or so again now as a refugee." He shakes his head, running his hand over his beard as he drops his eyes to his sandals. "Her entire pack was wiped out in a single night. She was the only one who survived because she'd been at home healing from an injury while the rest of the pack were in their meeting hall. She wandered the woods, trying to stay hidden, and was eventually taken in by another pack and sent here, to the Deadlands, where refugee camps were being set up for the displaced packs during the war. That's how I met her. I was just a hunter at the time. A few of us left Endova to go check out the camps, and when I saw her, I knew I had to have her, and somehow, she felt the same way about me."

He continues, "She was a beautiful, loving woman. I never deserved her, but she loved me and gave me Mercy and then Aviva. We thought our blessings from the Goddess were over, but then she gave me Shoshannah, and Lora." He sucks in a breath, shaking his head. "The younger girls only ever had Mercy and Aviva. Mercy is so like me. Tough. Quick to anger. Righteous. But Aviva... she is Gemma's daughter through and through. When Gemma died, Aviva bottled it up instead of grieving with the rest of us. She started disappearing into the woods every chance she could get. She moved on from hunting for food to hunting for sport, killing rogues and other beasts. We only ever knew because the other hunters would find their charred remains, sometimes with her arrows nearby. It caused a rift between Mercy and Aviva. Mercy stays awake at night, pacing the house, waiting for Aviva to return. She won't admit her love for Aviva because her fear over Aviva's death overshadows it."

My muscles tense as I look back at my wife, who is now kneeling next to Mercy, the two sisters doing their best to comfort the youngest. Jerrod continues, "Aviva can't remain here in Endova because she'll die in those woods one day. She isn't afraid. That's her only fault. Other men have come to me asking for her hand, but I knew, deep down, that even sending her to another pack out here wouldn't keep her alive. She'd end up back in those woods, chasing death. But then you came."

"I'm not the man you think I am."

"I think you chase the same kind of demons my daughter hunts every night when she sneaks out of my house," he says pointedly, his gaze boring into the side of my face. "I know what they say about you, Alpha Ryan. That you're cursed. That you have a heart of stone. And… maybe you are. Maybe you do. But I look at my daughter and see the same hurt I see in your eyes."

"Then why force her to marry me?"

"In time, both of you will understand." He claps me on the shoulder. "Safe travels, Alpha. I'll see you at the festival in three months."

"Wait–"

Howls cut through the air, echoing under the gathering clouds. A few drops of rain start to fall, and my attention is stolen by the scouts I sent out this morning to make sure our route back to Silverhide was clear. Jerrod slips away, and I'm left pondering his last words while watching Andrew and Jacob meet up with the scouts.

"Don't go!" Lora howls as Mercy lifts her off the ground. She kicks her little legs, thrashing. "Don't go, Aviva!"

"I'm only thirty miles away," my wife says tearfully, hugging herself as Mercy clutches a sobbing Lora to her chest. "It's–it's a day's travel, Lora, I'll visit as often as I can."

The young girl's scream rips through my heart as Mercy carries her away.

"Please take care of them," Aviva says loudly, directing her words at Mercy, who turns to her with dry eyes but an expression that rocks me to my core.

This isn't right. This *feels* so wrong, but Jerrod's words still echo through my mind as Mercy nods, swallowing hard, and cradles Lora tightly, walking back toward the village.

I look at my devastated wife as she gapes after her family. Her eyes meet mine, and she shakes her head, turning from me the moment I open my mouth to say something, anything, to make this better.

"Don't worry about it," Freya's voice says somewhere behind me. I whirl as she bustles past me, a heavy bag slung over her shoulders. She turns to me, walking backward. "I've seen worse goodbyes. Everyone will be just fine."

I'm truly at a loss for words as I watch Freya fall in step with a distraught Aviva, both of them dressed in pants and shirts sewn with those strange loops and strings that pull apart when they shift. Freya ropes an arm around Aviva's shoulder and says with remarkable casualness, "So, how was it? Better yet, how big–"

Aviva shoves her away, but Freya laughs, and to my immense relief, Aviva looks at her with a ghost of a smile on her trembling lips.

I roll my lower lip between my teeth while I watch the women walk toward the rest of our group, which has gathered on the rugged trail leading back to Silverhide. Aviva doesn't look back at me. She joins the ranks, Jacob leading the pack. I'm sure some members of the party will shift after a while, but right now, everyone is tired from not only the hunt, but two nights of partying in a row.

We should be home by sundown. That's the plan, but we're walking into a storm that I'm sure will force us to make a camp somewhere along the way. I doubt I'll be able to avoid sharing a tent with my wife this time.

Honestly, I'm not sure I want to avoid it. I need to talk to her. I have to know she's all right. Because all of this is my fault.

* * *

"THIS ISN'T LOOKING GOOD," JACOB SAYS AS I CATCH UP TO HIM ON A hill halfway between Endova and the new Silverhide territory. The creek below us is three times as wide as it had been when we crossed it four days ago on our way to the village. "We're going to lose the carts if we try to cross here."

I grit my teeth, my gaze sweeping over the seemingly endless rolling hills. To the west, the dark forest stretches as far as the eye can see. "We need to find shelter tonight to ride out the storm. That's all we can do right now." The woods are going to be our best bet in that department. I'm not going to risk my men sleeping out in the open, storm or no.

Jacobs nods and walks down the hill toward the group standing below us. I spot Aviva in the small crowd, still standing with Freya. She's wet, but whole, and right now, that's all that matters to me.

Jacob starts shouting commands, and the group begins to move again, following the swollen creek to the west.

I stay behind the group, using the mind-link to tell Andrew and Jacob to send scouts ahead. Three wolves dart away, taking off at the speed of light, and fall out of sight as more rain pours over us in never-ending sheets.

With the incoming night, the air starts to take on a fresh chill that makes me want to strip out of my clothes and shift just to stay warm, but we're nearing the forest with every second that passes, and the only thing on my mind is sitting by a fire and eating something for the first time since last night during our wedding party.

I also need to talk to Aviva and make sure she's okay, but I'm not sure what I can even say at this point. "I'm sorry," doesn't feel like enough.

I keep myself busy for the next two hours as night falls. We set up camp at the very edge of the forest under the shelter of a crop of towering oak trees. Soon, four small fires are burning, and food is being prepared.

But I'm standing with Jacob and Andrew instead of sitting with my wife.

"The creek is shallower here," I tell them, looking down at a crude map as thunder booms overhead. "I just don't trust this storm, and the creek is being fed from the mountains at the far edge of the forest."

"It might be shallow now, but there's no telling what things could look like in an hour if this continues," Andrew murmurs in agreement, nodding his head.

"I'll take two scouts and cross the creek," Jacob says, dragging his finger over the map to Silverhide. "We'll reach Silverhide in... two hours, I'm guessing. It's only fifteen miles."

"Once you reach Silverhide, send a group back to help us get the supply carts across the creek. If worst comes to worst, we'll have to float them across. We'll need men on the other side to help with that." I run my fingers through my wet hair, shaking my head. I'd kill for a weather app on a working cell phone right now. There's no infrastructure for that here—not yet, anyway.

Jacob rolls up the map and heads out, gathering two men along the way. I stand under a tree and watch the three of them shift and take off into the swirling, rain-soaked darkness.

"You okay?" Andrew asks.

"Make sure everyone is either sheltered tonight by tents or sleeping in their wolf forms. We're hunkering down for the night." I kick off the tree but pause, looking around the camp. Freya is fast asleep leaning on one of the supply carts, but she's alone. "Where's Aviva?"

Andrew steps up to my side. "I haven't seen her in a while."

I scan the camp slowly, taking in every detail. "Does she have a scent to you?" I ask.

"Uh, I guess. She just smells like a girl. Why, you don't know her scent?"

"I've never been able to pick it up. I think she masks it somehow."

Andrew shrugs helplessly. I notice Aviva's bag sitting next to Freya. She hadn't been wearing her knife belt during our journey today. I'd noticed it hanging out of the bag earlier.

It's gone now.

I look toward the dark, stormy woods.

She's fucking hunting, isn't she?

An hour later, I find her in a hilly stretch of open fields in the center of the forest. I stand at the top of one of the hills and watch in silent awe, and horror, as she darts in her wolf form behind a massive, mangled rogue wolf and shifts as she leaps off the tips of her claws, her blade outstretched.

It doesn't even know she's there. She lands on her human feet, sliding over the rain soaked grass, and silently slits its throat before shifting again and chasing after the second. She takes the second one down in a similar manner but uses its body to leap onto the back of the third rogue, shifting back into her human form again to pierce its skull through the base of its neck.

I've never seen anyone move like she can. I've never seen anyone able to shift back and forth with such skill and ease.

I'm impressed but also furious as I sit back on my haunches and watch my wife kill, over and over again, stone faced and emotionless, like she can't even feel her blade doing awful, but necessary, work.

She ensures each rogue is completely dead before sheathing her blade and falling to her knees in the center of the three beasts, then she screams. Loud and furious, her scream pierces the air over the torrents of cold rain and rumbling thunder.

When she's done, she slowly lifts her head, her eyes meeting mine. I turn and head back to camp.

13

OFF TO A GREAT START

Aviva

THE CAMP IS QUIET WHEN I RETURN. I'M SOAKING WET, BUT thankfully clean of rogue blood, because of the rain. Everyone gave up on sleeping outside in their wolf forms, choosing to sleep in tents instead in their human forms. Everything is soaked. Tarps cover the supply carts, nailed to the ground to prevent any sudden gusts of wind from ripping the tarps off completely and soaking everything my village traded for Ryan's wares.

I walk by each tent and find Freya curled inside one of them, fast asleep. I start to kneel to crawl inside when Ryan's voice cuts toward me, emotionlessly rasping, "Get over here."

I rise and turn to him. He pitched a tent several yards away from the rest of the camp, further into the forest. Its entrance faces the forest, in fact, and I think he means to stay up all night under the shelter of the canvas to make sure none of the beasts within make any moves on his people.

I chew my lower lip as I follow him. He holds the tent flap open for me. I don't argue as I kick off my water-logged boots and crawl inside.

"Change into something dry," he says, exits, and snaps the flap closed.

I kneel for a moment, wiping rain from my face. My bag isn't in here. It's probably in Freya's tent, and the only thing available to change into is one of Ryan's shirts, which is so large on me it brushes my knees and I have to roll the sleeves several times. I'm not sure what to do with my wet clothes, so I leave them near the entrance and sit down on the bedroll on one side of the tent and start untangling my curls.

He's going to scold me for going after those rogues, I already know it. I knew the second I saw him standing in his wolf form on top of that hill that I was in trouble.

I don't know how to be his wife. We're not even friends. He's still a stranger, and today has just… been hard.

"Are you dressed?"

"Yes–"

He opens the tent flap and slides inside, closing it quickly behind him. Thunder booms overhead, and lightning cracks the sky in two, illuminating the darkness all around us in vibrant blue light.

There's a soft click, then muted yellow light erupts all around me. It startles me, and I jump. "What is that?"

"A solar powered lantern," he murmurs. He's soaking wet. Water drips from his hair as he rolls out a second sleeping mat and begins to unbutton his shirt. The fabric clings to his body as he roughly tears it off and tosses it in the corner with my wet clothes. His eyes slide to mine then inspect the shirt I'm wearing.

"I didn't have anything else."

"It's fine. Your bag is with Freya."

"I know."

"You'll be sleeping–housing–with me, from now on." He holds my gaze for a second longer before digging through a large leather bag at the head of the tent, taking out some kind of sweater with a hood and pulls it over his large frame.

It's too quiet in here even with the pounding rain. We're also only inches apart. I'm waiting for him to rip into me, to forbid me from ever setting foot outside with the intent to hunt. He's my husband, after all. He can tell me what to do now. I am nothing more than his wife.

"How did you know the rogues were there?"

I hug my knees to my chest as he tosses a blanket onto my mat. "They've been tailing us for the last ten miles."

"I didn't see them or smell them."

"You can hear them if you know what they sound like." I swallow hard as he reaches into his bag for another thick sweater and rolls it up, reaching over the ten inches or so of space between us to lay it on my mat like a pillow. I chew my lip, watching him make… make me a bed, in silence. A bed I don't deserve, especially after sneaking off.

"What do they sound like?"

"They make little clicking sounds. Like bones tapping together, when they're walking. The–the birds get quiet when they're around. When we left the forest and came out into the plains, I noticed the birdsong didn't follow us. It'd been quiet for a while, for too long."

"You could hear these things over the rain?"

I nod, unsure what else to say.

He kneels only a few inches away from me, his hands resting on his thighs. "Don't ever do that again."

"But I–" He raises his head, his eyes a deep blue in the dim light. The expression behind them leaves me momentarily breathless. "Ryan–"

"This is the second time you've scared the fuck out of me, Aviva, and I've only known you for four days."

I scooch a little closer to him as all of the emotions I've been burying for those four days come bursting to the surface. "You didn't have to marry me. You could have left me in Endova. You could have taken Mercy."

"I didn't want Mercy."

"You didn't want me, either. Why do you care if I'm off dealing with rogues? They were hunting us. They would have found this camp and attacked the moment your people stopped to rest!"

"I know."

"Then what is your problem?"

He leans in so we're nose to nose. "The next time you decide to run off into the night, or scale a fucking mountain, tell me so I can go with you. So I can help you."

"I don't need or want your help."

"I don't want *my wife* dying."

The emotion in his voice rattles me to my core. He's taking this very seriously, isn't he? I think this goes beyond the fact we're hand-fasted. "What happened to you?" I don't know why I feel the need to ask. I noticed the dark look in his eyes the first time I encountered him in our wolf forms, the day Shosh shot him in the shoulder.

That darkness swells as he starts to pull away, but I stop him, my hand flying out and closing around the back of his head.

"Why did you kill your mate?"

He chuckles darkly, shaking his head. "We're getting right into that, then?" He tries to pull away again, but I tangle my fingers in his hair to tighten my grip. He grunts in pain but has a slight wry smile on his face as his eyes meet mine. "Why do you go out into the forest every night?"

"I asked you first." I pull his hair.

He lets out a soft sound that sends a ripple of warmth ghosting down my spine. My heart starts racing out of rhythm as his eyes, heavy with sudden heat, lock on mine. "She threatened someone I love."

"Then you understand why I spend so much time in the woods," I reply, giving his hair another pull for good measure. His mouth ticks into a heated smile that has me feeling... dizzy. I let him go, slowly raking my fingers through his wet, dark curls, but he catches my wrist, his thumb pressed to my pulse.

I'm not sure why, or how it happens, or why I even allow it, but he starts to pull me closer, and I don't shy away from him.

His lips hover just in front of mine, his face tilting slightly to one side, but he doesn't kiss me. His mouth brushes over my jaw before he dips his head, his curls brushing over my face and neck.

His breath is warm and tickles the crook where my neck meets my shoulder as he whispers over my skin, "Why can't I smell you? It's driving me insane."

I close my eyes, my lips parting as his free hand travels up my side.

"I don't know," I whisper. At least, I think I'm saying the words out loud. My spine loosens, and my body feels suddenly heavy as I instinctively lean into his touch.

He groans against my skin, and the noise ignites a feral, primal want that burrows through my lower belly. He lets go of my wrist, and I instinctively wrap my arms around his neck and pull him closer until we're chest to chest.

He pulls me onto his lap. This is crazy. What we're doing right now doesn't make any sense, but neither does anything that happened over the last four days, so I lean into it, tilting my head back as he buries his face in my hair and rocks his hips against mine and I'm...

A howl breaks through the night, over the pounding rain. Another howl follows, and Ryan goes wholly still.

Reality crashes down on us both, startling me out of the haze of delusion that's been clouding my judgment since last night when our mangled palms were tied together and we were blood bound.

Before I realize what I'm doing, my arm slides from his neck, and my hand pulls back, knocking him soundly on the top of the head.

"Ow, hey!" he snarls, teeth bared. "What the hell was that for?"

"For touching me!"

"You're on my lap," he growls, his nose pressed to the tip of mine.

Another howl breaks through the rain. "Aren't you going to go see who that is?"

"It's just my scouts returning and alerting their next watch."

My heart is pounding. Neither of us have moved. Neither of us have blinked, either.

"Your useless scouts who didn't see the rogues?" The breath is knocked out of me as he rolls with me in his arms, pinning me to the sleeping mat. I thrash, but Ryan is strong as hell. He drives his knee between my thighs and… fuck, it feels good, but it also stops me from trying to squirm out of his grasp because any movement against his knee sends… heat–pure, white hot pleasure–settling in my lower belly.

He's smirking down at me now. I refuse to give him the fucking satisfaction. So, I bare my teeth, my canines lengthening.

"Are you going to shift and rip my throat out, little wolf?"

"Don't tempt me with a good time," I growl.

His eyes twinkle with amusement before he gives me a rough shove for good measure and straightens up, letting go of my arms. He pulls his hood over his head. "Go to sleep, Aviva," he chuckles, then roughly switches off the lamp.

Darkness swells, heavy and cold. I watch his shadow leave the tent and disappear into the thundering rain, and I'm alone.

I rarely ever sleep alone. If I'm alone, I'm sure as hell not fully asleep. Especially since being alone would mean I'm sleeping in the woods somewhere, preferably my hideout in the ruins of the old temple… not on a sleeping mat with a pillow and blanket that smell like *him*.

My new reality hits me like an arrow to the heart.

I'm alone. Utterly alone. Freya is my only lifeline in this storm, and I can't go to her right now, can I?

If I did, Ryan would probably use that against me. He'd see it as a weakness.

I'm here, in his tent, because, to his people at least, I'm his wife. This is where I belong.

I curl into the blanket and hold my eyes open. I will not cry. *I will not cry.*

I do fall asleep at some point which I detest immensely, especially when I wake up to early morning sunlight, and I'm warm to the bone, heavy with a peaceful, enriching kind of sleep and… Ryan's arm is roped over my side, pinning my arm to my chest. His breath tickles my hair. He's nuzzled so close, and he's shirtless… pantless. His knee rests between my bare legs.

I slowly untangle myself from him and hop up, ducking out of the way of the ceiling of the tent, and give him a little nudge with my foot. "Wake up."

He murmurs something. He looks rather cute with his stubble and his hair all wild and mussed from sleep, but I give him another nudge, harder this time.

"What do you want, Aviva?"

"It's morning."

"Sleep in while you have the chance. Jacob won't be back until noon."

"How do you know?" I nudge him in the stomach again with my foot, and he grabs my ankle.

"Mind-link," he murmurs, his eyes still closed, and his face relaxed. "Go back to sleep."

"Scoot over, then."

He groans as he rolls over, taking the blanket with him.

Well, this marriage is off to a great start already, isn't it?

14
STOW AWAY

Aviva

THE MOMENT RYAN STIRS AGAIN, I LAUNCH INTO MOTION. I'M OUT OF the tent the second he begins to stretch like he's the only one on the sleeping mat. I run at a full sprint through the center of the camp, wearing nothing but his shirt.

I jump into Freya's tent and land with a crunch on top of her. She squeals, swatting me as she tries to untangle herself from the quilt she bundled herself up in last night. "What the hell are you doing, Aviva?"

I grab her cheeks. She blinks sleepily up at me, her eyes cloudy with confusion. "I need you to tell me everything about men. Everything."

* * *

"LOOK AT THOSE IDIOTS," FREYA GIGGLES AS SHE POPS ANOTHER perfect, sweet strawberry into her mouth.

I lick strawberry juice from my fingers and turn to look over my shoulder at the group of men on opposite sides of the creek below, yelling and arguing with each other as they try to get the two heavy, overladen carts across the swollen creek. I smirk down at them. I doubt they've even noticed us watching them. It's well into the afternoon on the second day of what should have been a day-long journey.

From our perch on the flat peak of a huge boulder sticking out of a hill nearby, we can see the entire hilarious scene below and have no plans or desire to help them.

Instead, we spent the day roaming the hills and picking the sweetest strawberries I think I've ever tasted with no plans to share our bounty with the tired, increasingly grumpy men below.

I bite into another strawberry. The bright flavor explodes on my tongue. I groan around it, happy with our decision not to give them any.

"Should we help?" Freya asks, tilting her head. "It's been three hours since they started."

I peer down at the center of the creek where a soaking wet Ryan is shouting at Jacob, who is waist deep and using a rope to try to pull one of the carts across. Four other men are pushing it, slipping on the rocks into the swift current.

"Nah," I reply, fishing for the last of the strawberries in a huge basket between us. "They'll use those big, male brains of theirs to figure this out eventually."

"They could have made a raft, at least. It wouldn't have taken that much time."

"They're showing off for us," I laugh, pointing at Andrew, who has his shirt off as he jumps into the water with a second rope and swims to attach it to the cart.

Freya shakes her head, smirking. "You know, everyone back home is so jealous we got to go. Rochel was in a fucking tizzy about it. Miriam told me she cried through your entire wedding and not because the ceremony moved her to tears."

I roll my eyes. "Why does everyone want to get married so badly? I had to share a tent with Ryan last night–"

She gives my leg a little nudge with her foot. "Yeah, you did. And you also burst into my tent this morning acting desperate to understand why just sleeping next to him had you all worked up… warm, and wet–"

I pinch her, and she yelps. "I never said I was–"

"Oh, please." She waves a hand in dismissal. "It's okay to be attracted to your husband. You're lucky, honestly. I'm sure not everyone is half as lucky as you, Aviva, having such a handsome man to share a bed with." She sighs dramatically and rests her chin on her fist, batting her eyelashes at the men now fighting for their lives as the cart slips into the current and starts tilting sideways. "I'm honestly shocked he hasn't, you know…"

"I thought maybe last night–" I bite my tongue. Okay, first of all, why do I care? I shouldn't be tangled in knots over the idea that Ryan and I have been married for two days, and he hasn't taken me to bed yet–not in that way, anyhow. Secondly, I should be thankful for it, especially after catching a glimpse of him in nothing but his undershorts this morning.

My throat goes dry at the thought of his thick, muscular thighs and chiseled abs with that sharp V leading toward–

"Look, they got the first one across." Freya giggles. We both clap and whistle enthusiastically.

Andrew beams, waving at us. Jacob and Ryan exchange glances, and while Jacob chuckles and says something under his breath, we're too far away to hear, Ryan scowls directly at me, his eyes shining with annoyance over the gurgling howl of the swift creek.

Eventually the second cart floats over the creek, and Freya and I have to leave our perch, now covered with the leafy, discarded strawberry tops, and hike down to the creek. Andrew offers to carry Freya on his shoulders as to not, "get her pretty dress wet," which he says with a wink that makes Freya blush, and of course she obliges. She throws a look over her shoulder and waves as she clutches Andrew's head between her thighs and I know, without a shadow of a doubt, that he's loving every second of it.

Ryan doesn't offer me the same treatment. He's waiting on a large rock in the very center of the creek, crouching, resting his elbows on his knees. "Go ahead," he says, his voice low and dripping with remnants of frustration left over from an honestly arduous task I didn't help with.

In my defense, no one asked for my help.

I'm sure he's hoping I fall in.

I skip across the creek like it's nothing, carrying my sandals under my arm as my bare feet find the taller, flatter rocks none of these men saw under the current, apparently. When I pass Ryan, forgoing his center rock, he frowns at me. That frown singes the back of my head as I leap off the last of the rocks and land on the other side of the creek, totally dry above the ankles.

I walk beside Freya for the rest of the afternoon, arm in arm, too busy listening to her rattling on about all of the gossip she gathered during my wedding to even bother shifting. Eventually, we leave the rolling, open plains again and start walking along a well packed dirt road into the forest. It's straight and narrow. Old, actually. I know exactly where we are, even though I've never been this far away from Endova.

This is the road leading to the Roguelands. Beyond this forest, the Deadlands become nothing but barren, gray hills. Once, refugee camps dotted those plains. Sometimes the elders tell stories about that time, over two decades ago now. War and famine. Unimaginable hardship. My heart begins beating so fast I start to lose the ability to take a full breath. Freya keeps talking, going on and on about how someone we know kissed someone else we know at the wedding party.

For some reason unknown to me, I look over my shoulder. We're in the center of the group, following the carts, and Ryan is far back.

He's walking in his human form, following his people. His eyes meet mine as my heart rate continues to skyrocket. For a split second, his eyes shine with sudden understanding. He looks momentarily concerned and straightens his shoulders. I doubt he can sense the way my heart is beating out of rhythm, but he searches my face, then tilts his head to the side. *'You're not scared, are you, little wolf?'*

'*Stay out of my head,*' I fire back through the mind-link, and face forward again.

A few minutes later, the group ahead of us turns sharply to the left, no longer following the well packed road to the Roguelands. Instead, we pick our way along a more rural road that's still fresh and obviously seldom used. A mile later, the forest gives way, and a valley so green it's blinding erupts before us.

Freya gasps, and so do I. We hold each other a little tighter as shock ripples through us both. "What is this place?" She gapes, looking around as rolling farmland hugs either side of the narrow road.

"Silverhide," I whisper in disbelief.

Cattle graze lazily in a field nearby. More fields come into view. We climb higher into the valley, eventually following another shallow creek. Some are tilled and freshly planted with who knows what, but I can see the first outlines of fields of grain sprouting in the distance, golden blades swaying in a soft, warm breeze.

I'm not sure what I expected. When father visited this pack for the first time, he'd come home telling stories of a village of canvas tents, not large stone houses with blue shutters. Not barns and cabins made of logs that gleam like gold in the sunlight. Not the village now standing toward the back of the valley, built on either side of the creek, and connected by a wooden bridge.

Some of the buildings are two stories tall. Glass windows shine in the sunlight. Smoke flows toward the sky from several neat, stone chimneys on several of the larger buildings.

Gardens spread wide over the rolling hills. A small wooden building with a stippled roof has several children playing in the yard. They see our group and start shouting, laughing deliriously as they run forward and watch us walk by. A woman calls the children back, but waves excitedly.

A school, perhaps?

I didn't realize there were so many children here.

Several women are doing laundry in the creek, which is shallow enough the water only reaches their knees in some spots. Their clothes are different compared to back home. Thick fabric woven so tightly I can barely make out the threads. Warm, fluffy sweaters made of what looks like fine wool.

Freya clears her throat as we pass the women, who stare at us and whisper.

We pass them and soon we're stepping into the village proper and... I'm shocked. This place is lovely.

"Took you long enough," says a deep, male voice somewhere ahead of us.

Ryan walks past us. I turn around, wondering how long he'd been gaining on Freya and I, and notice most of the group we've traveled with has dispersed. Several of the men are walking toward small houses dotted along the road, further away from the village. When I turn to look forward, practically dragging an absolutely stunned Freya by her arm, I realize we're part of the few left in the group to actually walk into the center of the village.

Ryan clasps elbows with a tall, dark haired man as we come to a stop. The man's eyes slide to mine, then back to Ryan's as he steps closer and says, "Jacob mentioned–"

"I was so worried!" A soft, lifted female voice hits my ear, and the most pregnant woman I've ever seen comes to stop at the stranger's side, steadying herself on his arm.

"Oh, Dahlia," Ryan sighs, shaking his head. "I was really hoping you'd have had the baby by the time I got back."

She frowns, tucking her light brown hair behind her ears, which have gone pink. "The baby is stubborn. I have nothing else to say about it."

The stranger purses his lips, gently wrapping his arm around her back. He must be Ryan's Beta. I remember hearing that he had one, someone who acts as his second, or something like that. I also remember that he didn't come on the hunt because his mate was due to have their baby any day.

Mate. The word rings through my head as I stare at the couple. I've never met a set of mates before.

Ryan slowly turns his attention to me, grimacing a bit. "Uh, so, this is Aviva. My *wife*."

Dahlia looks at me cheerfully, but her mate doesn't give me a smile. So, I don't give either of them one in return, and stay stone-faced and skeptical.

Ryan sighs, his eyes locked on mine, and turns back to his Beta to say something else when a commotion directly behind us has everyone turning toward the carts. Andrew, who was raising the tarp off one of them, jumps back with a grunt of surprise.

"What?" Ryan asks coldly, stomping toward him.

"Shit, man, we gotta problem–"

The tarp starts to move, which causes several people to yelp in alarm, and then flies back to reveal…

"SHOSHANNAH?" I shriek as my sister pops her head up, smiling like the little demon she is.

15

FEEL YOU

Aviva

RAGE AND WORRY FIGHT FOR CONTROL AS SHOSHANNAH STARES AT US, glancing from face to face. Her mouth and fingers are stained red from feasting from a basket of berries sitting next to her in the cart, but one quick scan of her body in whole shows me she's dry and uninjured.

I think of crossing the creek only a few hours ago, how easily the current could have swept the cart away with her in it, and my chest convulses.

I open my mouth to say something, anything, but a muffled groan comes out instead.

Freya is the first to act. She brushes past me, her face twisted in confusion, and storms up to Shosh, picking her up and throwing her over her shoulder like a sack of grain. Freya turns to James and Dahlia, who are watching the scene play out in shocked silence, Freya's blonde hair is wild and coming loose from the long braid down her back as Shosh thrashes and kicks. "Where will I be staying?" she asks politely, smiling kindly at the couple.

"Uhm, I had a room set up for you at our house," Dahlia squeaks, casting a quick glance at Ryan before motioning for Freya to follow. "I'll show you."

"Put me down!" Shoshannah rages, but Freya tightens her grip and walks away.

I move to follow, but Ryan grabs my arm. "Let her go."

I whirl. "She could have died in that creek. She slept all night alone in the rain and I–" I suck in a breath, shaking as I continue, "Mercy and father are probably frantic right now–"

"James, get Grey and Hunter and send them back to Endova, now." Ryan's voice rips through the air as he starts tugging me away from the cart. "Tell them they're not stopping until they get there." Ryan holds James's gaze, and I wonder if they're sharing a separate conversation over the mind-link as Ryan continues to back away from the cart, taking me with him. Jacob and Andrew motion to a few other men standing around to start unloading the supplies, and things simply… move on.

But I'm fuming. I look over my shoulder in the direction Freya disappeared with Shoshannah, the opposite direction Ryan is leading me in now. "Hey! I need to talk to her!"

"Not right now," Ryan growls, his hand clutching my forearm so tight it begins to burn as I try to yank free of his grasp.

"That's my sister!"

"I understand," he snaps, his voice low and rumbling. We leave what I believe is the center of the village and walk around a two-story wooden building where a narrow dirt road leads toward a trio of small houses. One of them is further away than the others, built on a rise with a deck that overlooks the village. Tall trees brush the deck railing, and a trail of rock leads to a plain, wooden door.

"Where are we going?"

"Home."

"Shoshannah–"

"Is fine and will be returned to your father." He practically drags me up the stone trail, which looks like stairs cut directly out of rock, all while I fight to get out of his grasp.

My feet slide across the smooth floorboards of the deck as he drags me toward the door, opens it, and quickly shuts us inside.

Everything is made of warm toned, smooth wood. The walls, the furniture. A small kitchen with nothing more than a work table and some cabinets greets us immediately. A large fireplace made of stone sits on the far side of the room, dormant. That's it, other than a narrow, short hallway leading to a door, with two more doors facing each other.

Ryan's scent is heavy here. This is his house. His things.

Well, this is my house now, too, I guess.

The adrenaline pumping through my veins makes it impossible to really take in my surroundings, however. I whirl on him, sending my fist flying toward his face. He catches it and squeezes until I yelp and back away.

"You need to calm down!" he snarls.

Panting, I shout, "My sister is here. Do you realize what's probably happening in Endova right now? They're missing a child–"

"I understand, which is why I just sent two of my best scouts in that direction. They'll be in Endova shortly after sundown. It's only thirty miles–"

"She needs to be returned immediately!"

He points to a window overlooking the deck. Dark clouds move swiftly into the valley, swirling toward the sun. "It's going to rain again. I can't take her back to Endova until this storm passes."

I shake my head, frantic. "Why would she do this?"

"You really don't know?"

That raw emotion flares behind his eyes. It's grief, I realize with a start. Grief–and anguish, things I hadn't thought someone like him would feel. Not when he has all of *this*. This beautiful village. Pack members who obviously adore him. Friends.

Emotions I've kept buried since we left Endova burst to the surface, and I find myself gritting my teeth to keep a torrent of sharp words from falling from my tongue.

He steps toward me, but I move away. Shaking his head, he says calmly, "Shoshannah loves you. I knew something was off when she didn't say goodbye–"

"You don't know her–"

"She is your spitting image. I thought she was your daughter the first time I met you, when you were defending them from me," he says through gritted teeth. "I'm not surprised at all that she pulled this stunt because it's something *you* would have done."

I see red.

"Don't look at me like that." He edges toward me, his hands balled into fists.

"I need to talk to her. You can't keep me from her–"

"I'm not separating you. You just need to chill the fuck out for a minute and think. You've been on the road all day. We had a long night–"

I'm trembling with rage as Ryan postures in front of me, widening his stance like he's preparing to catch me when I attempt to barrel through him for the door.

"She is my sister!"

"And you're going to go down there and yell at her, scold her for what she did!" he shouts. "I'm the Alpha here, Aviva. I'm not going to allow that."

"I wouldn't–I wouldn't yell at her like you're yelling at me now! She is my responsibility!"

"And you're mine," he cuts in harshly. "You are my wife. Shoshannah is my family now, too. No harm is going to come to her here, and once these storms pass, I will take her back to Endova-personally. Right now, you need to rest."

"You don't know–"

"I can feel you," he rasps. His eyes darken, turning from that fresh, clear blue to something stormy and depthless.

His words catch me off guard. I'm not sure I understand what he means.

He takes a shallow breath and shakes his head as if to clear it. "I can feel you... wanting to... break something, I don't know. I don't know how else to explain it, but you're worked up, and you're fucking exhausted. I am too, okay? This–" he motions between us. "I don't know what to do with this, how to act, how to treat you. But I'm not going to put myself through watching another scene play out like when I had to watch you saying goodbye to Lora."

My lips part in surprise. There's an edge to his voice–heavy and raw. His eyes shine in the soft evening daylight still whispering through the clouds, bleeding through the windows.

He takes a single step in my direction. My heart is beating erratically as he comes to a stop only a foot from where I stand. "I have a twin brother," he says, his voice taking on a softer edge. "Sydney. He's older by a few minutes. You can only imagine how we used to butt heads when we were young."

I scan his face, unable to read the emotions playing behind his eyes.

"We have a younger sister, Misty. She's turning twenty in a few months. I know what it's like to have a little sister, especially one like Shoshannah. Misty and Shoshannah aren't that different. I get it, okay? That feeling like you're not in control? I understand."

I stare at him. He stares at me with the same intensity.

"You don't know me," I whisper.

"I don't, you're right. I don't know you, but I know you love your sisters, and I know you're pissed that she put herself in harm's way. I would be too."

"She's ten. She doesn't understand what she's done. The other tribes–if my father has already acted thinking she was taken by Navvan–"

"I'm doing what I can, okay?" Ryan's voice wavers on the words like he's just as anxious as I am. This is probably why he dragged me here, locking us into the solitude of his own home, where no one is going to overhear or interrupt us. He just told me he needs me to calm down and think. He needs to, too, apparently. "Grey and Hunter will be in Endova in a few hours, I'm sure. It won't take them long to get there."

Silence settles between us like a wet blanket–cold and suffocating.

But then he asks, "Why did you scream after killing those rogues?"

I blink. I'd forgotten about that. "It just felt good. I needed to. I don't know."

He nods, a faraway look in his eyes as he turns and heads for the door. "Someone will come up to fetch you in a little while. I'm sure dinner is almost ready at the pack house; that's where we eat together every night." He doesn't look at me as he tilts his head toward the little hallway of doors. "I'll bring your bag up later. There's a bedroom on the left. Dahlia had some clothing brought up for you before we arrived. You can change, if you want. It's colder here than in Endova." He looks at me, his gaze sweeping from my face down to my legs, where the short, wrapped dress I'm wearing hits me mid-thigh.

With that, he tears himself from the house and shuts the door behind him.

I stand in the center of the room for several minutes unable to move. My mind is in knots as I go over our conversation several times. I do wonder why he thought it was best that he separated me from Shoshannah for the time being. She's with Freya. She'll be fine, but I'm...

I'm not okay. I blink back tears I haven't allowed myself to shed since leaving my village–my home. My people. My family.

Had he known that I would crumble the second I arrived? That this would hit me so hard I'd find it hard to breathe, and that matters have been made worse by Shoshannah's deception now, too?

I wipe my eyes on the back of my hands, refusing to cry. Not now. Not yet. Maybe not ever.

And then I do what anyone in my situation would do–I go through all my new husband's things. I open every drawer in the dresser in his bedroom. He has more clothes than I've ever seen one person possess. He likes dark blue and gray the best, apparently. Even the quilt on his bed, which is lifted off the ground on a frame, is a deep, dark sapphire in color. The top drawer of his dresser is a mess of random things–trinkets. I pick up an odd block of what might be metal with a glass cover on one side, turning it over in my hand. It suddenly lights up. I toss it onto the bed with a yelp.

Edging closer, I see... Ryan, and what must be Sydney, reflected on the glass. Ryan's smiling and Sydney, who looks like a less rugged, more polished version of him, has his eyes closed in a laugh. The image disappears, and the glass goes black. Weird. I decide not to touch it again in the event it's some magic relic that might curse me if I accidentally summon its light and move on from the bedroom.

I find a simple bathroom with a huge tub made of copper. I close the door, deciding there's nothing inside worth snooping through, and open the third door. I expect to find another bedroom, for me, but it's totally, completely dark in here. I open the door wider to let in some sunlight, but I'm met with a thick, coppery smell that makes my nose wrinkle.

"Hello? Aviva?" Jacob's voice drifts toward me. "I'm here to take you to the pack house for dinner."

I step out of the strange room, every hair on my body standing on end. What's in there? Why does it smell so… weird? Why is it so dark?

I turn to Jacob, trying to smile to hide the fact I've just spent at least an hour going through every drawer and cabinet in this house.

He sets a stack of clothes on the kitchen table, smiling kindly at me. "Ryan told me to give these to you. He said you might like them."

"Give me what?"

16

SHE'S NOT MINE

Ryan

RAIN PELTS THE ROOF OF THE PACK HOUSE. IT'S THE LARGEST BUILDING, other than the barns we erected last year, in Silverhide. It's an exact model of our pack house back in Crescent Falls but made with cruder materials instead of things like steel and concrete. The log walls still smell like cedar as I walk around, making the rounds, checking in on my pack.

Everyone has questions about my wife, of course. Jacob, after being sent to Silverhide to gather help with the carts, spread the word. Now I'm being showered in clipped congratulations, everyone sounding a little unsure. I'm sure the strained smile on my face doesn't help.

Aviva is seated at the end of one of the three long, wooden tables. She has a plate of food in front of her, and I've been watching her eat as I weave from pack member to pack member, making sure she's actually touching her food. She's seated next to Shoshannah, who's a bit pale, like she had a firm talking to from not only Freya but her sister.

But Aviva looks somewhat at ease. I doubt she rested like I ordered, but I knew she needed a minute alone. Don't ask me how because I don't fucking know. I just felt it. Felt it like her emotions are my own. My hand curls into a fist around the mark—now barely visible—where our hands had been joined. I wonder if this strange sensation has something to do with the ceremony. I wonder if we're now bound in some way that goes beyond our vows to each other, which I honestly don't even know because they were in a different language.

Aviva's eyes briefly meet mine as I walk past their end of the table. She looks away first, and I find a seat next to Jacob and Andrew, who are sitting with some other single men, enjoying plates of roast venison and mashed potatoes with a dark, rick gravy.

I pile food onto my own plate in silence as Andrew carries on a conversation with the men in our group. He's telling them about the spring hunt we went on, of course. Everyone wants to know how it went.

I eat, occasionally glancing down the table toward Aviva. Dahlia has joined them, her hands resting on the curve of her swollen belly as she and Aviva converse, which is nice to see. I'm hoping Aviva will take to Dahlia. Dahlia is easy going and loving, easy to befriend. Having her join my pack was a blessing in disguise. She brings everyone together even in the worst circumstances.

James sits down beside me and sets a glass of whiskey in front of me.

"Thanks," I mumble around a bite of food.

"You look like you could use it." He sips his own drink as he glances down at his mate, but I notice the worry in his eyes.

"What's up?"

"Dahlia's been having contractions all day. The midwife believes she's getting close. Early labor, she called it. She could finally have that baby tonight."

"How do you feel about it?"

"She's miserable. Can't get comfortable; can't sleep. I'm ready for her to be done, you know? I just hate seeing her in pain."

I nod, even though I have nothing to add. I've thought about having kids but not about being a father, if that makes sense. I feel like some people, like my brother, are meant for it. He's so hands on with Blake, and their second son, Liam. My nephews are only a year apart.

Evander drifts into my mind and I smile to myself a bit. Evander, who is scary as hell, dotes on his kids. Brie, who is three and about as wild as they come, has him wrapped around her tiny finger. Then there's Aris, two and more subdued, like Blake. The boys are nearly the same age and can just hangout instead of needing constant stimulation. Kenna had a daughter last year, Maeve. Life moved on when I left. I'm okay with it. I needed the distance.

"Where'd you go?" James asks.

I shake myself out of my mind and take a sip of the whiskey. "Just thinking about everyone back in Crescent Falls and Moonrise."

"Does your family know about the wedding? That you have a wife?"

It feels weird talking to James about this. He never knew Hadley was my mate. I wasn't even the one to tell him after Hadley died. Sarah spilled the beans. I'm not mad about it. James and I both dealt with the grief of losing her in a similar way—not talking about it ever again.

The worst part, I think, is that neither of us knew what she'd gotten herself into until it was too late, and then Sydney killed Gabriel without getting the full story of why.

"No, they don't. I still have to go to Moonrise next month for a bit. I'll tell them then. My parents will be there, and it'll save me a trip back to Crescent Falls."

James nods, but his attention is back on Dahlia, who is a little pale as she tries to carry on a conversation with Aviva and Freya. Justine, the midwife, and the mate of one of my warriors, comes to talk to her, bending to whisper in her ear. Justine is pregnant, too. In fact, our pack will have at least five new babies born this summer.

Again, I glance at Aviva, and my mind wanders toward the possibility of... having a child with her.

I banish the thought. I find that I constantly have to remind myself that she's not really mine. I'm just holding space for her mate when she finds him.

"When the weather clears," I tell James, derailing the subject away from me and Aviva, "I'm going to escort my wife's sister back to Endova personally. I'll take Jacob with me. It'll be faster just the two of us and the girl." I take another sip of whiskey. "I'm going to put Freya up in her own house nearby."

"The cottage next to the blacksmith shop is finished and unoccupied," James says with a nod. "I can get Andrew to set it up for her tonight. He's been talking about her non-stop."

I smile despite the heavy feeling in my chest. "Well, she'll be his neighbor. But I already told him to leave her alone. I'm on good terms with Jerrod, but the rest of the elders in Endova are still skeptical of me."

"She's still welcome to stay in our house, of course. But if Dahlia is having the baby tonight, I don't Freya's going to get much sleep. I know I won't."

Justine moves toward us, giving me an apologetic smile. "Alpha Ryan," she says with a bob of her head, then turns to James. "Beta, Dahlia and I are going back to your house. I need to see if she's progressing."

James immediately straightens up, his face going a little pale. Justine gives him a tight smile as she lays a hand on his shoulder.

"Don't worry, she's not going to have the baby in the pack house. I told her to eat a little more, and then we'll walk back, taking the long way. It's good for her to be up and moving right now, even if it's uncomfortable."

James nods, his eyes going a little hazy with concern. "How long, do you think?"

She tilts her head from side to side. "Tomorrow afternoon, probably. Her contractions are still very far apart. We'll see, though. The most important thing you can do for her tonight is get her to rest as much as she can."

"I'll, uhm, I'll come with you," he says, then claps me on the shoulder in farewell.

I watch them move down the table. He lovingly helps Dahlia off the bench and walks her out of the pack house, using his jacket to shield her from the rain.

Aviva is watching the scene as well. My eyes meet hers. She looks concerned, too, but quickly looks away again.

I feel bad for being so hard on her earlier, but I didn't know what else to do. The Shoshannah situation sucks and the last thing I wanted was for a rift to form between the sisters before I had to separate them again. Now, she's sitting easily beside Shoshannah, putting more food on Shoshannah's plate, and Shoshannah's face is alight with excitement as she looks around in awe and chats happily with Freya.

These women haven't ever left Endova. I have to remember that when I look at Aviva and only see heartache and uncertainty behind her eyes.

People start leaving as the night drags on. My pack is on a rotating set of chores, and those in charge of dishes have started gathering plates by the time Andrew goes to fetch Freya and Shoshannah to lead them to what will be Freya's house for the summer. I told him what to do over the mind-link, of course, and he was more than happy to move her into the cottage right next door to his blacksmith shop where his own living quarters are housed behind it. Aviva rises and watches them go, but stands there, picking at the fabric of the pants I found for her today. Dahlia was worried the clothes she brought up to the house before we arrived would be too big for her after seeing her for the first time, so I found some myself. The sage green wool cardigan Aviva's wearing covers a simple cream colored shirt, and she's wearing thick, blue socks with her sandals. It's an odd outfit, but I chose the sweater for a reason. One of my pack members knits them using wool from the herd of sheep we keep in the valley but adds her own unique flare. Little white beads are dotted throughout. They remind me of the shells she wore in her hair during those first few encounters we shared.

Right now, her hair is completely loose and wild as she turns to me looking defeated.

"Let's go home," I tell her, and my stomach twists in a way I hadn't expected when I take her hand in mine.

* * *

"It's a cell phone," I tell her ten minutes later, standing in my bedroom–our bedroom, even though I plan to sleep on the couch until further notice. I click the button that makes the screen come to life, and Aviva jumps back. "That's Sydney, my brother."

"What kind of weapon is it?"

"It's not a weapon, not really. I guess it depends on how shitty you are to the person you're talking to." I press it to my ear. "It doesn't work out here. No service."

She stares blankly at me.

"You can talk to people on it. You can also send them text messages, like little letters, back and forth."

"Oh."

"Yeah." I put the phone back in the top drawer. I noticed immediately that she rifled through my things, but I expected that. I was kind of looking forward to seeing what dirt she thought she could dig up on me, which items she was most curious about.

I rest my hands on the top of my dresser and turn to look at her. She looks... different. Unsure. Tired. That fearlessness behind her eyes has waned, replaced by something shockingly empty and cold. It guts me, and I sigh heavily. "This is your room now. I won't be sharing a bed with you, don't worry."

I expect her to say something back to me, something sharp and cutting, but her brows draw together. "Uh, okay–"

"Are you all right? I know this is a lot to take in."

"I'm fine," she lies.

I'm not sure what to do. I never really got to know girls. I honestly never really dated past that first date kind of thing. I truly didn't emotionally connect with a woman I wasn't related to until Sarah came along, but this is obviously a different situation entirely.

"Well, goodnight–"

"What's in that room?" She points through the open bedroom door. The door across the hall is slightly ajar, meaning she went inside.

I roll my lower lip between my teeth. "Nothing, really."

"It stinks in there, and it's dark. There's no windows."

"It doesn't stink," I chuckle, closing the top drawer of the dresser and crossing my arms over my chest. "Why were you looking around? What did you think you'd find?"

Finally, a glimmer of that cutting attitude I've come to really enjoy flares to life behind her eyes. I'm fucking relieved, too.

"What'd you think you'd find? A body? My deepest, darkest secrets come to life?"

Her jaw flexes. She says nothing, but I can tell something's bothering her, so I shrug. "I'll show you, come on."

I brush past her. She turns to follow me, her footsteps light and agile on the floorboards, like she's standing on her toes to peer over my shoulder into the darkness as I open the door.

I flip on a light switch, and my uncle's weird powers dimly light the room, swirling in those odd lightbulbs I had to purchase and have shipped from Moonrise.

She makes a small noise in her throat behind me.

"See, it's nothing."

"What are those?"

"Photographs." I step deeper into the room, which is so snug that Aviva and I are standing side by side, touching. "This is my darkroom."

She scans the length of twine running from one side of the room to the other. Photographs hang from the twine, fully dry and developed since I hung them up before I left for Endova last week. Containers of water mixed with developing chemicals rest on a table, which is likely where the scent she smelled is coming from.

On instinct, I start taking the photographs down. She stops me with a hand on my arm.

"Where is that?" she asks, pointing to a photograph of a heavily wooded landscape with several pools of milky water in the center, surrounded by rock. The image is in black and white.

"There's a hot spring nearby, deeper in the valley." I take the picture down, feeling suddenly self-conscious.

I've never shown anyone this before. Even back in Crescent Falls, I kept this hobby a secret. It was easier there, since everything was digitized. I have to do everything by hand here, though.

It's… calming. It clears my head in a way nothing else does.

"It's a… a painting?" She smooths a finger over the glossy film paper and reels back, confused. Her eyes meet mine, and I smile a little bit. All of this—all the things I might have taken for granted when I lived in the excessively modern Crescent Falls—are wholly new to Aviva.

"No, it's not a painting. I have a camera."

"I don't know what that is."

"I'll show you sometime." No, I can't. I can't show her. I can't take her to the places I photograph and let her see this part of me that no one else knows because she's… not mine.

She looks up at me with such softness that I… I just can't. I can't do this.

I reach behind her and shut off the light. "Goodnight, Aviva."

17

SO YOU'RE THE LUNA?

Aviva

"You know, there's this thing called sleep, and it's fantastic." Freya tilts her face toward the pocket of sunlight dancing over us. "You just lay down, shut your eyes, and then you wake up several hours later feeling refreshed. You should try it sometime."

I throw her a cutting look as I pick at the grass. "I did sleep."

"Well, you look like shit, so I know you didn't sleep well. How many days has it been? Three? Four nights without sleeping? I'm shocked you're able to function."

I let out a breath and watch the scene playing out before us on the shore of the shallow, calm creek. Someone built a little wall of rocks just past the bridge, creating a man-made eddy. Shoshannah shrieks with laughter as she splashes with three other little girls her age, all of them soaked to the neck.

Freya smiles, her blue eyes creasing as she watches Shosh. "I remember being ten."

"So do I." I smile despite the exhaustion weighing me down. I didn't sleep well last night. I curled up in Ryan's bed, surrounded by his scent. I laid there alone, unable to relax, listening to the new sounds of a new village, unsure what was a threat and what was normal.

At some point, sleep did reach for me, and I let it sweep me away, but I woke up on the floor in front of the couch, half covered by the blanket Ryan had been using, while he slept soundly on the couch totally oblivious to the fact that I'd likely wandered in there seeking the company of someone, anyone, to get me through the night.

I shake my head to try to banish the memory and close my eyes for a moment, breathing in the soft, clean scent of the flowers blooming all around us.

"I'm a little worried about you," Freya says to me.

"You shouldn't be. I'm fine."

"You look so tired, Aviva. I know this is stressful but–"

"I'm fine." I try to assure her, but she doesn't look convinced. She sighs and looks past me as two lean wolves come rushing down the road toward the village, bursting through the pockets of sunlight left behind by the thunderstorm that rolled through the valley last night. They run right past us at an insane rate of speed.

The girls playing in the creek stop splashing for a moment to watch them but quickly go back to their game.

"Those must be the scouts returning from Endova," Freya says. We turn to watch them speed into the village proper. Freya glances at Shoshannah. "You should go find out what happened. I'll stay with her."

I nod, wiping my hands on the fabric of the pale pink cotton dress I changed into this morning. It's very pretty, but it's a little big on me. The straps keep sliding off, revealing my shoulders. It's warm this morning though, compared to last night. I slide my feet back into my sandals and walk along the road into the village proper and see the door to the pack house is open, and male voices drift outside.

I step inside without knocking. Jacob, Ryan, and James are standing with the scouts, now in their human forms and dressed. The scouts are drinking water, panting.

Ryan is talking in low tones to Jacob when he sees me walk in. For a split second, I swear his eyes soften with relief, maybe even excitement that I'm here, but I know I'm just hallucinating from lack of sleep. "Next week, then," Ryan says in conclusion, nodding in farewell to the men standing in the empty pack house, and walks toward me.

My lips part, questions dancing on my tongue, but Ryan gives me a smirk and leads me back into the sun.

"Everything is fine in Endova. Your father knows now that Shoshannah is here, and next week, once the spring storms are over and the creek is less temperamental, she'll be returning home."

"Oh." I clear my throat, relieved but also a little on edge because of how close he's standing to me right now.

"So, everything is fine now," he says with a bit of a sigh as he squints through the suddenly blinding sun peeking through the clouds. "Which means you can actually sleep–"

"Why is everyone so concerned about that?" I ask sharply.

Ryan looks down at me, the corner of his mouth ticking up in that cocky, boyish smile that makes me want to punch him–or kiss him–I don't know. My fatigued mind seems to favor both possibilities, unfortunately. "Because you haven't slept since we returned from the hunt. It's been days since then."

"I slept last night."

"No, you didn't."

"How do you know? Were you watching me?"

"I woke up early this morning, cold, wondering what happened to the blanket I brought onto the couch with me and found you with it, curled up on the floor beneath me." There's a teasing glint to his tone that sends a shiver up my spine.

"I'm not used to sleeping alone." I whirl and walk away, my cheek burning red, and curse at myself. I need to lock myself into the bedroom tonight, apparently. I don't question why he won't share a bed with me or why it bothers me. I should be grateful, right? I'm sure some women leave their villages, and their new husbands don't leave them alone whatsoever. Mine doesn't seem to want much to do with me, and that... that should feel better than it does.

"Aviva!" he calls out.

I halt in my tracks, halfway back to the creek where Freya is still sitting in the sun. I turn to look at Ryan over my shoulder. "What?"

"Tonight, after dinner, I'll take you to see the valley. We can shift. I think you could use the run." With that, he turns to go back into the pack house, and I huff a breath and go back to sitting beside Freya, who smirks at me but doesn't ask any questions.

* * *

DAHLIA LOOKS EXCEEDINGLY UNCOMFORTABLE AS SHE SITS DOWN WITH us at the end of a long, wooden table. She's a bit flushed and puffy as she picks at her food with her fork, pushing a grain of rice around her plate.

It's been a strange day. I'm not sure what to do here, honestly. Freya has taken Shoshannah under her wing while I try to adjust. I haven't seen Ryan since he told me my father was informed of Shoshannah's whereabouts. I'm sure he has a lot to do as Alpha. My father was always busy as patriarch, and I'm sure it's one and the same, but still.

I feel like I'm floating in a directionless body of water, unsure how to move, how to act, or what to think.

Freya and Shosh are taking to village life, however.

"Shoshannah made some friends today. See?" she says, pointing to the group of little girls playing in one corner of the pack house. Shoshannah is with them, bright eyed and oblivious to the strife she's caused. I haven't had the heart nor the energy to talk to her about it yet, and she's avoiding me in turn, likely knowing the fight coming her way.

"She's settling in better than I am, I suppose," I say, accepting a bowl of salad with what I think might be kale and spinach, as well as roasted nuts and dried berries. I give myself a huge scoop and look at Dahlia, meaning to pass the bowl to her next, but she flushes again, closing her eyes.

She doesn't look so good. I look down the table where I'd seen Ryan sitting with her mate last night, but neither man is anywhere to be found.

"Dahlia," Freya says lightly, reaching across the table to rest her hand on the woman's wrist. "I think you should go home and lie down."

Dahlia nods wordlessly and allows Freya to help her upright.

I shift my position on the bench, unsure what to do. My only experience with pregnant women, especially one in obvious labor, was my–my mother.

A pang of grief lights in my heart, sending a dull ache through my body. Freya calls out to Shoshannah as she leaves, and Shoshannah follows, leaving me totally alone at the end of the table.

So, I pick at my salad, suddenly unable to eat. I notice movement at another table, however. A group of young women are talking amongst themselves and occasionally throwing glances over their shoulders at me. I noticed them last night, too. They're the same women I saw doing laundry in the creek.

No one, other than Dahlia and James, has spoken to me yet. In all fairness, I haven't made much of an attempt to introduce myself, and Ryan hasn't either, so….

One of them rises, laughing with her companions before smoothing her dark, glossy hair away from her face and striding over to my table. Her group watches her, talking in low whispers as she struts over to where I'm sitting and smoothly sits down, propping her chin on her fist.

"Uhm, hello," I say, feeling more than a little odd. Her dark eyes scan mine.

"So, you're Aviva." She smiles, kindly, I think. "Our new Luna, right?"

"I believe so."

Her smile widens. "I'm Natalie. I thought I should probably introduce myself since our Alpha hasn't publicly announced his… marriage." She throws her hair over her shoulder and glances down the table, probably looking for the man in question. "When Jacob came back to Silverhide in a fuss, we all thought Alpha Ryan died or something. Turns out, he just has a wife now."

I'm not sure what to say or think, but I know women. There's a lot of young, competitive women in Endova with the same glimmer of cattiness in their eyes that Natalie has now.

I roll my shoulders before tightening them and fix Natalie with a look. "Ryan has been busy, as you can imagine, after coming home from a successful spring hunt. Did you need him for something?"

Her eyes shine for a moment before she shakes her head. "No. Like I said, I just wanted to introduce myself. As our new Luna, you're probably going to want some woman in your inner circle to help run things, you know."

"Oh, thank you for offering your services." My voice is clipped but edges on sincere, which is enough for her. Her smile widens, but this is some kind of standoff. I don't know this woman at all, which makes it different to determine what her motive is right now. Did she really come to introduce herself, to get into her Luna's good graces, or is she hoping to stir up drama?

Part of me hopes it's the latter, just to give me something to focus on.

"You know," she laughs, shaking her head, "I just can't believe Alpha Ryan is married. It's so strange to us. He's such a—such a—oh, what's the word I'm looking for?"

"I have no idea." I take a bite of my salad.

She frowns a bite at my bored tone. "He's just never one to be in a relationship."

She wants me to ask what she means so she can tell me something sordid about my new husband, but I'm not going to give her the satisfaction. I know men as well as I know women. I know the cocky smile, the posturing, and sharp wit likely won Ryan any girl he ever wanted. He's the most handsome man I've ever seen, and being the Alpha of a pack with so many young women of marrying age means he's probably enjoyed his fair share of attention from them.

Maybe even from Natalie.

I take another bite of my salad and smile around my fork before setting it down, clearing my throat, and fixing her with a look that's both kind, and knowing, dripping with ulterior motives. "Perhaps Alpha Ryan finally found what he was looking for in Endova, and that was me." Another smile, with teeth this time.

Natalie's frown grows into something edged with faint rage, but she contains it in a practiced manner. "I guess we'll see, won't we?"

I rise, leaving her at the table, and walk out into the night, buzzing with nervous energy.

Admittedly, I don't like the notion that Ryan lays it on thick with other women when he can barely look in my direction without either glaring at me or looking at me like I'm something so fragile that if he touches me, I'll break.

I'm supposed to be his wife. I'm supposed to be the wife of an Alpha, for Goddess' sake. He hasn't even so much as kissed me.

I huff a breath and look around to distract myself from the conflicting emotions fighting for majority. Ryan said he'd take me for a run tonight, but he's nowhere to be seen, and I don't see Freya or Shoshannah, either. So, I go back to his house to change into my clothes from Endova. I'll take myself running. I'll shift and go hunt to clear my head. Maybe then I'll be able to sleep.

I throw open the door to go inside, cursing under my breath. An intake of air and a sharp hiss of pain greets me, followed by Ryan's shadow crossing over me in the faint moonlight.

He rubs his jaw, frowning at me.

"Did you just get hit with the door?" I laugh. "You didn't hear me walking across the porch?"

"You threw it open hard enough for it to come off the hinges." He roughly rubs the side of his face as he steps past me onto the porch. "I was just coming to get you. Are you ready to go?"

"I was going to change, first."

"It doesn't matter. We're not going that far. There's clothing caches all over the place." He adjusts a black strap across his chest, and I notice the strange object hanging from it.

"Is that the camera?" I ask, the word sounding strange on my tongue.

He looks into my eyes, running his tongue along his lower lip like he's debating something, then nods. "Come on," he says, turning from me. "We're burning moonlight."

18

YOUR MATE IS OUT THERE

Aviva

RYAN TURNS AWAY AS I STRIP OUT OF MY DRESS IN A POCKET OF TREES toward the very back of the village. I hang it on a tree branch before shifting into my wolf form, feeling naked despite my thick fur. I'm used to having my knife belt and bow slung across my back even in wolf form, but now I'm in my skin, and I'm not giving Ryan the same courtesy as he strips off his clothes. I do turn my head to avoid watching him take off his boxers, however. I'm not that desperate.

He clutches the camera in his mouth, protected by a little leather bag, and leads me through a network of wolf trails that weave through a rather dense forest that hugs the back of the village.

We follow the creek at one point, which weaves through the forest. It's the only sound other than the rustling of the leaves overhead.

It's beautiful here, I have to admit. The forest is thick as we start gaining in elevation toward the very back of the valley where the mountains Silverhide is nestled between finally join. A small lake glistens in the moonlight as he leads me out of the forest, and we follow a trail along its shore.

A small building rests along the rocks on stilts. It's dark inside as we pass, but I pick up several different scents. It's likely his pack members come to the lake to fish and swim, so I'm not nervous, nor surprised by the different, foreign smells.

But we don't stop at the lake. I follow him along the trail in silence as it feeds back into another wooden area with less wolf trails than the first. Time ticks by, and soon, the entire area is drenched in moonlight, signaling the late hour.

The trail becomes more rocky and hard to navigate. He eventually leads me off the main trail, dipping into a shadowed cove of thick, old growth trees.

I don't sense that there's others nearby, friend or foe. We're totally alone out here, but I find it hard to relax. He hasn't spoken to me through the mind-link, and I haven't spoken to him. In all honesty, I'm just enjoying being in my wolf form and getting some exercise.

He looks back at me from time to time to make sure I haven't wandered off, but that's it.

Eventually he leads me toward a group of large rock formations in the depths of the forest, and when we pass them, the forest ceases to exist, revealing a second valley overlooking the first.

If I could gasp as a wolf, I would.

I look down at the valley below, at the little village twinkling in the moonlight in the distance. Ryan makes a noise in his throat that tears my attention back to him, and he tilts his head, motioning me for me to keep following.

There's still trees up here, though nothing compared to the forest below, but when he leads me toward the left of the valley, where a small waterfall laps down the side of the mountain, I see the place he captured with his camera and somehow memorialized on that weird, shiny paper.

The hot springs.

The waterfall feeds into the largest bath, sending steam billowing toward the starlit sky. Smaller baths send wisps of steam across the rocky ground beneath us as I follow me around it and climb up onto the strange, flat rocks. He comes to a stop near the largest bath, a pond, really. I'm not sure how deep it is, but I tip my paw into it, expecting the water to be scalding hot, but it's actually comfortable enough to swim in.

But then Ryan is in his human form pulling a pair of sweatpants on. He tosses a leather bag toward me, which hits the ground and spills over with random clothing. Did he really come all this way with no intentions of jumping in?

"This is the place from the picture," he says, but my splash as I shift and jump into the pool of warm water overwhelms his voice.

It is a little deep, but nothing too scary. I swim to the surface and suck in a breath, laughing as I smooth my hair away from my face.

Ryan is gaping at me. "Are you insane?"

"What?" I laugh as the warmth of the water works its way into every muscle. "You've never swam in it before?"

"It's going to cook you alive!"

I tread water and point to the small waterfall. "It's fed by snowmelt. It's barely even hot. It's like a bath after waiting for twenty minutes for the water to cool down."

Ryan doesn't look convinced. So, I splash him, soaking his sweatpants. "Hey!" But he's not glaring at me for once. In fact, that ice between us that's been festering for days melts in the steam rising from the hot spring.

I realize with a start what our problem is. Ryan and I have only ever bonded in the wild–outside of the constraints of village life. He brought me to his home and has barely spoken to me since, barely looked in my direction, but now his eyes are on mine and he's... smiling.

"Close your eyes."

"Why?" I ask as he sets his camera bag down several feet away and slides his thumbs into his waistband. "I'm your wife, aren't I? Shouldn't I have seen you naked by now?"

He stares at me with that unflinching, unwavering gaze that rocks me to my core. I'd thought once that this man has never been prey in his life, and I'm right. This look–the look that makes me feel things I can't explain–is the look of a predator debating their next move to make a swift kill.

But then I think of the women he's used this look on in the past and crack, lowering my gaze to water and turning around, my toes barely brushing the bottom of the pool.

Ryan jumps in with a splash that sends waves rushing toward me and spilling over the rocky edge of the pool. He pops up a few feet away, wincing a bit at the hot bite of the water, and blows out a surprised breath. He can stand, but the water is up to his neck. His hair is wet and slicked back, and he looks... relaxed. Relaxed for the first time in days, I realize.

We look at each other for a moment. I'm not sure what to say, but I know we have a lot to talk about, so I tread water, enjoying the slight burn of exertion in my muscles.

"You're pretty short, huh? Can't touch the bottom?" The corners of his mouth twitch into a taunting smile.

I suck in a breath and sink down until my feet are flat on the sandy ground then shoot up again. He's still smiling as I smooth my hair away from my face. "Nope, can't. What's the view like from all the way up there?" I tease, and he gives me that cocky grin again as I swim a little closer.

I feel better than I have in days. Maybe it's the warmth of the water, the exercise, being away from everyone else and in the sanctuary of the wilderness, but I feel... good. Unburdened. Myself.

He must see that flash of relief behind my eyes because he says, "I haven't been avoiding you, you know. I've been busy since I got back. Especially with... Shoshannah's situation."

"I understand–"

"I didn't know I'd be bringing home a wife," he cuts in, his eyes holding on mine. He licks his lips and leans his back against the edge of the pool. "I don't really know what to do with you, honestly."

"Are you asking me? Because I don't know what I'm supposed to do either."

He rolls his eyes to the sky, to the stars burning bright above us. "I've never been married before."

"Neither have I."

"I know," he says pointedly. "I just... what exactly do you need from me?"

"I don't really understand what you mean by that." I start swimming toward him, resting my arm along the rocky edge of the pool to give my legs a break. "I'm just a wife–"

"*Just a wife*," he says sardonically under his breath, closing his eyes.

"Yeah... I'm meant to... make you food and have your babies, or whatever."

"Well, you already mentioned you don't cook."

"And you won't even touch me." The words slip out before I can stop them. He opens his eyes and looks right at me, and I... edge away, putting a few feet of distance between us. Stupidly, my dumb, big mouth continues, "It's fine if you think I'm ugly, but don't you want to carry on your bloodline?"

He gapes at me for a minute, shocked. Truly shocked.

I shrug, unable to backpedal. "I can put a pillow over my head so you don't have to look at me–"

"Aviva, what the fuck are you talking about?"

"We haven't...you know."

"Had sex?"

"Yeah, that."

"We've known each other for a week." He looks a little shocked, but now I'm confused and feeling the effects of bottling my conflicting emotions for days.

I think of Natalie and every other woman he's probably, theoretically, been with. "You sleep with women you're not married to all the time."

His eyes narrow. "What?"

I nod. "Like... Natalie?"

"Natalie?" His eyes are mere slits as he slowly edges toward me.

"She came to talk to me today, during dinner. So, is it true? She looked like she was ready to scratch my eyes out."

He laughs–low and angry. "That's none of your business."

"I feel like it is, seeing as you married me and won't touch me, but you'll touch practically every other woman."

"You're not every other woman." He's closing in on me with every passing second. "I didn't realize you wanted that so badly."

"I–I don't," I stammer.

I roll my lower lip between my teeth as he cages me in against the edge of the pool. I'd have to duck under him to move, and he's just as naked as I am. So far, he's had the decency to keep his eyes on my face and not my breasts, but with this little distance between us, it's hard to ignore the fact there's nothing separating us but water.

"Why haven't you done your husbandly duties?" I ask, tilting my chin up to look him in the eyes, but my voice shakes.

He hums, biting down on his lower lip, and I feel... too hot all of the sudden. "Is the anticipation killing you, Aviva? Do you think I'll corner you one day and force you into bed? Taking what I want, when I want it? Is that really what you think of me?"

My heart is racing as his gaze drops to my lips. He moves closer, and my arm drops from the edge. I start to slip into the water, but he snakes an arm around my naked waist and pulls me close until my breasts are flush with his chest. The sensation is immediate and mind-boggling. My nipples harden, heat rushing to my core. He splays his hand wide across my lower back and leans in, whispering against the top of my ear, "I'm not your mate. I'm not the one who's supposed to touch you, to take you to bed."

I shove him away. He retreats, but his eyes are locked on mine, swimming with stars.

"I don't have a mate."

"You do. You just haven't met him yet."

I shake my head. "How do you know you're not my mate?"

That breaks something in him, and I instantly regret it. He swims toward me again, caging me back in, but instead of the heated tone he'd used when he whispered against my ear only moments before, he growls, "You called me cursed once. I'm not entirely convinced you were wrong. Whatever bond you think is between us, it's because our hands were sliced open and pressed together when we married. That's it. Imprinting, I believe, is what your people call it?"

I shiver at his tone, which drips with malice.

The tip of his nose brushes over my cheek as he says, "I don't get a second chance at having a mate, Aviva. Your mate is still out there. You might be my wife, but you do not belong to me." His hands grip my waist, and I whimper as his thumbs drag over my hip bones. He hisses like touching me is painful, but he doesn't let go. "I can't stand being around you," he whispers, closing his eyes and groaning as his hands drift further back, traveling down over my ass. My eyes nearly roll back in my head despite his harsh words. "I can't even look at you," he says, guiding me closer, his mouth hovering over mine. "Anything you feel for me is just your body reacting."

His lips barely touch mine. Just barely. My heart cracks into pieces. This rejection… stings. More than stings. It hurts physically, like the water is suddenly too hot, burning my skin. It shouldn't bother me. The only reason I want him, want him to take me to bed, is because that's what I've told I'm supposed to do… right? Ryan goes very still, opening his eyes and looking over the top of my head.

I search for something to say. Something mean, something dry and cutting, but come up short.

He pushes away and says roughly, his voice like gravel, "We need to go back, now." He gets out of the water and stands–totally naked–looking down at the clothing cache. I watch as his hand hovers over the camera bag before he shifts in a muted blur of light. I climb out of the pool, my body numb and my heart in shambles, and shift as well, confused, hurt, and unable to process what just happened between us.

It doesn't matter, though, because he says, 'There's a situation in Silverhide. We need to get there as soon as possible.'

19

JUST LIKE MOTHER

Aviva

I BARELY HAVE TIME TO PULL MY DRESS OVER MY BODY BEFORE RYAN IS running again, hastily pulling on his shirt. I leave my sandals behind and sprint toward him, my bare feet slipping over rock that turns to gravel as we reach the village. My heart is thundering when I finally reach his side.

We sprinted down into the valley. It took mere minutes compared to the long climb up to the spring. I've never run so fast, and so far, and my legs burn as I reach for Ryan's arm but–

People are gathered around one of the houses near the center of the village. I see Shoshannah in the crowd and rush out a desperate prayer, thanking the Goddess for keeping her safe from… whatever we hurried here for.

But then a scream rips through the night, hollow and anguished. My blood runs cold as a memory slips through my mind, burning to light. The sound of the scream is so familiar and so fresh, even though it's been several years since I heard that same scream.

"Shoshannah," I whisper as she flies into my arms.

Ryan talks animatedly with Jacob and Andrew, gesturing wildly as he points to the house where the cries are coming from.

Jacob nods, his face slightly pale, and starts motioning for the crowd to disperse. "Everyone go home now. Your Beta doesn't need this–"

"Back to your houses. Give them space," Andrew echoes in a gentler tone.

A few women crowd Ryan, who listens to them, nodding along with whatever they're saying, but I can't hear over the blood rushing in my ears. I hold Shoshannah so tight she starts to squirm, but then a hand is on my shoulder, and I look up into a woman's eyes, someone I recognize from the village but I've never met.

"Let her stay with us tonight. I'm Opal. I'm Maggie's mother. She and Shoshannah have been playing together, and our home is about half a mile away, down the road. She'll be fine."

"Oh, I–"

Ryan is suddenly beside me shoving a set of keys into my hand. He eyes Opal, who backs away with Shoshannah. "Take her to your house, Opal, that's fine–"

Another scream tears through the air. My hands shake as I watch my sister turn with the woman.

What the hell is going on?

"Ryan?" I croak, looking up at him.

"In my bedroom, under the bed, there's a lockbox." He wraps his hand around mine, the keys biting into my palm. "You'll see a little wooden box inside. Take one of the vials out of it. Be very, very careful with it." His eyes are wide and wild as he scans my face. "Go."

I turn and run for the house, but my mind is on one thing–my knife belt. I wish I had a new bow. Breaking mine in that fall... I think about it every day. But if someone is hurt–hurt enough to be screaming in agony like that, whatever attacked them has to be nearby, right?

Adrenaline keeps my feet moving faster than my mind is reeling, and soon I'm on my knees and frantically testing each key on the lockbox. Finally it opens, and the only thing inside is the wooden box Ryan mentioned.

I claw it open and find six small glass vials of... something. I lift one to the light. The liquid inside glows the palest, almost translucent blue. It shimmers with golden swirls that momentarily mesmerize me.

But the adrenaline in my veins has me on my feet again, the vial clutched in one hand as I sling my knife belt over my shoulder, moving too swiftly toward the door to bother looping it around my waist. I fly down the steps, running as fast as I can toward the house where the crowd had been gathering when we first arrived and make a critical error upon charging inside.

* * *

RYAN

"JAMES." I TAKE JAMES BY THE ARM AND PULL HIM AWAY FROM THE BED where his mate is slack with pain. "James, look at me, take the baby and sit outside for a minute, please. Let Justine–"

"That's my fucking mate," James snarls in my face, teeth bared. "My wife!" The baby girl in his arms chokes on a cry. She was born shortly before we arrived and is still damp, still red, wrapped roughly in a thick blanket.

"Go outside, now," I growl, taking him by the collar. I start dragging him out of the bedroom. "If you shift right now, you're going to hurt your daughter. She needs you, okay? They both do. You need to sit out here and calm down–"

Aviva is standing in the hallway leading to the bedroom where Justine is doing everything she can to stabilize Dahlia. I didn't even see her there. I didn't hear her come in. She's totally, completely still and has a faraway look in her eyes.

Freya rushes to the doorway of the bedroom, her eyes wide and expression contorted as she looks at Aviva. "No. No, Aviva. You can't be here."

Aviva's face drains of all color. Her eyes are locked on the bed, just visible behind Freya, the sheets damp and stained with blood.

Even James, who two seconds ago had been on the verge of shifting with his newborn, perfectly healthy daughter in his arms, stills as he notices the sudden anguish playing behind Aviva's eyes.

She looks like… she looks like she's about to faint. I don't think she's breathing. "Aviva? Hey–"

She blinks, a single tear rolling down her cheek. I've never seen her cry. Not even when she said goodbye to Lora. No, she hadn't cried.

And she hadn't looked like *this*.

I notice the knife belt slung over her shoulder. She'd thought someone had gotten attacked. She was ready to defend us if it came to that. The vial is clutched in her hand, though, but her hand doesn't tremble as her eyes stay locked and unseeing on the bloody sheets. Freya pushes past me, prying the vial out her hand and tossing it to me casually, like it means nothing, like the tears inside won't heal Dahlia, who is just bleeding more than expected and had a really rough go of it, from what I hear. Neither of these women could have known about the tears, though. Aviva knows nothing about my family's powers. At least, I don't think she does.

"Aviva," Freya whispers desperately, smoothing Aviva's wild hair away from her face. "Hey, she's fine. Dahlia is fine. She's going to be okay."

Aviva takes a shallow breath then turns and sprints from the house.

"What–"

"How could you bring her here?" Freya screams at me, which startles both me and James. I hand James the vial, and he quickly goes back into the bedroom, closing the door behind him. Freya looks toward the door where Aviva disappeared, her chest rapidly rising and falling. "How could you?" she sneers, teeth bared.

"What are you talking about?"

"Her mother," she croaks, her eyes full of tears.

I shake my head, not following.

Freya gapes at me. "You didn't know?"

"Didn't know what? What's wrong with Aviva?"

Freya sniffles, shaking her head. "Her mother died having Lora. It was horrible. It was… days of this, but so much worse." She waves a hand toward the room where Dahlia is recovering, which is now being sped up by the tears. "Oh, Goddess, I can't even… I can't even put into words." She shakes her head. "Aviva was sixteen. She was there for all of it. It was awful, Ryan. I don't think she ever really recovered from it–"

I'm out the door before Freya can finish.

I had no idea. I'm a fucking asshole, I already know that. I can still taste the horrible things I said to Aviva moments before we came back to the village. I shouldn't have said them. I want her to hate me, to keep her distance. I think I do. I think that's what I want but…

"Is Dahlia okay?"

"How is she? The baby?"

A few pack members stop me in the center of the village. I look around in the dark. I can't see Aviva anywhere. Did she shift and run? She had to have shifted. That's what she does, isn't it? When the memories become too much? Isn't that what her own father tried to tell me?

"She's fine," I say, brushing past everyone starting to gather again even though I had Jacob and Andrew tell them to go home. Dahlia and James just had the first of the babies born on the soil of our new territory. It's an exciting, but nerve wracking, time. We're so far from help if we were to need it.

My feet carry me on their own accord, and soon, I'm pushing through the door of my house. "Aviva?"

I'm answered by silence, by darkness. The bedroom door is open a crack, though. I slip inside. "Aviva?"

She's sitting on the floor with her head between her knees. She's shaking, choking on silent sobs.

I kneel in front of her, hesitating before I lay my hand on her shoulder. She flinches so hard her back slams against the foot of the bed. It has to hurt based on the crunching sound that follows. "Hey, it's me, Aviva–"

"Let go!" She swats me, and I get a glimpse of her face as she gasps for breath. "Let-let go of me–" She gasps again, painfully this time, like she can't find the air she needs. "I don't–want–you–here–"

What's left of my heart shatters as she struggles to breathe, her face ghostly white. "Look at me," I beg, grabbing her arms and pulling her toward me. "Aviva, look at me. You're having a panic attack–" She fights, whimpering and trying to swat out of my hold, but I get my arms around her and haul her into my lap.

She begs me to let her go, but I cross my arms over her chest, pinning her arms down. I grunt with effort as I rise to my knees then stand, carrying her two steps to the bed.

She's shaking so hard her teeth chatter as I lie down on the bed and roll so I'm lying on my side with her back to my chest. Her cheek rests on my arm. I can feel her tears sliding down her cheek and onto my skin.

"You're going to be okay," I tell her, tears stinging my own eyes. "You're okay. Everything is okay."

She whimpers and shakes so badly the bed is shaking, but I hang on, curling around her body and pressing my weight against her, sheltering her.

I lick my lips before burying my face in her hair, pressing my mouth against her shoulder. Goddess, I wish I knew what she smelled like. I hate that I don't know. I don't understand why I can't pick up her scent.

Her heart is beating so fucking fast as I press a kiss to the spot where her shoulder meets her neck. She's slightly damp with sweat, her hair sticking to her skin.

"I wish you would have told me," I whisper, hating myself for what I said to her earlier. It's the only thing on my mind. "I'm sorry, Aviva. I'm sorry."

She's starting to calm down, her breathing regulating. I hold her closer though, taking in her warmth, the feel of her against my chest.

She fits perfectly here with me curled around her. I want to just...
stay here, beside her.

I lie there for a long time with my arms hooked around her,
holding onto her like she's the anchor in a storm. When her father
said we chased the same demons, he was right. As I fall asleep beside
her, I have the same dream I have every night. Hadley's blood stains
my mouth and my hands as Sarah pulls me away and looks into my
eyes, horrified and scared, and I'm... empty. Unfeeling. I stay that way
for years. I feel *nothing* for years.

Until that day in the clearing near the creek when that red wolf
burst into my life and an arrow pierced that impenetrable wall I'd
built around my heart.

2 0

DON'T MOVE

Aviva

WARMTH. I FEEL WARM TO THE BONE AND HEAVY AS I ROLL TO THE SIDE AND snuggle deeper against the body beside me. My hands drift up his stomach to his chest, tracing taut muscles until I reach the half-moon shaped scar on his shoulder. He stirs, rolling over and running his calloused hand over the slope of my naked hip, over my thigh.

When he kisses me, it's unhurried, his tongue sweeping over mine and exploring any place he hasn't yet discovered. My breasts ache as he rolls my peaked nipples between his fingers, stirring that desperate, unending want between my legs.

His tongue dances with mine as he slides a hand down over my belly, his fingers reaching for my slit, and he finds me wet and aching for him.

He hums with satisfaction, his mouth still on mine, and whispers, "What have you done to me, little wolf? I can't get enough."

I gasp, my eyes flying open to pale gray daylight streaming through the window over the bed. It's raining hard, pelting the window in little rivers that flow down the glass.

I'm in Ryan's bed. I slept for hours, I'm sure, because, for once, my

151

brain doesn't feel clouded by fog, and I'm acutely aware that I'm not alone. Ryan's arm is draped over my waist, his hand clutching the slope of my hip, warm and tender.

I shift my weight, trying to slip out of his embrace, but my thighs slide together from the wetness pooled between them. The friction is enough to send a jolt of heat licking up my spine, igniting more of that nonsensical desire that's making things exceedingly difficult for me right now. Memories of last night start to trickle in, but it's not enough. It's not enough to break me out of the haze of the dream I just had, of the faded details that I'm trying to clutch and hang onto, just so I don't have to feel anything else.

What Ryan said to me last night at the hot spring isn't lost on me, but he was there when I spiraled out of control, when I couldn't breathe, when any rational thought in my mind left the building, and I lost myself entirely.

Now, I'm in his arms, and I don't know what to do.

"You okay?"

I turn to look at him. His face is cast in shadow, but his eyes are open and locked on mine. "I don't want to talk about it."

"I don't even get a thank you?"

"For what?" I scowl at him, and he smiles softly, sleepily. His gaze drops from my eyes to my lips, swollen from biting down on them last night, I'm sure, and then down to my... breasts.

My nipples are peaked, and it's evident through the thin fabric of my dress. He looks back up at me. My breath hitches in my throat as the hand still resting on my hip moves upward just a touch, just enough for the sensation of his touch to bloom across my skin, and I fold.

I cup his cheek, his stubble tickling my palm as I run my fingers into his hair. He leans into the touch. He likes this, I realize. He likes having his hair played with, pulled. I wonder if he knows how his lips part, and he makes that little sound in his throat that has my heart skipping beats when I gently tug on the strands.

He closes his eyes and groans as I rack my nails over his scalp, his hand sliding up my side and over my chest. He palms my breast, dragging his thumb over my nipples in slow, deliberate strokes that leave me panting. My lips part as he opens his eyes to slits, his gaze heavy and heated. "Aviva," he groans, flicking his thumb over my nipple, and I moan.

He groans low in his throat, and then his mouth is on mine–hot and reckless. Our teeth clash as he rolls over on top of me, his tongue dragging over my lower lip. He bites down, moaning, and I open my mouth in invitation.

He takes it, and the kiss turns feral in a way I didn't know it could. His tongue swirls around mine while he tangles his hands in my hair, his knee drawing up between my thighs, and I'm... a goner.

This man can kiss. At least, I'm pretty sure this isn't normal. This can't be what everyone feels. If it is, why don't people talk about it? Why would I have had any reason to be nervous to share a bed with him when my body *wants* this?

His hands drop from my hair to explore other places. His fingers glide over my collarbone and back down to my breasts, thumbing my nipples before dipping lower, and lower, until he moves his knee and cups me between my legs.

I arch my back off the bed as feeling explodes through me, showering me in pleasure I've never experienced.

"Fuck, Aviva," he growls, releasing me from the kiss and gazing down at me. He props himself on one elbow as he rubs the heel of his hand up and down over that sweet, aching spot between my thighs.

I bite down on my lip, my eyes fluttering shut as sensation builds and builds.

He dips his head down again, sucking a bruise into the crook of my neck. I grab his arms, writhing beneath him.

He's still in his clothes from last night. I wish he wasn't. All I want right now is to feel his skin, to smell him, to bury myself against him, and again, I'm reminded that this isn't normal. This can't be. This feeling like I'll die unless he touches me where no one has ever touched me before.

The sensation dies, and I'm left wanting when his hand drags over my thigh, bunching up the fabric of my dress.

"Do you touch yourself?" he rasps against my neck, his teeth nibbling the tender skin there.

"Yes," I nod as his fingers move in a featherlight touch toward my inner thigh.

"Show me."

All of the air leaves my lungs as he straightens, his eyes dark with need. He nudges my legs apart, kneeling between them, all while keeping his eyes locked on mine.

I can barely catch my breath but my hand moves on its own accord, traveling over my breasts, down my belly, toward my sex. He watches every move I make with a predator's gaze—sharp and focused. My hand slips beneath my dress, now bunched over my hips. My fingers slide between my wet, aching folds, and the sound I make is guttural and far away, something I've never heard before.

I stroke my clit with easy, slow circles, all while he watches. Slowly, his hands run up my thighs. He grips them, his head bent as I speed up, chasing the feeling he started.

"More," he commands, and his tone is nearly even to send me over the edge.

One of his hands slips down as his eyes meet mine again. He slowly presses a finger through my folds and I swear he trembles when he realizes how wet I am. With his gaze locked on mine, his lips parting, he presses his finger inside of me.

"Ohhh." I arch into the feeling, the stretch, my walls clenching around him.

He adds a second finger, and it's almost too much. I inhale sharply, slowing my own fingers.

"You can take it," he says in a low whisper that sets my soul aflame. He thrusts his fingers inside of me, hooking them, drawing out a moan as I tremble around him. Every part of me is focused on his touch, of the feeling of him slowly dragging his fingers in, and out, hitting a place deep within that has my muscles coiling with tension. His thumb slides over my swollen clit, and I almost come. He chuckles, low and dark. "Not yet, little wolf."

"Bossy," I manage to say, but my voice is ragged and broken by a sharp intake of breath as he lowers his head and...

I grab his head, tangling my fingers in his hair and pulling hard, but his tongue swirls over my clit while his fingers stay fixed inside of me. "Ryan!"

He growls, his voice sending exquisite vibrations through my center. "I want you to scream my name the next time you say it."

He sucks and licks, sometimes using his teeth, and I'm losing my will to even breathe as my body succumbs to his touch. I draw my knees up, his head lodged between my shaking thighs as he picks up the pace, working me into a frenzy that leaves me dizzy and gasping.

He pulls out his fingers and grips my thighs, pulling them apart so I'm laid out like a meal before him, and he *feasts*.

White-hot, blinding pleasure rips through me. I bite down on my lip to stop from screaming as I come undone. My legs shake as I arch my back, twisting to the side as pleasure explodes through my thighs, my lower back, and my core.

"Ryan!" I gasp, my eyes squeezed shut, my lungs burning for air.

This isn't what I thought this would be like. Whatever this was... I want it again. And again.

He keeps going, groaning as I ride out the orgasm on his tongue. He kisses my inner thigh then rises, crawling over me to press a firm kiss to my lips, his tongue sliding over mine.

His cock grinds into my thigh, but he's still clothed. That's what comes next, right? He's going to break me apart, I can already tell.

I reach down and clasp him over his pants. He makes a sound deep in his throat, hissing out a breath as I run the heel of my hand down his length, and back up again.

"What have you done to me?" he asks against my lips.

Goddess, I need him inside of me. I have to have him. I'm going to cry if I can't have him. Right. Now.

But he kisses me again, softer this time, a gentle peck that leaves me... confused.

He pulls away, resting his hands on the bed for a moment with his hand bent so I can't see his face.

"Stay here." He's gone in a flash, but he doesn't leave the house. His footsteps sound in the darkroom, and when he returns, looking mussed from sleep, his lips slightly puffy and cheeks a ruddy pink, he's carrying something in his hand.

"Stay right where you are, don't move," he rasps like someone took a rake to his vocal cords. The notion that I affected him so greatly whirls through my body, sending a shimmering sense of pride and possession coasting through me, unlocking parts of me I hadn't known were there. He climbs back onto the bed and straddles me, reaching to part the curtains, then pulls them back again, adjusting the way the morning light plays over my face.

"Don't move," he whispers, looking down at the thing in his hands. It's square, metal, with sharp lines and a strange... *nose* of sorts that sticks out from the center. He raises it to his face.

My lips part in anticipation for what this thing can do, why he has it, and why it's covering his eyes, but then a soft click echoes between us. This is his camera, I think.

His whole body is relaxed in a way I haven't even seen when he's asleep, like this object is his lifeline in some way, just like... just like my bow, which is gone now.

He reaches for me, twisting a curl around his finger before letting it go against my cheek, but his hand lingers there, his thumb resting on my lower lip, slightly dragging it down. Another soft click fills the space between us, the sound only broken by our heartbeats.

"We have a lot to do today," he says softly, lowering the camera.

"Can I take your picture?"

He holds my gaze, his mouth twitching softly, like he's trying to decide what his answer might be.

"Sure. Some time. Right now... I want you to spend the day with Shoshannah."

I frown.

21
NO SECOND CHANCES

Ryan

I LEAVE AVIVA IN THE BEDROOM AND IMMEDIATELY WALK OUTSIDE INTO the cool, rainy morning air. I clutch the railing of the deck and hang my head, trying to steady my thundering heart. I can't go into the village like this. I can barely walk in a straight line with this ache between my legs, but I sure as fuck can't go back inside because I'll rip her dress off and pin her to the bed like I wanted to only moments ago.

That little sliver of restraint is all I have left at this point.

I run my fingers through my hair, now wet from the rain. A thick fog hugs the valley, and only the outlines and pitched roofs are visible as my gaze sweeps the village. I had a long list of things to do this morning that are nearly impossible in my condition, and it's my own damn fault. I didn't mean to fall asleep with Aviva in my arms last night, but I did, sucked into a kind of peace I don't think I've ever known, and now I'm paying the price in droves.

I can't get the taste of her out of my mouth, and honestly, I'm not sure I want to. I think of awful things to try to calm myself down, to ease this raging erection that has only one thing on its mind, the woman in my bed. My fucking wife.

I close my eyes and imagine the worst possible thing I think could happen to me; being told Sydney doesn't want to be king, and suddenly I'm the heir apparent to my father's title. Even the thought of wearing a stuffy tuxedo and mingling with the rich, wealthy, and powerful Alphas of Crescent Falls does nothing for my condition, because I think of laying Aviva down on the couch in the library and fucking her brains out, her moans echoing throughout the castle, all while she wears a pretty little tiara in her wild hair..

I think of her falling while hunting that goat, and thankfully, that does the trick. With a long, drawn out sigh, I trudge down to the pack house and try not to think of Aviva for the rest of the morning.

Andrew derails that plan the moment I step into his blacksmith shop, of course.

"Well, well, well–"

"Shut the fuck up," I say by way of greeting and sit down on an old crate. He takes off the thick gloves he wears while working with the forge and sets them down on his work table. It's not even 8:00 in the morning, and he's already smeared with soot.

"Bright eyed and bushy tailed as usual," he grumbles, grabbing his old Wellington University thermos and drinking deeply. The logo is nearly worn off the side of the burgundy colored thermos. It's strange seeing it here, thousands of miles away from the campus where I met him.

"That thing I asked you to do?" I begin, crossing my arms over my chest as he looks me up and down. I roll my slightly swollen lower lip between my teeth and wonder, as he scans my face, if he can tell how I chose to wake up this morning.

In heaven. Burying my face between Aviva's legs.

"Aviva's bow? Yeah, it's nearly done. I have Seth working on the woodwork because I don't know shit about it, you know. His dad has him working the saw mill, and he's getting pretty good at it. He's talking about building himself a house now."

I picture eighteen-year-old Seth in my mind, one of our packs only teenagers. His family came to me a few years ago wanting to leave the Crescent City pack and join mine, and I accepted them, which was honestly the beginning of my issues with our neighbors in Crescent Falls. Seth's dad, Mark, is one of maybe three men older than forty in my entire pack, and he ranked pretty high in the Alpha of Crescent City's ranks.

Seth is also one of three teenage boys with no women around close in age. At all.

"He wants to build a house so he can have a wife," I deadpan, meeting Andrew's gaze as he slips his gloves back on and adjusts the thick, heat proof apron over his chest and waist. I notice the door-knobs and hinges on his worktable, some still smoking from being pulled from the fire. Summer is our only chance to build, and it's all hands on deck.

"Look, people have been talking, especially the men. You came home with a wife and… for a lot of us, it's been two years, you know, since…"

"I get it. But I don't want people thinking this is going to become the norm. We're not in the Deadlands to take women from the tribes."

"But if our guys started paying bride prices?" Andrew examines one of the hinges, taking a particular interest in it. "For example, if I paid Freya's bride price, she could stay. Be my wife."

I sigh and run my hand over my face. Maybe staying in bed and exploring every sweet inch of Aviva's body wasn't such a bad idea despite the fact that she's not, and will never be, mine. "We'll be going to the Harvest Festival as a pack this fall. It's likely some of our people will find their mates there, and next year, after the snow melts, the Roguelands hold a mating festival during the spring." I didn't realize bringing home a wife was going to cause such a splash, honestly, but I get it. My pack has a lot of single men of mating age who are building their own houses, farming their own land, living the dream I sold them years ago, with empty houses and cold beds to show for it. My guys… they want families. They want companionship and meaning.

"Just putting the idea into your head. No rush."

"Well it sounds like there's a rush."

"Have you had any coffee today, like, at all?" Andrew toys with his gloves and narrows his eyes at me. "What's up with you?"

"It was a long night."

"Ah, yeah, Dahlia and all that." He looks around the room. "Is Aviva okay? I heard–"

"She's fine." I think she's fine. Watching her spiral into a full blown panic attack had been awful. Guilt sweeps over me, rendering my mind useless as I stare blankly into the forge.

Andrew toys with one of the hinges, watching me. "Can I ask you something without you getting pissed off?"

"What, Andrew?"

He sighs, taking off his gloves again and arranging them neatly on the table just to do something, anything, with his hands. "What's your deal with Aviva?"

I chew the inside of my cheek, unable to even make eye contact with him.

"Do you like her?"

"What does that have to do with anything?"

"I just...." He sucks in an annoyed breath and postures, puffing out his chest a bit. "Look, dude. That night you made her that wager, before the hunt? I've never seen anyone, and I mean anyone, especially not a girl, step up to you like that and win. I don't even think you let her win that one, man. The look on her face when she told you the two of you were hunting in whatever the fuck that valley is called...your life flashed before your eyes. You looked like–"

Don't say it. Don't fucking say it.

"You looked like a guy who just saw their mate for the first time."

I look down at my boots. "I have a mate."

"Had."

I look up at him, running my tongue over my teeth. "I don't get a second chance at the mate bond."

"Yeah, you do. Plenty of people lose their mates and find new ones–"

"I didn't lose my mate. I killed Hadley."

Andrew holds my gaze, unblinking. "That's the first time I've ever heard you say her name."

"We're not having this conversation."

"Then why did you come here this morning?" His tone takes on an edge I'm not used to hearing from him. "You come here, smelling like Aviva, like your fucking wife, acting like this isn't significant."

"I don't know her scent. Do you get what that means?" I stand, gesturing to my chest. "I killed my fucking mate, Andrew. I tore out her throat. That goes against everything the Goddess stands for. I was supposed to protect her. I do not get a second chance."

"She was going to kill Sarah. Probably your nephew, too, if he'd been there. She was going to kill Dahlia!"

I cover my face with my hands and fight the urge to scream. The scream would have come from a deep, dark place I buried over two years ago when I looked up at Sarah and saw the horror and anguish on her face as she reached for me, tears in her eyes. Not tears for her traitorous friend. No, tears at what I'd done. What I'd sacrificed.

No one has looked at me the same since then.

Andrew clutches the work table and turns from me, his head hanging. "There's been talk."

"About what?" I croak, smoothing my hair out of my face. "Me still being capable of being Alpha?"

"No, never that." He exhales, long and slow. "Between me, Jacob, and James."

The mention of James spurs fresh, hot, displaced anger. I curl my hands into fists.

"You need to move on. We thought–Jacob and I–when we watched you get married… the way you looked at her." His eyes meet mine. "I never saw you look at anyone like that. I never saw you look at *Hadley* like that."

"It doesn't matter. I'm not Aviva's mate, Andrew. She's twenty-two. She'd feel it–"

"Not if you're not able to feel it."

I grit my teeth, shaking my head. "She isn't my mate. Her mate is out there."

"And you're going to do what? Go hunt for him? Unite them, and spend the rest of your life in fucking purgatory?" He takes a single step in my direction, his hands raised in surrender. "I fucking hate this, man. I hate seeing you like this. Jacob–fuck, man–we all want you back. The old Ryan would've been fucking grinning from ear to ear right now after what you were up to this morning. You'd be telling us about it. Talking the same old shit–"

"That's my fucking wife you're talking about right now. That's my business."

For whatever reason, his mouth ticks into a smile. "Like I said, don't act like whatever we just went through in Endova wasn't significant."

I didn't need this this morning. This was the last fucking thing I needed. I'm acutely aware how people see me now. Hadley's murder wasn't kept a secret. Word spread like wildfire through my family, through my own pack, and no one said a fucking thing.

I'm treated like a head case, like something people have to be careful around. My brother is the worst offender, which is why when Ryatt came to me and asked if I wanted to leave, if I wanted to claim this territory as my own and be as far away from everyone, and everything, I accepted.

He understands what it's like to be the outcast, the cursed one, the enemy.

The last thing I ever wanted was for anyone to worry about me. Now my friends were staging an intervention.

"Jacob and I are going to Endova the second this rain clears. We'll leave tonight if we have to. I need you to step in for James while we're gone. He deserves the break."

Andrew grumbles under his breath, turning from me.

"That's what I came here for," I grind out, turning for the door. "You're the Beta until James feels that Dahlia and the baby are settled."

"Does he know?"

He's about to. I leave Andrew's shop and walk in the direction of James's house just as the fog begins to lift, and the sun peeks through the clouds. Green grass sparkles in the early morning sunlight, setting everyone out and about in a soft glow.

Aviva walks with Shoshannah toward the field where we keep the sheep, falling in step with Freya, who spins in the lifting fog. Aviva turns to look over her shoulder, spotting me. Her cheeks go slightly pink, but her lips... they curve into a smile that instantly lifts the heavy feelings weighing down my chest.

This isn't fair to her in the slightest. We got married. I am her husband. I made her a vow. I made her people, her family, a vow that I'd be good to her, and I haven't been.

I keep walking as she disappears into the rolling fog and quietly enter James's house. Justine is just leaving, smiling kindly at me as she tells me to keep quiet, that Dahlia and the baby girl are asleep.

I slowly, carefully open the door to their bedroom, and I'm met with a sight that makes my heart squeeze with both happiness, and admittedly, a pang of jealousy.

James sits on the side of the bed, his hand resting on the swell of Dahlia's hip as she sleeps on her side. The baby is sleeping beside Dahlia, her small, round face washed in dreary sunlight. James looks up at me as I hang back in the doorway, and I speak into his mind without meaning to. Maybe it's because Andrew just ripped me a new one, or there's just something in the air after his daughter's. It's summer. A season of change. A season of decisions that affect the outcome of the months, and years, to follow.

'Can we talk?' I ask through the mind-link, and he nods.

2 2

NOT THE OLD WAYS

Aviva

"I KNOW THAT FEELS BETTER," FREYA SAYS, FROWNING AT THE frantically bleating sheep, who is now sheared clean and pretty much naked as it gallops off to join its herd. She wipes her brow, squinting into the sunlight as she gathers up an enormous handful of raw wool and carries it over to the creek where I'm crouching in the water, rinsing another batch of wool until it shines a soft white. "Who's next?"

"That one," I laugh, tilting my head to the giant, gray and black ram with spiraling horns that looks like he wants nothing more than to kill us both. He stamps his hooves and lowers his head in emphasis, snorting and shaking his fuzzy head.

"That fucker," Freya growls, tucking her hair behind her hairs and stretching out her arms over her head. "He's been getting in my way all morning."

"I can take him, if you want."

She shakes her head and picks up the shears. "No, thanks. He's mine. We have a score to settle." I watch her stride off, posturing

165

toward the ram as he aggressively bleats and tries to ram his horns into her thighs, but Freya grabs him by the horns and wrestles him to his side.

"Freya's tough, huh?" Shosh says as she grabs a handful of wet wool and hangs it over the rock wall creating the smooth eddy we're wading in.

"The toughest," I echo, watching with a smile as Freya pins the ram down, her muffled curses drifting through the air toward us.

"I'm going to be tough like you guys."

"Well, you can be as tough as you want, but we behave ourselves and don't run away from our villages." I jiggle the mass of wool between my hands before lifting small strands out of the cold water, laying them out to dry in the sun. Shoshannah frowns at me and continues to work beside me, occasionally muttering to herself. She's spent the last few days expecting a severe scolding from me, but luckily for her, I haven't been in the right state of mind.

Now, when I finally have my chance, I'm too damn relaxed to even care. Not after what Ryan did to me earlier this morning.

My cheeks blaze red despite my best efforts to remain casual and not think about that moment over, and over, turning it into something it wasn't.

"I didn't want you to leave," Shoshannah bites out. "That's why I left."

"I was going to have to leave eventually, regardless of whether it was with Ryan or someone else. One day, you'll leave Endova, too. You know how this works." I look at my little sister and the way her face has changed over the last year. She's only ten, but in a few years, her body will transform, and she'll shed what remains of childhood and turn into a woman. Dolls won't matter. Her friends will start talking about boys instead of wanting to pretend to be fairies in the woods. She'll catch someone's eye, he'll pay her bride price, and she will be gone.

I blink back sudden tears and look back at my task, licking my lips. "What you did was reckless."

"I was fine–"

"You could have died in more ways than one. Rogues in the woods. Catching a chill from the rain. Being swept away by the creek."

Shosh angrily squeezes the wool but drapes it gently over the rocks. "I don't want to go back. I want to stay with you and Freya."

"You can't." My throat closes around the words. "This isn't your home."

"It's not your home either!"

"It is now. I know you don't understand, but one day, you'll be bound to your husband, and you will turn his village into your new home, and you'll find that you like it there, and that you're happy. That's all I want for you, but it's not your time. You need to be with Father. You have Lora to think about."

She screws up her face. "You don't seem happy."

"I will be." I hope. I hope I'll be content here, eventually, even if Ryan continues to keep me at arm's length. Whatever happened between us this morning didn't mean anything. I feel it as sharply as I'm sure he did. What had he said to me in the hot springs? Is it just my body reacting?

Freya walks over dripping with sweat and dumps a pile of thick, black wool on the creek bank, huffing out a breath as her eyes shine with pride. "That's the last of 'em. Good job, girls."

"These sheep are smaller than the one's back home. That's why it didn't take long," Shosh says, looking up her nose at Freya, her tone sharp enough to slice. Freya crouches, her eyes sliding to mine, then she scoops her hand through the water and absolutely drenches Shosh with a splash that sends a tidal wave rippling to the opposite bank of the creek.

Shosh finally breaks out of her awful mood and proceeds to splash her back, all while I watch, thankful for fine weather and the chance to just be with them for a morning.

"Andrew says he's going to put a loom in my cottage at some point this week," Freya says as she helps us finish washing the rest of the wool. "This black wool is so fine and soft. No wonder they're using that ram to breed."

"You and Andrew seem pretty cozy lately," I murmur as Shoshannah catches the attention of her new friends and darts away to catch up to them as they go to pick berries or something, all four of the girls carrying baskets as they head in the direction of the gardens and greenhouses at the far edge of the village.

"I don't mind him at all. Isn't that weird?" Freya smiles, sitting on the creek bank and turning her cheeks to the sun. "I've never met a man I liked."

"But do you *like* him?"

"Well, he's not my type," she says with a little laugh as I sit on the bank beside her. "He's so–he's so blond."

"Blond? So are you."

She cuts me a teasing look. "I like them tall, dark, and handsome."

"He's tall and handsome."

"He also lives here." She sighs, stretching her legs out and dipping her toes in the water. "Plus, you know I'm spoken for."

Her tone drops, edging on disappointment. I purse my lips and look out at the sweeping green hills hugging the village, watching as the group of girls runs up one of them. "So was I, apparently, but no one had paid my bride price yet. It was all talk between my father and the patriarch of Navvan before that from what Mercy told me. Your father and the patriarch of Teshka haven't come to any agreements yet either."

"It doesn't matter, does it? I have a few months here. Maybe Andrew will... never mind."

I lean against her, smiling at my closest, dearest friend. "You do like him, don't you? You're thinking about the possibility of him paying your bride price, I can tell."

"I like to look at him," she huffs, closing her eyes against the sun. "This morning, real early, before the sun rose, I got up and went to the pack house to grab some breakfast for me and Shosh and walked by this building, and the doors were open wide, and you'll never believe I saw."

"What did you see?"

"A bunch of guys lifting these things... heavy things, by the look of it. Most of them had their shirts off. It was quite a sight. I lingered, of course, and Andrew caught me, asking if I wanted to come inside and *work out*, whatever that means, or just stand and gawk at him. Honestly, I could have stood there all day."

"Why don't you tell him you like him?"

"Because none of these men know anything about our people and how this works. You got lucky, Aviva."

"You keep telling me that–"

"You're married to an *Alpha*. You would've been married to a patriarch's son had Hardan paid your bride price. I'm the daughter of an elder, so my price is just as high, and I don't think… I don't think your new people really understand the significance of all of this, and honestly, that does bother me." She wraps her arms around her knees. "I want to stay here, but I don't want to lose what I am and where I came from, even if someone like Andrew could come up with a satisfactory bride price, you know?"

We fall into silence as the clouds drift overhead, blocking out the warm spring sun for a moment. Shadows dance across the waving plains of green and gold as I take in the beauty of this village while also feeling the full brunt of Freya's words.

My people are spiritual–aligned with the Goddess and Her companions of old. We believe the ancient legends and say the ancient prayers. We follow the practices from a time when wolves were few and dangers were plenty.

When Ryan married me, he vowed to protect me, to protect our future children, our family line. He vowed to honor me before the Goddess, to hold me in his prayers, and to spill the blood of those who ever crossed me, ever threatened me.

He made those vows to my village without realizing it, because he doesn't know the old tongue. He comes from a land of mates. Mates, which is a concept I still haven't been able to wrap my mind around. My feelings for him run so deep it hurts, and I can't get him out of my mind, but that has to be because he won't let me in.

This marriage is just business to him. To me, it's my entire life. My entire purpose.

Freya understands without having to voice it. Whether she sees an actual future with Andrew doesn't matter as much as her hopes that he'd do it in the old way, offer her bride price, and say the vows beneath the Harvest Moon like it's been done for centuries upon centuries.

But these men are modern and come from a land neither of us can fathom. They must do things differently there. They must not feel in the same way we do. They must not take these roles as seriously at all.

Freya is just starting to rise to gather the wool when Ryan appears, walking in tandem with Jacob, their heads bent in conversation. I haven't said a word to him since this morning, when he'd taken my picture in a bed we should be sharing more than we have.

The men come to a stop on the opposite bank. Ryan's eyes meet mine, and for a brief moment, I feel like we're sharing the same thought, the same memory of being in bed. I feel my cheeks heat again but banish it, burying that longing until I feel nothing at all.

Jacob crosses his arms over his chest and looks at the sheep in the distance, nodding his approval. "You even got the ram. He's a real bastard. No one has ever been able to shear him since we got him last summer."

"We're best friends now," Freya chuckles, motioning to the bruises starting to show along her legs and arms. "I just had to convince him."

Ryan keeps his eyes on mine, however. "Aviva, I need to talk to you for a moment."

Great. I bet he's going to give me a lecture about how what happened this morning won't be happening again, how he can't even look at me, how touching me is painful, something along those lines.

I fight the urge to shift and run far into the hills as I cross the creek, barefoot, and walk by his side back into the village while Jacob wades into the water to help Freya with the wool. We don't go back to his house, however. He pulls me into the shade of the pack house, his hand gripping the back of my neck as he leans down and… kisses me.

2 3

AMBUSH

Ryan

"WHAT WAS THAT FOR?" AVIVA ASKS BREATHLESSLY AS I PULL AWAY.

"I'm not sure. Sorry." I clear my throat–clear my head, more like it. I've been out in the sun all day helping stack stone for a new house being built in the village, and apparently, that hadn't been enough to wash Aviva's taste from my mouth, and my body decided it needed more.

We stare at each other for a moment. Her eyes shine like fine whiskey in the sunlight cutting through the shadow all around us. The clouds move swiftly to the south, which is why I had to talk to her.

"Jacob and I are leaving in an hour with Shoshannah. I sent scouts in every direction to monitor the weather, and it looks like there'll be a break from the rain tonight."

"You said a week–"

"I don't really have a week to spare," I admit, when in reality I need to get away from her before I do anything else I'll regret. "I also need you and Freya fully available to help out. Making sure Shoshannah

171

stays out of trouble isn't in the best interest of my pack at the moment."

She runs her tongue along her lower lip, right where I'd just kissed her. No wonder Andrew chewed me out this morning. Every time I look at her, I feel like my body is at odds with my mind. I want to catch the tongue between my teeth. I want to press her to the wall of the pack house and run my hand up her inner thigh until I find–I need to fucking chill.

"But I'm going with you back to Endova."

"No, you're staying here."

She shakes her head. "I'm going.

I arch a brow. "You're staying. That's final."

"Why?"

"Because I can be there in less than four hours if Shoshannah rides on Jacob's back. I don't want you running off to hunt or chase rogues and slowing us down. You're also the Luna now. You need to be here–with our pack. I've already spoken to some of the women, and they're eager to learn from you."

"Learn what?" She sneers, crossing her arms under her breasts. "How to hunt? That's all I know how to do."

I lean back and run my hand through my hair. "Freya is really good with a loom, I've heard."

"Well, I'm not very good at it. She can teach them."

"I have something for you," I cut in, closing my eyes as the words spill out in a tone I hadn't intended, rushed and edged with frustration, and when I open my eyes, I notice the hurt on Aviva's face. I take her by the arm, trying to pull her from the wall, but she digs in her heels. "You're going to want to see this, okay?"

She grunts with annoyance but follows me up to our house. Afternoon sunlight spills over the floorboards as I close the door behind us, closeting us in silence.

Aviva has already seen what I brought her here for, though. Her shoulders go rigid, and she takes an excited breath before snatching the bow off the kitchen table and wrapping her fingers around it. She examines it closely, studying the craftsmanship on the limb and back, running her fingertips over the wood and metal details. The bowstring is reinforced, thanks to Andrew. He also made several arrows, some totally metal, and Seth carved wooden ones with metal tips. The grip was my design. It's small enough for her hand and made from a piece of leather that came from the mountain goat we brought back from Fell Valley.

I'd been planning this gift since then, designing it in my mind. I'd never seen someone look so hurt like she had when I watched her gathering the pieces of her broken bow.

Silence hangs in the air between us for several minutes as I watch her take it in. I can practically see the gears turning behind her eyes as her fingers dance over the bowstring. Quick as lightning, she reaches for an arrow resting in the quiver on the table and loads it, the tip pointed at my heart.

I don't even flinch. I'd be a happy man if she was the one who cast my final blow. I'd probably deserve it.

"Do you like it?"

"It's smaller than my old one."

"Your old bow was too big for you," I tell her, walking around to get a better look at the bow now that she has it flexed. Her muscles are tight as she pulls back on the arrow, a metal one, which Andrew told me would be heavier than she's used to. The arrow sings through the air as she lets it fly. It pierces through a log near the front door, sticking out by a few inches. "Thank you," I growl. "I needed a new coat hook."

But Aviva lets out her breath, her shoulders relaxing as she looks up at me and I see.... Thank the Goddess, that's happiness in her eyes.

"So you like it?"

"I do. Thank you."

"I figured since I didn't have a ring for you, I owed you something for our very brief engagement."

She furrows her brows. "A ring?"

"Back in Crescent Falls, when people get married, they exchange rings." I reach for her, gently pinching her left ring finger. "They wear them here as a signal that they're taken."

She slings the bow over her back with practiced grace. "We get tattoos."

Now I'm furrowing my brows. "Really? Where?"

"Same place. If you mean to stay married to me, you'll have a tattoo on your finger, a symbol of our own design to signify our union." She holds my gaze without blinking, like she's testing me.

"I mean to stay married until you find your mate."

"It won't matter if I do."

"You say that now, but you don't know–"

"What it feels like? I don't." She huffs a breath and turns from me, picking up the new quiver and examining the leather straps that will fit along her back. "Do mates wear rings as well?"

"No." I feel like I'm suddenly in front of a hot flame. "They don't."

"What do they do, then?" She looks over her shoulder at me. She's still wearing that long, pink dress, but has it bunched up around her waist to show off her calves, the excess fabric tucked into her knife belt. The straps slip off her slim shoulder, showing off her golden skin and the constellations of freckles I'd love to count one day. Her hair, normally wild, is tied back with a ribbon at the base of her neck with little red curls forming a halo around her face, and I'm... drowning.

I lick my lip to stop them from trembling as I say, "They bite each other."

"How romantic."

"They bite to leave a mark." I touch her shoulder, smoothing a finger toward the crook of her neck. "Usually here. Or along the shoulder blade, or the spine." I feel her pulse quicken as she slowly turns to face me, and my finger dips along her collarbone, lower, lower.... "Sometimes in places far more intimate. Wherever it feels right."

"Where did you mark your mate?"

Fuck, Aviva knows exactly where and how to hurt me.

"I didn't mark her."

"Then was she really your mate?"

"It's something you feel."

"You need to be more specific." She bats my hand away and turns back to the quiver, sifting through the arrows.

Standing behind her, I take a breath and let it out through my nose. Are mates so rare in this part of the world that people have really forgotten what it feels like?

"It's like… tasting color. Seeing things you could only feel before."

"That doesn't make any sense."

"Neither does the bond." I notice the way her hands tighten on the arrows. "Don't go too far away from the village tonight, but you have my permission to hunt, not that telling you no would have done anything. Take Freya with you."

"You think Freya is going to protect me in the event I get into trouble?" She looks at me over her shoulder, the corner of her mouth ticking into a smile.

"No, but you'd be too busy keeping her safe to even think about doing anything stupid."

Her smile grows into something real, something with feeling, and that's enough for me.

* * *

WE LEFT SILVERHIDE IN THE LATE AFTERNOON. SHOSHANNAH RODE ON Jacob's back, and I was thankful that there hadn't been a tearful goodbye between the sisters. If anything, I think Shoshannah decided that it was best she leave instead of allowing the anger Aviva obviously felt toward what she'd done fester any more than it had to.

Shoshannah stayed quiet and serious for the first half of the journey until we had to cross the creek, which had, thankfully, gone down quite a bit, but then demanded to walk for a while, citing numb legs and boredom.

So, now we're walking, two wolves and a ten-year-old girl who can talk like no one I've ever met before.

"Aviva can beat up anybody," she says as we reach the forest wrapped around her village, which means, in ten miles, she'll be home and safe as long as she doesn't run away again. "But I'm going to be stronger than her one day. Father thinks I'll be tall like Mercy, so that means I'll be taller than Aviva. Mother wasn't very tall, I guess, so I'll get my height from Father. And then I'll be about to beat up Aviva, and she won't be able to do anything about it."

Jacob glances at me with a wolfish grin on his face as we continue to flank either side of the young girl, who is now talking about birds and frogs, and how she once caught a frog and put it under Mercy's pillow.

But I notice something that makes my fur stand on end. Aviva had mentioned something to me that night when she killed those rogues. The birdsong. How the birdsong quieted to nothing, and that's how she knew we weren't alone anymore.

It's silent in the woods right now other than Shoshannah's lifted voice. I glance at Jacob. *'Something's wrong.'*

"Mercy chased me around with a broom, but I'm faster than her, so she couldn't catch me. She scared the frog so bad it peed in her bed because she screamed at it, but I hid from her so I wouldn't have to wash her blankets. Now, when she sees a frog, she screams–"

Something whizzes through the air right above my head and lodges itself in a tree nearby. Jacob sees it too, a second too late. More arrows fly toward us, but Shoshannah is still talking, unaware that we're suddenly under attack.

Then a yell rips through the air, followed by the sound of thundering feet and paws, and I grab Shoshannah by the fabric of her dress and toss her headlong into a thicket of heather before turning toward our attackers with a snarl.

'These aren't Endovian warriors!' Jacob shouts through the mind-link as the first wolf jumps out of the woods with its jaw open wide as it careens through the air and knocks into my side.

'Get Shoshannah and GO!' I shout, rolling with the enemy wolf, its teeth ripping into my thick fur. More arrows follow, and we're trapped, unable to run, and Shoshannah is still in the bushes. Jacob barrels over the wolf currently clamped down on my shoulder, sending it rolling into a tree. A sharp yelp follows as I rush to my feet

and face the five warriors, all in their human forms, jumping out of the dense trees.

Arrows are pointed in my face. Blades are drawn. Jacob can't safely get Shoshannah and run until we deal with these men.

A sick, twisting feeling settles in my gut. Is Endova under attack too? This is their territory, after all. Did we walk right into a conflict with a child in tow?

I bare my teeth, snarling, and Jacob does the same a few feet away from me as the warriors close in, grinning from ear to ear.

'I'll take two, you take the rest,' Jacob says into my mind.

'Once they're down, get her out of here.'

We lunge at the same time, crashing into the warriors, ignoring the blades and arrows, and tear them to shreds.

It's a madhouse. The first man I take down tries to shift, but I close my teeth around his throat before he can do it, his blood filling my mouth. Jacob roars as he barrels through the two warriors he called dibs on, tearing them to pieces in a matter of seconds.

Something sharp grazes my back as I turn to the final enemy in the group. Jacob steps to my side, his mouth dark red with blood as we snarl at the man only a few feet away, holding a spear with my blood staining the tip.

I hear Shoshannah sobbing as I lunge at the man, and he shifts in a burst of light before tearing through the woods and out of sight, the spear left behind.

My heart races as I turn and run back to where we left Shoshannah. I lift her out of the bushes, nudging her with my snout.

'Your back is flayed open,' Jacob says into my mind.

'It's a flesh wound. It's nothing.'

Jacob steps beside me anyway, nudging Shoshannah until she grabs his fur and hoists herself onto his back, her cheeks wet with tears and eyes wide with terror, but she's safe and whole, not a single scratch on her skin.

'What the fuck was that about?'

'I don't know,' I reply, turning back toward the road. *'But we need to get to Endova, now.'*

24

FAMILY KILLER

Ryan

We're met in Endova by warriors armed to the teeth. The sun has set, and the village is glowing with torches, the fire at the village center burning brighter than usual. I'd sent scouts ahead of us by several hours to inform Jerrod of our earlier than anticipated arrival, but they're nowhere to be seen, and that sinking sensation in my stomach explodes as we walk into the village, and Jerrod rushes toward us, his eyes wide with both stress and relief to see Shoshannah safe and sound.

The wound on my back throbs as Jerrod wordlessly ushers us into his meeting hall. Still in our wolf forms, Jacob and I are given clothes and left alone to change while Jerrod scoops up Shoshannah and takes her away to be tended to.

"Let me see it," Jacob insists, grabbing my arm to turn me around. He hisses out a breath. "It's deep, man."

"It doesn't hurt that bad," I lie, pulling my shirt over the long, jagged gash on the left side of my back. I'm not sure if it was the bloody spear or an arrow that caused the wound, but it doesn't matter. Something happened here within the last six hours since we left Silverhide and our best scouts, Grey and Hunter, are presumably missing.

Just as I assume the worst, Hunter strides through the door, followed by Grey. Hunter, with short, dark hair and even darker eyes, nods to us in hello, breathless. Grey looks equally as stressed, running his fingers through his sandy blond hair.

"What happened?" I ask roughly, pouring myself a drink from a random pitcher on one of the long tables where a meal was laid out and quickly abandoned. I chug what tastes like mead—flat, but sweet—letting the alcohol numb the ache in my back.

"It was quiet until an hour ago," Grey says, panting.

Hunter adds, "Everyone was sitting down for dinner. We were outside the meeting hall, talking with a few of the Endovian warriors, shooting the shit, when screaming interrupted us. A group of what the elders believe are Navvan warriors tore through the outer ring of the village."

Jacob glances at me before asking, "Why?"

"No one knows yet. It was chaos trying to get the women and children to safety. The Endovian warriors put up a fight and pushed them out, and me and Grey were able to chase one down that tried to run and dragged him back." Hunter crouches, and I notice both of my scouts are totally out of breath.

Grey adds, "The hostage was being interrogated by the elders when we left the village to try to track the Navvan warriors. They have a camp about six miles east of here, in the woods."

"Were you seen?" I ask, and the men shake their heads.

"We stayed down wind. They had no idea we were there."

"How many strong?" Jacob asks.

The tension in the room is so thick I could cut it with a knife as Hunter replies, "Twenty at the camp."

"We just faced five," Jacob says to me.

I run my hand over my face. I was warned that the tribes occasionally fight, but Jacob and I were brutally attacked less than half an hour ago with a child in tow. For whatever reason, this seems like more than infighting.

The door to the meeting hall opens wide, and Jerrod walks in, followed by several elders, including Freya's father. Jerrod runs his hand over his beard before motioning with his hands for us to sit down, lazily motioning to the food, but I shake my head. "What happened here?"

"Navvan has a new patriarch. Their elders are dead, from what we just learned," Jerrod rushes out, looking exhausted. "I've just sent scouts to Teshka to inform them."

"What do you mean the elders in Navvan are dead?" I say through gritted teeth. What I know about the tribal packs in these lands is that someone like Jerrod isn't necessarily an Alpha. He's the leader, the patriarch, but his council of elders back him up, helping to guide his decisions for the good of the pack. The elders are elected officials, and the patriarch is chosen from among them.

Jerrod grits his teeth, anger flaring behind his pale green eyes. Something isn't right.

I turn to Jacob, tilting my head to our scouts, who are now sitting on the benches, drinking whatever they can get their hands on to cool their burning lungs. "Try to get in touch with Andrew and James through the mind-link. I want every man up, out of bed, and preparing to defend my territory if Navvan makes a move on us. If you can't get ahold of them, send Grey back to Silverhide. Hunter can lead us to the Navvan camp nearby."

Jacob nods and turns away, motioning for Grey and Hunter to follow him out of the meeting hall. I pace in front of the group of elderly men now cloistered nearby, watching my every movie. "What do you mean the elders are dead?" I repeat, my eyes meeting Jerrod's.

"They were murdered by Hardan of Navvan, the patriarch's eldest son. He staged a coup and is now calling himself patriarch," Jerrod breathes. "He killed his own father. An ally of mine. Dead."

"He's not a patriarch. He wasn't elected to the role," another elder cuts in coldly, spitting on the floor.

"You're correct," I rasp. "He just made himself an Alpha." I look up at the ceiling, trying to clear my head. "What did the warrior from Navvan say about why they were attacking Endova?"

Jerrod makes a small noise in his throat and dismisses the other elders, telling them in passing to keep their warriors around the perimeter of the village. I watch them leave, tucking my hands behind my aching back. I know blood is starting to seep through the shirt I was given. It's sticking to my skin.

Jerrod closes the massive doors and turns to me, his eyes downcast as he tucks his hands in the pockets of his cloak. "Hardan attempted to pay Aviva's bride price several months ago in anticipation for the upcoming Harvest Festival, but I said no."

His eyes meet mine, holding my gaze. He continues, "He offered again a few days ago and made it very clear that he'd have her, one way or another. He came here with his band of misfit warriors and demanded a presence with her. I refused. He didn't take kindly to that." He takes a breath as he begins to pace, picking up random goblets and setting them back on the table. "Aviva knew about Hardan's desire to wed her, but she didn't know the details. I kept that from her and Mercy."

"What details?" My blood runs cold at the pained look on his face.

"Hardan is the worst kind of man." He clears his throat, closing his eyes as he shakes his head. "Before he came to me asking for Aviva, he'd gone to Teshka to pursue the daughter of the patriarch there. Hardan's reputation for being uncontrollable and rash had spread, and he was denied. Instead of leaving Teshka, he had the poor girl kidnapped from her bed and... he passed her around to his men." He grits his teeth, cursing under his breath in the old tongue. "She never recovered. She died from her injuries a few weeks later after suffering endlessly. When Hardan came to me, talking about how he'd heard of Aviva, our huntress, our warrior princess, he wanted her. Not in the way a husband wants a wife, but he wanted to dominate her, bend her until she broke, and I could see it in his eyes. So I refused him, twice. And that second time, he told me I'd come to regret it. Then you showed up."

He holds my gaze as my stomach twists. "You told me Aviva would die in those woods, but you weren't talking about getting killed by rogues, were you?"

"No," he says, nodding in confirmation.

"Why didn't you tell me? My pack is at risk now. You realize that, right?"

"I didn't tell you because, at the time, it didn't matter. Hardan was still under the yoke of his father's command. I knew he was a stain on our kind, but I didn't know he was capable of killing his own family, his younger brothers included."

"So he came here to punish you for not giving him *my wife?*" I can't think of Aviva in any other way. The idea of harm coming to her–of her, theoretically–being given to this man before I'd come into her life… it rips me to shreds. Aviva is tough as nails, but only on the outside. Inside, she's soft, hiding her sensitivity behind a rock-hard shell of strength she can barely contain.

Jerrod nods, but fury coasts through my veins, burning my skin.

I step toward him, seething. "We are allies. You and I, Jerrod. I promised I'd take care of your daughter, and I won't stand by and let a madman threaten her life and my pack. I have to act, which means Endova will be in the middle."

"He killed four of our warriors tonight and maimed several villagers. We're missing five of our women. He's already declared war. We are on your side. You have my warriors behind you if you choose to pursue him."

Rage licks up my spine, blurring the pain of the wound throbbing on my back. "I need forty of your men. I need them ready to leave in ten minutes."

Jerrod nods but gives me a distant, empty look. "Navvan has the most skilled warriors out of the tribal packs." He looks right at me, his expression cast in shadow as he asks, "If you don't come back from their camp tonight, what will happen to Aviva?"

I think of my family, my mom especially. I'm not sure why. Maybe it's because, deep down, I know Mom would love her, would be so happy for us both, and there's a chance they'll never meet. "Aviva will return here, to her home."

I leave the meeting hall with a sour taste in my mouth. Jacob steps up to me looking hard and ready for whatever comes next, but out of the corner of my eye, I notice Mercy hanging around nearby, her eyes wide with worry as she watches Jacob cross the distance between us. He looks at her, takes a shallow breath, and turns his attention to me.

"Grey is on his way back to Silverhide. I told him not to stop. I couldn't get through to anyone. I need him to do what he has to do to stop any Navvan warriors that might be headed that way."

Fuck me, this is really bad. "We're leaving in a few minutes for the camp. I asked for forty warriors from Endova. You and Hunter need to gather and prepare them. We're taking out that entire fucking camp."

Jacob nods and runs off, grabbing a slightly delirious and exhausted Hunter by the arm as they fall out of sight, swallowed by darkness.

But Mercy is suddenly beside me, clutching the sleeve of my shirt. She swallows so hard I wonder if she's trying to choke back a sob as she asks, "How is she?" She looks up at me with eyes identical to her father's. She and Aviva look so different, but that look... that sheltered look that hides the mass of roiling, conflicting emotions, is the same.

"She's adjusting."

Mercy nods, letting go of my sleeve to wipe her nose on the back of her hand. She looks at the spot between two earthen houses where Jacob disappeared, and I wonder, deep down, if something might have happened between the two of them. I've seen the same knowing look on Sarah and Kenna's before. That same ache that comes with worrying about one's... mate.

"I'll bring him back," I tell her, giving her a cocky smile as my fury is replaced by adrenaline.

There's one thing I've always loved more than women.

A fucking good fight.

2 5

THAT'S HIS MATE

Aviva

MOONLIGHT GHOSTS OVER MY SKIN AS I STAND AT THE HIGHEST POINT of the valley that overlooks Silverhide. Wind whispers through my fur, and my keen eyes scan the valley below for movement before I move along the narrow rocks, careful of the steep drop-offs hidden in the shadows. The stars are out in full overhead, bright and wild against ribbons of deep, swirling purple.

It's a perfect night. The kind of night I always longed for after days of rain and clouds. But I've realized why Ryan and his men came to Endova to join the spring hunt and get their fill of deer in a single night. The valley of Silverhide is empty, save for small critters like rabbits. I won't be bringing home a deer tonight, not if I stay within the valley like I promised.

But it feels good to be out in the wild after a very long day of village chores. All of the wool we sheared and washed this morning is hanging to dry so we can brush it out and spin it into yarn tomorrow. Freya offered to teach some of the women in the village how to weave using the loom Andrew started building for her within hours of our

185

arrival in the village several days ago. He should have it finished by tomorrow night. At least, that's what Freya told me over dinner tonight, her cheeks stained with a blush.

My heart aches at my friend's turmoil over her desperate crush on Andrew, which I find a bit hilarious, because he's obviously head over heels for her.

I edge down the mountain, taking my time, adjusting to the new fit of the bow and quiver against my back.

I reach what I really came here for, the hot springs. I shift back into my human form and shed my knife belt and the harness keeping the bow in place and jump into the big pool, gasping at the hot bite of the water. Heat instantly numbs my skin as I swim to the side, staying close to the falls so the water isn't blindingly hot, and proceed to just… float. Alone and content.

I haven't gotten past it, though. I'm absolutely pissed that Ryan made me stay in Silverhide while we went back to Endova. Thankfully, today was so busy that the hours felt like minutes, and before I knew it, night fell, and everyone went to sleep, which meant I could rage in privacy.

I went through all of Ryan's things again, moving them around. I took all of his socks out of the second drawer in his dresser where he keeps them and took the pairs apart, matching them with socks that were a different color, a different feel, before putting them back again. I dragged the blanket he'd been sleeping with at night over the floor in every room, and even out on the deck, before tossing it in a ball on the couch.

Petty, I know. But he left me here, and I've never been alone before.

The water works its way into my muscles and relieves some of the tension in my body. I start to feel the effects of the water and the fatigue of a long, hard day. My head starts to nod as I cross my arms over the edge of the pool, resting my cheek against my skin.

I'll wash his blanket tomorrow. I'll rematch his socks. I'll put his little trinkets back where I found them. Tomorrow. I'll do it tomorrow before he comes home.

Because he's supposed to come tomorrow, not that I care when he gets here.

I groan as I pinch my eyes shut. I missed his stupid little comments all day. I missed how he looks at me, that little flex of his jaw. I missed him, and I shouldn't be feeling like my world is crumbling apart just because he's gone. Am I missing something? Does everyone feel this way when they're hand-fasted?

A pain like I've never felt before rips through my chest so hard that I jerk and gasp. I choke on my own breath, fighting to get air back into my lungs. Frantically, I let go of the edge of the pool and tread water, running a hand over my bare chest. It feels like someone stabbed me, or punched me so hard they broke all of my ribs, but the pain passes nearly as quickly as it came.

I haul myself out of the water, still gasping for breath as my muscles go rigid with echoes of what I can only describe as pain. I turn my head toward the overhanging rock that overlooks the massive, sweeping view of not only the valley by the plains beyond, all the way to the forest that hugs Endova far in the distance.

I'm imagining Ryan's voice rasping my name right now. It drifts over me, whispered by the wind, making all the fine, down hair on my body stand on end. I feel the sudden urge to run to wherever he is, but bury the feeling, and rise, shifting, and start heading home.

* * *

RYAN

"YOU'RE OKAY," I TELL THE TRIO OF YOUNG WOMEN TIED TOGETHER around a tree as I slice through the rope. "You're okay." They're all in tears, their faces washed in terror as I pull the rope free and notice the raw skin on their arms and wrists where they'd been rubbing against the rope for over two hours now, trying to loosen it. I look around the clear, at the bloodshed and shattered bodies. "Where are the other two?"

"Here," Jacob says gruffly, carrying one young woman in his arms while another walks beside him. I recognize the one that's walking, and another who was tied to the tree. They're the only ones with murderous looks in their eyes instead of terror–Aviva's companions. These women had joined the men on the spring hunt.

Several Endovian warriors walk up to us, whispering to the women in low, comforting tones as they gather them up and start herding them out of the clearing. Jacob passes the woman he's carrying to one of the warriors at the same moment a bellow of pain and frustration echoes toward us through the woods.

The fighting isn't over. We stormed their camp twenty minutes ago, surprising the Navvan warriors who'd set up camp a few miles from Endova, likely in preparation to attack again at daylight. We'd pushed them into the woods where they scattered, using the thickly wooded forest to their advantage as the Endova forces swept through them.

"Come on," I say to Jacob, picking up a random Navvan blade lying on the ground next to one of the bodies.

The wound on my back is in rough shape. I haven't been able to shift. I'm not about to bust it open and make it any worse while actively engaged in combat. Unlike not only the Endovian and Navvan people, however, I was trained in hand to hand combat from a young age, as was Jacob. That's what warrior training was all about back in Crescent Falls, being able to defend yourself in both forms, as well as perform offensively.

Jacob shifts and stalks into the woods with me right behind him, and soon, we find the active battle taking place. Wolves and men dart between the trees. The air smells like copper–the metallic tang of blood–as the first Navvan warrior makes a move toward us. Jacob lunges, taking the man down at the knees. I finish him off with the blade.

It goes on like this for some time. I'm coated in blood and dirt by the time we reach the center of the battle. Hunter weaves between the trees in his wolf form, chasing several Navvan warriors.

We group up with a few Endovian men and a few of their wolves, standing back to back as the Navvan men charge us from the trees.

"Keep at least two alive," I snarl, looking toward the trees, into the darkness where all I can see is eyes looking back at me. "I want the Alpha of Navvan to know what happened here and what's to come if he steps a single foot outside of his territory."

We charge forward, meeting the Navvan warriors halfway, and all hell breaks loose.

I slash my way through the fray. Claws rip over my skin. Teeth leave punctures on my arms and legs, but I stay standing, stay moving forward, cutting my way toward one man in particular who seems to be shouting orders to the other Navvan men.

He's tall, with dirty brown hair and wild eyes full of vengeance. He doesn't give off the Alpha vibe, though, not entirely. I'm certain, without knowing anything about this man, that he's not Hardan.

His eyes meet mine, and he smiles wickedly before screaming so loud it echoes over the chaos behind me, and then he runs toward me, still in his human form, twin blades drawn.

We collide. My mind goes blank, my senses focused on this one man, this one fight. He's a commander of sorts. If he goes down, his men will fall into disarray, and we've won.

I block his strikes, our forearms clashing as I knock one of his blades from his hand and twist his arm until it pops out of his shoulder socket. He falls to his knees with a sharp grunt of pain, and then I'm behind him, forcing him onto his stomach with my blade pressed against his throat and my free hand tangled in his hair, pulling violently.

"Fuck you," he snarls.

I dig my knee into his spine, and he hisses out a breath, chuckling darkly.

"Is something funny?"

He spits blood. I dig my blade a little deeper into his neck.

"Are you Hardan?"

"No. You wouldn't be talking if you'd already met him. Your head would be so far from your body–ahh!" My blade digs into his throat enough to draw blood.

"What does he want?" I already know the answer. All of this is because Jerrod refused to give him Aviva.

"That bitch belongs to him."

My blade draws more blood, and he goes still, taking several panicked breaths. Behind me, the battle continues, but right now, it feels like this stranger and me are the only people in this blood-soaked clearing.

"I should cut out your tongue for talking about my wife that way," I seethe, yanking on his hair until his head is nearly bent backward.

"That fucking whore is Hardan's mate. She belongs to him."

My heart stops beating. I don't even feel the arrow pierce my back from behind. I don't feel it exit through my chest and lodge into the base of the man's neck, killing him instantly.

"RYAN!" Jacob screams as I fall forward, my vision going completely black before I can process what's happening.

I see her then in vivid color, smiling as she looks up at me in the hazy starlight of the ruined temple, those silly shells clinking together in her hair. I wanted to reach out and touch her then, to run my fingers through her wild, unruly hair, just to know what it felt like. I say her name, not realizing it's the last words that will ever leave my lips.

Noise explodes through my ears. Jacob screaming my name. Feet moving in on me. The warm, soft touch of small hands ripping my shirt from my skin.

I should be dead, but I'm not. So I should be able to feel my body, but I can't. I'm numb. Totally, completely numb, trapped in my head as darkness swells around me.

"It was a silver arrow coated in wolfsbane. There's not much we can do."

26

I'M SAVING HIM

Aviva

I WAKE IN A COLD SWEAT, FINDING IT IMPOSSIBLE TO CATCH MY BREATH. I didn't dream last night, but I feel like my mind has been moving a hundred miles per hour without a moment's stop in the hours I spent sleeping beside… sleeping beside Freya.

I look around, pushing a patchwork quilt down to my feet as I take in a new space, a new room, memories of last night flooding back to the forefront of my mind. I'm in Freya's cottage in the village. I came here instead of sleeping alone in Ryan's house. I curled up in bed beside her after leaving the mountain, after swimming in the hot spring, after I felt like I had something sharp lodged in my chest….

A shout echoes from outside. More shouts, all male, follow. It's an argument.

"Freya?" I hiss, feeling over the bed. It's still warm, like she'd only been here moments ago, but it's so early that the sun hasn't even reached the mountain peaks. Silverhide is still blanketed in foggy darkness.

I start to slide out of bed when the front door of the snug, stone cottage opens, and hurried footsteps move to the bedroom. Freya bursts through the bedroom door, in a nightdress, her shoulders covered by a beautiful woven blue and white shawl.

Her blonde hair is wild, curling around her face and falling out of her braid as she rushes toward me, her mouth opening and closing like a fish.

I know at that moment that something is terribly wrong. "Aviva–"

"What happened?" I leap out of bed wearing a similar nightdress I found in her dresser. I move toward the door as she gapes behind me, trying to find words to explain the thick, crackling tension in the air.

She left the exterior door open, and now the male voices are more clear. I immediately see the foggy, shadowed figures of two men standing in the center of the village, surrounding a fourth man. I run toward them through the fog as they turn to me, their faces coming into startling clarity.

Grey has his hands on his knees, bent at the waist. "I was halfway here when Jacob called me back through the mind-link. I went back to Endova but Ryan was–Alpha Ryan–"

"Aviva," Andrew says breathlessly as I step out of the fog. James turns to look at me, his face cast in unreadable shadows, but their body language is clear.

"What happened to my husband?" I ask, not recognizing my own voice. "Where is Ryan?" If Grey, one of the pack's best scouts, is here, and Hunter isn't….

Andrew steps toward me, glancing at James. "Navvan warriors attacked Endova last night."

The breath catches in my throat as he continues, "Endova is secure now–"

"Secure for now," James cuts in, his expression ice cold. "Grey, go get some rest. Andrew, start gathering our men–"

"What happened to my husband?" I snarl, looking between them. "Where is Ryan?"

James looks stern, but Andrew's expression cracks enough that I can see the uncertainty in his eyes.

"Ryan took an arrow to the chest. It's bad." Andrew licks his lips before cursing under his breath. "I'm sending men–"

"We're sending men to ensure our territory is secure," James says, giving Andrew a look.

My heart beats erratically as I look from man to man, noticing the stark differences between them, behind their eyes. I barely notice Freya stepping up beside me, her hand resting on my shoulder.

"Is Ryan alive?" My voice is like boots crunching over gravel.

Andrew nearly breaks, and even James shudders. That's how I know he is horribly wounded. Wounded and on the edge of death. My throat closes up as I wait on pins and needles for their answer, for their confirmation to what I realize is my worst fear.

Losing Ryan. Losing the very man who can't seem to decide what he wants from his own wife.

But suddenly they start arguing, talking over each other.

"Ryan made it clear–"

"It was a silver arrow coated in wolfsbane, James!"

"He made us vow–"

"He will die," Andrew bites out. Freya squeezing my shoulder as I go completely, utterly still. "If we don't do something, he will die."

"I'm not going against our Alpha's direct orders."

"His powers can't keep up with the poison. He won't be able to heal himself–"

"What did you just say?" My voice cracks as I look from man to man. "What powers?"

Andrew chews the inside of his cheek, throwing James a look. James shakes his head as he crosses his arms over his chest, looking down at his boots. It's Andrew who speaks, his voice strained as he says, "Ryan and his family... I don't really get it, okay? But Ryan can heal pretty fast from his wounds. His grandma, and his brother, his cousin... they have this ability–"

"He made us promise not to use the tears on him, Andrew," James rasps, but his voice finally breaks, giving me a glimpse of the emotion tearing through his body.

"We don't have a fucking choice. He's dying. Grey said so. Grey said the healer in Endova isn't sure he'll make it through the day–"

"The tears?" I whisper the words, completely and utterly confused. Powers? What powers? Like magic? Like the kind of powers the Queen of Eastonia and the Shadow King possess?

"His grandmother's tears," James answers. "The vials. It's medicine. It can heal… anything."

"Ryan has the ability to heal on his own pretty quickly without them, but with silver and wolfsbane in his system… he was shot through the heart, Aviva. He can't heal from that on his own."

"But the tears could save his life?" I ask, desperation clinging to every syllable.

Andrew and James look at each other, some internal debate swirling between them. Andrew looks at me, shaking his head. "He made us promise we wouldn't waste them on him–"

"Waste?" I choke. "He's dying–my husband is dying, and you're debating whether or not to give him what can save his life?"

"It might not be enough. We only have so much," James argues. "We made a vow to our Alpha–"

I turn and sprint, my feet sliding over wet gravel. Andrew curses and runs after me, but I'm faster, and I reach Ryan's house and run inside before he even reaches the stairs to the porch.

I rip the lockbox from under the bed and realize I don't have the keys. Andrew runs into the room, and I whirl, snarling, "Where are they? Give me the keys–"

"I don't have them."

"Who does?"

"I don't know–"

I snatch one of my blades off the bedside table where I'd placed it before deciding to sleep at Freya's cottage instead. Before Andrew can even take a breath, my blade is pressed against his throat, his eyes going wide.

"Aviva," he whispers, raising his hands in surrender. "Ryan wouldn't want you to do this."

"Slit your throat, or save his life?"

"Both. He made us promise to save the tears for our pack members and to never use them on him, even if he was dying–"

"I never made such a promise. Where are the fucking keys?"

"Ryan might have taken them with him. I don't have them, James doesn't have them."

I snarl and shove him away, turning back to the lockbox. It's heavy as fuck, but I lift it, grunting with effort as I walk out of the room and drop it on the kitchen table. Ryan has a wide variety of tools and weapons in the cabinets in the kitchen instead of pots and pans. I find a hammer, slamming it against the locking mechanism over, and over again until it finally pops open.

Andrew stands and watches, not saying a single word to me as I roughly pull the little wood box out of its haven and fist one of the vials.

"Aviva, please, just listen to me–"

"Do you want him to die? Does James? Because that's what it sounds like."

"We don't," he says heavily.

I turn to look at him over my shoulder. "Is James hoping Ryan loses his life so he can be Alpha? Is that why you've been standing around debating this when the answer is so fucking simple it makes my head spin?" I bare my teeth.

Andrew shakes his head. "You don't know Ryan well enough yet to understand–"

"I am the Luna here, am I not?" I rage, clutching the vial. It's warm to the touch, and I swear it vibrates, but maybe that's just the anger coursing through me.

"You are," he admits.

"Then as Luna, I command you to get out of my fucking way so I can save my husband, your Alpha, before he dies."

I turn and walk back into the bedroom, slamming the door shut. Andrew is still in the living room, his eyes downcast, when I emerge dressed in one of my outfits from Endova, the loops already loosened for shifting. My bow and quiver rest on my back in a harness, and my knife belt hangs around my waist. I don't need shoes because I won't be in my human form again until I reach Endova. I won't be stopping, no matter what greets me in the plains and forest between our two villages.

"I'll kill James if he makes any moves to take over in my absence," I tell Andrew roughly, my voice dripping with malice. "I'll kill you, too."

"I know," he says, barely able to meet my eyes as I cross the room and throw open the front door. I clutch the vial between my teeth and shift without another word, sprinting off into the early morning fog.

I'm a blur, my body parting the fog, as I run through the village. People are starting to leave her houses. Men are shifting, following what has to be directives from James to start guarding the village. They look up as I pass in a whirl of red fur and weapons. I don't even look at them. I can't spare the time.

Thirty miles. I could run that in an hour if I stay at this speed. Maybe less.

The forest lined road leading out of the valley is a blur of deep green. The road leading to the Roguelands fades behind me. The plains open up, painted gray and deep gold, free of the fog cloaking Silverhide in darkness. The stars turn from bright bulbs to streaks of light at this speed. I chase the sunrise, my paws pounding over raw earth, kicking up dust. I leap over the width of the creek, my heart pounding, and land on the opposite bank, my claws curling into the rough, solid ground of Endova.

The next ten miles are a golden blur as the sun rises, casting the distant village in streaks of light. Smoke rises, blanketing the village in a haze as I sprint out of the plains and into the village proper. I shift mid-step, pulling on the strings to tighten the loops on my dress so it hugs my body again, and spit the vial into the palm of my hand just as Mercy runs out of our house, sensing my presence.

"Aviva, thank the Goddess–"

"Where is he?" The fear and utter grief I haven't had a chance to feel since waking up this morning come rushing to the surface, causing my thundering heart to crack into pieces. "Where is my husband?"

Mercy looks so broken as she shakes her head, mouthing, "I'm sorry," but I push past her toward the healer's cottage, ignoring the shattering sensation in my chest that tells me I'm too late.

Ryan's dead.

27

MAKE NO PROMISES

Ryan

Hadley's blood is everywhere, coating the wallpaper, the floor, the fine furniture and gilded frames in the foyer of my brother's house. Her neck snapped so easily. It bent like a blade of grass between my fingers. I'm still holding her. Her neck is limp between my jaws.

Sarah's voice is lifted in a scream. It echoes through my ears as pain ignites deep in my chest.

I let go of my mate. She drops onto the floorboards with a smack, her arms limp at her sides. I feel dizzy, like my heart has stopped beating, and all of my blood is rushing to my head. I make the mistake of looking down at her before falling over on my side, her blood soaking into my fur.

A white wolf stands in the shadow of the formal dining room just visible down the hall. It's totally still, it's glowing, silver eyes holding mine as it turns and disappears like it hadn't been there at all. Inside, I feel my heart... twisting. Twisting like someone is flaying me open and jabbing a heated blade through my chest, twisting and yanking apart the golden threads of the mate bond, one by one.

I've known people who've rejected and also been rejected by their mates. I know it hurts, both mentally and physically, but this is not what was ever described to me. This is pain so severe I can't think past it. Pain so strong it blinds me to the room around me, to Sarah's screams as she calls out my name, to Hadley lying dead and cold only a few feet away.

I deserved this. I thought I was Hadley's mate, yet I still took pleasure in other women. I didn't settle down when I felt the first inklings of the bond. I thought it just wasn't strong enough, that Hadley was too young. I thought I'd get the leg-wobbling sensation one day, when she came into her wolf, that finally made me see her as my mate. I thought one day, her scent would be overwhelming, her touch like a flame, and I wouldn't be able to ever get her out of my head, but when she kissed me in my car that night I felt... like it wasn't right. Like maybe I was confused, and it was wrong, and I needed more time. I had more time. One day, soon, she'd be twenty-one, and I'd know for sure that that stupid golden thread between us wasn't just a figment of my imagination.

But that day hadn't come, and it wouldn't now, because I'd killed her. I killed my own mate. I killed my own mate.

More pain drifts through me, hot and endless as I melt into the floor, praying for not only forgiveness but for the Goddess to just strike me where I am, putting an end to the confusion and suffering I've felt for years.

That huge white wolf fills my vision again as I open my eyes to slits. It's standing in the hallway leading to the dining room now, standing totally, utterly still as it watches me with glowing silver eyes. That golden thread binding me to Hadley finally snaps, and I scream at the pain, of it, at the regret of it. I could have saved her from this madness.

But I hadn't wanted to after seeing her in that video footage, laughing and smiling while talking to the very man responsible for so much of my family's suffering.

Small hands touch on my face, trying to turn my head. I keep my eyes on the wolf. It starts to walk toward me, glowing, fragments of magic pouring from its long, flawless fur. An angel. The Goddess, perhaps, come to take me away to whatever hell awaits.

I'm sure there are ramifications for killing your own mate. There has to be.

I deserve it. Whatever comes, I deserve it.

"Look at me. Open your eyes." Sarah's voice is pleading as she yanks on my face. "Look at me, Ryan. Please, look at me. Open your eyes. I'm begging you, don't go yet. Please don't go."

The white wolf continues walking toward me but stops, tilting her snout toward the ground. A rush of numbness skitters through me, blurring the pain, and then the heat of a fire warms my chilled skin.

"Ryan, please!"

More voices whisper around me, turning to violent noise that hurts my ears as Sydney's foyer fades, and the wolf blurs to nothing but bright light. I turn to look at Sarah, knowing I'll find her violet eyes full of tears for me, when she should be crying for Hadley.

But it's not Sarah pulling me out of the darkness.

"Aviva?"

Aviva lets out her breath, her red, curly hair forming a halo around her face as she looks down at me in disbelief. The room comes into view. Walls of stone. A fire in the clay hearth. People I don't know gathered around me wearing Endovian robes.

The firelight catches on the glass of a small vial in Aviva's trembling fist. She clutches it so hard the glass shatters in her grip, blood dripping between her fingers. I feel the pain, the sharp sting, like it's my own.

I look up at her, my vision slightly hazy, and see my own reflection in her amber eyes. "Aviva–"

She pulls her hand back and slaps me so hard it brings me out of my dream-like stupor in an instant. Pain burns through my chest and back, and the injuries heal rapidly, but the burning sensation on my cheek is fresh. I feel everything. I see everything in vivid color. I smell... her, for the first time.

She's straddling me, her weight pressed against my bare stomach as she shakes with what I hope is relief but know is fury. But she smells... so fucking good... like everything I love, everything that draws me in, all in one. Like the first cup of coffee on a rainy morning. Like blades of grass in the plains after a storm. Like lying in a warm bed with her curled against my chest, her skin warm and scented like ozone and a tang of sweat, rich like whiskey.

How did I not notice before?

Her chest heaves as she looks down at me, the disbelief in her eyes shattering, replaced by white-hot rage.

"You fucking bastard!" she screams, tears streaming down her cheeks. The crowd around us gasps, murmuring to themselves as Aviva is dragged off me by two Endovian warriors who struggle to keep their hands on her.

"Get her out of here!" Jerrod shouts somewhere in the crowd, but Aviva is snarling like the wild animal she is.

"Fuck you, Ryan! You fucking prick! You were dead! You were fucking dead!" Her voice breaks around the heartache in her tone, but she continues to struggle against the hold of the warriors. My wife is the strongest person in the room, and she's livid. Mad at me, actually.

My mouth ticks into a smile as she's lost in the crowd, but she screams in frustration, and I hear the tail-tell sound of flesh meeting flesh, then a grunt of pain I imagine came from her fist meeting the jaw of one of the warriors tasked with subduing her.

"Fuck you!" she screams again, then she's silenced as she's dragged through the door.

People start to move as I regain feeling in my legs and arms. I'm beat to shit. I can feel the healing powers knitting slash marks together and healing bruises that cover every inch of my body. I feel the gaping, bloody hole in my chest start to close as Jerrod's face comes into view, looking down at me apologetically.

"I think she brought you back to life so she could kill you herself this time."

"I am aware," I rasp, my voice deep and scratchy as the magic moves through me, fixing whatever was broken. "What happened?"

"You took a silver arrow to the chest. It was coated in wolfsbane for good measure, I assume. Such weapons are banned in Endova and Teshka. You were on death's door when she got here. You had mere minutes, Alpha Ryan, if that. We were doing what we could to stop the poison from spreading until then."

"You shouldn't have let her in here."

"Do you really think any of us would have been able to stop her?" he replies with a wry smile. "She ran all the way here from Silverhide with that potion clutched between her teeth."

"She needs to eat and rest."

"So do you," he says, pursing his lips as his eyes fall to where the magic is currently knitting the wound on my chest back together, slowly because of the poison in my veins. He pulls up a stool and sits, turning his head to nod in dismissal to the few people left in the room. They leave, and I grunt as I sit up, resting my back against the stone wall. It's a single room with a door leading directly outside. Rough, homespun curtains block out the light of day, of morning.

"How many men did we lose?"

"Six out of forty. Those are good numbers."

"Are they still out there?" I look for a shirt on the bed, meaning to dress and head back to the Navvan camp to finish what they started, but Jerrod shakes his head.

"Your man, Jacob, left one of the Navvan's warriors alive to send a message back to Hardan." The mention of his name brings a memory rushing back, reminding me that that man I'd been battling when I was shot through the chest by an arrow said that Aviva is Hardan's mate. It sinks into me, festering into something cold and deadly I can't shake, even if I tried. "The rest of the Navvan warriors are dead. It's over for now."

"Jacob will stay here. I can't spare any more of my men to guard Endova. We don't have the numbers and I need them in Silverhide."

"I have enough warriors to keep my territory safe, but Jacob is welcome to stay. The patriarch of Teshka sent scouts who arrived this morning after we alerted them to the battle and will be sending twenty of his own forces to our aid. We will be fine here."

My mind is numb. The only thing clear enough to focus on is the word *mate* bouncing around in my skull. I'll kill Hardan before I give Aviva up, even if they are mates. My hand curls over the scar on my hand that never healed despite the minuscule amount of healing power I naturally possess. It's nothing compared to my brother, Kenna, or my grandmother. "Will you bring her back in? I need to talk to her."

"Are you sure?" he asks, his lips straightening into a ghost of a smile.

"I'd rather fall on one of her blades than anyone from Navvan. If your daughter killed me, it would be an honorable death."

He chuckles, shrugging as he stands and nods.

A few moments later, the door opens again, and Aviva steps into the room with a shell shocked, pale look on her face.

I hold her gaze. "Come here."

She walks toward me slowly, a bandage wrapped around her left hand from where the shards of glass from the vial cut into her skin. She licks her lips, looking me up and down, before sitting on the stool beside the bed.

I reach over and pull her to me so she's on top of me, balanced with her knees on either side of my waist.

The only thing in my head as I pull her down to kiss her roughly, our teeth clashing, is that she's mine. I don't give a fuck about whether she has a mate. Whether it's Hardan, or some other bastard. I'll kill him before I give her up.

"Never do that again," she says breathlessly, her hand sliding up to clutch my neck. "Never fucking do that again."

"I'll try not to die again, but I can't make any promises."

"I want you to swear on the Goddess."

"I can't do that."

She lets go of my throat and pushes away. The look on her face crushes me, and she doesn't look back as she storms out of the door.

28

HE'S MY MATE

Aviva

THE AIR IN MY OLD HOME IS HUMID. THE SUCKING, STICKY KIND THAT makes me feel dirty and uncomfortable. Summer swept through the Deadlands last night after what felt like weeks of rain, and now, what's left of the moisture hangs in the heated air, weighing me down, making me sweat, stopping the tears from completely drying on my cheeks.

I brush them away with the backs of my hands and press my back to the cool, stone wall in the center hall, trying to gather myself. My heart is still beating rapidly. I arrived in Endova less than an hour ago. Far less. I still can't catch my breath, and my legs are on fire from running like my life depended on it–because Ryan's life was in my hands… clenched between my teeth.

I run my fingers over my knife belt, counting hilts. I absently reach over my shoulder and count each arrow in my quiver. I make note of the press of the bow against my back, the strength of the leather of my new halter.

Run. My mind is telling me to run. To go far, far into the hills. To run into the forest until my legs eventually give out. I'll meet the sea eventually. I'll outrun this. I'll outrun him, and the feelings skittering around in my heart trying to find a home. I'll outrun the crushing weight of this new feeling in my chest that festers into something so painfully raw it takes my breath away.

It's a feeling I can't name. It's the same feeling I felt when I watched the light dim behind my mother's eyes six years ago. The same empty desperation. The same crushing grief.

I'd come so close to losing Ryan. Now, I'm not sure how to feel. I don't want to feel like this… like I have something to lose.

The front door swings open, sending in a fresh spray of hot daylight. The shadow that darkens the doorway is one I expected, but I hadn't expected Mercy to be wearing the expression currently engraved on her face like it was cut from stone.

She looks me up and down, drinking me in, her gaze roving over my weapons before her eyes finally meet mine. She reaches behind her back and firmly shuts the door. "I know what you're thinking."

"You don't," I try to say, but she shakes her head violently, her head lurching as she struggles to swallow.

She keeps her hand curled around the doorknob, her knuckles white. "I'm not letting you go."

I straighten up, my heart thundering. I haven't made the decision yet, but she must see the answer written in my eyes.

"*You're not leaving.*"

"That's not up to you."

"I'm not going to stand by and watch you run away again, not this time."

Fresh fury ripples to life as I square up to my sister. "I don't run–"

"That's all you've ever done. For six years." She heaves a breath, and her beautiful face shatters, revealing guttingly raw emotion I don't think I've ever seen in her before.

"You don't understand." The words wobble off my tongue. "Mercy, I can't–I can't do this–"

"You have to." She lets go of the door knob and raises her hands in surrender, but her tears spill over her lashes.

"Ryan–he didn't want a wife. He was forced into it, just like I was. He doesn't want this, with me. He nearly died tonight and would have just–just let it happen." I think of the powers Andrew mentioned. I assume they're healing powers. Why hadn't he just healed himself? Why would he go head first into battle without a care in the world about who he was leaving behind and then allow himself to go so easily into death without a fight?

I'd seen the peaceful look on his face as he took a single, rattling breath the moment I rushed through the healer's door. He was ready. Unburdened. Ready to let go and say fuck it.

I hadn't been ready to let him go, which burns through me, the truth tangling through my soul and undoing the stone fortress I'd built around my heart, brick by brick.

So, I didn't let him go.

"You went into the woods the morning after Mother died," Mercy whispers, the words broken by stifled sobs. "I followed you after Father said you'd gone hunting. I watched you standing at the bank of the creek, sightless, for hours. I stood there with you, and you had no idea I was even there."

She shakes her head, finally breaking from my gaze to look down at her feet. "It was the shock of it. I told myself that. You needed some time to get over the shock of losing our mother so violently, so unexpectedly. I understood. I understood until months passed and you were still gone, still hunting, still chasing down the god of death every night to enact some form of sick revenge, to take back what he took from you. *From us.*"

My lower lip begins to tremble as her face twists with despair and grief. I've never seen her like this. Never. Mercy has always been so cold, so domineering. So scary, honestly.

But she breaks. Completely, utterly breaks. "You left us. You left me with two little girls, Aviva. You had sixteen years with Mother, but Shoshannah? She only had four. She didn't understand what was happening. Lora didn't even have a chance to know her face. I didn't have a chance to grieve for our mother. I couldn't grieve for you both. I couldn't do it."

"Mercy," I choke, tears blurring her image.

"You ran from all of it. You ran from us."

"I didn't-"

"You did. You did run. When it got hard, you'd run. I haven't slept in six years," she admits painfully, hugging herself with her arms as her voice splits over every syllable. "I haven't slept at all. I lie awake at night wondering if I'll find you in bed with the girls or if your bed will be empty, if I'll finally find your body in the woods, and I hated–I hated feeling like when that happened, I'd finally know peace because you would have found peace."

I strangle myself on a sob that nearly splits my throat in two. Mercy sniffles, growing quiet. A heavy silence permeates the air around us for several long, drawn out seconds. Maybe minutes. Then, she says, "When Alpha Ryan came here… it was the first time in years I'd seen light in your eyes again. And honestly I felt… angry. I wanted to ruin it. I wanted to hurt you in the same way I've been hurting for years. I spent so long trying to bring you back to us, to find my sister again, and suddenly, you were just… you were alive again."

"Don't," I rush out, breathless.

"You've been running away for years. Today was the first time you've run *toward* something. And you ran toward him."

I close my eyes.

"Now you're going to run again, aren't you?"

"I don't know what else to do." The admission is brutal. It crushes me.

"You're going to go back to Silverhide with him," she says gently, motherly. I feel the ghost of her touch, but her hands stay raised, like she's afraid to move, like a single twitch of movement will have me sprinting toward the door. Like I'm a nervous, wild animal, and she's doing everything in her power to finally tame me.

I meet her soft green eyes. Her cheeks are raw with tears. For once, she doesn't look perfect. She's let that mask drop, showing me a face I recognize from a time when we were close, the best of friends.

"I can't be what he needs."

"I think he just needs you," she whispers with a shrug, trying to smile. She fails miserably. "Maybe *you* just need *him*."

"You don't know him."

"I know enough to understand that people don't usually look at each other the way he looked at you during your wedding."

I drop my gaze. She risks a single shuffled footstep in my direction but stops. "You have to go back. You are his wife... maybe more."

"More?" I laugh bitterly. "More, what?" I think of those few intimate moments between us when his touch set me on fire in a way I hadn't thought possible. Like he was built for me, and I for him. Like he understood me in a way others didn't. That he can see things others can't.

"I can't be there without you."

"What?" When I meet her eyes again, they're clearer, sharper. Her smile softens the sharp planes of her face.

"I'm going to Silverhide. With my... *my mate*."

My stomach hollows out as my sister's eyes soften and drop to her sandals. She lowers her hands and folds them neatly across her waist, taking a soft breath.

"Who?" I already know the answer, but I ask anyway, watching her face with feline focus. Her mouth twitches at the corners. Her brow pinches together as if in disbelief. Her eyes shine as she meets my gaze again, heavy with surprise and a deep, clear happiness that edges on relief.

"Jacob."

I roll my eyes to the ceiling before closing them and taking an audible breath. I want to tell her mates aren't real. I want to drill that into her skull, reminding her that to be fated to someone, and especially to find them, is so rare it's nothing but legend.

"Does father know that he imprinted on you?"

"Aviva," she says, shaking her head. Her hand comes to rest over her chest, her heart. "He didn't imprint on me. We felt–I felt it. Here."

My nostrils flare on impulse. I hadn't noticed before, but her scent is different. Her usually soft, sweet, clean scent is punctuated by something heavier–something sharper and more masculine. Jacob, I realize. That woodsy scent he carries that reminds me of walking by the sawmill in Silverhide–rich, sharp cedar.

Jealousy strikes me in the chest. I can't fight it.

She curls her hand into a fist over her heart. "We haven't even touched–"

"How do you know?" I swallow past the bite in the words, trying to hide the fact that I'm begging to know what she felt, how she knew he was her mate, and it wasn't just a visceral attraction.

"That night, when Alpha Ryan gave Father the Golden Elk pelt, I stormed out of the meeting hall. I was so mad. I wasn't even sure why I was angry, but I was. Everyone was in the meeting hall, and I thought I'd be able to be alone for a minute to gather myself, but I wasn't the only one standing near the bonfire. I looked up, and he was there. I felt... lost, for a moment. Then it just snapped–something here, in my chest. Like a piece of me had been missing, and I didn't realize it, and suddenly, I had it back, and it was overwhelming."

She goes on to explain how they stood there in silence for several minutes just looking at each other. She hadn't been sure what was happening, but Jacob voiced it, lowering his voice to tell her that he'd talk to her father. He'd been so gentle about it, she explains. He didn't touch her, didn't tell her she had to come away with him or leave her family. In fact, they didn't speak for days until the night after the wedding, when Jacob told her he'd find a way to offer her bride price.

"Seeing him leave for Silverhide was the most painful thing I'd ever felt," she says weakly. "That distance just wrecked me. I barely know him, but I know him, if that makes sense. I know it doesn't." She looks down at her toes. "I feel like I'll die if he doesn't just... touch me. Touch me anywhere. Stroke my cheek, lay his hand on my shoulder…. His touch is like fire, Aviva. Like I was made for him."

Her words echo through me, untangling the knots in my brain.

Why is that what she feels for Jacob is the same way I feel for Ryan?

Why doesn't Ryan feel what I feel, if that's the case?

"Has he spoken to Father about the bride price?"

"I don't think so," she says hurriedly as voices approach the front door. "There's so much that needs to be discussed and decided upon. The girls, more than anything. I don't think–I wouldn't feel right about leaving them here."

I lick my lips and nod. The sudden shift in conversation away from me and cowardice is a welcome relief, but it highlights several painful truths. We love our Father, but in our culture, the mother's do the childrearing. The men are warriors and hunters–leaders. Our mother taught us everything we know.

If both of us are gone, someone else would have to step in for Lora and Shoshannah while Father runs our pack.

"Father will want them to be with us." I meet her eyes. "They'd come with us."

"It feels wrong taking them from home. From Father."

"He wouldn't see it like that. He'd want us all together."

The voices draw closer, and the door opens, revealing two shadows I recognize without turning to look at their faces.

Jacob, I'm not surprised by.

Ryan?

"Aviva?" Ryan's voice is steady but edging on pained. "We need to talk." I hold Mercy's gaze for a few seconds before turning toward Ryan, but then he says, "You too, Mercy."

2 9

YOU KNEW ALL ALONG

Ryan

I watch Jacob lead Mercy away. He's careful not to touch her, but his hand hovers over her lower back as she lifts her skirts to pick her way out of the forest. I let out my breath and turn to Aviva, who has been sitting silently on a ledge surrounding the remains of the temple ruins she was guarding like a dragon defending its horde the first time we were ever able to speak to each other.

I look at her like I looked at her that night after her father gave her to me in marriage. She's still wild, still beautiful, and has an echo of that same furious look that cloaked her face during our first few days together.

My heart beats slightly of rhythm as her scent is carried on the wind—lovely, soft, sweet. A scent that makes me curl my hands into fists to stop from touching her.

This is remarkably unfair. To both of us.

Because now I know what's happening, and I still can't bring myself to accept it.

"Do you think they're really mates?" Aviva asks. Is the first time she's spoken to me since she arrived this morning, at least, in a tone that edges on friendly. Screaming at me? Yeah, I'd deserved it. I'd deserved the slap, too.

"I do."

"Why? Can you tell?"

"Her scent is mingled with his," I say as I turn toward her, leaning on an old column I pray holds my weight. "The way he looks at her is telling. His pupils grow larger and he's... rather protective of her right now, regardless of the circumstances."

Aviva won't meet my eyes. How fucked up of me. That's all I can think about. My mind is a tangle of regret. I've been so awful to her. I've pushed her away and taken advantage of her when it suited me, reminding her that she belongs to me when I knew, deep down, she didn't.

But now she does and I can't... fuck, I just can't accept it. I don't deserve this, and part of me wonders if this is a test from the Goddess Herself. To give me something soft and beautiful and rip it away the moment I acknowledge it as a lesson, as karma, for killing the first gift She bestowed upon me.

"Aviva," I begin before I can stop myself. Her eyes turn up to meet mine, bathed in sunlight, gleaming that incredible whiskey color that makes me dizzy. "I was told that Hardan believes you're his mate."

Her eyes crease as she smiles, which quickly turns to a bitter laugh. "What a way to try to win over my father. Pillaging my people, and all."

I want to smile back but grit my teeth. "Have you ever met him?"

"No."

"So you've never been face to face?"

"Are you asking me if I've ever felt the mate bond? Because you know my answer." But her eyes change. They darken to a rich bronze the same color as the freckles dotted across the bridge of her crinkled nose as she turns that radiant smile into a frown. "He isn't my mate."

"I know," I whisper, and the words crush me.

She takes a breath and looks toward the pocket of sunlight where

Jacob and Mercy faded out of view, shaking her head. "What now? Mercy comes back to Silverhide with us?"

"No, not for a while. Jacob will offer her bride price, and Silverhide will pay it. He's going to stay here for the time being to act as an... emissary for me, of sorts, to manage any threats from Hardan and Navvan. He has my permission to marry–to hand-fast with her, if they choose."

"Does he really need your permission?"

"No, but I gave him my blessing anyway."

"Are you going soft, Alpha?" The teasing glint in her tone wobbles, like she's unsure. Like she's trying to stay mad, and I kind of wish she would.

"Aviva, I..."

"We're mates, aren't we?"

I close my eyes. My blood simmers in my veins. Hearing the words come out of her mouth ignites that pull, finally. A pull so strong it's enough to knock me off my feet, but I stay standing by some miracle.

"I believe so."

Silence hugs the clearing between us, and when I finally open my eyes, she's gone, leaving so silently and swiftly I hadn't heard her footsteps crunching in the dry, dead leaves leftover from a brutal winter.

I return to the village a few minutes later after barely gathering myself. My head is in shambles, and my body thrums with a dull ache. I can't shift right now, even with the vial of tears in my system. Someone my size with my strength would have needed three to fully heal.

One vial brought me back, but I welcome the suffering of my sore, aching muscles flexing against the wounds littering my broken body. It'll keep my mind off me... mate. For now.

The day passes in a blur of activity. I meet with Jerrod to discuss not only Navvan but the prospect of his eldest daughter marrying into my pack. Jerrod is elated, telling me that Mercy's bride price was paid in droves by Jacob's action in the skirmish, no other action needed besides a swift hand-fasting ceremony. Jacob is confirmed to be staying in Endova for the time being, which I think is smart, even though we'll miss him in Silverhide during the busiest season of the year.

I send Hunter back to Silverhide in the late afternoon with news of my survival and my impending arrival. I decide after little deliberation that Aviva and I will set off in the morning for Silverhide, alone. And on foot, unless by some miracle the poison dampening my powers is metabolized by then.

I don't go to the feast in the meeting hall held in celebration of our triumph over Navvan. It wasn't really a win, was it? Not when I can feel the threat of Hardan in my bones. He's just one man, though. Right now, the only thing on my mind is sleep... and Aviva.

I haven't seen her all day at this point. I'm not going to push her to accept our bond because I honestly can't bring myself to acknowledge it yet. What a cruel twist of fate. I wish I'd known the moment I met her. I wish I'd realized that this feeling inside of me every time I look at her, this desperate want, wasn't just a superficial attraction and something far, far deeper.

I can't take back the way I treated her.

I'm almost asleep when the door to the healer's cottage opens and shuts. I blink into the darkness as Aviva's scent fills the room, broken by the acrid smell of a match being struck. She lights an oil lantern and walks over to me, sitting with a sigh at the foot of the bed.

I sit up, balancing on an elbow. The thin blanket slips over my bare chest as she turns to look at me.

"Aviva–"

"Before you say anything," she whispers, swallowing against the bite in her voice. She takes another breath, closing her eyes for a moment before setting the lantern down on a table near the bed. "Before you say anything, I need to know why we didn't know we were mates from the beginning. Did you know the whole time?"

"No, I didn't."

"You didn't think–"

"I couldn't feel anything for you other than..." Other than I wanted her. I wanted her in my bed. I wanted to do unimaginable things to her. "Other than lust, honestly. Lust, and curiosity."

She doesn't seem surprised by this admission at all. "But something changed, didn't it?"

I nod and sit up completely, leaning back against the headboard. She turns to me, sitting in an almost identical position. "I shouldn't have been able to speak to you through the mind-link, during that hunt. When you fell, I felt everything... I felt the wind getting knocked out of you. I felt you being hunted by that Hellhound. I chalked it up to adrenaline."

She holds my gaze, her eyes round and dark in the lantern light.

I look into her eyes, sighing. "Then we were hand-fasted. I thought it was some form of imprinting, and it is, isn't it?"

She shrugs, then nods, unsure. "Anyway," I continue, "That... want. It only grew. That pull–it was stronger, and I told myself it was because of that. Wanting to touch you, wanting to be near you, to be inside of you." I hold her eyes as she scans my face, emotionless, still as a predator, "I told myself it was just my body reacting."

"And you told me the same thing."

"I did."

"You couldn't pick up my scent," she says, her voice hoarse.

"No, I couldn't. I asked around about it. Andrew could smell you. Jacob, Ryan... I was the only one who couldn't."

"Why?"

"I wish I knew." I think of the white wolf again, of the feeling of my bond with Hadley snapping piece, by piece. I reach up and touch the bare skin over my heart. I feel both empty and full. Empty in a way I've never felt before and full in a way that makes my skin tingle with knowing. There's something new taking up space I'd locked away and buried. A new bond. New strings being plucked every time Aviva's own heart hammers in her chest only a few feet away.

"It's because I saved you."

I close my eyes. "I don't know."

"You didn't feel it because she was still there. You hadn't been able to let her go."

"Aviva–"

"You think you're so incapable of love," her tone drops to something cold and deadly. "You–you shoved me away and made me believe that what I felt, what you knew I felt, was nothing. A byproduct of our hand-fasting."

I finally meet her eyes again and find them full of tears.

"You still don't want me."

"It has nothing to do with wanting you," I grind out, but she shakes her head.

"You don't believe–you don't believe you deserve this. So you refuse to have it."

Bingo. "I killed someone," I remind her. "I killed my own mate."

"I don't care." The words ring out between us. She holds my gaze, unwavering. I can see the desperation behind her eyes. "I've never cared."

"I care. I care that you're stuck with me in an even deeper way now."

She looks hurt, which guts me. I used to be able to just… lay it on thick. Tell a girl whatever she wanted to hear. Make her feel like she was the most desirable, beautiful thing in the world, but I've never been able to do that to Aviva. She makes me want to be honest, to be myself, to tell her exactly what I'm thinking even if it hurts her and show her parts of me no one else has ever known.

It's because she sees right through my bullshit and always has, and I don't think that has anything to do with the mate bond.

"So, what now?"

"You reject me," I deadpan. She's still as stone as she scans my face.

"I don't want to."

"I'd like you to."

"Why not just reject me?"

I lick my lips. "I don't want to."

"Then we're fucking *mates*," she says with an arch of the brow.

"We're fucking mates."

"I guess." She leans back to inspect me.

"Sure." I cross my arms over my chest to stop from touching her.

She chews her lip. I flex my jaw.

The Goddess tethered the two most fucking stubborn people in Her kingdom together for Her sick, twisted entertainment, I'm sure.

Aviva stands up and dusts invisible dirt off her thighs. "Well, this isn't what I anticipated, but I guess it's nice to know that if I throw myself off a ledge tonight, you'll feel it too."

"Please–" I hold out a hand before I can stop myself. "Please don't do that."

"I wouldn't give you the satisfaction." Something breaks in her voice. I'm reminded instantly that Aviva's hard as nails exterior is all for show. Deep down, she's hurt. Hurt bad. And it's my fault.

I swing my legs out of bed and grab her by the arm before she can turn for the door.

"Don't," she whispers, yanking her arm out of my grasp. "I know you don't want this. I know you don't like me, that you can't–"

"You're the only thing I've ever wanted," I admit, and it's true. Nothing has ever been more out of reach than the one thing I know was made for me, and that's her.

She takes a shallow breath and turns to me, her eyes glowing a soft amber in the dim light. "Then show me already."

30

DESERVE IT OR NOT

Aviva

RYAN LOOKS CONFLICTED, AND I IMMEDIATELY CHANGE MY MIND. AT first, I'd been more than willing to lie down on this rickety bed and let him have me just to know what it would feel like to lie with my mate. The legends painted this as something so incredibly life-altering. Finding your mate was supposed to be like having your heart torn out and remade, melded with theirs. In a way, I can feel the "heart torn out" part clearly. I get it because I feel that sensation right now in droves.

"Never mind," I manage to say and tear myself away from him. It takes every fiber of my being to do so, but I step into the cool night air and walk at a steady pace toward the outer ring of the village.

I should go home... *not home*. My old house. I should go there; I even plan to go there, but my feet carry me out of the village all together, and within minutes, I'm back in the woods, passing the old ruins, walking up along the creek into the hilly, moonlight clearings that follow the base of the mountains.

I'm not alone. Ryan has been following me since I left the healer's cottage, making his presence known by cursing under his breath and mumbling as he picks through the increasingly dense forest.

He hasn't spoken to me though. I'm not sure what he could say at this point. He'd laid out his truth. We're mates, but he doesn't want me in that way. Sure, we're bonded now in more ways than one, but that doesn't matter to him. Something is holding him back, and his only explanation is that he doesn't deserve me, or whatever.

I've had enough.

I whirl on him the moment my feet brush over the soft, moon-drenched grass of a small, tree lined clearing, roughly a mile outside of the village. "Do you mind?"

He huffs a breath and balls his hands into fists at his side—still naked from the waist up, still giving me those sad, puppy-dog eyes despite the tightness on his jaw and his bared teeth.

"We're going to talk about this—"

"So talk," I snap, reaching for my blades, reminded I'm not wearing my belt or bow.

He grinds his teeth and shakes his head.

"Don't waste my time," I say, rolling my eyes to the moon. "Say what you want to say or go."

"I'm sorry this isn't a magical, mind-altering experience for you," he says flatly.

I meet his eyes in a glare. "Is that your problem with me? That I'm not drooling and fawning over you, professing my undying love?"

"You deserve someone who's capable of being like that for you—"

"You think that's what I want?" I take a step toward him on impulse, shocked. "Do I seem like someone who can appreciate a grand gesture of romance or even has the desire for it?"

His brow arches as the tension between us reaches deadly heights. "You liked when I gave you your new bow."

Now I'm the one talking through gritted teeth. "You owed me one."

"I didn't owe you anything. It was your own stupid fault you fell off a cliff ledge!"

"What do you want from me?" My thundering voice echoes

through the woods, bouncing from tree to tree. "You just told me I was the only thing you ever wanted, but when I told you to show me—to finally show me what you feel—to prove it to me, you just looked… you looked like you'd rather be anywhere else."

He edges a step in my direction, his battered muscles rigid and flexed. "I don't know what to do with you. From the moment I met you, Aviva, I haven't known what the fuck to do with you."

"Do something because I can't take this anymore. Reject me."

"No."

"Kill me."

He closes his eyes and takes a single, shallow breath. "That's not funny."

"It's obvious you want out of this."

"You're wrong. I do want this, Aviva. I want you. I've wanted you since you nearly ripped my throat out for charging at you and the girls when Shoshannah shot me with one of your arrows." I stay totally, completely still. He opens his eyes. "You mentioned once, a while ago, that I'd come here because I was cast out of my homeland by the king. That's not true. I'm a prince in Crescent Falls. My father is the Alpha King there. He didn't force me out. I chose to come here under the guise of what was best for my pack, but that's not the whole truth."

His eyes momentarily rise to scan the forest behind me. He continues softly, "I wasn't ready for the mate bond when I felt it for the first time—with Hadley. It was days after my twenty-first birthday. I'd been running Silverhide for two years. I had my garage to think about, employees, new pack members every day…. Hadley was my Beta's little sister. She came to Silverhide one day to live with James, and the moment I saw her, I felt it. It was faint, just a glimmer of what it should have been, but she wasn't twenty-one yet. She wasn't able to feel it all."

His eyes meet mine, dark and depthless. "I wasn't ready. I don't think I was ever ready to be mated. I don't think I wanted it at all. Not with her. That's why… that's why I… felt so fucking horrible about how it all ended."

His voice is so low, it's nearly a whisper, like he isn't meaning to say the words out loud. "I'd decided at that point that I would reject her. It was a touchy subject because her brother was, and still is, my Beta. I love James like a brother, but he can be an asshole, the kind of guy who holds a grudge, and I was too much of a coward to just tell him about the bond, let him know I have no intentions of pursuing any kind of relationship with Hadley. I don't know why I was so at odds with it. I grew up believing the mate bond was everything. It was the foundation of everything my family built and is, and I... didn't want it."

He's barely a foot away now, his eyes downcast on the ground between us. His fists relax. "My aunt, your Firestone Queen, left my grandparents and my father behind to join her mate here. Ryatt, my uncle, he... he understood something I didn't at the time. That the bond isn't always the bone-breaking, out-of-this-world experience when you see them for the first time. It's confusing and messy. Sometimes it's just wrong." His eyes meet mine. "Sometimes it's just... a lot. Too much."

My voice quakes as I choke out, "And how does it feel now?" I'm trying not to feel his past mate's presence between us. Maybe that swelling, aching feeling in the air is simply his doubts, his reservations. He's experienced this before, but I haven't.

"Like I've been given a second chance, and I don't know how to reach you, keep you, and... be with you while reckoning with what I've done."

I take in his words and let them sink into my mind. He's being brutally honest with me right now. In the woods, in the shelter and solitude of the night sky... this is where we can just be us. No walls to constrain us. No listening ears. No wonder I came here.

No wonder he followed.

He closes the distance between us, breathing deeply, his hands trembling as they close around my arms. "You've never been with anyone."

"And you've been with... everyone?"

He licks his lips before he chuckles, low and deep, the corner of his mouth ticking into a smile. "Yeah. Pretty much. Does that bother you?"

"It's not like you can take it back."

He groans slightly, but the air between us isn't choked with tension anymore. It's actively lifting as he runs his hands up and down my arms, my skin pebbling with gooseflesh. I close my eyes against the feeling, letting myself soak it in.

"I've never been with anyone I trusted with my life," he says heavily.

I'm slightly surprised by this admission. I look into his eyes. "You trust me with your life?"

"I do, even though you have a temper and an affinity for weapons." He takes a shuddering breath as his hands link with mine, holding there. "Aviva, this feeling... it's new to me too. Not being mated, but *wanting* it. Being thankful for it. Wanting to... explore it." Heat laces through every syllable, and my wolf claws to the surface of my mind, begging. Begging for him, I realize. Those brand new threads in the very fiber of my being pluck as his touch warms my skin.

"But it's up to you. Whatever you want... I'll do it. If you don't want this, if you don't want me, I can walk away from it. I wouldn't hold it against you, and I sure as hell won't force you to be with me, mate bond or not."

I do want him. I want his jagged, broken pieces. But part of me wonders if this is just the bond talking.

He was honest with me. I should be honest with him, tell him how I feel, but... I'm not very good at that. How else could I say that I want him so badly it hurts? That I understand him. I want him broken, rough, slowly healing, because that's what makes him... him. And I like that.

I rise on my toes and kiss him—light, a faint brush of my lips against his. The tension in his body softens to the point he leans in, brushing an equally soft kiss to the corner of my mouth. It's not enough. We both know it. We can feel it. My heart starts to race as he draws me closer, his breath tickling my cheek. "I swear to the Goddess, Aviva, the way you take up every thought in my mind is... a curse. Or a blessing. I'm not entirely sure but–" He inhales deeply as his lips brush over my cheek and into my hair. "Your scent is overwhelming. I can't–get enough–" He growls low in his throat as he pins me against his chest, his hands grazing up my back, bunching the fabric of the thin linen night dress I'd put on less than an hour ago.

I couldn't go to bed without talking to him first. Without confirming the feeling in the pit of my stomach, the feeling that blooms to life whenever I look at him.

Mine. He is mine. I'm not ready to give him up. I wasn't ready for him to die. I'll never be ready for that. The thought of bursting into the cottage and seeing him nearly lifeless scorches through my head. I tighten my grip on him, curling my fingers into his back and relishing in the way his muscles go tense. He's sore. I know I'm hurting him right now, but I have to know that he's here, he's safe, he's whole.

He swipes his leg against my ankles, and I yelp in surprise as I lose my balance. I'm flat on my back in an instant, and he's on top of me, tugging me across the grass to position me exactly where he wants me.

My body warms as he presses his weight against me, closing me in, not a single inch of space between us.

But he stops moving and looks down at me, the tip of his nose touching mine. I meet his gaze, hold it, barely able to catch my breath in the heat of the moment.

"Are we doing this?" I ask hesitantly. Doing what, I'm not entirely sure. Being mates? Well, we don't have much of a choice. You can be mates and not be... be in love... right?

Being married? Well, we didn't have much of a choice about that either.

Finally getting this desperate, aching *want* out of our systems...?

"I'd really like to fuck you now," Ryan rasps, and my answer comes in the form of a deep, heated kiss.

31

THAT'S NOT SO BAD

Aviva

RYAN'S HANDS ARE HUGE. HE CAN COVER EACH OF MY BREASTS entirely. He can curl his thumb and forefinger around my wrists without issue. He could break my neck into splinters without even feeling the damage he's doing.

For a moment, I feel that rush of adrenaline. Fight or flight–just because of his sheer size compared to mine and his strength. It's simultaneously terrifying and alluring.

We've done this once before but not... all the way. I've gotten a glimpse of his cock once or twice, but never... I'm in over my fucking head already, and he's done nothing more than kiss me so far.

"You're all right," he coaxes, noticing the tension starting to coil through my body. "At any point, you can tell me to stop."

"I won't," I whisper, licking my lips as he draws away and looks down at my body. I'm bathed in moonlight. Pure beams of silver-white coast over my skin, setting every freckle and scar glowing. His eyes drop from my face to my neck, and his fingertips brush over the thin, sensitive skin just above my sternum. I wish I knew what was going through his head right now. I'm thankful, honestly, that he knows what he's doing. It could be worse, far worse.

"I heard–" I rasp, desperately needing to clear my throat. "Freya told me a story about some woman who married into our village a few years ago."

He arches a brow but doesn't look at me as I lie motionless. He drags his hand down my side, toward the hem of my dress.

"She–she laid with her new husband of course, after their wedding at the Harvest Festival, and the next day, he wouldn't even look in her direction, and she was beet red and went to the healer to ask for… direction…." My lips part, and my eyes narrow to heavy slits as his hand slips beneath my dress, ghosting over my heated skin.

"Do you ever wear underwear, Aviva?" he groans with a slight tremor in his voice as he clutches my naked hip, his thumb stroking just below my navel. I'm on fire.

"You interrupted me."

"Sorry. Continue," he says lazily, chuckling darkly as he nudges my legs apart to continue his exploration of my body.

"I can't remember where I was."

He starts to pull my dress over my hips and belly, and I just lie there, letting him do it, unable and unwilling to move. He places his hand over the flat of my belly, his eyes meeting mine. "She went to the healer?"

"Ohhh…" I suck in a breath as he pulls my dress over my head, tossing the fabric aside. The cool summer night air sends a chill rippling over my skin. My nipples harden, my skin pebbling with gooseflesh, and I'm… hyper aware of every touch.

"Her new husband didn't know what to do in the marriage bed, and neither did she. I can imagine how… how awkward that must have been for both of them."

He chuckles again, lying down beside me on his side. He thumbs one of my nipples, tracing a line between my breasts until he reaches the apex of my thighs.

I remember his mouth there, his tongue, the way his teeth gently nibbled my folds until I completely, utterly unraveled.

"If you're trying to ask if I know where to *put it*, I guarantee that I do." He drags his fingers through my folds, and I am soaking wet already. He exhales deeply, satisfied. "Do you know what happens now?"

"You fuck me with your cock."

"Holy shit." He trembles, stifling his shock as he presses two fingers inside of me, stretching me out. "Aviva if you talk to me like that the whole time, I'm not going to last very long."

"Will it hurt?"

"Yeah, for you." There isn't an ounce of pity in his voice, and I'm thankful for it. "Not for long, though. It should feel good. If it doesn't, you need to tell me."

I finally open my eyes and look up at him. He's hovering over me, fucking me with his fingers while I pant and start to writhe beneath him. I feel heavy in the most delicious way. Excited and nervous. "I'm so glad it's you."

Those words do something to him. His eyes briefly shine with what I can only describe as pride before he dips his head to suck one of my nipples into his hot, eager mouth. I tangle my fingers in his thick hair and rake my nails over his scalp, alternating between gentle strokes and vicious tugs that make him bite down on me and drive his fingers harder, hooking them, which makes me arch into his touch and want to beg for more.

But when he starts to kiss down my belly, I pull his hair hard. "No. No I want… I want…"

"You want to fuck," he finishes, pressing a wet kiss to my stomach. "Needy little wolf." His teeth catch my skin, and I moan around the slight pain of it. It doesn't hurt. It's a sharp contrast to the deep ache between my legs that makes that coiling sensation feel brighter.

"Take off your pants," I demand, but he chuckles and lifts his head, his hand snaking around my neck as he climbs on top of me.

"I need to make one thing clear, Aviva. Wife. *Mate.*" Each word is clipped, but his eyes dance with heat as he continues, "You might be able to boss me around and bend me to your every whim, *and I will bend*, but not here. Not in bed, or on the forest floor, or wherever I choose to have you. I am in control. Do you understand?"

I nod, but he can see the silent challenge in my eyes. He smirks—deadly and wry—before letting go of my throat and making a show of unbuttoning his pants, too slowly for my liking. I'm thrumming with anticipation, the need to be touched, for relief.

"Please. Hurry. Up."

"So eager," he says, clicking his tongue. "Bossy, like usual. Like I said, I am in control. This is my domain. Your body is *mine*, Aviva. I will do as I please, and there is *so much* I want to do to you."

Oh, my Goddess, his tone and his words work their way through my body like ribbons of heat. I tremble, arching my back to find any friction I can between my thighs, but Ryan is amused by my neediness, my desperation to be touched.

"You're in heat, aren't you?"

I open my eyes just as he leans down again, covering me with his now totally naked body, his skin so warm it feels fevered. He buries his face in the side of my neck, pinning my skin between his teeth as his hands travel down my sides, my hips, to my ass and roughly pulls my legs apart. The head of his cock is bigger than three of his fingers. Smooth and hot, it presses against my entrance, and he lets out a guttural groan after the briefest of touches. "You're so fucking wet for me, Aviva."

I wrap my arms around his shoulders as he balances on an elbow, reaching between us to guide his cock through my folds, the wetness pooled between my legs catching the moonlight showering over us.

"You're perfect," he rasps into my hair, the words laced over the top of my ear. "That night I saw you standing on that arch with your arrow pointed at my chest, I imagined how good it would feel to bend you over those ruins and fuck you in the moonlight. Goddess, I wanted it. You have no idea what you've done to me," he whispers against my cheek before catching my mouth in a kiss that knocks the air from my lungs. His tongue dances over mine, his teeth closing on my lower lip.

He slides the head in slowly. The stretch is insane. I buck off the ground, the muscles in my legs going tight.

I trust him. Even when he's saying the filthiest things I've ever heard in my ear, telling me all the ways he wants to use my body, all the things he wants to make me feel.

I'm suddenly unsure if he's going to fit, and it breaks my heart. What if he hates this? What if he doesn't actually like doing this with me and I'm–

"Look at me," he commands, and I do. His eyes are hooded and heavy with desire so palpable I can taste it. "Aviva, I swear that I will make this good for you. More than good."

I nod. That's all I can do. I can feel his own doubt for a split second as he tries to guide the head of his cock back inside of me. I tense up again.

"I don't think it'll fit," I whimper when the stretch edges on too much.

The corner of Ryan's mouth lifts in a wry smile. "You can take it."

He kisses me at the very moment he thrusts with all of his strength, and I choke on a scream.

"*Fuck,*" he breathes, his eyes closed as he holds himself there. The pain is both dizzying and electric. The way my heart is beating out of rhythm reminds me of hunting. It's the same full bodied thrill.

"You're such a good girl for me," he soothes as he rocks against my hips, slow and rhythmic, giving me a chance to adjust to him, which I'm not sure I ever will. "You're so tight. So good, Aviva. You're taking me so well."

My eyes roll back in my head. He loops an arm around behind my lower back to keep it arched as he pulls out slowly, groaning loudly, like he can't help but soak in the feeling of my walls clutching him all the way down.

The emptiness that follows is excruciating. "Ryan, please, come back–"

"Slowly, baby," he coaxes, "We have time." His next kiss is gentle, his lips pressed against mine as he guides himself in, and out, in, and out, until I relax enough to handle the rhythmic jerks and thrusts that follow. His breathing picks up. He unwinds his arm and holds himself upright with his palms planted on the grass beside my shoulders, his head bent to watch the place where we're joined.

When I bend my knee and arch my back to take more of him, to take him deeper, his body rattles with delight. *"Fuck..."* He draws out the word, gritting his teeth and slightly shaking his head.

"Is it not–does it not feel good–" I pant, sweat dripping between my breasts.

"Your pussy is fucking paradise," he grinds out, grunting as he clutches my hip to grind into me so deeply it makes my toes curl.

A warmth starts to expand in my lower back, making it hard to focus. The sounds coming from my lips are shattered and far, far away as I start to beg. For what, I don't rightfully know, but Ryan somehow understands.

"Very good," he praises, pleased, pressing a kiss to the top of my knee. But I wipe the smug ass grin off his face the second I tense my inner muscles around his cock. He chokes out a breath, his hand curling into a fist in the grass beside me. "If you do that again, I'll come, and you'll be disappointed."

My breath grows heavy and quick as the warmth spreads from my lower back to my belly, shimmering deep under my skin.

"Oh, you're so close," he whispers, closing his eyes as his movements slow. His free hand splays over my lower belly, warm and huge, his thumb drawing sweet circles around my aching clit. "That's it."

"Ryan," I whimper, biting down on my lower lip to stop from screaming his name. He's so large inside of me. I can feel everything. It feels amazing everywhere, and I'm–I'm losing control. Is this how it's supposed to feel? "Ryan?"

"You're all right," he soothes, his movements gaining speed again, his thumb pressing and dragging over my clit in a way that has my legs locking up. He licks his lips, his cheeks a ruddy pink with exertion. "Come for me, sweetheart."

I look up into his eyes, depthless and a deep, dark blue in the moonlight. *Mate.* This is my mate. The person the Goddess designed for me, for life.

So I say it, the word tasting as sweet as sugar on my tongue. "Mate. My mate. My–" I scream his name, squeezing my eyes shut as blinding release erupts between my legs and expands everywhere, untangling every tense muscle and filling me with pleasure that makes me feel hot and tingly.

My inner walls spasm, clutching his cock, and Ryan growls with satisfaction before pumping into me once, twice, so hard my back slides over the grass. He pulls out swiftly, spilling himself on my lower belly. His muscles are locked as he hisses out his breath, shuddering.

Then he collapses on top of me.

I wrap my arms around him and squeeze.

That wasn't so bad.

I can't wait to tell Freya.

32
SWALLOWED WHOLE

Aviva

EXHAUSTIONS HUGS EVERY MUSCLE AS I FOLLOW RYAN DOWN THE wooded trail leading from the hot springs to the village. It's midday, and the sky is wide and crystal blue as I peek up through the trees, wiping sweat from my brow.

We didn't sleep last night. Not a wink. The soreness blooming between my legs with each step is a constant reminder of that, and I can't help but smile as I look down at my sandals. We left Endova the morning after we slept together for the first time. We'd walked back into the village together, silently, both of us thrumming with nervous energy. He'd gone to sleep in the healer's cottage, and the moment I crossed the threshold of my old home, planning to curl up in bed with the girls, he said into my mind, *'Goodnight, Aviva.'*

'Goodnight,' I'd replied through the mind-link, which felt so much sharper and clearer. Before, it had been like he was speaking to me underwater, but now, it's like he's standing in front of me speaking out loud.

I woke to Shosh and Lora curled up around me and Mercy gently knocking on my door, telling me it was time to go, so I went, walking beside Ryan into a cool, foggy morning.

We hiked through the woods up the valley parallel to Silverhide instead of following the main road. It took all day, and well into the night, to reach the peak of the valley. We dropped down into Silverhide territory when the first glimmers of morning breached the lazy, misty pools of the hot springs. Ryan couldn't shift, not with poison still working its way out of his veins, but it hadn't slowed him down.

I thought we were stopping to rest and maybe eat at the springs, but he had other plans, and soon, he was grinding against me, his cock stretching and filling me, while I kept my legs wrapped around his waist and my back against the side of the pool.

Then we... came home, and the veil of dizzying, sex-fueled delusion lifted in a heartbeat.

Sore, tired, and hungry, we walk into the village to the delight and relief of Ryan's entire pack.

He's immediately bombarded, and I'm bustled out of the way, falling back as people rush to encircle him, their voices carrying into the stiflingly hot summer air.

But then I spot Freya running toward me, her eyes wide with concern. She skids to a stop, noticing what must be a very odd look on my face. I glance back at Ryan, who has disappeared in the fray, and stalk toward her.

I take her by the wrist and wordlessly hustle her toward the closest building with an open door. Heat bursts toward us, hot enough to singe my eyelashes. I yelp just as Freya pulls me back into the doorway, facing us toward the cool morning air instead of the furiously hot forge.

Freya grabs my cheeks, turning my face from side to side as she inspects me for harm. Then, she smirks, rolling her eyes to the bright morning sky. "Well?" she says, smacking her lips. "What have you been up to the last few days?"

My cheeks burn, and not from the heat in Andrew's shop. "Is it that obvious?"

"Something's different about you," she says, scanning my face. She turns back to the crowd in the center of the village. I spot James motioning to the crowd, telling people to go back to work and chores. Andrew and Ryan walk side-by-side in our direction, and I realize quite suddenly that if I'm going to tell Freya anything, it needs to be right now, while they're still out of earshot.

"We slept together," I rush out.

"Well it's about damn time–"

"He's my mate."

Freya's brows raise so high they almost touch her hairline. She blinks slowly, then shakes her head, reaching for my hand. "Because of being hand-fast–"

"Actual mates. Fated, like the legends–"

"How–"

"Welcome back, Aviva. We… *missed* you," Andrew drawls, rubbing his neck as if he can still feel my blade pressed to his skin.

"Sure," I growl at him but catch the slightly amused look on Ryan's face and quickly press my lips together and try to turn them into a smile. "Sorry. I missed you as well."

Andrew smirks, but Freya throws him a look that immediately has him looking down at his boots. Now, I'm the one smirking.

Ryan clears his throat, directing his words at Freya and Andrew. "I'm taking Aviva home to rest for a while."

"Don't worry about it. I'll go with her," Freya says brightly, her hand curling around my upper arm. "Everyone is in a frenzy, Alpha Ryan, I'm sure–" Freya's voice fades as my gaze fastens on Ryan's face, on his eyes, which are locked on Freya's hand.

His pupils expand, and his jaw flexes. It's almost like–like he's about to shift. "Ryan?" My voice sounds small, confused.

"We do need to debrief," Andrew says, but he's looking at Freya this entire time, of course, watching the way her full lips move as speaks. Now, however, he's narrowing his eyes at Ryan. Andrew takes a single step between Ryan and Freya, squaring his shoulders.

What the hell is happening right now? I close my hand around Freya's. "Yeah, I could use a minute with Freya to help–to help braid my hair."

Freya makes a face, shaking her head. "You know I'm useless when it comes to braids–"

"Alpha, let's talk." Andrew claps Ryan on the shoulder, which seems to have broken him out of whatever bizarre trance he'd fallen into.

Ryan scowls, gives Andrew a shove, and storms out of the shop. Andrew gives me a look over his shoulder, rolling his eyes and whispering, "I fucking knew it," under his breath before taking off after Ryan.

"What was that all about?" Freya murmurs, meeting my eyes.

"I have no idea."

* * *

Freya sits on the floor beside the huge bathtub, resting her head against the wall as she finger-weaves what I believe might be a pair of socks. "What does it feel like knowing he had a mate before you?"

I sink up to my nose in the overly soapy water. Freya went a little nuts on the soaps and oils, I'm afraid, but after several days in Endova, and then hiking through the forest, I definitely needed a good, hot soak.

I consider her question. I debate telling her the truth–that I hate it. That it makes me jealous and I can't stop the feeling from festering whenever it crosses my mind. "I don't really care. She's dead."

"You sound like you care," she taunts, giving me a teasing look over the rim of the tub.

"I don't like it, of course. But they weren't close. At all."

"Well, I'd assume they weren't, given that he killed her."

We shouldn't be joking about this, but damn, it does feel kind of good. I don't even know Ryan's family, but the idea of anyone hurting them, or him, makes me want to go scorched-earth. I dunk my head underwater and reemerge, slicking my hair away from my face.

Freya sighs heavily as she focuses on her knitting while I let my mind wander. I spent the last half hour telling her almost everything.

I left out the juicer details about sleeping with Ryan, of course. I want that to stay something that's mine.

But she knows Jacob and Mercy are mates, and that Ryan and I are mates, and that the mate bond is drastically different from couple to couple.

Speaking of possible mates, we both turn to the sound of boots on the floorboards in the main room, and then Andrew's voice rings out, "Freya? Aviva?"

"Give us a second," Freya calls back with a bit of a smirk. She rises, sets her project on the counter, and unfurls a towel for me.

"I can do that," I murmur, but she rolls her eyes at me.

"This is the most time I've had to sit around and do nothing since you left. I don't mind."

Wrapped in a towel, I dry my hair in another one and hang back in the bathroom for a moment while Freya fetches me something to wear and briefly talks to Andrew. When I finally emerge from the bathroom in another flowy, calf length dress made of thin linen to combat the sudden stifling heat of summer, Andrew and Freya are waiting for me in the main room. He's leaning an elbow on the kitchen table as he watches me approach.

"Don't tell your mate I'm here," he grinds out.

I brush my wet curls over my shoulders and fix him with a look. "So, he told you?"

"He didn't have to. He was ready to rip Freya's arm off for touching you."

"What? Andrew, of course he wouldn't," Freya butts in, but Andrew and I are holding each other's gaze.

Freya hadn't seen the look Ryan gave her, but we had.

"Why?" I ask.

He fiddles with the busted lockbox that was left on the table after I ravaged it with a hammer a few days ago. "Look, you guys are mates. That's great. I'm honestly not surprised. None of us are, the guys at least. But you don't know much about mates from what I understand." He looks between us. "Right?"

We nod.

"Mates, the males, get really… territorial after… you know."

"After what?" Freya asks innocently.

Andrew winces, his cheeks going pink as he cuts a quick glance in my direction. "Being friendly with each other."

Freya looks confused.

"Fucking," I tell her.

"Oh. You could have just said that, Andrew."

He runs a hand over his face, cursing under his breath. "Ryan is going to be a little on edge for a while, okay? Just don't–don't put him in a position where he feels like he has to defend you, or anything. So no more touching."

Freya steps away from me, but I find this entire thing ridiculous. "Why is this happening? What's the reason?"

"Uh, well, some people say it's because of breeding, but that practice is ancient, you know. Like, he wants you…. You know what? I can't talk about this with you. Either of you." He throws his hands in the air in surrender.

"Just tell us," Freya begs, giving him a pouty face.

It's Andrew's undoing. He watches her lower lip tremble and finally breaks, saying, "Ryan wants you bred. It has nothing to do with his actual feelings about the matter. It's just a biological thing that happens to all newly mated guys, and they go a little feral for a while, but it'll pass. At least, it should."

"He wants me to be pregnant?"

"No, but his wolf does, and it will snap on anyone who even looks in your direction."

"Does he know this is happening to him?"

"Oh, trust me, he's well aware." Andrew blows out his breath and runs his fingers through his hair. "He's busy. We have him occupied, but you two should stay away from each other." He points to me and Freya. "And you," his eyes slid to mine. "You need to stay up here, away from everyone. Just until he works through this."

"So because I'm his mate, I'm now his prisoner too?"

"He didn't mark you, did he?" he asks with a sigh. "No fucking wonder. Okay, look, if he marks you, this will pass quicker–"

"Why? How?" Freya presses, enraptured by the line of conversation.

I feel sorry for Andrew. He looks like he'd rather be anywhere else. "Freya, please, your father would gut me if he found out I'm telling you all of this."

"I'm a grown woman."

"Yeah you… are."

I scoff at the two of them. "Where is Ryan right now?"

"Hopefully where I left him, in the woods, hunting with James. He'll be back tonight, and you seriously can't leave. We'll bring food up for you, okay?" He grabs Freya's arm and tugs her toward the door. "Clean up in here if you can. Open all the windows so he doesn't pick up my scent in here with yours."

"Why? You think he'd hurt you for just–just talking to me?"

"You don't know anything about being mated, do you?" he says with a wry laugh then leads Freya out the door, closing me in. Alone.

I consider shouting at Ryan through the mind-link to come back and explain this to me but decide I'm a little curious. Do I feel territorial right now? I guess… maybe. I guess I don't feel any different, or maybe I do.

Maybe I just need sleep. Definitely.

I fall asleep on the couch shortly thereafter, basking in the hot sun coming through all of the windows I opened for Andrew's sake. I sleep harder than I ever have, and I don't wake until night falls, and the door opens and closes.

Ryan locks the door. I notice a few containers and bowls of what must be food on the kitchen table, untouched. I hadn't even heard anyone come in to drop them off.

Ryan slowly turns to look at me as I sit up on the couch, smoothing my curls away from my cheeks. He silently scans my face, my body, lingering on the slope of my thighs beneath my dress.

"I heard you've gone feral," I say sleepily.

He licks his lips. He's still as stone, quieter than I've ever heard him.

"You need to stay away from me for a few days, until this—whatever this is—passes."

"No," I tell him with a smile.

"There's something I need to tell you."

"Have you changed your mind?"

"No." He takes a single step into the house and stops. "About my powers."

"You can shoot light out of your fingertips, can't you?"

He huffs a breath, obviously annoyed by my teasing. "I think it's better if I just show you."

A burst of black mist erupts and swallows me whole.

33

THE BEAST WITHIN

Ryan

AVIVA DOESN'T SCREAM. SHE STARES UP AT ME WITH HER NORMAL, slightly bored, yet skeptical, expression she naturally wears. I'm relieved, but a little unsure, as she goes perfectly still.

The mist fades until there's nothing between us, nothing blocking her view of the power, the gift, that makes me incredibly unique and horribly deadly.

This is only the third time I've ever done it.

It feels... great. Needed, especially after everything that happened over the last few days.

I hold her gaze. She scans my eyes, relieved to find them the familiar blue I see in the mirror every morning. But nothing else about me is familiar.

'I can't shift back for a few minutes. I needed this,' I say into her mind.

'What is this?'

'My... I'm not sure what to call it. My father and my uncle call it a beast form.' I do my best to stay perfectly still so I don't leave talon marks

243

on the wood floor. My fur–now black as night and thick–trembles with each breath I take.

"Are you a hellhound?" She asks this out loud as she takes a cautious step forward, her hands curled into fists at her sides.

I shake my head.

Her eyes flick to mine, a curious glimmer passing behind them. 'Can I touch you?'

'Be... be careful. The fur is–

'Sharp,' she muses, her voice a soft flutter in my head. Her hands are small in normal circumstances, but now they're impossibly so. My back brushes the ceiling as she runs the palm of her hand over my front leg, the hard, thick fur flicking across her skin. 'Like a knife tip.'

She carefully reaches deeper into the fur, meeting the hard, scale-like armor covering my skin. Out of the corner of my vision, I notice her looking up into my eyes, perplexed but ravenously curious. Then she reaches up, standing on her tiptoes, and tries to pull up my upper lip but can't quite reach. I lower my head, allowing her to lift my jowl to inspect my teeth.

'Goddess. Your teeth are as long as my forearm.'

'Longer.'

She continues her inspection in silence, moving behind me so I can't see her anymore, which makes me nervous. I feel her tugging on my tail, then moving on, walking around my other side. Her fingers moving through my fur sends ripples of pleasure dancing through me but not in a sexual way. It's… it's not what I expected to feel. It feels good. It feels good that she's not afraid of me, that she's curious.

I feel the power start to simmer as she rounds to face me again, her hands on her hips as she looks me up and down, her eyes lingering on the impossible sharp, elongated talons on my massive paws. Black and shimmering, they're sharper than any blade, made from something stronger than bone.

'Did you need to shift into this because of me?'

This is hard to explain, but I try. 'This is only the third time I've been able to do this. I felt the... shift, I guess, when Freya grabbed your arm *earlier. I had to stay away from you until it passed but seeing you again... I just needed to.'*

She looks smug. *'I didn't realize I had this kind of effect on you.'*

'You're not scared of me?'

She tilts her head from side to side. *'You shifted into this when you fought that hellhound, didn't you? I couldn't see you fully in the dark, but I thought you were bigger than usual.'*

"*I did.*" Memories of barreling through the woods in my usual wolf form ripple through my mind. The shift hadn't been voluntary. One second I was a wolf, the next I was... Still wolf, but changed. Bigger. Dark as a shadow. All sharp lines and hard edges. Full of deadly rage. The only thing on my mind that night had been protecting her.

'Does it hurt?'

'It doesn't feel good,' I admit. *'I feel heavy if I stand still like this.'*

'I want to go hunting with you like this.'

'I don't know if I'm ready for you to see that.'

'You think I'd be scared?'

'I think you'd think of me differently. I'm not in my right mind in this form.'

'You seem pretty normal to me. Nicer, actually.'

I smile internally, and maybe it's because she's not blubbering in fear and trying to get as far away from me as possible, but my powers start to simmer, and I feel the yoke of the magic loosen enough to snap out of it. Shifting back hurts. It hurts like hell. Another burst of black mist coats the room and fades as I fold back into my human form, panting, bent at the waist with my hands on my knees as my spine snaps back into place.

Aviva drapes a blanket over my back. "Thanks."

"Who knows about this?"

"You, my dad, and my uncle. I'm sure my mom knows, but she's never brought it up to me."

"Why haven't you told anyone else?" She gathers my shredded clothing, torn beyond repair based on the look on her face.

I find it hard to find the words to explain. I chalk it up to the fact my brain is still stuck in that form. She notices my inability to continue and dumps my shredded clothes near the front door. "Bed?"

"Bed," I manage to say, nodding tiredly. A few minutes later, I'm curled up beside her listening to the warm wind rustling through the trees outside our window. She's facing the wall, her back to my chest, her fingers drawing lazy circles on my forearm. I know she must be waiting for an explanation, so I finally say, "I was sixteen when it happened for the first time."

"That's early to shift."

"Not for my family. Sydney and I both came into our wolves at sixteen, just before our birthday. Our dad did, as well, young like that. He wasn't surprised, but I was a little different. That summer, he took me to Eastonia, alone, to visit my uncle. I thought it was weird going alone, just the two of us. Being a twin, I was used to doing everything with Sydney, but I'd noticed how big my wolf was, how differently I had to train compared to Sydney and our friends, our fellow warriors. I was... a headstrong, surly teenager."

"Me too."

I gather her a little closer, resting my chin on the crook of her shoulder. She smells amazing. Like soap and toothpaste, but the undertone of her natural scent is still there, laced through her hair. Warm and sweet, calming, honestly.

"I can imagine." I close my eyes as my tired, aching body starts to grow heavy with impending sleep. "I overheard them talking about me one night. I'd come down to Uncle Ryatt's office hoping to sneak back to my room with a bottle of whiskey to share with my friend Evander the next day, but they were in there, talking about me, my wolf, my dad's concerns. I was so angry they'd been talking about me, behind my back, like I was a problem." I know she has no idea who Evander is, or has ever met my family, but I continue, "The next morning before sunrise, Dad woke me up, told me to get dressed. We were going to go shift. I got in a fight with him, telling him I'd overheard him talking with Ryatt. Ryatt ended up coming into the room and diffusing things and promised a large breakfast if I went with them. I was a sixteen year old boy, so food was the answer to everything, and I eventually agreed, but I was still pissed off. They took me into the forest surrounding Moonrise, and I got more and more angry. Looking back, I realized Dad was egging me on, and I know he hated it, but he wanted me to stay mad, to get more mad. He did everything he could to rile me up, and it... worked. I couldn't keep up with them, and they knew it. I was a large, lumbering fool still getting used to shifting and was a wolf twice their size, so I fell behind several times, and they were dicks about it. Ryatt laughed at me, and that was it. I snapped and... confirmed what they took me out there for, what my dad brought me to Eastonia for."

Aviva continues drawing circles on my arm, slow and lazy. "You must have been terrified."

"I was," I admit, and it's hard to do. "I didn't know what was happening. I panicked, started attacking myself, and Ryatt had to use his powers on me to subdue me. He's a powerful bastard, I don't even understand how he can do what he can do, but even his powers could barely keep me down. Dad talked me through it, telling me it was okay, that I was safe, that he was sorry. He sounded so broken. I've never heard him like that, and I haven't since. Afterward, when I'd calmed down enough to shift back, they took me back to the castle and gave me the breakfast they promised. I took a nap, and when I woke up, Ryatt summoned me to his office."

Aviva curls her hand around my arm, nestling it to her chest. Her breathing is rhythmic and steady. She says nothing, just listens.

"Dad never told me about his ability to shift into something similar until that day. Ryatt knew, of course, and we spent the rest of the night talking about what this meant for me. Dad offered to let me stay in Eastonia to train my new powers with Ryatt and my aunt Ella, but I refused. I wanted to be back in Crescent Falls with my friends. I wanted to go to Wellington University. I didn't want the power I possessed, and they allowed me to make the final decision."

"You can't just summon it, can you?"

"I never learned. It's fully based on emotion, currently. You falling to your death, then sensing that hellhound hunting you in the aftermath… that did the trick. I didn't even feel it happen. Today was the first time I felt it and had to keep it under control."

"Because we had sex?"

"Because we're mates, and I…. Yeah, that."

"Andrew said if you marked me, this would pass quicker."

I sigh against her shoulder, my teeth grazing her skin on instinct. I want to. Everything in my body is screaming to just bite down, to draw blood. "Not yet."

She doesn't protest, which I'm thankful for. I don't think I'd be able to control myself if she begged for it. I'd do it roughly. I'd make it hurt just to see the look of pleasure and pain mingling behind her eyes.

But not tonight. Not while I'm like this.

"I have to go to Moonrise in a few days," I tell her, closing my eyes. "For a week, at least. I'd like you to come with me, to meet my family."

She doesn't reply. She sighs into sleep, her heartbeat slowing to a gentle thump. I curl into her, nestled against her touch, her warmth, and feel… whole.

It's the best and also the worst feeling.

Having something to lose.

34

GONE FISHIN'

Aviva

SOMETHING CHANGED AFTER THAT NIGHT. THERE WAS A SHIFT BETWEEN me and Ryan. He showed me a part of himself that only two other people have seen. Something he locks away, guards, and hides. I don't know if he's ashamed of it. I wouldn't be. If I had the power to shift into a beast like that? Oh, gods, everyone would be sick of me. I'd never shift back. I'd stay like that, ruling the forests, enacting the sick, twisted judgment I crave when it comes to rogues and hellhounds.

Maybe not, but it would be difficult to come back to my human form. I could tell, when he was in that startling form, that he was uncomfortable. I think it hurts him, honestly. The grotesque shape of his spine. The hard as rock muscles covered in tight, scaled armor. Fur sharp enough to tear skin.

It was the coolest thing I'd ever seen.

But I understand the weight of it. What he carries every day in his heart. He's sensitive, deep down. I should probably be nicer to him... but taunting him is so easy and *fun*.

"Put me down!" I screech, banging my fists on his back as he carries me to the edge of the dock at the lake above the village. He's shirtless, which means I have nothing to grab onto but his skin, which is slick with sweat.

Without ceremony, he tosses me into the water.

"Ryan!" I gulp water on accident, sputtering a cough.

"Have you learned your lesson yet?" he asks, trying to look mad.

I'm in trouble for probably the third time today. It's been several days since we came back from Endova, since he showed me his beast form. We've been moving through time like it's always been this way. Like it's been the two of us, living together, running a village, our pack. He has a routine that I've been trying to follow the best I can. He wakes up early, before the sun. He shifts, running in his wolf form for several miles around the perimeter of the valley. Then, he goes to what he calls "the gym" with his friends, and they lift heavy things with their shirts off, just like Freya said.

After that, it's breakfast at the pack house, which he never skips. Then he goes to work—building structures and houses. Tending to his people if there's issues. Taking stock of the cattle, the gardens, the fields of wheat and corn.

While he does all of that, I stick to the sheep. We have sheep in Endova, and it was the only thing I enjoyed about my duties to my pack. Herding the sheep to the plains to graze; herding them back when the sun set. Guarding them, protecting them, making sure they didn't fall behind or get lost. I'm good at it. I understand their tiny brains.

Freya has been teaching the women how to use a loom. Andrew built her one shortly after we came here for the first time. She's making friends and integrating herself in the pack, but I don't have that skill. I like being alone. I like only having to hear my own thoughts because they're more than enough. They're overwhelming enough.

It hasn't stopped his pack from trying to seek me out. Dahlia and her baby have spent the past few days with me out in the fields. The unnamed baby girl is very cute, I can admit. She looks like her father—dark hair, dark eyes. Dahlia already wants another one.

I can't even bring myself to hold the baby when she offers. I don't know what's wrong with me. I used to hold Lora when she was a baby all the time. I raised those girls with Mercy. I know what it takes to be a mother.

I guess I just never saw myself as one, even though I knew that was part of my destiny as a woman. I never let myself think past being pregnant because I'd have to bring the baby into the world at some point. I always imagine my mother then, and shove the idea away, refusing to dwell on it.

This morning started out completely different from the rest. Ryan went straight to work, skipping breakfast and his run, and returned to our house a few hours later before I'd even gotten ready for the day.

It's a hot morning. Blindingly so. The thin linen dress I chose for the day stuck to my skin the second I put it on. He took one look at me and told me we were going to the lake.

To fish.

I tread water, scowling at him. "You're doing it all wrong."

"I know how to catch a fucking fish, Aviva," he says, gesturing with his hands toward a fishing pole resting on the dock. "And you pestering me isn't helping."

"There's barely any fish in this lake." I float on my back, bored, but the water is sharp and cool, a bright contrast to the heat of summer. "If you'd listened to me, we would've had a feast of trout for dinner. But no, what does Aviva know? I've only lived near streams for my entire life!"

He huffs a breath from the dock. "Get out of the water."

"No."

"Aviva."

"You threw me in here."

"Get out of the water."

I relax back into an upright position. "Make me."

Heat and a touch of frustration flashes behind his eyes. He doesn't move, though.

"Oh, are you afraid to get your hair wet? Poor baby with your pretty curls–" the splash he creates causes me to roll underwater, drifting several feet away from where I was swimming just a few seconds ago. I screech as he starts swimming toward me, but he's a powerful swimmer, which I hadn't expected. He dives under and barrels toward me so fast I have no choice but to suck in a breath and prepare for what's about to happen.

He grabs me around the waist, dunking me underwater for emphasis, and starts hauling me back to the shore. I gasp for breath and dig my nails into his shoulder. "I can swim just fine, you know."

He pants out a breath as he reaches the shallow part of the lake, able to stand. "I wanted a nice, peaceful morning. This has been the opposite of peaceful."

"I'm having fun." I wrap my legs around his waist beneath the water, my dress billowing out around me. "You're the one who's been uptight and grumpy all morning. What's wrong with you?"

"Nothing."

"Because I told you you wouldn't be able to catch any fish here today? It's too sunny. They're all at the bottom, and the better fish are in the stream up the valley–"

"I know," he grinds out, holding my gaze.

I slide around his waist to face him, comfortably supported by the cool water all around us.

"Then what is the matter?"

He sighs and rests his forehead against mine. "We're leaving for Moonrise in a few hours, remember?"

I chew my lower lip. We haven't talked about this very much. I knew he had to leave, and he wanted me to go with him. But I hadn't noticed any preparations being made for the journey, which would take several days, I was sure. I've never been to Moonrise. I've never traveled through the Roguelands and up into the mountains where the witch coven claims its territory. But, I know for a fact we'll be on the road for a while.

"My bag is packed," I tell him. "I'm ready to go whenever you are."

"We need to shower and dress," he says, more to himself, like he's mentally checking off a list. I find it odd he's worried about looking presentable when we're going to be camping out every night and covered in road dust, but what do I know about traveling through the Roguelands?

"I'm sorry I ruined your fishing trip," I murmur.

"You didn't ruin it. I ruined it. I just woke up in a bad mood."

"I know. Your grumbling while you got dressed this morning woke me up."

He smiles softly, his eyes downcast on the water between us.

Honestly, this is the closest we've been to each other in days. Ryan needs space to work through the... the mate stuff. We sleep in the same bed, sure. I wake up with his arm resting over my hips in the morning. I know he hesitates before he gets out of bed, probably wondering the same things I am. Wanting the same things but holding back.

Now, we're only inches apart, and the tension between us is stronger than I've ever felt it.

"I don't like the idea of being gone for this long while things are still so uncertain in Endova," he admits.

"The tribes fight all the time. This is nothing new."

He eyes me, scanning my face. "You know Hardan is going to continue to be a problem."

I shrug, "He could be, but you taught him a lesson, for sure. We would have heard by now if he made any more moves on Endova or Teshka. Anyway, if we do have to go to battle with Navvan again, you can just shift into your beast." I tighten my legs around his waist. "I'll ride on your back into battle. They'll be so scared they won't even fight."

He smiles boyishly, the corners of his mouth twitching as he fights his lips back into a straight, serious line. For some reason, I don't believe his terrible mood is because I made fun of his inability to catch fish all morning or because the tribes are fighting.

"Are you nervous about seeing your family?"

"It's been over a year since I had the chance to see them, so yeah. I guess I am." He sounds a little broken up about it. A year without seeing my family... I can't fathom it.

His hands slide up my thighs to my ass, squeezing on impulse, like he can't help it. I bite my lower lip, my mouth only a few inches from his. "We need to go back and get ready."

"Are you sure?" I lean in, brushing the words across his cheek as my breasts press against his chest.

He shudders, gripping my ass even tighter as he holds me there—close—my body flush with his. Having sex with him twice hasn't been enough. It's all I think about. This must be because of the bond. That constant ache of his absence between my legs....

"We can't," he says against my ear, his teeth catching my earlobe.

I close my eyes as a shiver of longing licks down my spine. "Why not?"

"You're in heat, Aviva, I can feel it."

"So?"

"So, you're not on a contraceptive tonic, and I could get you pregnant." He pulls away enough to look at me fully. "We'll pick some up in Moonrise. My cousin is a midwife. She'll be there, and she has everything you'll need."

"How can you tell I'm in heat?"

"Because—" He grits his teeth as he adjusts my position against him, like I'm too close, but he's also searching for any kind of friction to satisfy his own desire. "I just can. It's a mate thing. Feeling the mate bond with you... I can feel other things too now. Sense things. Like every morning when I wake up next to you, and you're warm, soft in my hands and wet..."

My heart skips as he leans in to nip at my neck. I squirm in his grasp, desperate for him to touch me. I'm ready to beg for it.

"I was barely able to control myself the last two times, but I don't think I could again."

"Please," I beg, whimpering as I grind against him.

He rolls his neck, groaning. "Not here. Soon, I promise."

Somehow, we untangle ourselves. I trudge behind him back to the house where he orders me to take a bath and change my clothes. He leaves in a huff, and an hour later, I'm dressed, my hair clean and air-drying as I sharpen my knives at the kitchen table.

I wasn't sure what to wear. I had a feeling we wouldn't be leaving until tonight, after nightfall. It's far safer to shift and travel under the cover of darkness, anyway, since it would only be the two of us. So I picked another pretty dress that hugs my breasts and hangs loosely around my waist, soft and airy to combat the heat. This will do until I need to change into my dresses from Endova when we set out to travel.

But two male voices drift toward me through the open windows. Ryan's is familiar, but I can't place the other. It's new… but familiar in a strange way that immediately sets me on edge.

The door opens.

35
MIGHT AS WELL JUMP

Aviva

RYAN WALKS IN ALONE, HIS UNFAMILIAR COMPANION RUSHING BACK down the stairs away from the house. He's slightly unkempt, like he'd been to the sawmill, wood shavings sticking to his clothes and hair.

There's a new scent being carried on his clothes–male. Familiar, yet unplaceable.

"Hey," he says with a smile, pressing a kiss to my temple as he walks past me toward the bathroom.

I whirl, following him. "Who was that?"

He turns on the shower. "I have to make this quick. We're leaving in a few minutes."

"Oh–"

He rushes out of his clothes, stepping into the bathtub and pulling the curtain. I chew my lower lip as I walk out of the bathroom, edging toward the window to look outside. In the distance, a group has gathered in the center of the village around a stranger that I can't see clearly. I have an odd feeling about this. I glance back at the supplies I have laid out on the table in anticipation for our trip *tonight*, not in a few *minutes*.

Tapping my foot, I go into our bedroom and pull one of my dresses from Endova out of the drawer with the rest of my clothing, a mix of both styles—the looping, shiftable dresses from my old village, and the new, soft, flowing dresses I've grown to like wearing here.

"I like the dress you have on," Ryan says, towel drying his hair as he steps into the room. He has boxers on already as he reaches past me, pulling a pair of pants I'd never seen him wear out of the drawer. They're a dark gray and made from a thick, complicated fabric that doesn't look handmade. He pulls them on, fishes for some socks, and then walks to the closet.

"Why are we leaving early?"

"Sydney got here early."

"Your brother? He's here?" Nervous excitement blooms in my chest. Why? Why would Sydney be here? "Is he traveling with us?"

"Yeah." Ryan shrugs into an off-white long sleeve shirt, turning to face me. It has buttons all the way up the chest—tiny ones, which he deftly secures into place without missing a beat. He shaved, too. His hair is brushed away from his face like he tried to tame the curls he usually ignores.

I turn to the mirror over the dresser, hastily pulling my hair away from my face and securing it in a bun at the nape of my neck with a ribbon.

My mind keeps dragging me back to why he's dressed like this. He looks so different. He looks, I realize, like a prince. At least, what I imagine the Prince of Crescent Falls would look like.

There's a knock on the door. He curses under his breath, turning toward the closet for a pair of shoes—again, a pair I've never seen him wear. He slides them on. "I'm coming."

I follow him into the living room just as he opens the door, and his twin steps inside, smiling brightly.

Sydney is exactly what I expected. He looks like Ryan... kind of. Not totally. Ryan is larger overall, but not by much. Ryan's roughness is accentuated by Sydney's polished looks, however.

Their eyes are exactly the same.

Sydney notices me and smiles kindly, which catches me off guard.

"This is Aviva. The one I told you about when you got here."

"You're in so much trouble when we get to Moonrise," he replies with a nudge of his elbow into Ryan's ribs. Suddenly, Sydney's walking toward me, his hand outstretched. "It's nice to meet you."

I don't know what to do, so I tuck my hands behind my back.

Sydney bites down on his lip, nods, and curls his hand into a fist before letting it drop to his side. "Well, uh, we should get going. Mom's waiting for us. She told me to be back in time for dinner."

What? Back where? Moonrise is days away…?

"Yeah, sure. You can do this, right? You've been practicing?"

"I jumped here from Moonrise. It's fine."

"But with two extra people–"

"I got Sarah and the boys to Moonrise from Crescent Falls–"

"Sarah has these powers too–"

"It's fine, I'm not going to kill you." Sydney's eyes slide to mine. "Or your *wife*, I promise."

I have no idea what's happening as Ryan gives his brother one final, skeptical look and reaches for my bag on the table, hauling it over his shoulder. I step toward my bow, hand outstretched, but he catches my hand in his, knitting our fingers together. One second, I'm standing with my feet planted on solid ground. The next, Sydney claps a hand on Ryan's shoulder, and the room spins out of control.

I scream.

"Oh, fuck I didn't warn–" Ryan's voice breaks, replaced by a whirling, roaring sound that blasts through my ears at the same moment I fall to pieces, pulled apart.

Everything goes dark. That spinning sensation remains. I can't make sense of up or down. I think I might be screaming for help because new voices are breaking through the darkness, lifted in excitement and…

"Ryan! It's been so long–oh, my Goddess, is she okay?"

Bright light erupts in my eyes. I'm blinded, my knees buckling as the scream chokes out of my throat. I can't catch my breath as my vision tunnels, the brightness fading, replaced by gold. Golden walls, light flooring. Sunlight beaming toward me.

"Fuck," Ryan growls, scooping me up. My stomach pitches as I grip his shirt for dear life. "Aviva, I'm sorry, I forgot–"

"Who is that?" A bright female voice hisses nearby, but I can barely keep my eyes open.

Oh, gods, I feel so sick. I'm going to throw up. I need to–

"Did you even warn her? Oh, Goddess, Ryan, get her to the infirmary–" Another female voice I don't recognize bursts toward us, followed by rushed footsteps.

"Sydney, who is that woman?" the first female voice repeats, but her voice is far away as Ryan clutches me to his chest and starts to run.

I catch a single glimpse of the two women before I'm forced to close my eyes again against the twisting, sick pain in my stomach. One woman is very short, with thick, dark brown hair that falls nearly to her waist. The other is tall with hair so blonde it's nearly white as she gapes after us. I see her swat Sydney on the chest before my vision starts to fade again.

Where am I?

Ryan kicks a door open, and suddenly the expansive, gaping nothingness surrounding us shifts. It's dark in here, wherever we are. It smells like… him. His things. His clothes. I'm so confused as I blink up at the domed ceiling, painted a deep, dark green and trimmed with dark wood. He rushes me into a new room where a light bursts to life, and the nausea returns.

"I can't–" I whimper, trying to roll out of his arms. "I don't feel well–"

He unceremoniously dumps me in front of a toilet and kicks what I realize is the door leading into a bathroom closed against the voice rushing in our direction.

I clutch the rug, crawling toward a porcelain bathtub, and press my cheek to its cool surface, closing my eyes.

"I am so sorry," Ryan grinds out.

I don't even open my eyes. I'm still spinning. "What the fuck just happened?"

"We're in Moonrise."

"What?"

"I didn't think–I wasn't thinking," he exhales. "You're going to be okay. Jumping is hard for people who don't have powers."

"What?" That's all I can manage. I slowly start to feel my body again, and the light doesn't feel so painful to my eyes. When I finally lift my head, Ryan is sitting on the ground with his back against the door, resting his arms on his knees. He doesn't look so great either, like he's fighting the same dizziness that has my body in a chokehold.

I take the opportunity to look around. We're definitely not in Silverhide anymore.

* * *

RYAN

I CLOSE THE DOOR TO MY BEDROOM IN MOONRISE BEHIND ME, HOLDING it closed as the two men waiting nearby watch me with similar expressions of disbelief and curiosity. My private apartment in the castle is exactly how I left it the last time I was here, which was probably close to a year ago now, when I'd last visited the family.

"She's asleep," I tell Sydney and Evander.

Evander glances at Sydney, rolling his eyes. "She's going to be out for a while. You can't just jump with someone like us and expect us to land on our feet." He's talking about the fact that he, and my mate, don't have the same kind of powers we do. I can jump all over the place, and it barely affects me. I get a bit of a headache afterward, but nothing major. I don't have the power to do it myself, which is probably why I feel a little sick to my stomach right now too.

Or, that's the guilt of straight up neglecting to tell Aviva how we were traveling to Moonrise.

I run my hands over my face, shaking my head.

Sydney takes a breath in preparation to say something, but I cut him off with a wave of my hand.

"Nobody say anything to me for a minute, okay?"

Evander smirks down at his boots, crossing his arms over his chest.

Seconds tick by. The questions haunting the room fester between us.

"Fine, what do you want to know?"

"How'd you end up with a wife, Ryan?" Sydney grinds out. Back in Silverhide, I'd told him the news and then promptly followed up by telling him to shut up about it until I had a moment to explain in length.

"She's my mate, first of all."

Evander stiffens, and Sydney looks perplexed.

"You're sure?" Syd asks, lowering his voice.

I glance between the men and nod. "It just happened a few days ago, all right? I'm just as shocked as you are and still processing."

Evander runs his tongue along his lower lip. "So you married her right away?"

"That came before. It was a… a fuck up, on my part. I didn't fully understand the customs of her people and accidentally paid her bride price."

Neither man understands what I'm talking about, but at this point, the last thing I want to do is explain myself, especially since it's a matter of minutes before my parents find out we're here.

"This is a lot for me," I admit. "It's even harder for her, so please, rein in your wives tonight."

Evander chokes a laugh. "Kenna is already bombarding the mind-link right as we speak. They want an explanation."

"They'll get one, but I'm not going to totally overwhelm Aviva, not tonight. Just give us a minute. I need to talk to Mom and Dad," I tell Sydney. "I need to talk to them about this first. Ryatt, too, since she'll be queen of the Deadlands." The words fall from my tongue. I hadn't even thought of it that way yet.

I feel sorry for her. Neither of us had any idea what would happen to us the night I gave her father that pelt.

Evander nods. Sydney, too, slumps his shoulders and relents by saying, "Do you want to come see the boys? Blake has been asking about you."

"Yeah," I reply, rolling out my shoulders. "Uh, in a bit. I'm going to stay with her for a minute, make sure she feels okay."

Evander steps forward, tilting his head toward the bedroom door. "I'll have some tea sent up. Kenna has a special blend for me that I use when I have to travel. It helps with the nausea and headaches." He claps me on the arm.

"Thanks, man."

I watch them leave and lock the door behind them, making sure the exterior entrance is locked as well, and creep back into the bedroom.

But Aviva isn't in bed. She's standing at one of the windows, the shadows cast by the tall trees right outside dancing across her face.

I walk to her side, resting my hand on her lower back and watch her gaze out at the sparkling, golden city and the turquoise lake beyond.

"Is this real?" she asks.

"Yeah, we're really here."

She looks up at me, a bit flushed and pale. "They're not going to like me. I'm not a princess."

"Have you ever cared if people like you or not?"

"I care if *they* do." She holds my gaze, and I can see the doubt behind her eyes.

I cup her cheek and lean down, brushing my lips over hers before taking her mouth in an open, heated kiss. The kind I've been dreaming out.

"UNCLE RYAN!" Tiny fists pound on the door in the next room that leads into the castle proper. "UNCLE–" A yelp, then a sucking, angry cry as the voice is carried away. "NOOOOO! I WANNA SEE UNCLE RYAN! RIGHT! NOWWWW!"

"That's Brie," I laugh, resting my forehead against Aviva's. "Are you ready?"

"I don't think we have a choice." She laughs and allows me to take her hand and lead her out of the room.

36

MEETING THE FAMILY

Aviva

I EXPECTED TO BE LED INTO A THRONE ROOM GUARDED BY WOLVES. I expected gold finishes, ball gowns, crowns made of precious gems. I expected to see their powers at work and feel tiny in comparison.

I wasn't expecting the woman who greeted me in the doorway of a very simple, open sitting room in the depths of the castle, yellow wallpaper illuminating her face in a soft glow.

She sucks in her breath and absolutely beams at me, her dark blue eyes widening with... joy. Or maybe it's utter relief. I'm not sure. Whatever it is, she's happy to see me, and she doesn't even know me.

"The girls said you had red hair, but this–wow, you are just stunning."

"Mom, can you at least let us come into the room first?" Ryan smiles down at the woman, his mother, his hand flat against the small of my back.

I see the resemblance now. Ryan doesn't look like her other than the eyes. His features are much more striking, harder, sharper. But she's soft and lovely, her hair a deep, wine red. It's pulled back in a long ponytail that drapes over her shoulder as she takes my hand and tugs me forward. "Look at her, Ryan. Oh my Goddess. You have incredible hair."

I clear my throat. I'd caught my reflection in a trio of mirrors while we walked across what felt like an entire city on our way to this room. My hair was crazier than usual, practically standing on end at all angles, tightly curled. A lion's mane, honestly.

I look back at Ryan as his hand slips from my back. He tucks his hands in his pockets, smiling softly as his mom guides me toward several couches arranged around the room. But just as I'm about to turn back to his mother, several tiny people rush for him, crashing into his legs at full speed.

Ryan dramatically falls to the ground, groaning like he's injured, much to the delight of the four children climbing him like a tree.

"I thought the girls were joking when they told me Ryan brought home a wife," she says, her hand still locked on mine as we reach the center of the room. She finally releases me, motioning for me to sit. I do, wondering if I'm dreaming up this incredibly weird day. "It sounds like, from what Sydney said, that you didn't have a choice. Is that true?"

"Can we not get into this right now?" I hear Ryan say from across the room. He has one of the toddlers, a little boy, tucked under one arm, while another, a boy of a similar age with bright blond hair and silver eyes, climbs over his back. The little girl with curly brown hair, Brie, I assume, is busy knotting Ryan's shoe laces together, while the fourth, the youngest of the group, stands by and innocently sucks his thumb. "Let me guess," Ryan chokes out, trying to stand, "Sydney told you everything?"

"I forced him to, in his defense," she retorts, but smiles at me nonetheless. "I'm Maddy, by the way. Welcome to the family."

Is that it? No interrogation? No arguments about whether I'm suited for her son or capable of ruling beside him as Luna, carrying on his family name and lineage?

"Blake, that's enough. Uncle Ryan isn't a jungle gym, remember? We talked about this." The blonde woman from earlier enters the room wearing an outfit made of silk, I believe. It's a deep, muted violet, matching pants and a flowing shirt that hangs off her shoulders. She scoops up the little boy who was sucking his thumb and adjusts his weight on her hip before she sets her sights on me.

I go rigid when her eyes meet mine. Her eyes are pure violet. "Aviva," she says brightly, her wide smile lighting the room. "I'm so sorry my idiot brother-in-law and thoughtless mate didn't have the wherewithal to warn you about *jumping*."

My mouth pops open in a perfect O. No, this wasn't what I was expecting at all, and now I feel incredibly unprepared.

"She handled it just fine," a blond man, who I hadn't realized had been standing in the room the entire time, says from the corner near the window. He's standing with two other men, older, Maddy's age, by my estimation.

I stand on instinct, something reminiscent of fear coiling through my veins as the dark haired man turns around to look at me. Silver eyes drift over my face. Tattoos cover his neck and his forearms, down to his fingers.

Holy shit.

That's Ryatt, Alpha King of Eastonia.

My legs wobble. I nearly drop to my knees and hang my head in a bow. I'd heard about him, the legends about him. I guess I never really let the truth of the matter settle in.

I'm mated to his nephew.

How is this real?

Ryan is behind me suddenly, turning me to face the men fully. The second man is most definitely Ryan's father. The resemblance is uncanny. Now that I've seen King Isaac in person, I can also imagine the differences between Sydney and Ryan more clearly. Sydney takes after Maddy.

Ryan is his father's son, through and through.

King Isaac walks toward me, smiling kindly if not a little skeptically, and extends his hand. Unlike with Sydney, I take it, wondering if I'm meant to kiss his knuckles or shake his hand.

He chooses the latter. "Aviva. That's a unique name."

I'm speechless.

"It's Endovian," Ryan says as Isaac releases my hand.

Everyone is looking at me. My heart starts to beat out of rhythm. I feel that twisting ache in my chest again, making it hard to breathe. Ryan notices, giving his mom a look before turning me toward the door in an attempt to get me out of here, but then the little girl is in front of us, peering up at me with large, hazel eyes the size of tea saucers.

"Who are you?" she asks politely.

"I'm—I'm Aviva," I croak, embarrassed, feeling like a tinier version of myself.

"I like you," she says with conviction and then darts away.

"Okay," I whisper to myself, feeling faint. I'm going to faint. I am, in fact, losing my vision around the edges.

"Okay, that's enough," Ryan practically growls, cursing under his breath as he starts to nudge me toward the door over the voices blurring around us.

"She's just feeling the effects of jumping, you meathead." A cup of tea is suddenly thrust into my hand, and I'm seated before I can blink or form another rational thought. Silver eyes fill my vision, and then she's there, the small, dark haired woman I'd seen very briefly when I arrived. She smiles kindly at me as she bounces a baby on her hip. "Drink it. You'll feel better. It always makes Evander feel better."

Evander. That name is familiar. Why is it familiar? Ryan mentioned him a few nights ago, of course. His childhood friend or something.

I blink a few times and sip the tea. It's lukewarm, meant to be finished right away. The silver-eyed woman watches me tip it back and drain the cup, pleased when I hand it back to her with trembling hands.

Ryan ropes an arm around my shoulders as the room continues to spin. It takes several minutes for it to slow down, for the voices and faces to stop blurring. A bright warmth flows through my body, making my skin tingle. On instinct, I look for the woman who gave me the tea and find her seated nearby with the blonde woman with violet eyes.

Everyone has dipped back into their own conversations, leaving me and Ryan alone for a moment. When I sigh heavily, taking a much needed breath, Ryan asks softly, "Are you okay?"

"I'm really confused."

"I know, I'm sorry. I could have prepared you better. It's just been so busy in Silverhide the last few days."

"I know." I rest my hand on his thigh, squeezing, feeling instantly better knowing he's actually here, and I'm not hallucinating all of this. "I'm not upset with you."

"You should be. I'd deserve it." He licks his lips, looking around. "Goddess, there are so many of us now." He adjusts his position, turning to point to the group of four men standing in the corner by the window. "That's my uncle, Ryatt. My dad, obviously. You met Sydney already. And the blond, scary guy is Evander."

He does look kind of scary. Deadly is a better descriptor.

"Evander is mated to Kenna, who gave you the tea. She's Ryatt's daughter, my cousin. Sydney's mate is Sarah, the one with the blonde hair."

He goes on to explain whose children belong to whom. Brie, Aris, and Maeve, the baby, are Kenna and Evander's children. Blake and Liam are his nephews, belonging to Sydney and Sarah.

My head spins, but I take it all in.

"Ryan," King Isaac says with a tilt of his head toward the door as the men move out of the room.

Ryan flexes his jaw, his fingers tightening their grip on my arm.

"I'm being summoned. I'll walk you back to my apartment—"

"No, don't take her away yet," Kenna argues from across the room. Sarah shakes her head in emphasis.

Ryan looks down at me as he stands, his eyes searching mine for confirmation that being left here with his family is okay with me.

"I'm fine," I tell him, wondering if I am, in fact, fine.

"This shouldn't take long." He grumbles, bending to kiss me right on the mouth in front of his mother. I go bright red as he pulls away.

Kenna and Sarah move in on me without prompting. Maddy is busy with the children, looking like she's in the Goddess's Kingdom in the clouds. I don't think she even realized the men left.

Kenna sits on one side of me, and Sarah takes the other, so I'm trapped.

I think of Natalie and her friends in Silverhide. Women who like Freya but don't look in my direction if they can help it. I'm not the kind of person who can make friends naturally, but Kenna and Sarah aren't really giving me a choice.

"So, you're Ryan's mate?" Sarah asks, smiling around the words. Again, I notice the relief in her eyes that I also noticed in Maddy's. I nod, and her smile widens.

Kenna lets out her breath with a sad smile, her eyes slightly glassy.

"He seems much happier," she says absently, nodding to herself. "Good."

I notice their expressions, the deeply seeded grief. It strikes me in the chest. I know Ryan has been through a lot, likely pushed people away like I'd been doing since my mother died, but I didn't realize how it affected his family.

How deeply must he have been hurting for them to look beyond relieved that he'd found me?

"I know this is a lot to take in," Sarah whispers as Kenna gets up to tend to Aris, who bumped his head on a coffee table while playing with one of the other boys. "I'm an in-law too."

"There's just a lot of people."

"Oh, you can be honest. It's totally overwhelming, but you get used to it. Sydney and I often end up in another room, enjoying the quiet, after a family dinner." She smiles prettily, her strange eyes seeming to glow. "It could be worse," she continues with a shrug. "You and Ryan seemed to have just found each other naturally, *pre-forced-marriage* aside."

I smile a bit, which makes her smile even wider. "Is that how you and Sydney–"

"Oh, no. I wiped his memories of me after the first night we met and conceived Blake, then–"

A rushed intake of air travels through the room as two new women appear in the doorway. I stand on impulse as Ella enters... Queen Ella. Her power radiates off her just like her mate's. She's smiling at me though, but then looks... shocked. The woman beside her with copper-blonde hair rushes forward, coming to an abrupt stop only a few feet from where I'm standing.

"Amanda, what's the matter?" Maddy asks as she stands with baby Maeve in her arms.

Amanda. She looks like Evander. She must be his mother.

Queen Ella and Amanda stare at me so hard I go red.

"Who is your mother?" Amanda rasps, tears in her eyes.

"My mother?" I echo, confused.

"There's no way," Queen Ella says to herself, but Amanda shakes her head, several tears sliding down her cheeks.

"Who is your mother?" she repeats in a desperate tone that has everyone rising from their chairs in confusion.

Sarah grabs my hand. I barely feel her touch out of the shock of this moment, but it's comforting.

"Gemma. Her name was Gemma."

Amanda crumbles, covering her face with her hands. Queen Ella looks suspicious as she edges toward me, her fingers gently touching my cheek, turning my face to the side. "Is she still alive?"

"No," my heart begins to crack. I ask myself, for the thousandth time today, what's going on. "She died six years ago."

"How?" Queen Ella's voice is totally, completely serious. Hard, and stern.

"Mom?" Kenna asks behind me. "What's wrong?"

"She died having my sister. Lora is six now. Shoshannah is ten, and there's me, and Mercy." I'm not sure why I'm telling them this, but at the mention of the four of us, Queen Ella's eyes soften, and Amanda steps toward me, scanning my face before pulling me in for the tightest embrace I've ever received.

"Ella," Sarah says cautiously. "What–"

"I thought I was the only one left," Amanda says, holding me tight. "You look like us. Our pack. Gemma was–"

"Gemma was a friend," Ella says tightly, obviously resisting the urge to cry. She turns just as Maddy reaches her side. "Dinner's ready."

37

IS RYAN BACK?

Ryan

THE FAMILY DINING ROOM IN THE PRIVATE QUARTERS OF THE CASTLE where Ella and Ryatt spend their time outside of their royal duties is washed in starlight and the faint glow of a chandelier.

It's probably edging on 9:00 PM, by my estimation. The dinner was long, drawn out, conversations yelled down the impossibly crowded wooden table.

Now, I sit on one end, nursing a glass of scotch, while my mate sits surrounded by my family on the other end, her eyes rapt as she watches Ella's mouth move.

I've barely spoken to her in the past two hours. She was herded to a seat and immediately surrounded, and I ended up on the other side of the table from my mate, stuck between Sydney and Granger, Evander's father. Granger eventually moved down the table as well, joining whatever conversation I was being excluded from, apparently. The kids were scooped up and tossed in bed an hour ago. It's quiet now, which is rare for my family when we all get together.

Well, not all of us. We're missing Grandma and Grandpa and

Ryatt's parents, all of them held up in Maatua for some reason. Misty isn't here either, which I knew would be the case. She's in Tarsian, spending her summer digging in the sand doing some research study for her degree program.

I take another sip of scotch, watching Aviva prop her chin in her hand as Amanda leans in, laughing at something Ella said.

Something obviously happened after I left the room with the men. I'd been cloistered away in Ryatt's office and was interrogated about my marriage, how it came about, if I tried to stop it, for her sake, of course. Only after the rest of the guys left when dinner was announced did my dad pull me aside and ask if I truly felt the mate bond with Aviva.

I take another sip of my scotch, draining it this time.

I told him I did, and I do. It's just… confusing. I'm trying to reckon with why my bond with Aviva feels so much different than it did with Hadley. Should I feel as guilty as I do about that?

"Here." Fresh amber-hued liquid splashes into my glass. Sydney sits down beside me with a sigh, looking worse for wear, his shirt a little ruffled. He pours himself a dram, knocks it back, and pours a second.

"What happened to you?" I chuckle as I lift my drink to my lips.

"Blake," he grumbles. "Putting him to bed has been a nightmare lately. Someone, we're not sure who, probably a kid in his preschool class, has him convinced monsters live under his bed and are going to eat him the second we leave the room. He gets Liam all wound up, too." Despite his frustrated tone, he smiles against the rim of his glass. "I wake up every morning and roll over to kiss my wife and find Blake between us, stretched out like a starfish in nothing but his undies, sleeping like a baby."

I smile a bit wistfully at the image dancing through my mind. I'm happy for Sydney. I knew Sarah was the one for him the first time I met her. They just fit together like pieces of a puzzle. She understands his weird, tangled brain, and he soaks up her light.

"Are you guys thinking of having another one?"

"Another kid? Hell no." Sydney sucks in a laugh, shaking his head.

"Not for a while, at least. Liam's a handful. Two boys is hard. It's like a war zone every time I get home from the firm. Cosette keeps threatening to retire and move so far away we'll never be able to find her. I'd love a daughter, though. Seeing Sarah with a girl... one that looks like her, acts like her...." His lips thin into a gentle, dreamy smile. "Yeah, I'd have another kid. A hundred of them. She's the best mother. Evander and Kenna are done for sure, though."

"Oh?"

"Yeah, Maeve hasn't been... easy."

"She's only one. How hard can that be? She can't even walk yet."

Sydney grits his teeth. "You know why we're here, right?"

I sigh, crossing my arms over my chest as I slouch in my chair and look down the table at my wife. "Dad mentioned something about the plan for succession for this new generation. That's what Ryatt called this... *reunion* for, I assumed."

Sydney chews his lip, his eyes ghosting over Evander. Kenna must be with their kids right now. "Maeve has powers."

"Already?"

Sydney nods. "You've missed a lot, Ryan."

Before I can ask what he means by powers, Sarah slides into a seat beside Sydney, giving him a look. "Your sons are driving me up the wall."

"Are they asleep?"

"Blake tried to stall, but he's out, for now." She reaches for his glass and takes a sip, winces, and sets it back on the table. "What are they talking about down there?"

I shrug. "I have no idea. I haven't been able to talk to my own mate all evening."

As if summoned, Evander starts walking toward us down the length of the long table. He sits down across from me, scratching his jaw as he reaches for the bottle of scotch resting between us. Sarah rises to investigate the group at the far end, bored with us already.

Sydney leans forward, sliding a glass in Evander's direction. I notice the lost look in his eyes, though, and ask, "What's everyone talking about down there?"

Evander drags his tongue across his lower lip. "Your mate," he says, his sharp green eyes meeting mine. "Her mother."

"What about her mom?" I remember Jerrod telling me about Gemma, who'd been a refugee from the Roguelands during the great war.

"She was loosely related to my mom," he says like he isn't sure he believes it yet. "A distant cousin, part of the same pack. Mom thought her entire pack was wiped out, that everyone died when Granite Rise was attacked by Kane's army. Gemma was a very close friend, and even Ella knew her. I guess they traveled together for a short time, before Ella and Ryatt linked up. Gemma was attacked by a hellhound trying to get… what was her name? Hannah, that's right. Trying to get Hannah to the coven."

I raise my brows. I've heard this story before. Ella used to tell us stories of her early adventures in Eastonia when we were kids whenever we gathered in Maatua for the Winter Solstice.

"Gemma was the friend who couldn't travel with them again because she was injured, so she stayed behind while Ella and Amanda left alone and got picked up by bandits, right?" Sydney asks.

Evander nods. "Mom still talks about her sometimes, so this is… shocking, to say the least."

I look down the table at Aviva, tucked between Amanda and Ella, Amanda's hand resting on her shoulder.

"I should have it seen right away," Evander says with a sigh. "The red hair, the dark, coppery eyes… they were pack traits. According to my mom, she and Gemma were the only ones without the red hair their pack was known for."

Aviva mentioned to me once, lying side by side in bed, that Mercy took after her mother with her dark, thick brown hair.

"Is Aviva doing okay?" I ask thickly. This has to be a lot to take in. Hell, I'm struggling with it myself. Is this why we're mates? It's a silly thing to wonder… why certain people are matched. Why people like Kenna and Evander became mates when they grew up in the same castles, raised by parents who were friends and also ruled together. There has to be more to it than fate, right?

Was Aviva chosen for me so I could lead her back to Amanda, giving Amanda and Ella a sense of peace they hadn't known for over two decades?

"She's tired," Evander says, tilting his head down the table.

"Yeah," I say into my drink, draining it, feeling the effects of it starting to hit my head, numbing the anxiety that's been simmering in my chest all day.

I rise, and Aviva instantly senses my movement and looks at me. She says something to Ella, Amanda, and my mother that I can't hear, and starts walking in my direction. I look around the room, taking in the familiar faces. Weeks ago, when I found out about this meeting, I'd dreaded it. The idea of being here with my family, the people who worried for me, cared about me... it was a lot. It was too much for me because, if I couldn't see past what I'd done to Hadley, how could they?

But no one looks at me like I'm a head case, like they still have to tread lightly around me, biting their tongues. In fact, I briefly meet my mom's eyes as I rest my hand on Aviva's back to guide her out of the room, and her smile mends something I hadn't realized was broken.

We walk through the private home of Ryatt and Ella, a mansion built within the castle itself. I guide an exhausted Aviva through the network of hallways and stairways leading to the levels of private apartments on the west side of the castle where my family has their own lodgings.

"How come you don't stay with your parents when you're here?" she asks sleepily, rubbing her eyes as I open the door to my private apartment. It's nothing more than a bedroom, a sitting room, and a bathroom, but it's beautiful.

"Getting your own quarters here in Moonrise was kind of a rite of passage in my family when we were growing up," I tell her, guiding her through the dark into the bedroom.

She moans slightly, shrugging out of her dress. "I've felt weird all day."

"It's the travel and... meeting my family, and all."

"Bed?"

This is something Aviva asks every night. It's like a reflex, and I'm not sure she even knows she's saying it to me when she does, but I nod. "Bed."

She falls asleep practically before she even hits the pillows, but I'm thrumming with nervous energy. I leave her in bed and head back out, walking three entire floors down to the sweeping veranda overlooking the city and the lake.

I'm not shocked to find my brother, Sarah, Kenna, and Evander on the veranda, resting in lounge chairs in the warm, night air.

"I thought you went to bed," Sarah says with a smile.

"Thought about it. I figured I'd find you all out here." I sit down on one of the plush chairs, rubbing my face before running a hand through my hair. They're all looking at me. I know what they're waiting for. Am I back? The old Ryan? "So, what do you think about her?"

Kenna and Sarah beam smiles bright enough to light the night sky. Evander and Sydney just stare at me, slightly smug, smirking their approval.

"I think we should go out to celebrate," Kenna says brightly, shifting her position to look at Sarah and Sydney. "A new club opened up this summer."

"Your father's been complaining about it," Evander cuts in, shaking his head at his mate. "He says it's seedy, and I agree."

"It is not! It's beautiful!"

"I could use a night out." Sarah breathes, clutching Sydney's hand. "I know you could, too."

Kenna is on pins and needles. I can't remember the last time we did this together—went out on the town. Danced. Partied.

It would have been that ball several years ago, when Sydney snuck Sarah back to my house, and Kenna nearly got kidnapped by Gabriel and was then saved by Evander.

"Wait, are you pregnant by chance?" Kenna asks Sarah.

"No. I'm not." Sarah shakes her head furiously in emphasis. Sydney snorts a laugh. "Are you?"

"Goddess, no."

"This is the first time in a long time one of us hasn't been pregnant," Sarah says, grabbing Kenna's hand. "We have to go out. There's no question about it."

Evander throws me and Sydney a pleading look to help put an end to this, but….

"I'm in."

"Me too." Sydney's eyes slide to Evander, the only hold out.

"Fine," he says, grumbling, but I can tell he's trying not to smile as he looks at his mate.

"Does Aviva like to dance?" Kenna asks.

I've only seen her dance once, at our hand-fasting. It was the most beautiful thing I've ever seen. "Yeah, she does."

38

NOT MY CIRCUS

Aviva

I WAKE TO FULL SUNLIGHT BURSTING THROUGH CEILING HEIGHT windows, warming the sheets covering a four poster bed. A cool morning breeze drifts through the open windows, ruffling the lace curtains as birdsong floats through the air.

It's like something out of a dream. I stretch, groaning with delight as my skin slides over satin sheets, and relax with a slump.

I slept like the dead.

But as I feel toward the opposite side of the bed, the sheets are cool and empty. I roll over and reach for the bedside table where a piece of paper is propped against a vase full of fresh flowers.

"There's breakfast down the hall in the pink room. I'll see you later this afternoon." I lie back with the note, smoothing my fingertip over the scribbles. Ryan has *terrible* handwriting. With a sigh, I roll out of bed and pad across the wide room. The carpet is soft, and the wallpaper is heavily detailed with intricate green and alabaster scrolls, trimmed with dark wood. The furniture is ancient. I run my fingers across a beautifully designed dresser, taking in the little carvings and details.

This place–this castle–it's incredible. It's something out of the legends told around the fire when I was a child.

I change into a loose fitting shirt I packed from the village. It's dark blue and hangs off one shoulder. I pull on what Ryan calls "shorts," which he explained are simply pants cut off around the knees. They're odd, but it's far too hot to wear much else. I slide my feet into my sandals and leave the room.

I have no idea what the "pink room" is, but I've barely stepped through the door when a flash of white-blonde hair catches my attention.

"Oh! I didn't think you were in there!" Sarah rushes toward me, carrying her youngest son, Liam, I think. He has a teddy bear clutched to his chest and a skeptical look on his cute face as they approach. "What are you up to?"

"Oh–breakfast, I think. Ryan left a note saying to go to the pink room."

"We're headed there now. Walk with me. You'll get lost otherwise." She chuckles. I fall in step beside her, and as we turn the corner, I spot Blake tumbling his way down the long, seemingly endless, hallway. Sarah smirks, rolling her eyes to mine as she motions to her oldest son. "I make them run around the halls first thing in the morning to burn some energy. This place is huge if you haven't noticed."

I look around, wondering just how far this one particular hallway stretches.

"Blake, right here," Sarah calls out, pointing toward a stairway that came out of nowhere. Blake slides across a red carpet runner and climbs up the stairs on all fours. Sarah sighs, giving me a wry smile. "You mentioned you have a six-year-old sister?"

"I do. Lora." A pang of grief strikes my chest. Goddess, I miss her. "She's just like him. Full of energy."

"So it never ends, does it?"

"No, I think it gets worse. I have a ten-year-old sister, too."

"Great," Sarah mumbles, but her eyes dance with amusement as we reach the top of the stairs and turn again, down another long hallway, but the smell of food is thick in the air, and voices drift from a set of open double doors.

Aris runs right into my legs in an attempt to tackle Blake, and before I even have a chance to step fully into the room, a riotous game of chase begins.

Kenna waves us over to a table drenched in sunshine. Glass doors overlook a deck with incredible views of the city below. I sit beside Sarah and feel…. "What is that?" I point to an almost transparent, glimmering sheet of light covering the open space where the doors to the balcony should be.

"It's to keep the kids off the deck." Kenna snaps her fingers, and the strange glimmers of light disappear. She snaps them again, and they return.

I flush, my fingers tingling with adrenaline as I slowly look at her. She's not even looking at me. She's trying desperately to get Maeve to try a strawberry, but Maeve is far more interested in chewing on the edge of the table.

"When are the guys supposed to be done with their meeting this morning?" Sarah asks as she plops Liam in the center of her lap.

"I'm not entirely sure." Kenna sighs, giving up on the strawberry and setting Maeve down on the ground. She promptly crawls away. "Evander said not to expect him back until noon."

I timidly reach for a platter of eggs, glancing back and forth between the women. "What's going on?"

They look at me, their faces washed in similar looks of defeat and uncertainty. Kenna especially. She chews the inside of her cheek for a moment before saying, "Succession."

Sarah nods.

"Succession?"

"Ryatt and Isaac are setting up the kids with their inheritances this week, which also means their future titles are being decided." Sarah smiles faintly, pouring herself a cup of coffee while Liam continues to sit on her lap, picking at his teddy bear. "It's nothing too serious." She glances at Kenna, however.

Kenna inhales as she looks at Maeve, who's clutching an ottoman, shrieking excitedly at the other kids as they run around the room.

"Kenna, it's going to be okay," Sarah says in a soothing voice, but Kenna's eyes start to water.

I feel like maybe I shouldn't be here for whatever conversation is about to take place. I barely know them. Something is obviously bothering Kenna to the point she's about to cry.

"Kenna?" Sarah says.

Kenna shakes her head, forcing a smile. "I'm fine."

"What's wrong?" the words slip out before I can stop them. Kenna's silver eyes meet mine, glassy with tears.

"I–Maeve is the first full-blooded Firestone witch born in over a thousand years. We just had her tested." She sniffles, swallowing what looks like a sob as she continues, "Her powers are–a lot, for someone so little. We've been having some problems back in Veiled Valley and…." She meets Sarah's eyes in a pained grimace. "I don't know what to do."

Sarah glances at me apologetically as Kenna bursts into tears.

Unsure what to do, I reach over and pat her back while Sarah whispers soothing things in her ear, all while the kids run around, screaming excitedly and tossing toys across the room at each other.

"Your mom is going to figure this out. The mystics are helping, Kenna. Maeve is going to be fine."

"She b-bursts into silver flames when she's upset about–about anything," Kenna sobs. "What's going to happen when she starts throwing t-t-tantrums? Will she burn the c-castle down? What if she spirits away again?"

"That happened?" I gape at them.

Sarah sighs heavily, stroking Kenna's hair. "Yeah, a few weeks ago."

"She was two miles away in the woods," Kenna sputters. "It took us over an hour to find her."

I stand, rubbing her back with more effort. *Holy shit.* The idea of a baby going through what I did yesterday is unfathomable. The idea that a baby has the ability to do it herself is… terrifying.

"She's going to have to stay here with Mom and Dad," Kenna says in an exasperated tone. "There's no other option. She's going to have to be kept contained until she's old enough to start training her powers, and that's–that's years away. I can't…. She's stronger than me already! There's nothing I can do!"

I look at the baby in question. She's gnawing on the ottoman now, drooling like mad. Her eyes meet mine–a bright sea-green. She smiles widely at me, all gums, and laughs sharply. On the outside, she looks like a perfectly innocent little creature–a regular baby. A really cute one.

I immediately wonder what my future baby with Ryan will look like, smiling to myself, and instantly banish the thought when Kenna chokes on another sob.

"Nothing has been decided yet, Kenna." Sarah soothes her, but her eyes meet mine. Suddenly, Sarah's voice pings through my skull. *'I know you don't understand any of this yet, but thank you for being here right now.'*

I nod, holding her gaze, too stunned and confused to speak.

Sarah continues raking her fingers through Kenna's hair, "There will be a solution soon. I know it."

"I'm going to have to leave her here. She's so much calmer here in Moonrise. She's literally made for this-this place. Her powers are so much easier to control here."

"Kenna." Evander's voice cuts through the fray of emotions and screaming children.

She immediately looks up, sniffling, and her mate's face is… so *broken.* He exhales, taking a single second to gather himself before walking over to her.

Sarah and I step out of his way, watching as he leads her out of the room while leaving their kids behind to continue playing with their cousins. Before I can think about what I'm doing, I reach down and scoop Maeve into my arms, bouncing her on my hip as she begins to fuss.

Then I remember this baby can apparently *burst into silver flames,* whatever that means, and gently set her back down on the floor, taking a step away.

"Welcome to the circus," Sarah grumbles, her hands on her hips. Circus indeed.

* * *

RYAN LOOKS STRESSED AS HE RIFLES THROUGH THE CLOSET IN OUR bedroom, pulling out several options of shirts and pants for himself.

"So… Kenna can turn into a literal shadow and has… fire power?"

"Pretty much," he says absently.

"And Sarah can manipulate time?"

"Yep."

"You're saying this so casually!"

"The longer you know us, the less weird this will be, I promise."

I rise from my perch on the end of the bed, hugging myself with my arms. "And Maeve might have to be separated from her parents? Is that what's happening?"

"No." But Ryan sighs heavily, bracing his hands on the dresser. "I don't think that's going to happen. From what I was told today, it sounds like Ryatt and Ella are trying to find a solution, maybe sending Kenna and her family back to Veiled Valley with a few witches to help out with Maeve, to try to contain the issue."

I nod, but I can't wrap my head around anything that's going on. My brain is literal mush as he turns to me, sighing, his shoulder slumping. "Do you want to get out of here?"

"Out of the castle?"

He nods, rolling his lip between his teeth. "I want to show you the city. I thought I'd have time earlier today, but I was woken up by Ryatt's voice in my head telling me to get my ass down to his office. I'm sorry I pretty much abandoned you this morning."

"You had a very good reason to." I laugh. To my relief, he laughs too, agreeing that this is just… insane. Most people have family drama, but his family takes it to another level. "I had a good time with Sarah and all the kids, anyway."

"We're going out tonight."

"What does that mean?"

"I'm taking you to have dinner in the city, just the two of us, and then we're meeting up with my brother, Evander, and the girls to go clubbing."

I've come to realize that whenever *"the girls"* are mentioned, it's Sarah and Kenna. I'm sure I fall into this category now, too. "Clubbing?"

"Dancing," he says matter-of-factly.

I arch a brow, sitting back on the bed as he edges a few steps in my direction. "Do you even dance?"

"I danced at our wedding."

"I wouldn't call that dancing. It was more like… dragging you around in a circle, watching you trip over your own feet."

He leans over me, caging me in. "I'd known you for four days when we got married, if you care to remember. Do you think I had time to learn the stupidly complicated dances your pack is known for?"

"Endova isn't known for our dances." I giggle. The sound turns into a soft moan as he dips his head, brushing his mouth over the side of my neck. I close my eyes as heat thrums through me, igniting that desperate desire that's been building for days now, unsatisfied.

He nips my neck, one of his hands pressing on my lower back to stop me from lying down. He has me right where he wants me and I'm… drowning in him. Everything else fades. The room around us ceases to exist. It's just me, and him, and–

"She's going to need something to wear," Kenna's voice erupts in his sitting room.

"The blue one, I think. Neither of us can fit into it anymore, not after the kids." Sarah and Kenna laugh as they close in on the bedroom.

"Shit," Ryan whispers, clicking his tongue in annoyance. "Remind me to lock that fucking door when we come home tonight."

39

SHE CAN DEFEND HERSELF

Ryan

THE CLUB ISN'T WHAT I THOUGHT IT WOULD BE. SURE, I'D HAD MORE than a few rowdy nights at the ancient taverns and inns scattered around the Roguelands drinking homemade beer and young whiskey, but this is….

"They're serious about a road system, then?" I ask over the thumping music, a mix of dark synth that makes my body believe it's back in Crescent Falls, not standing in a sea of black velvet, gold finishes, and strobe lights in the center of Moonrise.

Sydney sips his whiskey cocktail, nodding as he squints through the crowd to where Sarah, Aviva, and Kenna are currently tearing up the dance floor. "Ryatt put a council of Alphas together a few years ago, and they finally voted to allow the road system. It'll connect at the border with Crescent Falls, lead here, and across the rivers to Tarsian."

"Tarsian is already preparing for their own super-highway," Evander says beside me, turning with Kenna's forgotten cherry-flavored concoction in his hand. He sips it, grimaces as he drains the glass, then continues, "They're digging a route through the desert from Rifthold to Oasia, then down to the coastal territories."

This is huge news. For the past twenty years, since the veil fell, the leaders of Eastonia have balked at change at every corner, and Ryatt and Ella have respected that.

But a new generation is coming of age. Our generation. Young wolves raised in the cover of Eastonia's magic and remoteness want more. They've started filling Crescent Falls universities and setting up new lives outside of the Roguelands, and vice versa. Moonrise has a stellar medical university that draws large numbers of students from Crescent Falls, and the Roguelands are modernizing with every passing day.

Then there's my territory, the Deadlands. I'm not sure how I feel about this kind of change.

I don't have time to dwell on it. It's hard to focus while watching Aviva move amidst the crowd. I slowly sip my drink, my eyes locked on the way she moves, like the music is part of her, thrumming through the very marrow of her bones.

I've never seen anyone move like her. I knew she was a good dancer after our wedding night, but she'd been doing the traditional dances–fast, intricate steps and twirls that followed standard rhythms. This is... not that. This is purely *her*, moving her body in a way that feels right, in the way the sensual music demands. She's graceful in a way that doesn't feel real. It makes me want to pick her up and carry her to the nearest closet to see how she moves on top of my lap instead of with her feet planted on the lit dance floor.

She's wearing a bralette in rich golds and pale blues with a matching mini skirt. An outfit like this would've caused looks in Crescent Falls, but Moonrise, despite its age, has fashion that shows off the skin with ethereal cuts and fabrics. Strips of pale blue silk fall from her shoulders, down her back, as she turns to the music, her hips swaying, her arms stretched above her head.

Her eyes are closed, and she looks... lost. Totally, completely, lost within herself.

It's the most alluring thing I've ever seen.

But I'm not the only one watching her.

Sydney straightens beside me watching a group of men stand nearby, watching the girls with a particular interest that hasn't gone unnoticed to us–their mates and husbands.

While Aviva sways beautifully, Sarah and Kenna are moving like they've been drinking, which they definitely have. Sarah grabs Kenna's arm while they both giggle frantically, neither of them aware they're being encroached on.

But Aviva's eyes open to slits, holding my gaze.

I tip my drink back. She knows the guys are starting to move closer. She knows one of them is coming up behind her, biting his lip as he scans her body with a predator's gaze. She's a hunter, but she's also been hunted. She knows how it feels. Kenna and Sarah are moving back in our direction though, still giggling, without a care or worry in the world.

Evander, Sydney, and I watch the man decide he might have a shot with *my wife.*

"Are you going to do anything about that?" Sydney asks as the guy places a hand on Aviva's hip.

I set my glass on the bar we've been leaning against for the last half hour while our girls enjoy themselves and say, "I'll finish whatever she starts."

Sydney gives me a curious glance as Sarah sways into his waiting arms, but Evander is watching with a blank stare I know means he's just as interested in what's about to happen as I am.

Aviva whirls on the man, giving him what I'd consider to be a polite, "I'm uninterested, thanks," kind of shove.

He leans in, curling his hand around her wrist to say something into her ear over the music.

"Ryan," Sydney says under his breath, as if I'm not watching every second of this man touching my mate, feeling the way his hand is tightening around her wrist like it's my own bones scraping together.

Aviva looks at me, though, her eyes wide and bright in the strobing, dim lighting. She knows I'm not going to save her unless she really wants me to. Her slightly mischievous smile fades to a sneer as she lets her free hand fly and rakes her nails across the man's face in a vicious slap that echoes over the music.

"Oh, my gods," Evander chokes under his breath, his tone dripping with pride.

The man rears back in shock, then looks murderous as he grabs her arm and yanks her toward him.

"That's my cue." I kick off the bar wondering what it would feel like to crush this man's skull between my hands. Evander follows, but Sydney stays behind with Kenna and Sarah, who still haven't noticed what's going on. I count each step I take to stop the urge to shift and rip this man to shreds in the center of the club. Ten. It takes me ten, steady steps before I'm in front of him, my hand curling around his throat. "Would you like to explain why you placed your hands on my mate?"

Blood coats the man's cheek from three gashes where Aviva's nails torn his skin. Good girl. I'll reward her for that later.

He tries to choke out a reply as his friends move in to defend him but quickly step back when they realize the commander of their Alpha King's Ghost army is standing at my side, dressed in his usual black, his eyes locked on their every move.

I let the man go. He takes a single wobbly step backward then swings on me against his better judgment. My fist locks against the underside of his chin before his punch can even graze the air I'm breathing, and he goes down, his eyes rolling back in his head before he even hits the floor.

No one is dancing right now. Security guards move in but stop as Evander turns to them, his face ever blank and deadly serious.

I look at the man's friends, smiling kindly. "Be sure to tell him how lucky he is that I didn't allow my wife to finish him off because he wouldn't be waking up otherwise." They gape at me as I take Aviva's hand and lead her back to our family, the crowd parting to allow us to leave the dance floor.

"What just happened?" Kenna gasps as we rejoin Sydney at the bar.

Sarah inspects Aviva's nails, her eyes wide with shock. Sydney eyes graze Aviva's face before turning to mine for explanation.

'I feel like you left something out when telling us about her,' he says into my mind.

'That didn't even scrape the surface.' I accept the drink Evander hands to me, barely tasting it. Aviva is leaning against me, her ass pressed against my groin as she talks in low tones over the music with Sarah and Kenna.

The dancing begins again as if nothing happened, but Sydney seems on edge as he watches the dance floor, his arm roped around an increasingly sleepy Sarah's shoulders.

"I'm taking Kenna home," Evander says as his mate clutches his shirt, whispering what I assume are absolutely filthy things in his ear based on the dark look in his eyes. She sits on a barstool beside where he's standing, pulling him down to her level.

"We'll go with you," Sydney says with a nod then looks at me.

Aviva sips another fruity, sweet drink, moving absently to the music.

"We're going to stay for a while. I owe her a dance." My hand rests against her hip, my fingers drawing lazy circles on her naked skin above the waistband of her skirt. "We'll see you guys in the morning."

We watch them leave, neither of us saying a thing until they're out of sight in the swell of the crowd.

Aviva timidly looks up at me, a bit of a blush staining her cheeks. "What?" I ask, smirking down at her.

"You're not going to say anything?"

"About you nearly gouging that guy's eyes out? No. You could've done worse."

"In front of your family. Kenna and Sarah don't behave like that."

"Kenna could have flattened this entire club, and Sarah would have attacked his mind."

She rolls her eyes, taking another long drink from her glass. It's pink liquid, something with cherry blossoms sticking from the ice on a little sprig. I take it from her, sipping experimentally. "Not bad."

"Were you serious about that dance? You haven't danced all night." She turns into me, weaving her arms around my waist and propping her chin on my sternum. She's not this… cuddly… ever. I can't remember a single moment where she'd put her arms around me or even looked at me like she more than tolerates me in the company of others. On impulse, my hand rests on her back, warm and solid, pressing her closer.

"You've had a bit to drink. Are you sure you're up for it?"

"I want to stay here forever." She closes her eyes, her lips parted, as the song changes to something deep and rumbling, the music working its way into her every muscle.

I don't pride myself on being a dancer. It's hard at my size, and at clubs in the past, I'd enjoyed being danced for, whether I'd been standing with a smug look on my face or seated at a booth in a VIP section, but Aviva makes me want to move… just not like this.

The only thing I can think about as she grinds against me is getting her somewhere private. Somewhere quiet and empty, where it's just us and not hundreds of prying eyes watching while I bend her over a sink, or a crate of booze, or right here, in the center of the crowded dance floor.

Her body is flush with mine, damp with sweat, and her touch is like fire as she turns to the music. Watching her has me in a trance I'm not sure I have the strength to snap out of.

Aviva is everything that ever peaked my interest, everything I'd lusted after, and everything I'd ever loved in one person. I am obsessed with her, to put it plainly, and I'm feeling pretty good about myself for being able to hold back and not keep her tied to my bed like I've been dreaming about.

But the second she turns to me again, her skin golden and glowing under the strobe lights, a bead of sweat rolling between her breasts…. "Come here," I manage to say, my voice gravelly and low as I guide her through the crowd.

I know she can feel it too. This insane, mind-numbing pull driving my actions. She hasn't stopped touching me since I let her guide me back to the dance floor. I can't take it anymore. Neither can she, which is apparent the moment I burst through a door in a back hallway that ends up being a private bathroom, where we scare the hell out of a couple that had a similar desire for privacy.

"*Out*," I snarl.

The man's eyes go wide as he yanks his date out of the room. A second later, Aviva's mouth is on mine, my back against the door, my fingers fumbling for the lock. The room is dimly lit with red walls and dark finishes. A faint glow comes from the light above the sink, but that's it.

I don't care about the room. I don't give a shit about the fact I'm about to fuck my wife in a bathroom at a seedy club when she deserves a bed, preferably with a nice, firm mattress and–

"What–Aviva–" I choke out when her teeth nip at my neck, her hands traveling down the length of my abdomen, toward my belt. But she's starting to kneel, dragging rough kisses down even further until her tongue drags over the V of muscles on my lower belly.

I grip her shoulder. "You don't have to do that."

"I want to."

"Do you know... how?"

"Freya told me."

"How would she know–*fuck*...." I grip her shoulders, preparing to haul her upright, as she pulls my pants down enough to free my cock. "Aviva–"

"You've done this for me." She purrs, and then her tongue is sliding up my length and I'm...

I'm in love.

I'm fucking head over heels in love with her.

4 0

ALL THE WAY IN

Ryan

My fingers wind through Aviva's hair as she kneels, rising on her knees. I should tell her to stop. A very small, insignificant part of me is begging to haul her upright and service her first, like a gentleman, but under the haze of the dim lighting and thrum of music vibrating up through the floor, I'm not feeling very gentlemanly.

My eyes flutter closed at the sensation of her hands pressing against my thighs, her nails pinching my skin. This has to be some kind of dream state. My entire body jerks as her tongue glides up my shaft a second time in a slow, drawn out taste. She's testing me. I know if I open my eyes, she'll be looking up at me with that whiskey gaze that will have me spilling myself on her chest within seconds, and she hasn't even fully taken me in her mouth yet.

I'm fucked.

"Aviva," I choke out, my head rolling to the side against the door at my back.

"Hmm?" She hums as she guides the head of my cock between her lips. It's enough to send a jolt of electricity shooting down my spine.

Beyond words, the only sounds that leave my mouth are guttural, choked groans. I tighten my grip on her hair in an effort to control her pace, to keep her from trying to take all of me. But I feel an odd sensation starting to burn to life in my chest. It's like there's a little voice in my head, whispering in my ear to let go, to let her do this, to unleash myself like she wants.

I saw that glint of curiosity in her eyes when I showed her my beast form. It had been against my will. I was going to shift into that form that night regardless of if I had a moment to warn her, and I feel that same sensation now.

She is my mate. *My fucking mate.* Those golden threads binding us together sing in triumph when I loosen my grip on her hair and allow her to swallow me whole.

"*Goddess, yes.*" I bite down on the words, groaning like the breath is being knocked from my lungs. Aviva's hands tighten their grip on my thighs as she holds me there, taking all of me like she's built for this, built for me, every inch.

She pulls back, the head of my cock sliding over her tongue in a way that has a pleasure I've never known rolling through my body, making it impossible to focus on anything but her, on her mouth, on the way her hands slide up to assist.

My hands find her hair again. I've lost control. I can feel my restraint slipping with each moan that escapes her lips around my cock as I start fucking her mouth.

I open my eyes to heavy slits, pulling hard on her hair so she has to open wider, taking me deeper. "Is this what you want?"

Her eyes water, but she nods, her body trembling with heat I can feel in my own body. Her pleasure is tuned to mine, and I've only slept with her... twice. Only twice—because this is insane. No one talks about this. This brutal, all-encompassing ache that makes me want to do depraved things to the woman worshiping me on her knees right now. I know she's wet as fuck at the moment. I watch with hooded, heavy eyes as she rubs her thighs together, mewling around my dick as I drag myself out again, hissing out a breath at the unreal suction she can create with that unhinged mouth of hers.

There isn't a single rational thought in my mind. I feel... overwhelmed. My wolf and the beast are at odds, both begging for their turn, one wanting to mark her... one wanting to consume her. To get under her skin.

It's too much. I'm losing my grip.

Pleasure builds in a blinding way, blooming through the base of my spine and causing my muscles to lock and shake.

"Wait," I choke, grabbing her shoulder to push her away, but she pumps her hands harder, swirling her tongue over the head of my cock before taking me so deep I swear I'm transported to heaven, to the gates of the Goddess's kingdom, and it's not a white wolf waiting for me.

It's Aviva, naked, tied to my bed.

I spill myself down her throat, crying out her name like it's the last word that'll ever leave my lips. She holds herself there with me buried all the way down her impossibly tight throat. She whimpers as I pull out, shaking with her own pleasure.

She rises, wiping her mouth on the back of her hand, and gazes into my eyes with a look that has blood rushing right back into my cock. I press my thumb against her swollen lower lip, fighting the insane urge to bend her over and take her right here on the floor.

Her heart is beating impossibly fast. She's in heat. That's been obvious from the moment I finally claimed her body as mine in the woods that day. Whether by coincidence, or something brought on by our bond clicking into place, this is happening now, and I don't think I can hold back this time.

* * *

Aviva

Ryan keeps his eyes locked on mine as he roughly pulls up his pants. He looks like he's on the verge of shifting–the way his eyes glow. The way his canine teeth are slightly elongated and gleaming in the dim amber light washing us both in gold. I can hear my heartbeat pounding in my ears, and inside, my wolf is begging, absolutely begging, for me to just get on my knees and turn around, to let him fuck me like an animal on the floor in a bathroom. To breed me.

I'm out of my mind.

His fingers lace with mine as he wordlessly leads me out of the bathroom, out of the club, and into the humid summer night air. The city passes in a blur. I can't tell if we're running or walking. My mind is locked on the idea of him being inside of me to the point I'm starting to physically ache from the absence of him buried between my legs.

I barely realize we're walking along the side of the castle, through a set of gates, and up a set of narrow, stone stairs until he pushes through a door, and his apartment fades into view.

His scent is overwhelming. Hot and spiced, it works its way through my body, causing me to tremble as he comes up behind me, nuzzling my hair away from my neck while his hands roughly grope my breasts, kneading through the fabric of the beaded bralette. He tears the fabric from my body like it's made of paper. Beads ping across the room, bouncing off the furniture. "Ryan, please," I beg, my voice high and tight as he rolls my nipples between his fingers.

His free hand moves down my belly, his fingers sliding between my skirt and my skin. "All I've been thinking about," he rasps against my ear, his body trembling as he roughly slides two fingers between my wet, aching folds, "is how easy it would have to been to fuck you in the middle of that dance floor, with all of those people around to watch."

My eyes roll back in my head as he hooks his fingers, the heel of his hand rubbing my clit in just the right way. His hand leaves my breasts to close around my throat. I tighten around his fingers, spasming already, pleasure washing through me and leaving me breathless. He rasps out a dark chuckle, nipping my earlobe. "Needy little wolf. I've been catching your scent all night. You want me inside of you, don't you?"

"I do!" Tears sting the corners of my eyes as he continues thrusting his fingers inside of me at a slow, teasing pace that has me writhing in his grasp.

"I'm going to knot in you," he warns, breathing heavily, his teeth racking down my teeth, sharp enough to break the skin if he's not careful.

But I don't want him to be careful. Not tonight. I want him rough and totally, utterly out of his mind.

"It'll hurt," he continues darkly, dragging his fingers out of me to slowly circle my swollen, aching clit with his thumb. "But I think you can handle it, can't you?"

He claps his hand over my mouth as he bites down hard on my shoulder. Not hard enough to break the skin, but enough to give me a taste of what's coming. He's going to mark me.

He suddenly lets me go, taking a step away from me. I turn, breathless, and find him slowly undoing the buttons on his shirt. "Take off your skirt."

I hook my thumbs under the waistband and pull, shimmying out of the fabric. My breasts bounce with the effort, and his eyes rake over my nearly naked body. He curses under his breath, his eyes going nearly black as his pupils expand. "Get on the bed. On your knees."

I think my heart might actually be stopping. I obey. All rational thought has left the building and my brain is totally, completely empty as I walk into the bedroom and crawl onto the bed, resting on my knees like he commanded.

I close my eyes to better feel the sensation ricocheting through my body, through my very soul. My mate is coming up behind me. I can feel his dark, unhinged desire and excitement through the bond. The bond thunders in my chest like it has its own heartbeat, like it's the only thing keeping me upright at the moment because my heart is beating out of control.

His hand presses firmly on my back so I'm forced down, my breasts pressing into the satin duvet. My nipples harden at the sensation of the cool, silken fabric brushing over my skin. I whimper a moan, trembling as he snaps the thin little pair of panties I'm wearing against my hip.

He rips them off. I almost come just from that.

Then, he's binding my wrists together with them, my arms crossed behind my back.

The first actual thought that has entered my mind since he closed us into that bathroom at the club whispers through my head. He's not going to hurt me. Well, I might feel pain, but he's not going to *hurt* me. I trust him. He trusts me. Whatever he does, I want equally as bad as he does. I can handle this. I can take this.

He climbs onto the bed behind me, taking a ragged breath as his hands move over the globes of my ass and down my back, checking that my wrists are still firmly bound together.

"I'm going to mark you."

"I know," I say shakily, finding it hard to swallow.

"Do you want a say in where?"

I shake my head from side to side, desperate for his cock. He has it resting against my ass. I feel it twitch–hard, hot, and heavy–and it's almost too much to bear.

"P-please," I whimper. I'm already so close to unraveling already, and he hasn't touched me in what feels like an entirety when it might have been only a minute or two.

Wetness slides down my thighs. I rub them together, grinding against him in emphasis. He grips my thighs, sliding his cock up, and down, through the wetness before thrusting into me with a groan that echoes off the walls. The bed quakes. He grips my thighs hard enough to leave bruises. One thrust, I'm done for.

I bite the sheets and arch my back, taking him deeper, loving the stretch and fullness of him buried inside of me.

He pulls out halfway and rocks into me again so deep I'm seeing stars. "The way you were dancing on me tonight, Aviva?" He hisses out the words as he pulls out slowly, drawing out a pitched moan from my lips. "I nearly lost control. I couldn't stop thinking about your pussy." He bites down on the words, cursing softly under his breath as I swirl my ass into his hips.

My toes curl as he starts getting rougher, his movements less fluid and spurred by pure feeling. He braces one hand on my hip while the other snakes up my neck and into my hair, tugging in the same way I know he likes his hair pulled, and I understand why. That glimmer of pain is a rush. It rewires my brain. It has pleasure blooming to life so deep in my body I feel it in the marrow of my bones, my soul.

"Gods, you're so fucking tight," he groans as my inner walls clench hard around his cock. "Oh, Baby, fuck, you have no idea what you're doing to me right now."

"More," I beg, panting the word like my lungs are begging for air. "I want more of you."

He chuckles low in his throat, slamming into me so hard the sound of skin meeting skin bounces through the room in rhythm with his thrusts.

Just as I'm starting to unravel again, he reaches down and unbinds my wrists. He lowers his body onto mine, pressing me into the mattress, rolling his hips against my ass, reaching the deepest parts of me that send pleasure I've never known coiling to life. "You like that, don't you?" He hums over the soft, pitched moans escaping my mouth. His lips brush over my shoulder as his muscles start to tighten, and his thrusts start to slow, like he's holding back all of the sudden.

But then he's pressing deep again, holding himself there while my hips arch upward on instinct. "Move with me," he says in a near whisper, breathless.

I do. I meet him thrust for thrust, loving the slow rhythm and the tender kisses he presses to my shoulders and back. He hooks an arm under me and nibbles at my shoulder blade, then along the base of my neck and upper spine.

Deep, aching pleasure ignites in my lower belly, spreading to the point I can't ignore it. He can feel it, too. He knows I'm close.

And he's close, too.

"It's going to hurt. I can't stop it once it starts."

"What will?"

41

KNOT NOW

Aviva

"I CAN'T–YOU'RE IN HEAT. IT'S MY BEAST. IT WANTS YOU BRED, AND I'm–" He starts to pull out, but I stop him, writhing in a way I know he loves. "Fuck, Aviva. Goddess, you're making this–impossible."

"I'm going to come," I whimper, begging him not to stop. "Please, don't stop–"

"You're not on contraceptives," he groans, sounding like himself for the first time since I led him out to dance. "I'll get you pregnant. Right now, Aviva. It'll happen now."

"Please?" Something in my voice breaks. It's like… like I'm letting go of something, something that I let myself bury. A fear of mine only he has ever seen.

But I trust him. Whatever comes. He'll be beside me. I meet his eyes over my shoulder. His lips part, and his gaze is depthless, full of emotion I can't name.

He pulls me close, pressing me into the sheets, and bites down on my shoulder blade so hard he breaks the skin. My vision goes white with blinding light, with what has to be actual stars, as pleasure explodes through my entire body. I scream his name to the ceiling as his teeth sink into my skin, drawing blood, and then I feel… pressure. An intense, almost painful stretch. He grunts, crushing me to his body and rolls us onto our sides with his cock still buried deep inside of me and growing… larger at the base. I can't move. We're locked together, and he's trembling, lacing his fingers in mine as he presses a shaky, tender kiss to the mark he just left on my skin.

He's knotting me. I've heard about this act. This ancient act between mates. *Only between mates, and not even all mates can do it.*

I draw in a sharp breath when the pain becomes too much. He slides a hand between my legs, drawing circles over my clit until that pain turns to pleasure.

"What a good girl," he rasps, gently rocking his hips against my ass. I start panting, losing my breath entirely. It's impossible that I'm about to come again, right? "Come for me one more time, Baby. I want to feel you come on my knot." His voice is deep and strained, like he's in pain or the deepest throes of pleasure, I'm not entirely sure which. I think it's the latter based on the way he trembles.

I lean into him, my back flush with his chest. We're slick with sweat, and my brain is in shambles as his fingers work me into another full-body stupor. My inner walls clench around him, and I cry out from the mingled pain and pleasure of it. It's like nothing I've ever felt before, and I'm drowning in ecstasy when I finally fall back into my body.

Ryan is beside himself as I slump against him, trembling like I'm fevered. He gathers me closer, if that's even possible, hooking his arms around my chest and burying his face in my hair.

I watch the curtains sway in the warm summer breeze. The stars are bright, and ribbons of purple lace through the air, the moon nearly full again. Has that much time passed since our wedding already? Exhaustion sweeps over my spent body. I fall asleep with his cock still buried inside of me and wake up several hours later to him curled around me, both of us totally naked on top of the duvet cover in the same positions we'd fallen asleep in.

It's raining. Sharp pinging sounds fill the room, creating the coziest setting. The colors of the opulent room are muted now in the first hours of the morning, but there's some light coming through the windows, enough for me to know we'd slept, at least for a little while.

Ryan's hand is splayed over my naked stomach. I move experimentally, not wanting to sacrifice any of his warmth, but wanting to know if he's still inside of me, stuck there, hours later. He's not.

My skin pebbles from the wet, rainy chill in the room. His hand tightens for a moment.

"Are you cold?" he whispers against my skin.

"Did I wake you up?"

"No, I don't think I've been totally asleep." He rises up on an elbow as I sit up, allowing him to shift our positions so we're under the covers instead of on top of them. Tucked up beside him in the warm sheets, I roll to face him, nestling my face in the crook of his shoulder.

But our hands are moving like we can't stop touching each other. He's hard again, his cock pressed against my belly. His mouth finds mine in a slow, tender kiss as he guides his cock through my folds. My breath catches in my throat. I'm sore and bruised, but he's slow and gentle this time. There's no blinding lust guiding our movements. He's not peppering me with praise. This… isn't because of our bond. We're not being driven by biology and other feelings neither of us can explain. This is just for us.

He rolls on top of me, moving his hips over mine in slow, deliberate thrusts honed to my pleasure. His eyes are heavy and hooded with sleep, but he's watching me with an expression so tender it nearly brings tears to my eyes. Another stroke of his cock has my muscles tightening and heat coiling through the base of my spine. When I arch into an orgasm, it's not blinding. It's soft and warm, making me feel relaxed all over. I'm not seeing stars this time as I come down from the clouds. I'm seeing him smiling sleepily down at me, his cheeks ruddy and eyes full of… full of…

"I love you, Aviva," he whispers, dipping his head to steal my moan with a kiss.

"I love–love you," I echo, tangling my fingers in his hair. He trembles as the words fall from my tongue. "I love you. I want to–to mark you."

Still moving inside of me, savoring me riding out my orgasm on his cock, he nods, his breath hitching as he starts to tremble with his own impending release.

I press gentle kisses to his neck and shoulder, dragging my teeth across his skin. I feel my canines lengthen. Later, I'll probably think back on the moment and wonder about the logistics of our bond, and how my body knows exactly what to do, but right the only thing taking up space in my mind is how he rasps my name as I break the skin just below his collarbone, biting and sucking a half moon scar while he comes inside of me.

He doesn't knot me. I don't think I could handle it again, not right now, but that doesn't mean I don't want it. I remind myself that we have time.

We have our entire lives.

We fall asleep again in each other's arms, and we don't wake until half of the day has passed, the world outside our bedroom moving on without us.

* * *

Ryan draws circles on my thigh. I'm sprawled over his lap in his uncle Ryatt's office, and Maeve is asleep on my chest. I'm not sure how we ended up in this position, but I'm nodding off to the conversation taking place in low, serious tones nearby, my head propped on the armrest.

Ryan's touch moves down to my ankles. I'm lying on him, in front of his family, but no one is paying me any mind, honestly. Plus, he was the one who decided to sit here after I'd claimed the couch, and Kenna had plopped an exhausted Maeve in my lap before leaving the room. He simply lifted up my legs, sat down, and righted them again.

He's watching Ryatt, Isaac, Granger, Sydney, and Evander stand in various positions around Ryatt's desk, where Ryatt is leaning, his hands braced on the dark wood as they look down at two huge maps.

"Sydney is first in line, obviously," Isaac says, drawing a finger over what I think is a map of Crescent Falls. "Blake is second in line to the throne, then Liam, and whatever children come next. Ryan still has a claim if the three of them, and any future children born to Sarah, step down."

"Liam will inherit Shadowcrest," Sydney says, and Isaac nods.

"Misty has no territory as it stands," Isaac says almost absently. "She hasn't shown interest yet."

"We don't need to worry about that until she marries," Ryatt replies, and apparently Isaac agrees.

The conversation moves on to Brie and Aris.

Ryatt seems conflicted about Brie, but Aris is being called the "Shadow Prince," which means little to me. I've never been to Veiled Valley and can barely comprehend the powers Ryatt and Kenna share, but it's obvious that Aris will inherit the secretive pack tucked far away in the mountains, cut off from the rest of Eastonia.

Ryatt seems keen to not talk about Brie quite yet. I watch the men begin to move away from the desk, mentioning something about dinner starting, that they'll continue this conversation there, but Ryan doesn't make any moves to join them.

Evander gently lifts Maeve off my chest. She doesn't wake up and slumps against his shoulder as he gives me a tight but thankful smile for my help.

I glance at Ryan and notice him holding Ryatt's gaze. Within seconds, it's just the three of us in the room.

"Obviously your future kids will rule the Deadlands," Ryatt says with a wave of his hand toward where we're sitting on the couch.

I straighten into a seated position, swinging my legs off my mate's lap.

Ryatt clears his throat as he moves to the front of his desk, leaning his hip against it as he crosses his arms. He checks his watch, glancing at the door as the knob turns, and Ella walks in, flipping her dark hair over her shoulder. She's wearing a nice outfit–pants and a sleeveless shirt in emerald green that brings out the stunning shade of her eyes. The same eyes Maeve has. A Firestone trait.

"Sorry I'm late," she rushes out, throwing us an apologetic smile before giving Ryatt a quick kiss on the cheek, but Ryatt and Ryan are still staring at each other like they're having a conversation through the mind-link.

Ryatt blinks, nods, and shrugs. I wonder if Ryan told him about everything happening between the tribal packs, not that Ryatt would see the need to intervene. It's not like our infighting affects his kingdom at all.

But my gaze sweeps from them to Ella. During dinner two nights ago, I'd noticed the fine, pale scars across her forehead. Now they seem to glow, giving me a better idea of what they are.

I can speak the old Firestone language, of course. Most people in the Deadlands can. Reading and writing it is a different story. It's complicated, and a lot of the symbols have been lost to time, but I made an effort to learn so I could be better than Mercy in something, anything, when it came to our schooling.

"The Firestone mask," I say out loud, then quickly pinch my lips shut.

Ella whips her head toward me, and I want nothing more than to run out of the room. "Yes." She runs her fingers over her forehead, looking slightly embarrassed.

My stupid mouth won't stop moving. "The divine system of charting."

She arches a brow. "What?"

"The symbols," I say, my voice breaking. I can feel Ryan looking at me. Ryatt, too, straightens. "Uh, on your forehead. It's a... map, kind of."

Ella looks at Ryatt with a confused but slightly excited expression before turning back to me. "You can read these symbols?"

"Yeah. Can't you?"

She shakes her head. Even Ryatt looks perplexed as he takes a step in my direction. "No one, not even our historians and mystics, knows what they mean. How do you?"

"We–We speak the old tongue in my village." *Why won't I just shut up?* "I'm not the best at reading the old language, but those symbols are obviously the numerical values of the Seven Forges. The entire Firestone numerical system is based on the… on the latitudinal and longitudinal locations of the forges… from the legends," I quickly add, wondering if they believe me. I'm not sure I believe in the forges, the mythical cauldrons where the early gods made their weapons and divine gifts.

"The forges?" Ella is stunned. "There're… seven?"

"I doubt there are anymore," I say with a nervous laugh. "They disappeared when the Firestone empire fell…." I feel everyone's gazes raking over my face. I look to Ryan, who seems stunned, and slightly… suspicious. "What? How do you all not know this and you rule? Does anyone in the Roguelands and Moonrise know how to read the old tongue?"

"No," Ryatt says gravely. "The previous Alpha Kings made sure of that."

I gape, unsure what to say.

"What do the symbols mean?" Ella asks politely, but I can feel the buzzing, nervous energy flooding off of her.

"Well… it's about the Divine Seven, the templars of the Goddess. One forge for each object. The Firestone Mask. The Diadem of Starlight. The Blade of Time. The… Shadow Sword." My eyes meet Ryatt's as he stiffens. "Then there's the Book of Whispers and the Gilded Bow, but not much is known about those. Uhm…"

"The seventh?" Ryatt holds my gaze.

"The Baetyl." The old tongue slides from my tongue. I swallow the word back. We're not even supposed to say the word out loud.

Ryatt doesn't even blink. His eyes hold mine. "The Gate of the Gods?"

I nod.

Ella looks at her mate in confusion. Ryatt rolls his lower lip between his teeth, pondering something.

Ryan looks from them, to me, and back to them. "What the fuck is happening right now?"

42

WHAT ARE HER POWERS?

Ryan

THERE ARE ONLY THREE THOUGHTS IN MY HEAD AT THE MOMENT, ALL OF them intertwined. The first being that I'm starving. The second, that I'd like to eat, preferably as soon as possible, so I can haul my wife over my shoulder and carry her back to our bed to continue what we'd started last night.

And finally, I do not like the look on Ryatt's face as he gazes at my mate like she's the answer to a riddle that's been plaguing his mind for decades.

At almost fifty, Ryatt still looks youthful and dangerous. He's at his most powerful, from the whispers I've heard from my parents and close family acquaintances. He looks like a walking, talking angel of death with his shadows creeping between his fingers as he grips his desk, his silver eyes locked on Aviva.

Something just changed, I know that for certain.

"The G-Gate of the Gods," Aviva says, standing, looking down at me with a pink sheen covering her cheeks like she's embarrassed, maybe even a little nervous to be speaking to my aunt and uncle. "It's a–well. The legends are all different, I guess. In most, the gate is a depthless well where the demons who hunted the Goddess and Her people were thrown and sealed inside, long ago. I don't know about the other legends, uhm, because it's bad luck to talk about it."

"Why?" Ryatt asks in a clipped tone that sends a shiver down my own spine.

Aviva tenses, rolling her lower lip between her teeth. I stand up beside her, not liking the feelings coasting through our bond right now. She's scared of Ryatt. She doesn't know him like I do.

"Because it's said to be a gate to the underworld, where everything was locked away just before the Firestone empire fell. Curses, dark magic, demons...." She tilts her head from side to side, glancing at Ella before continuing, "When I kill rogues, I say a prayer to the Goddess and ask for their souls to be sent to Her instead of the Baetyl. We believe rogues and hellhounds are created with some of the magic that might have escaped the Baetyl when it was sealed and... it's silly. It's something told to children if they're misbehaving," she rambles, laughing nervously. "It's not real."

Ella is watching her with rapt attention. She looks at Ryatt, letting him lead, probably putting questions in his head.

But Ryatt is stone faced and serious as he asks, "Where is it?"

"The Baetyl?" Aviva chokes on the word. "It's not real. I have no idea."

"But if it were, where would it be, based on the legends?"

"The land split by rivers," she says quietly, glancing nervously at Ella. "A land of plenty. A land where the springs never run dry. That's all I know. The legends never say. But... there is a song."

"A song?"

Aviva looks down at her feet, closing her eyes like she has to dig through her memories to find it. "I don't remember all the words, but it spoke of dark times when a curse swept through the sacred land and chased the magic away. The Goddess dropped Her veil of starlight to contain it, but it was too late. The curse turned the green hills and valleys to dust, where nothing grows, where the ground is too hot and the sun burns. The curse came from the Baetyl because someone opened it, and let it out." Aviva opens her eyes.

Ryatt is staring at her so intensely it makes my skin prickle with anger. Recognition flashes behind his eyes, and he nods, looking down at his shoes as he turns to his desk. "Thank you, Aviva. Ella, please take her to the dining room. I'm sure everyone is wondering where you are."

I start to turn with them to leave, but he says, "Not you, Ryan."

Ella catches my eyes as she and Aviva leave the office, throwing me an apologetic but tight smile, one that doesn't touch her eyes.

Dread burrows through my chest as I turn to face my uncle. "What the fuck was that about? You scared the hell out of her–"

"What are her powers, Ryan?"

"She doesn't have powers," I grind out, hating his tone. It's like ice, sharp and bitter cold.

He turns to me. "What are her powers?" he repeats sternly.

"You would be able to sense them in her," I bite out, losing my patience entirely. "You and I both know there's nothing there. She's my mate, for Goddess' sake! I would feel that in our bond."

"She's different from other wolves. You must feel that." He's speaking to me like a child right now which only fuels my growing anger. What the fuck is his problem?

"I don't know what you want me to say."

"What can she do?" His eyes are almost pleading. There's an edge to his voice I don't think I've ever heard before. Ryatt, while sometimes terrifying, has always been... *mostly* serious. He wasn't always stern, like Dad. He allowed some flickers of emotion to show behind his eyes, unlike Dad. Dad only allowed Mom to see that side of him, which now that I'm mated, I understand, but Ryatt?

He was the fun uncle. The one who built sandcastles and tossed us in the ocean when the family vacationed together in Maatua. He allowed us to be rough, annoying little boys and delinquent teenagers. He knew we'd come to Moonrise for visits and immediately sneak out to drink and party, and he allowed it, but always followed it up with a vicious training session the next morning that had me and Sydney regretting every sip we'd taken.

He was easy to read, at least to me. I gravitated to him growing up, often seeking his company and advice over others. I trusted him.

I still do.

But something's wrong.

And somehow, I suddenly know exactly what he wants me to say. "She's incredible, and I'm not just saying that because she's my mate, or because I love her, but she's…" I bite my lower lip and sink onto the couch, exhaling deeply. "The first time I saw her, she was teaching her younger sisters how to hunt. I ended up with an arrow in my shoulder and she defended those little girls from me. It didn't matter that I backed off the second I realized that it had been a child, an accident, but there was something in her eyes that made me feel… like I was in serious danger around her…" I trail off, pulling those early memories forward, dusting off the details. "We went hunting together. I'd been invited on her pack's spring hunt and chose to follow her against my better judgment and we both nearly got killed. There was a hellhound on her trail. It was hunting her…had been for a while, I believe. There was something different about this—this thing. It wasn't tethered to a witch. It was driven by something else, something instinctual. I shifted into my beast and killed it." I meet his eyes.

Ryatt watches me talk without so much as blinking.

I lick my lips, continuing, "After we were married, and I took her home to Silverhide, we had to spend the night on the road. That night, she left camp, and I found her a few miles away and watched her… kill three rogues and it was… not a normal sight."

"How did she do it?"

"She can shift like I've never seen anyone shift before. It's quick." I snap my fingers in emphasis. "That fast. She moved in both her human and wolf form, shifting between them in a millisecond, killing all three before they even realized she was there. She's drawn to bows and arrows, mostly, but skilled with her knife. She didn't kill them with teeth or her claws. She just moved in her wolf form and shifted back to make the kill, and then again, and again."

I remember feeling like I was dreaming when I watched her do that. I'm still not entirely sure I wasn't.

Ryatt turns from me and walks behind his desk, sitting down with a low groan. Finally, he drops that icy mask and levels me with a look as he blows out his breath. "There's a lot we don't know."

"About what?"

"Eastonia, and the early people who lived here before the veil. Alpha King Kane finished the crusades his predecessors started, destroying the history of our kind's origins. We know so little about the Firestone witches, so little about Shadowsyngers, and the mystics, and other shifters who once roamed alongside our wolves. But the Deadlands?" He grits his teeth. "Those tribal packs…? They were far enough away from the carnage taking place in the Roguelands, Rifthold, and Tarsian that they stayed untouched and cut off from the war. The Deadlands are dangerous, which you know. It's like the landscape protected them, kept them sheltered, when the rest of Eastonia went to war. They essentially live in a time capsule."

"What are you getting at?"

"That Aviva and her people are possibly an ancient type of wolf, something different from us." He leans forward over his desk, suddenly excited. "Your aunt has spent the last two decades trying to uncover what exactly she is, cataloging everything we can find out about the Firestone witches. We know they had guards… wolves with skills like the Ghosts have now, but with very little training needed. They were just like that–impeccable warriors. Strong. Fearless."

"Like my mate."

"Yeah." He leans back, tapping his knuckles on the desk as he loses himself in thought. "Ella mentioned being drawn to Aviva, like some natural force. I didn't think anything of it, chalking it up to Aviva being the daughter of her old friend, but then I saw her with Maeve just now. Maeve doesn't fall asleep in anyone's arms anymore, not even her own parents'. She's weary and skeptical of strangers. But she was comfortable with Aviva, trusting her enough to rest her cheek on your mate's chest, and sleep. She knew what the symbols on Ella's skin meant. There's so many books and ancient tomes in the library that we've never been able to translate–"

A heavy, twisting feeling settles in my stomach. "No."

Ryatt stares at me, conflicted. "She might belong here, with Ella and Maeve. She might be our answer to Maeve–"

"No," I repeat. "I don't care what she is, or what this means, or about the forges or the Bae–fuck, whatever it's called. She is not staying in Moonrise. She is not getting tested for powers. She is coming home with me."

"It should be her decision."

"And I will allow her to make it," I say in clipped tones that drop as I draw out the words. "But she won't. I already took her from her pack. I won't allow you to separate us. I already lost a mate, and I'm not doing it again."

Ryatt watches me stand up and turn for the door.

"There's been reports out of Tarsian," he says loud enough to stop me in my tracks. "Alpha King Jaxon says there's some unrest, but he has it handled. Your territory runs along their southern border."

"It sounds like that's Alpha Jaxon's problem–"

"There's been a shift, Ryan. Ever since Gabriel and his coven started making moves, both Ella and I have felt it. An unrest, an uneasy feeling in our magic, like a warning, and it didn't go away after Sydney killed Gabriel. I need you to be prepared."

"Prepared for what?" I turn to him with a scowl.

"Whatever's coming," he says, holding my gaze.

I want to ask him if he wants my mate as some kind of specialized warrior. If he wants to keep her here to take her apart and find out what makes her tick, what gives her her skills, and how it can benefit our family, his kingdom. To see if she can unlock the secrets of our kind and why our family has the power we do. Maybe my anger is displaced, but for the first time, I feel like I have something that's mine, just mine, and I intend to keep it that way.

"It's good that the Deadlands have been historically left out of conflict, then." I turn for the door again, throwing it open and storming out into the empty corridor.

43

AM I A MONSTER?

Aviva

THE NEXT THREE DAYS ARE EASY AND FULL OF CONVERSATION, FOOD, and children dictating our every waking hour. I've grown attached to Maeve despite the knowledge of her abilities, one of which is lighting herself on fire. She's beginning to seek me out in a room now, crawling as fast as she can to tug on my pants or my skirt, and enjoys just sitting on my lap watching the other children play.

Kenna watches us, not saying a word. Sarah has had a lot to say about it, however, going on and on about how there was finally another baby girl in the family but she wouldn't allow anyone to touch her or snuggle with her... except for me.

I wouldn't consider Maeve to be a snuggly baby. She much prefers sitting on my lap and chewing on my fingers with the two razor sharp teeth she's cutting in real time.

All the while, Ryan floats in and out of whatever space we're sharing with his family. He's gone on a few outings with us and the kids, but he's been quiet and a little grouchy, dropping back into the same slightly secretive and stern persona I knew when I first came to live with him in Silverhide.

I'm not sure what he talked about with his uncle in that office three days ago, but I have a hunch it was about me, and that's why he's being so standoffish now.

I shouldn't have said a word that night.

I'm walking through the city with Sarah, arm in arm, without the kids for the first time in days. Kenna and Evander had to rush back to Veiled Valley for some reason, leaving early this morning without a word of farewell and taking all three kids with them. Without Brie bossing all of us around, Aris backing her up as her trusty, loyal servant, and Maeve clamoring for my attention, it's been quiet.

We're walking toward the castle now in the warmth of late afternoon sunshine, my arms laden with shopping bags. I bought gifts. A doll with a porcelain face for Lora. A leather knife belt with little toy knives in each holster for Shosh. Several spools of the most beautiful, silken fabric I've ever seen for Mercy, which I intend to give to her as a wedding present, and two bags of brightly colored yarn and thread for Freya, who's going to freak when I give it to her.

I even picked up some new clothes for Dahlia's baby with the help of Sarah, who I learned knows Dahlia well.

What I didn't know was that Dahlia was there the night Ryan killed Hadley, and for some reason, that changes everything for me. I'd been so cold toward her, blanketing my own shyness and insecurities with an air of detachment when she tried to be my friend. Knowing that she was more than James's wife, that she knew Ryan before everything, well... I owe her an apology for my coldness.

"I love coming here," Sarah says as we walk up the steps toward a side entrance to the castle. "I feel at home in this city, but that's only because I'm a mystic, I think. I'd miss Shadowcrest so much if Sydney decided to move here, though."

"Is that even an option? He's the heir to Isaac's throne."

"Well, yeah, but that's years away. Decades, honestly. Uhm, well, there's been talk about us coming here for a year or two, just for him to learn more about Eastonia to more effectively rule in Crescent Falls when the time comes and for me to learn my powers a little better. Neither of the boys will be like me, we think, not entirely. But a daughter might. I want to be prepared for that when the time comes."

"You were born here, right?"

"Moonrise? No. I don't actually know exactly where I was born, but I'm from Eastonia, yeah. It's strange." She laughs, shaking her head, "I love Crescent Falls, but I come here and feel like I'm home. Honestly, I think that about everywhere I go with Sydney." Her cheeks go a little pink.

I smile to myself, feeling those exact sentiments toward Ryan. He is my home. I remind myself that as he comes into view talking to Sydney beside one of the countless staircases spiraling into the upper levels of the castle. He looks stressed, but he's looked like that for three entire days now.

"Where are the boys?" Sarah asks, looking around. "With Maddy, I hope?"

"Yes. She's helping get them packed up."

"You're leaving?" The words slip from my lips before I can stop them. I really need to get better at that.

"Tonight, yeah. Sarah and my parents are going to Maatua first to visit our grandparents while I take you guys home."

I turn to Ryan for an explanation. He hadn't mentioned anything about leaving today. In fact, we're supposed to leave in two days. "What happened?"

Sydney and Ryan exchange a look then turn from each other, Sydney guiding Sarah up the stairs while Ryan takes the shopping bags from my hands and tilts his head down one of the long, criss-crossed hallways. "Nothing happened. We just completed our business here and are going back to our lives." He doesn't sound like nothing happened.

I drag him to a stop. He refuses to even look at me. "What's wrong with you?"

"Nothing's wrong."

"You look–you look like you're either on the verge of tears or ready to break something in half."

He runs his tongue along his bottom teeth, looking down at me with an arch of his brow. "Would you like to be broken in half? I could probably arrange that."

I smack him on the arm. "I'm being serious. You've been moping around for three days. What's wrong with you?"

He grinds his teeth before shrugging and walking forward again. I have to jog to keep up with him as we wind through the castle toward our apartment. He says nothing until we're closed inside then turns to me, his hands planted on his hips. "My uncle Ryatt believes you're part of some strange, ancient race of wolves."

"Well, that means absolutely nothing to me."

He exhales deeply. "He made it sound like it could mean a whole lot, Aviva, and he wants you to stay here in Moonrise. There's a historian in Veiled Valley with this thing–this magic little dog bowl that can test your blood, categorize you into specific area of magical powers–"

"I'm not staying here. I'm going home with you."

He sinks into a chair, rubbing his face for a moment. "I told him that."

"When did this conversation take place?"

"Right after you so conveniently let it slip that you know not only how to speak but read and write the Firestone language, which makes you invaluable."

"There's others that can read it. Hell, most ten-year-olds in Endova can read it. That doesn't make me special."

"What this means is that all of the sudden, the Deadlands are very important." He hangs his head in thought. "I'm going to have to go talk to your father and possibly send someone who can read the language here to Moonrise." He shakes his head.

"Why does it matter? Do they need something translated?"

"I didn't ask."

"Why not?"

"Because quite frankly, it's none of my business. My business is in the Deadlands, in Silverhide, where our pack is currently preparing for another long, cold winter, and I'm here drinking cocktails and fucking my wife on a four-poster bed."

I roll my eyes to the ceiling and kneel, laying my cheek on his thigh. "You love your family."

"I know."

"They're just weird. It's all right to be frustrated."

He chuckles, finally breaking out of the haze of his terrible mood. "They are pretty weird."

"Well, so are you. You can turn into a big beast with fangs the length of my forearm, and now apparently, I have special gifts. I fit right in. That doesn't mean we have to be separated."

"I wouldn't have let that happen. But… if you do have powers–"

"I would have known by now, wouldn't I?"

"Yeah. I think you would have figured it out, given your propensity for getting in life or death situations on a regular basis." He smooths his fingers through my hair in a way that makes my spine relax and skin tingle. "Shit."

"What?" I lift my head.

"I forgot to ask Kenna about those contraceptive potions, and she left this morning."

"It's a little late now, isn't it?"

His cheeks flush a soft pink, but he frowns, a flash of guilt pinching his brows together. "We never talked about it."

"About having children?"

He nods, sliding off his chair onto the soft, carpeted floor beside me. We stare at the wall, at a mostly empty bookshelf, lost in a few moments of companionable silence.

I say the first thing that comes to my head, and it feels incredibly selfish, but I have to get it out before it festers again. "I don't want to die like my mother did."

"I wouldn't let that happen to you. We'd come here for the birth."

"I'm not sure I'd be a great mother."

"I'm not sure I'd be a great dad." His fingers knit in mine, warm and solid.

"You would be. The best, I think."

"I don't think you give yourself enough credit, Aviva, for the kind of mother you were to your sisters."

"I was barely around, and when I was there, I wasn't… I couldn't give them everything they needed."

"You didn't want them to see you grieve."

Tears sting my lower lashes. I blink them away, shaking my head. "Do you want children?"

"Yeah," he whispers, as if it's a secret he's never shared. "But with you. I didn't start thinking about it until I met you. Shortly after I met you, actually. I thought–that woman pointing an arrow at my head is going to be the mother of my children if I can somehow convince her to *make* one with me."

"So you were just thinking about getting me in bed?"

"Oh, Goddess, you have no idea," he laughs.

I feel warm and fuzzy all over as we sit side by side, surrounded by shopping bags, none of our things packed for our journey home tonight.

"I guess we'll find out," I whisper, leaning my head on his arm and close my eyes.

Later, we share a final dinner with his parents, his brother, Sarah and the boys. Ella is there, too, of course, but Ryatt is notably absent.

Maddy gushes over us for the millionth time, and Ryan promises she can come to the harvest festival to see us get married, for real this time, even though no one but me really understands the significance of our upcoming nuptials.

Goodbyes are said. Ryan wrestles with Blake and Liam, telling them they need to work on their moves for the next time their family gets together, which sounds like it will be a few months from now, in mysterious Maatua, which I can't even picture in my head based on their descriptions.

And when Ryan takes my hand, lacing his fingers in mine, I'm almost prepared for the feeling of my body spinning out of control as Sydney claps him on the shoulder.

My stomach pitches and whirls, but the next moment I'm standing in our house in Silverhide, and Ryan is dropping our things on the floorboards, and Sydney is disappearing again in a flash of golden light.

I fall to my hands and knees, pinching my eyes shut against the spinning sensation threatening to pull me into the abyss. Ryan hands me a thermos he'd brought back from Moonrise full of the magic tea Kenna gave me the first time this happened, and I happily drink it before curling into the fetal position on the floor.

"I'll be back in a little while," Ryan says softly as he carries me to our bed, laying me on the firm mattress that smells like him, like us.

But I wake to several male voices talking over each other in the living room. It's night still, and I can tell I haven't been asleep longer than an hour, maybe less.

I open the bedroom door and step out to find Andrew and James standing next to Ryan, who has his back to me. His shoulders are rigid, though, every muscle tense.

Dread washes over me as he turns around.

"What happened now?" I ask, my fingers tingling to get my hands on my bow.

"We're going hunting," Ryan says gruffly, anger draped over every word.

I arch a brow. "For what?"

4 4

A GOLDEN GLOW

Ryan

IT'S BARELY DAWN. FOUR HOURS AGO, I WAS TAKING A DEEP BREATH AS I tucked my mate into our bed, and now we're here, lying low in the grasslands ten miles from Silver, with twenty of my best warriors scattered behind me.

Stars still fill the sky, shining under a blanket of deep navy and vibrant violet. It's kind of hard to stay focused when the sunrise looks like this, the first echoes of gold casting Aviva, in wolf form, in a halo of light. She's crouched in the swaying grass just a few feet below where the rest of us are lying, hiding in the scant brush and scorched trees. I watch her edge forward a few inches, her body covered in weapons and leather–one of her special dresses from Endova.

A half dozen whispers ghost through my head, mingling with the thundering of my heartbeat in my ears as we watch, and watch, the dozen or so rogues passing by, moving in a lazy formation toward the forests we, and the tribal packs, call home.

'What are they doing?' Andrew lies on my left side, his golden ears flat on his head as his eyes lock on the rogues.

329

I can barely form a coherent response. rogues aren't usually found in groups this large. Two or three at a time is pretty normal, but any more than that is completely and utterly unsettling. rogues vary in size and condition, some the same height and weight as the average male wolf, but others are much, much bigger.

I've never really understood how these creatures come to be. The easiest answer is that rogues are simply… us–but changed. Wolf shifters who give up their souls to stay in their wolf forms forever, but who would do that? And why? These things aren't wolves… not to the naked eye. Mostly gray and decomposing, they move with a strange click, like their bones don't fit together properly anymore. Their eyes burn a deep bloody red in the dim morning light as they pass us, a mile away in the open plains, and cross into the forest.

I send a quick command through the mind-link to the warriors I have stationed on the road leading to Silverhide and another all the way to Jacob, who is in Endova with Jerrod's warriors, preparing to intercept the rogues if they head that far south.

But they're not moving south anymore.

Aviva lifts her head ever so slightly, her snout tilting toward the East, toward Navvan.

I heave a wolfish breath and watch as my mate rises and starts padding down the hill.

'*Aviva, wait.*'

She halts and turns her head to look at me over her shoulder. '*They're turning east and skirting through the woods to stay out of the sunlight.*'

'*I can see that. They're going in the direction of Navvan, aren't they?*'

She lowers her head in answer, her eyes holding mine. '*Yes, they're moving away from Silverhide and Endova, but I don't like this, Ryan. There's too many together at once.*'

The men behind me in their wolf forms start rising from their bellies, stretching out after several hours spent in watch. We've been out all night canvassing the woods and securing the village and our territory beyond. The second my feet touched the ground in Silverhide, I knew something was wrong. I felt it in the air when I stepped out of our house and walked into the village, which was silent, every window dark and home empty.

James had secured our people in the pack house like we'd planned in the event of an attack or emergency. Everyone was accounted for, except for the two scouts he'd sent to travel to Moonrise to find me. That was two days ago. They never made it to Moonrise. They never made it out of the Deadlands at all, and they didn't come home. James and Andrew have been watching the rogues' progress for days now after they were first spotted. Reports of rogues by our scouts were common, but not this many at a time. We'd grown used to sharing the forest with them over the past two years.

But two of my scouts are gone—vanished. Andrew, sitting on my couch and trying to explain what honestly is unexplainable, mentioned how a few days ago, some of the younger wolves had gone out into the woods to shift and hunt and came tearing back into the village saying they'd heard what they believed were people screaming in the Endovian language, the old Firestone tongue. But when Andrew and James went to investigate, there was nothing there, and Jacob relayed that everyone was accounted for in Endova, that nothing was amiss.

Someone is messing with us. *Something* is messing with my pack.

Fury blasts through my veins. Aviva feels it through our bond and blows out a breath. *'Let me do it.'*

'Not alone.'

'You need to command your men. I can handle this.'

'There're twelve rogues.'

'I'm aware.' Silence hangs throughout our bond, but I can feel her nerves and absolute bloodlust like it's my own body reacting.

'Why are they moving together like this?' I ask.

'They're on something's trail,' she replies and turns back to the sprawling forest below where their grayish bodies are just visibly in the tree line. Just as the sun comes up, pouring bands of light across the plains, the rogues start running.

My heart quakes at the sight. My body rises in answer to their

grizzly, keening screeches. Birds erupt from the trees and then…
screaming, in the distance.

Aviva's ears prick up, her red coat rising. My wolves are totally silent right now as we watch the forest in confusion and horror.

'What is that sound?' Andrew snarls in my head. *'That sounds like a woman—'* His voice cuts off as the scream echoes again, sharper and closer. *'Freya?'*

He leaps out from the grass and starts hurtling down the hill toward the forest. Aviva tackles him, shifting into her human form in the blink of an eye, and rolls with him down the hill.

'Everyone go back to Silverhide, now!' I shout through the mind-link to the wolves behind me, then tear after Aviva and Andrew, who are still rolling together.

"That's not Freya!" Aviva shouts out loud as they come to a stop. She has her arms wrapped around Andrew's neck, trying to drag him back to the ground, but he's pulling her across the grass in his haste to reach the forest.

Gray figures moving swiftly toward the forest catch my eye. *'There's more,'* I say, and Aviva turns her head to the plains where another seven rogues dash out of the encroaching sunlight at a speed that seems impossible.

Aviva grimaces, baring her teeth in effort while swinging her legs over Andrew's back. She roughly pulls him to the side, sinking her heels into the meat of his belly, and then they're rolling again, violently bouncing down the remainder of the hill toward a grassy, shallow valley at the very base of the woods.

The screaming hasn't stopped. It grows louder and louder, like it's coming toward us. More birds lift from the trees as the canopy sways like something larger than the forest itself is barreling in our direction.

'AVIVA!' I howl, but she's still struggling to subdue Andrew, who is desperately trying to get her off him so he can run toward the screams echoing over us in waves that make my ears pop and skin tingle with terror. *ANDREW!*

Suddenly it goes completely silent.

"Stop it!" Aviva hisses, her arm locked around Andrew's thick neck. She hisses with fury as she forces his snout to his chest, pinning him down with her weight. I drop into the grass, watching with my heart hammering as the new rogues stop at the very edge of the forest. The golden sunlight draws over them, showing off their tangled, deformed bodies in a new way. They're ugly and mottled. Walking dead.

One of them turns to where Aviva and Andrew are lying in the grass, just out of sight.

But this one doesn't have red eyes. They're… green.

An uneasy feeling sweeps over me. Ryatt's words echo through my head, *"I need you to be prepared for whatever's coming."*

Suddenly, Aviva's standing. I watch in slow motion as one of the rogues in this new group starts creeping in her direction. His wolfish head lowers and his jaws open in a deranged smile, thick saliva dripping from his yellow teeth. Aviva reaches back for her bow just as the first rays of sunlight hit the valley.

I launch through the air, landing in front of her as the rogues split up, sprinting in every direction. Her arrow slices the skull of the first rogue at the same moment she grabs the rough of my neck and swings her legs over my back.

Andrew is a blur of gold through the grass as he weaves toward us, leaping in wolf form and tackling one of the smaller rogues heading in the direction where our warriors are moving out, on their way back to Silverhide to defend the village.

'Tell me what to do,' I say to Aviva through the mind-link.

But she doesn't need to. I'm barreling toward another rogue, a very big one, when she stands on my back and leaps off me, shifting in midair. She sails through the air in her wolf form, shifting again a blade in each hand. She slices the rogue's head clean off its neck and shifts back into her wolf before she even hits the ground, then she's off again.

'Well, what the fuck does she need us for, huh?' There's an obvious smirk in Andrew's words as he slows to a trot, then sits down on his haunches, licking black blood from his front paws.

I watch in horror and amazement as Aviva cuts through rogue after rogue. She doesn't need help. In fact, I think she might be enjoying it.

'*Four,*' she hums into my head, leaping from her most recent kill, shifting into her human form and sending an arrow through the base of the neck of her next. '*Five.*'

'*Goddess above,*' Andrew whispers in awe.

S-six.' Aviva slips for the first time, her human body slick with blood that's not her own as she stumbles back into her wolf form and tears after the seventh rogue, the last, which is barreling right toward her.

Something is different about this one, though. Something is off. It's not as big as the others but it's... new. That's the only way I can describe it. It's more like us than its counterparts. It moves with the grace of a wolf, but looks... wrong. Just wrong. Everything about it has my powers going haywire as Aviva runs toward it, blinded by blood and adrenaline.

Another blood curdling scream rushes from the forest. The rogue stops in its tracks and turns toward the noise.

Its sudden stillness startles Aviva. She skids to a stop, all of her fur standing on end as the rogue slowly turns its head back to look at us. It opens its jaw so wide I can see every tooth and all the way down its throat. It lets out a similarly blood boiling screech that causes the grass all around us to tremble. The sound is painful. Andrew grunts and buries his head in his chest, and Aviva bows as well, covering one ear with a paw.

She shifts back into her human form like she wasn't meaning to. It catches her off guard. She stumbles back with a choking inhale as the rogue continues to wail.

'*Aviva—*'

The rogue turns and sprints into the woods.

'*Aviva!*' I shout through the mind-link, feeling a yank on the threads of our bond. A warning.

She's trembling, shaking so violently her arrows are falling free of her quiver. I'm frozen as she slowly turns to me, her face smeared with black blood, and she....

Her eyes. Her eyes are glowing gold.

Andrew gets up and moves toward her. Her head whips in his direction.

'*Aviva*,' I say calmly as Ryatt's words from several days ago work through my head again, the same question that's been plaguing me for weeks.

I wasn't totally honest with him. Maybe he wasn't totally honest with me, either. He could sense what I could feel on this small, feral woman from the moment I met her.

Aviva has powers.

She just doesn't know it yet.

She bares her teeth at us, her eyes swirling with golden light, and shifts into her wolf form, disappearing after the rogue.

45

THE BOOK OF WHISPERS

Ryan

"She's not here, Ryan," Mercy hisses as I run through the village. She's hot on my heels, grabbing my fur to try to pull me to a stop but I'm not in my right mind.

It's been five hours since I last saw Aviva. Andrew and I have been scouring the forest and plains for any sign of her, but I lost her scent, and my desperate attempts to mind-link with her have come up empty and silent.

I shift into my human form the second I cross into the pack house and immediately crash into one of the tables, tripping over the bench and landing on my side with a crunch. I've been in my wolf form since last night. Exhaustion sings through my bones as my vision spins. I hear Andrew similarly falling to the ground with a choked groan before hurried footsteps reach the pack house. Someone throws a blanket over me with a scoff, followed by Mercy's sharp, soprano voice ripping through the air as she starts shouting orders to the others in the room.

337

"Get them clothes and water, right NOW!" she shrieks, and the other footsteps hurry back out of the pack house.

I turn my head, fighting to catch my breath, and watch as she kneels beside Andrew, turning his face from side to side as he goes limp with fatigue.

"Mercy," I croak, my mouth and throat dry and raw.

Mercy rises with a sigh and turns to me, her hands tucked in the pockets of a worn olive-colored apron. Dark circles line her under eyes and her normally perfect braided dark hair is falling in tangled sheets over her shoulders. "Jacob isn't here."

My eyes close against my will. I can feel the last echoes of my wolf power flickering before extinguishing. I need a charge. Food, water, and sleep. Hours upon hours of it, but we don't have that kind of time.

I feel Mercy laying a hand on the blanket covering my body, her fingers light on my chest. "Our warriors have been watching the rogues move in from the north and northwest for several days now. Hunters were the first to spot them, then we got the same reports from your pack. More rogues, moving in from the northern Dead-lands." I blink up at her, her profile a blur. "The patriarch of Teskha sent scouts to us yesterday with reports of over twenty rogues heading east. An entire pack of them. We sent warriors to intercept them, but night fell, and there was a battle..." She inhales sharply, shaking her head. "We lost ten of our best warriors."

"Where is Jacob?" My voice sounds like someone punched me repeatedly in the throat.

"I don't know. I haven't been able to connect with him over the mind-link." Her face fades and I notice the pink blush staining her cheeks and the way the tips of her ears go bright red. I assume they haven't been hand-fast yet, not with Aviva present, so if they can normally mind-link, Jacob marked her. That's a conversation for another time.

"So they're both missing." It's not a question. My blood simmers at the thought of my wife and my best friend out in the forest hunting rogues at best, dead at the worst. The latter is becoming more and more likely the longer I go without hearing from either of them.

"Night won't fall for another few hours," Mercy says with a shallow breath. "We have time to find them, but you need to rest."

"I'm aware." Guilt rages through my body as I let my eyes flutter closed again. I listen to new footsteps entering the pack house, the smell of roasted meat and the heavy, bitter home brew Endova is known for whispering through the air and mingling with new voices, new bodies in the room.

I sense Mercy's departure, her soft, floral scent replaced by new smells, new hands on my body. Someone tilts my head up so I can drink water. Someone replaces the water with something else, whiskey so young it burns my throat and jolts me back to awareness. I'm not sure how much time has passed by this point, but now I'm sitting with my back braced on the overturned bench, facing Andrew, while ripping into a turkey leg like I haven't eaten in days. Andrew's a hot mess. His blond hair sticks up at all angles as his eyes remain glassy and locked on the floor between his knees, still wearing nothing but a blanket covering his body.

There's a commotion outside. Male voices drift in, carrying word of rogues being taken down near the border of Endova and Navvan. It's an active, bloody battle.

But there hasn't been a single sighting of Navvan warriors or even civilians, which is a bad sign. Suddenly, Navvan is no longer the threat, and based on the conversation taking place just outside the doors to the pack house, the elders and warriors are making plans to reach the Navvan village to help defend the people there.

Because the rogues are headed right for it.

"At least a hundred," one of the warriors says, his voice muffled by the closed door. "But the Teshkan warriors we intercepted said they counted another sixty moving north east toward Navvan."

A hundred and sixty rogues. Impossible.

I look at Andrew and find him looking right at me, listening just as keenly to the conversation outside the door. *This is bad,* he says into my mind.

'*This is war,*' I reply gravely.

Ryatt warned me about rogues in the Deadlands. Even if someone turns into a rogue in Moonrise, or the Roguelands, or even as far east as Tarsian, they come here for whatever reason. Something about this place draws them in.

Part of our agreement about me coming here to carve out my own place in the world was to help Ryatt eliminate the rogue problem. Neither of us could have predicted there were this many.

"Hellhounds, at least four of them..."

I hold Andrew's gaze as the conversation continues, but then the door opens so silently I would have missed it had it not been for the tiny, pale fingers clutching the door. For a split second, Aviva was here. Then Shoshannah turns to me, her red curls and dark eyes so similar to my mate's that my heart stops, then breaks.

She closes the door and moves swiftly into the center of the room, dropping clothes in front of Andrew, then in front of me. But she crouches in front of me with her tiny child-sized bow on her back, her dark whiskey-brown eyes bright and sharp. "I need to show you something."

Her tone sends goosebumps whispering over my skin. I can't do more than nod as she walks across the room and turns to face a shadowed corner while Andrew and I dress.

I feel faint but better than before as we follow the little girl out of the pack house. It's almost sunset. The sky is fading from bright, cloudless blue to violet as we skirt through the village a few paces behind Shoshannah, who walks with her shoulders squared and her neck high and tight just like Aviva.

So much like Aviva. Where the fuck is she? The bond between us is still there. I can feel her, but she's far away. She's alive. For now. Any anger I feel toward her vanishes when I remember how her eyes glowed before she disappeared into the dark forest.

Powers. My mate has powers. Whatever she's doing out there, well, she better be learning how to use them.

We reach the forest a few minutes later. We follow Shoshannah up the creek until we reach the ruins. Shoshannah reaches the entrance and crawls inside. Andrew glances at me before following. But I'm stuck outside, my eyes locked on the remains of the archway. I imagine Aviva standing there, her arrow locked and honed on my skull while the moon rises behind her, just like that night several weeks ago.

"You better still be alive," I whisper through our bond and follow them inside.

The ceiling is so low I have to bend at the waist to fit. Andrew is crouched a few feet away, looking through the shadows at the knick-knacks scattered throughout.

"Aviva thinks this place used to be a temple," Shosh says quietly. She's looking for something, that's clear, as she runs her fingers over the stones and pulls crystals and blade tips from clefts in the rock. "The entrance to one. I used to help her dig, but we gave up a few years ago. She thought there might be stairs leading down into the ground, like the forest covered the temple up long ago."

"What did you want to show us?"

"I just didn't want anyone to hear," she says, turning to face us. "Aviva told me I wasn't allowed to tell anyone."

"Tell anyone what?" Andrew asks.

She lowers herself to her knees, gripping the crystals in her tiny fists. "She used to tell me stories to help me fall asleep after Mama died. About the Firestone cities in the Deadlands, and the magical forges where magic was made."

Unease settles heavy in my chest as I kneel, resting my hands on my knees.

"There was one story I liked the most, though she wasn't supposed to be telling me these tales anyway, but I'd beg and beg for it and...." Her eyes glaze with a distant memory. "I promised not to tell, but somethings wrong, isn't it? Mercy won't tell me anything. I'm supposed to be in the house right now."

"Can we hear the story?" Andrew asks softly, smiling at her. Andrew's always been good with kids. All I can think about right now is that this child is the kid-version of my missing wife, and my heart is actively shattering as she purses her lips just like Aviva does, tilts her head in the same way, and smiles while biting her lip.

"*The Book of Whispers* was said to have been hidden here, in the Deadlands, when the Firestone cities fell. The Firestone witches scattered the templars of their Goddess, the Moon Goddess, so the old gods couldn't find them and use the book to unleash things even worse than the curse they released when they opened the Baetyl. The Goddess and her daughter vanished, and Eastonia fell into the dark times, and the book remained here, hidden away in an ancient temple."

Something clicks into place in my head. The Diadem of Starlight, with the Diamond of Faith as part of the Diadem, were found in Crescent Falls. The Firestone Mask is now under Ella's control. The Blade of Time…that was the knife Gabriel used to torture Sarah as a child and then used to try to kill Sydney and is now in Sarah's control. The Shadow Sword belongs to Ryatt and Kenna.

My family is tied to this somehow. Like these pieces of history belong to us, for whatever reason.

"Is *The Book of Whispers* here?" I ask, motioning to the ruins all around us.

Shoshannah shakes her head. "Aviva told me it's in the temple in Navvan. It's buried there, and their village was built around it. They're meant to protect it…." She trails off, hugging her knees to her chest. "In one of the stories, the book was used to cast a spell on a pack as punishment by the old gods for failing to worship them. They were turned into soulless creatures who would spend eternity trying to find their way back to their human forms again, forced to do the bidding of the one who cast the spell."

"Rogues," Andrew whispers to himself.

"Someone used *The Book of Whispers*, didn't they?" I ask, and Shosh turns teary eyes to mine.

She nods.

"Is Aviva going after the book?" Why hadn't she told me, let alone my family, about this when we were in Moonrise? I bite down the confusion and betrayal starting to simmer in my blood, hating the idea that she kept this from me.

"No. She's looking for her bow."

Her bow? "She has her bow with her."

"The one that's meant for her," she says with a trembling voice.

The fucking Gilded Bow. I close my eyes, shaking my head. "Andrew, we need to go to Navvan, now."

46

ROUNDING UP ROGUES

Aviva

I'M HAVING THE TIME OF MY LIFE.

I zigzag through the woods in my wolf form after three rogues who've decided they want nothing to do with me. In fact, the rogues have stopped hunting me over the past several hours and instead are trying to get as far away from me as possible. Their prey has become their biggest predator.

I did my best to lead the horde away from Endova. That was my goal–the reason I made the snap decision to leave my mate behind and race into the jaws of death itself. Now, I have the horde moving away from the tribal pack lands all together, herding them back into the open plains like a shepherd, and they're my sheep–if a shepherd killed their sheep, that is.

I've lost count of how many there are. My red fur is completely black with their blood. I catch my reflection in another small, burbling creek as I leap, seeing only my eyes shining like polished amber against a blanket of black night.

I've become a shadow, like Kenna. I blend into the darkness, silent

345

as a ghost and faster than the rolling, incoming gloom of night as the rogues chase the sunset. I launch into the air, shift to my human form, and lean into my twin blades, driving them down into the spine of the first rogue. It falls with a crack, black blood spraying through the air. I'm off its back before it even touches the ground, sending an arrow through the neck of the rogue beside it.

Down it falls, landing on the body of its counterpart, and the third rogue takes off in a sprint, bellowing in fear and warning to the other rogues seeking refuge from the sunlight in the shadowed forest.

It's too late to double back to ensure the rest of the rogues have been herded to the plains. Sunlight will have weakened the ones I chased there earlier, but night is falling. I know once the sun dips below the distant horizon, they'll turn back toward the forest, rushing toward the small villages and hunting camps stretching from here all the way to Teshka.

I've killed dozens, but it's not enough. My hands cramp as I send one more arrow whizzing through the air. It lodges itself in the ear of that third rogue and travels through its skull, lodging itself in a nearby tree. The rogue falls, dead and crumpled.

I lower my bow, panting, as the last glimmers of sunlight fade and total darkness falls all around me, the forest growing so silent I can hear my own heartbeat.

'*Where the FUCK ARE YOU?!*' Ryan's voice echoes through my head, clearer than it has been in hours.

'*Please tell me you have warriors with you,*' I rush out, turning in a circle as wind rustles the canopy of leaves. '*Ryan?*'

'*Where are you, Aviva?*' He sounds desperate but relieved to hear my voice. I run my hand over my face, wiping rogue blood off my mouth, hating the salty, acrid taste of it.

'*Near the edge of the forest, due east. I'm ten miles outside of Navvan.*'

'*Stay there–*'

'*I can't. I have to–*'

A bellowing echoes toward me, causing birds and small creatures in the wood to scurry, seeking refuge. The rogues are coming back. This is the moment I've been coming to terms with all day long. The rogues gathered, forming an army, and I did my best to push them away from the tribal packs so their warriors would have time to prepare for the fight that's coming now.

Dread plucks the fine, golden threads binding me to Ryan. I know he can feel it. I know he knows I can't stay where I am.

'*Aviva*,' he says calmly.

'*I'm here.*' I look around as clicking, growling noises funnel around me. Eyes glow in the darkness-red. Red, and honed on mine. I raise my body as a chill coasts over my body.

'*I love you.*'

I blink back tears. '*I love you.*'

The first of the rogues breaches the forest again as I send the words through the mind-link, letting every feeling of love, of longing and devotion go with them. I might die here tonight. That thought has crossed my mind a few times already, especially since my fingers are sore and raw, and my skin is damp and slick with blood, making it easier to screw up. One wrong move, one missed arrow, and I'm gone.

In the distance, over the clicking of rogue teeth, I hear the first shouts of the warriors. High pitched, their war cries echo through the forest, and a pinch of hope replaces the dread coursing through my veins.

I'm moving again in my human form, sending arrow after arrow flying, gathering them from the skulls of necks of the rogues I kill and pass. My body aches from almost constant transformation, but something in my bones is making it impossible to take a break. There's always been a drive within me to protect. It's something ingrained in my soul, something woven through every vein into the very fiber of my being. I think of my sisters as I slash into a rogue with my knives. I think of Ryan as I shift into my wolf form and sink my teeth into the shoulder of another rogue, shifting to slice through its neck. I think of Freya and Andrew, praying the blood coating my hands gives them enough time to find each other again, giving them the time they deserve.

I think of Ella as I launch into the air and send an arrow soaring, piercing one rogue and then another. I think of Kenna as I skirt the edge of the forest, preventing rogue after rogue from entering as the warriors' calls get closer and closer. I think of Maeve, my future queen, when the first sounds of a bloody battle reach me only a mile outside of Navvan.

Tethered. I am tethered to the Firestone queens. I am their warrior, their protector. I can't fail. I won't. I refuse.

The village of Navvan is totally overrun and on fire when I reach the outer ring of stone buildings. Toppled stone blocks my progress. I'm running out of arrows as I bring down a rogue chasing a trio of warriors. My bow string threatens to snap, and my bloody fingers slip, sending the arrow flying into its ribs instead, but it gives the warriors time to regroup and turn on it.

'I made it to Navvan!' I shout through the mind-link to Ryan or his warriors, whoever's closest. I shift into my wolf form and barrel into the fray, leaping over burning rubble and clawing the backs of two large rogues chasing wolves that smell like they belong to Teshka. But there're so many scents here that mingle. I have no idea who belongs to what pack as I reach the front lines where over fifty wolves hold off a sea of rogues.

I shift into my human form, panting as pain stretches through my body with the transformation. "SURROUND THEM!" I scream, motioning wildly to the wolves. "SURROUND THE ROGUES! GET BEHIND THEM!"

I'm not sure if they can hear me. I pitch forward, resting my hands on my knees as my lungs tremble and refuse air. "Please," I whisper to myself, to my aching body. "Don't give up now."

My wolf feels so far away as I try to force myself to shift again, having to reach deep for those Goddess given powers.

'Surround the rogues!' Ryan's voice cuts through the mind-link, which explodes with noise. *'You heard her! Surround them!'*

The wolves part and start running in an attempt to form a circle around the rogues still rushing in from the forest. Rogues break through the line, tossing wolves into the air as they barrel into the village, but I feel a nudge on my side as I fight for breath, feeling every bone in my body knitting together as I shift into my wolf form.

Andrew is here, standing beside me, nudging me with his snout.

'*Ryan?*' I gasp. '*Where is he?*'

'*Nearby,*' Andrew says, his voice muffled with chatter in the mind-link. '*He's trying to get to you. He wants you to rest.*'

'*I can't.*' I meet his eyes. '*We're being overrun.*'

A keening howl slices the air around us in two. Andrew lifts his head, his ear flat against his head. Another howl, and I'm moving again, drawn to the sound against my will.

Rogues fall dead all around me, covered in wolves and warriors in their human forms. I ignore the arrows, knives, claws, and teeth. I step over bodies of wolves, humans, and rogues as I walk toward the forest, following the calls of the *hellhound*.

Ryan killed one once.

Why not me?

I shift into my human form against my will, my powers finally exhausted. I pull my last arrow from my quiver. It's bent, something I would have normally discarded.

I reach the edge of the village and step into the silent woods as the battles rages behind me and edge into the darkness.

Silence swells all around me like I've just walked into a void. The sounds of death and war die out, replaced by the rustling of leaves and scared mice scurrying from bush to bush.

Leaves and twigs snap under my bare feet. I lost my shoes hours ago. I don't even feel the rocks biting into my skin.

Green, glowing eyes breach the darkness. The smell of decay clouds my senses, but I grip my bow and pull back an arrow.

A man steps out of the darkness wearing rags–the remains of Navvan's traditional warrior uniform. Tall, with dark hair and a chiseled face, he might have been handsome at one point, but now his features are distorted, the muscles in his face slack and his shoulders... hanging, like they've been snapped out of place.

Real fear grips me as he steps toward me, his thin mouth drawing up in a deranged smile.

"You," he growls in a gravely, deep voice. "I've been waiting for you." He comes to a stop, panting and drooling. He jerks, closing his eyes as he rolls his neck like he's in severe pain.

"Who are you?"

"Hardan," he breathes, curling his hands into fists. "You were supposed to be *mine*."

"Well, I'm mated, so that sucks for you."

A low laugh escapes him. I notice his cracked, bloody teeth. What the hell is wrong with him?

"You don't even know what you are, do you?"

I adjust my bow and aim my bent arrow at his face. "Whatever I am, I'm in far better shape than you."

"Enjoy it while it lasts," he laughs cruelly. "Soon this will spread here, to the tribal lands, and there will be nothing you can do about it, Firestone *pet*."

I narrow my eyes at him. "What will spread?"

His green eyes blaze. "They have *the book*."

My stomach hollows out. I know what he means. He can only mean one thing.

"No," I say. "Did you–" I think back to the battle with the Navvan warriors. Hardan killed his own father and brothers. He killed most of the elders. Navvan was the resting place of the *Book of Whispers*, but only a few people knew. My father knew, because he's our patriarch. Hardan's father was the patriarch of Navvan, and it was his duty to keep the *Book of Whispers* guarded and kept under a veil of secrecy.

"You used the book." I gasp, my eyes growing wide.

He smiles, his back cracking as he jerks into a bow. "Not me, pet. *They*."

"Who are *they*?"

"You'll find out soon."

"What have you done?" Tears well in my eyes before spilling down my cheeks.

Hardan straightens and his face is… wrong. Half transformed, his body starts to stretch, and his next words strain into nothing more than a rumbling growl. It's the growl of a hellhound. I catch a single word. *Baetyl*. The Gate of the Gods.

"NO!" My scream is absorbed by his howl. He's not a man or a wolf. He's a rogue. Worse, he's some kind of rogue–hellhound hybrid, and he's coming right at me, jaws open and teeth gleaming.

My eyes close as I brace myself for his impact. But when I open them again, when he's only inches away, I see a white wolf standing in the woods, watching me with a silver gaze that I can only describe as curious.

Something black and huge crashes into Hardan. Spiky, sharp fur brushes my front, knocking me flat on my ass.

47

ANGELS OF THE GODDESS

Ryan

I'VE BEEN DREAMING ABOUT TYING AVIVA TO MY BED, BUT I'M GOING TO make it a reality for entirely different reasons. Now, I'll be tying her to keep her there, forever. No more hunting. No more fighting. No more killing rogues barefoot in the woods.

No more putting herself in situations like this. I will do her dirty work. I will gladly do it.

I roll with Hardan in his… hellhound form? Whatever the fuck he is now. I wish, Goddess, *I wish* I could have faced him man to man instead of beast to beast. I would have loved to see the look on his face when I ripped out his heart for even thinking for a second he had some kind of claim to my mate, even before I found her.

We roll down a decline. I sink my talons into his belly, ripping hard, but I already know hellhounds aren't that easy to kill.

We crash into an oak tree. Leaves shower over us as he tries to claw free of my grasp. He's calling out, bellowing strange, high-pitched howls. The forest floor rumbles as I sink my claws into his neck in the promise of death.

'*He's calling the rogues back!*' Aviva shouts through the mind-link like she's out of breath. I can sense her coming nearer.

'*Get out of here, Aviva!*'

'*He's controlling the rogues!*'

I look up, past the tree, and notice we're only a few hundred yards from a cliff. An idea sparks to life in my mind, but now Aviva is racing toward me, her red hair dark and matted with black blood. '*Ryan, kill him! We have to get out of here!*'

I sink my claws deeper. Hardan bellows again, his calls echoing off trees and into the valley below us. The rumbling increases to the point Aviva yelps and crouches, bracing herself with her hands planted on the ground.

"Ryan?" she croaks, meeting my eyes. She looks over her shoulder at the tidal wave of shadows breaching the trees and heading in our direction.

'*Go,*' I beg her through the mind-link. She has seconds to move before it's too late. '*Please, Aviva, go.*'

"I'm not going without you," she says out loud, shaking her head as she rises on unsteady legs and walks toward me. Hardan snarls and lurches beneath me. I have him pinned against the tree, and just beyond is the drop off. If I can hold him here, the rogues will come rushing down the hill in his direction, his calls driven by whatever fear he had left in the human side of him, and they'll take us, tree and all, over the cliff.

The battle will be over.

'*James will be Alpha,*' I say into her mind. '*You will return to your family.*'

"No," she grinds out.

'*If you're—if you're pregnant,*' I begin, and it kills me, knowing I'd promised to be by her side, that we'd do this together, '*My family will help you. You won't be alone.*'

Her eyes fill with angry tears. "I'm not going anywhere! You'll have to get up and move me, Ryan. I'm not leaving without you. If you're doing this—if you're going over the cliff, I'm going too!"

'*Please!*'

Hardan takes advantage of my sudden distraction and lack of awareness about anything but my mate and gets a claw between us. I cry out in pain and frustration but fight it, keeping my eyes locked on my mate. This stubborn, bull-headed, sharp tongued woman I love and didn't have enough time with. Not nearly enough.

I won't lose another mate. I can't.

But Aviva was never going to give me the choice.

The rogues appear, toppling trees and leaving chaos and destruction in their wake. Aviva launches herself toward me at the same moment Harden wiggles loose. His claws stretch as I lift off him and shift to catch Aviva in my arms in my human form and curl around her.

The next moments are blurry. I roll with Aviva. I lock an arm around her as my free hand grasps for anything to grab as we careen toward the cliff edge. At the last moment, I catch a thick root coming from the willow tree hanging from the cliff. I curl my fingers around it as we fall and jerk to a stop, our bodies slamming against the rocky face of the cliff. I curl into Aviva, tucking her as close as possible while we hang, my head covering hers as bodies start to sail over us into the void of shadow and nothingness below.

Rogue after rogue falls from the cliff. Dozens. The last sounds are Hardan fighting for his footing before he topples over the edge, stuck between two of the beasts he was controlling, likely calling to Navvan to create a sick, twisted army he planned to unleash on the tribal lands.

The trunk of the willow tree snaps, falling over the side, its leaves brushing over the top of my head as it falls.

We hang in the silence. Aviva is completely still, her arms growing limp at my sides.

"RYAN?!" Jacob's voice echoes down to us, followed by Andrew and the voices of many, dozens of warriors racing to the cliff edge.

I look up into the light of the moon as people appear several feet above our heads. I am exhausted. I couldn't pull us up if I tried, and Aviva is...

"Aviva?" I rasp, clutching her as her hands hang at her sides. "Aviva–Aviva?!"

Her head falls back, her eyes open and unseeing. In the glare of the moon, I see the blood streaming down her neck and chest.

* * *

AVIVA

I'm standing at the edge of the cliff watching the warriors. They stand in somber silence as Ryan bends over my... my *body*, his hands clasped on either side of my face. Andrew falls to his knees beside Ryan while Jacob remains standing, repeatedly running his fingers through his short hair.

"No, no, no, no," Ryan rasps, choking on the words as he drags a hand over my torn neck and chest. "Aviva? Av-Aviva? Please–" He groans, choking out a sob that rips into my heart and shatters it.

I look down at my hands and it hits me.... I look back at Ryan, and my... my body. I'm not in my body right now. I'm standing outside of it, watching as my mate begs for me to take a breath.

"No," I say, trying to take a step forward, but my progress back to my mate, myself, is blocked by two white wolves standing on either side of me, their fur dripping with silver mist.

I try to shove against them but they herd me back every time I take a step.

"Stop," I command, grimacing as the scene playing out before me starts to fade, like I'm being pulled away. "Stop! No, no, no! I'm not ready to go, not without him! I'm supposed to go with him!" My voice is distorted and desperate as I fight against a preternatural pull yanking me further from my mate.

I tug on the bond between us. "Please! No! No, no!" My voice breaks as I watch Ryan scream as he bends over my body again, gathering me into his arms and rocking me back and forth.

Warriors lower their weapons as they kneel. Those in their wolf forms bow.

No. This isn't happening. I'm not ready. We won. I should be there, beside them. I should be going home with my mate to our village. I should be seeing my sisters again.

"Let me go!" I scream at the white wolves as they push me back into the black, starless night. I look at Ryan in a desperate attempt to get his attention, screaming his name as he cradles my limp body. *"I'm here!"* I plead, sending the words through our weakening bond. *"Please, I'm still here!"*

I feel myself starting to… *go*. I'm out of time.

Screaming with every ounce of my soul I have left, I reach for my bow like it would still be on my back. It's there. It's still there, even when I'm being carried away by the Goddess's angels. I pull it forward, loosing the single, bent arrow and pulling back with all of my earthy strength, and send it soaring.

The arrow is pure gold as it breaches the body Ryan's holding. My own body. Light explodes through my vision, viciously bright and unending. The feeling of nothingness is replaced by pain, sharp and deep, and then I'm opening my eyes and looking up at Ryan.

He looks down at me in confusion.

I'm holding the golden arrow in my gnarled, bloody fingers. I can feel my fingers gripping the solid metal. I can feel my back against the dirt. I can feel the slight, smoky breeze in the air and see my mate's face as he looks down at me, shaking his head like he doesn't believe it.

Bodies drop to their knees all around us, voices lifted in murmured prayers.

Ryan closes his hand over my cheek as he eyes drop to my neck, where Hardan's last act had been to flay me open.

Blood fills my mouth. I can't breathe. I sputter his name, choking as I fight the strange feeling starting to numb my body.

My wounds are knitting themselves back together–but slowly. My vision goes in and out, and Ryan's voice fades as shadows pass over me. Someone presses heavy fabric to my neck. Commands are shouted. My head lolls as I'm lifted and carried away from the cliff, warm and whole in my mate's arms. I refuse to give into the darkness swirling in my peripheral vision. I refuse to fall asleep, to risk seeing those white wolves again. Why did they change their minds? What exactly did I do?

"It'll take hours to reach Silverhide and return with the tears," Jacob says somewhere nearby as I'm laid down again. Ryan sits down beside me, arranging me so my head is in his lap. A blanket is laid over my mangled body, but I still can't see much of anything. I can't feel much, either. Another length of thick, folded fabric is pressed against my neck, but I'm so weak. I'm slowly dying, I realize. Those fucking angels gave me another chance just to revel in my suffering like it's some kind of punishment for not going with them willingly.

"What happened?" Jacob rasps. "How is she surviving this? Where did the arrow come from?"

"She found her bow," Andrew says softly. His words are a near whisper as I blink back the darkness trying to swallow me again.

"What are you talking about?" Jacob asks, exasperated.

My vision clears enough to see Ryan's profile against a backdrop of fire. He's resting his back against a patch of rubble. He looks so tired, so worn and empty as he holds Andrew's gaze, and nods gravely, closing his eyes. "I need scouts sent to the Roguelands, immediately. I need to get in touch with my uncle. He likely knows something of this magnitude just happened, somehow. But I need to get her out of here."

"We can try moving her to Endova," Andrew whispers, but Ryan shakes his head.

"She can't heal these wounds fast enough. We won't make it to help in time."

My eyes leave his face and fall to the remains of a building across from us, where the white wolves lurk, their eyes holding mine in challenge.

I refuse to die. I will suffer like this forever out of spite, unable to speak, unable to see my mate clearly, unable to take a full breath.

But that weakness creeps in again, making me shiver. Ryan holds me close but doesn't look at me, which breaks my heart.

I was given a second chance, and I'm losing it. I watch the white wolves move closer, and closer, waiting for me to just give up.

The sun is rising again when Ryan moves, lifting me into his arms. I'm not sure how long he's sat here with me, watching his mate slowly die. It must have been hours of me holding on and him tortured in silence.

My mouth fills with a metallic taste reminiscent of blood. Ryan's talking to someone, but all I can hear is my own heartbeat as I watch the wolves no one else can see. They're so close now. I could reach out and touch them if I wanted to.

"Maatua?" Ryatt's voice says in a distorted whisper, questioning whatever Ryan just said that I must have missed.

"Take her. I'll come as soon as I can."

Ryan puts me in Ryatt's arms, and I feel… safe. Safe enough to turn to the wolves as that horrible magic swirls around me, fracturing me into tiny little pieces.

I flip them off right as my vision goes black, and Ryatt spirits me away.

48

TIDES OF CHANGE

Aviva

I wake with a start to bright, warm sunshine and the smell of salty air. I grope white sheets, blinking several times to clear my vision as an unfamiliar bedroom fades to life around me. Warm white walls. Pale wood finishes and sleek furniture in soft browns and creams. White curtains drift in a salty breeze coming through several open windows, and a glass door opens to a deck with a view of... a view of the ocean.

I've never seen the ocean before. From where I lie, I can hear the waves crashing on a white sand beach. Music I don't recognize drifts toward me, carrying two voices with it, one male, and one female.

"Your parents worry about you endlessly, Misty."

"They have nothing to worry about. It's not like I'm ten anymore, Grandpa. I can make my own way in the world now. Plus, where was their worry when they shipped me here four years ago, huh?"

"You know full well that they did that for your own protection. They didn't have much of a choice, given that you were a target."

"I was sixteen, Grandpa. I'm twenty now. I've been living in

Tarsian for two years, and now they're asking me to come home, give up my degree program? I have a year left! They can't... they can't ask this of me. Not now."

"Misty–"

"No." A chair squeaks across the tile on the deck just out of view. "I'm fine in Tarsian. The university is perfectly safe. I'm nowhere near Oasia."

"Your Uncle Ryatt is in talks with the Alpha King of Tarsian as we speak about the issue–"

"It's none of my business, Grandpa. I don't care about the politics between the Allied Kingdoms. I really don't. I told Dad and Uncle Ryatt that a few weeks ago when they asked me to leave my internship and come to Moonrise for that big meeting about succession like they were going to carve out a piece of territory for me. For me. I'm not the heir to my dad's kingdom. I'm just Misty, and I'm going back to school!"

"They're not asking you to drop out of college."

I hear a scoff. I realize, as my numb mind starts to unthaw, that I must be in Maatua, and this lifted, pissed off female voice belongs to Ryan's little sister, the mysterious Misty, Princess of Crescent Falls.

"*They are.*"

"Wellington is an option. Hell, you could come back here and go to Maatua University."

"And study what? Nursing? Tell me, do Wellington and MU have Protohistory Archeology courses that I'm unaware of?"

The older man sighs heavily. "Misty, you're being unreasonable."

"They're being unreasonable."

"You are a princess, in case you've forgotten." His voice takes on an edge. "Even if you're far away from the conflict in Oasia, you're still in Tarsian, and that's too close for your parents' comfort."

"They're going to have to chain me up and drag me home," she says gruffly. I hear the chair squeak again like she had stood and is now seated again. "Grandpa, I'm fine there. Yeah, it sucks that my internship was cut short, and me and all the researchers were pulled off our dig site in the desert, but I have a year left. I'll graduate next spring, and I already promised Mom and Dad that I'd come back to Crescent Falls for a while. Nate got offered a job in Celestoria after he graduates, and we're talking about me going with him. Celestoria has such a rich history and I'm sure there's going to be work for me there."

"Nate? He's still around?"

Another scoff. "Why is that so surprising? You met him last year!"

"He's… a great man."

"You don't sound so convinced. Why? What have you heard? Is Dad trying to sell me to an Alpha? Oh, *Goddess*, does someone want me as a breeder? Like Grandma?" I can't help but smile at the sarcastic edge to her voice.

"Misty, that mouth is going to get you in a lot of trouble one day."

"I've been told that all my life, and so far, I'm unscathed." Her voice drips with amusement, but her grandfather isn't laughing.

"Trouble you can't get out of."

"I'll be fine, Grandpa. Please? Can you just back me up on this? I gave them my word that I'd stay in Maatua, but only for this week, because Grandma needed my help. But I'm going back to Tarsian in two days, all right?"

"None of us like it, Misty. Not when things are the way they are now."

"I'll be fine. If anyone is going to trust my judgment, I want it to be you. So can you just trust me? Please?"

The old man grumbles something I can't hear over the sound of the incoming tide, but the chair squeaks again, and light footsteps sound across the deck. A petite woman with sun kissed skin and hair the color of pure gold walks aimlessly through the open doors into my room, her eyes glued to what I remember being told is a cell phone. Large blue eyes fanned by dark brown lashes lift to meet mine, and she arches a perfectly manicured brow.

"Oh," she says. "You're awake."

Something about this woman puts me on edge in a way I don't think I've ever experienced. She is intimidating to the highest degree. She's slightly taller than I am, I think. She's probably the most beautiful person I've ever seen, but she doesn't look like either of her brothers. The furrowed brow and skepticism flaring behind her eyes is remarkably similar to the way Ryan occasionally looks at me, however.

"You should lie back down," she says without an ounce of emotion then looks back at her phone with a sigh.

I sink back against the cushions. She flicks her gaze to me again, looking me up and down with a slight smirk twitching the corners of her pink lips. "I'm Misty."

"I know."

She arches her other brow. "Do you know where you are?"

"Maatua."

"Very good," she smiles, suddenly relaxing her shoulders and dropping her phone on the foot of the bed. She sits on the corner, crossing her long, tan legs, and stares at me. I stare back, unsure what to say or do. She's not kind and soft spoken like Kenna, I can already tell. She's not cheerful and friendly like Sarah, who I hope is here as well, somewhere. Misty is different. I just can't place how. "Do you feel any pain?"

I reach up on impulse and feel over my neck and chest where I'd been bleeding out what feels like only minutes ago and find my skin totally intact, not even a scar. "No, I don't."

"Great, that's good news. Ryan will be happy." A soft chime echoes between us. She looks down at her phone, rolls her eyes, and looks back at me. "So, Aviva. I heard you went feral and killed like, sixty rogues. That's pretty cool."

"Cool?"

"Yeah" she says, rolling her beautiful, glacier blue eyes again. They're lighter than Ryan's eyes. "Bad ass, actually. My Aunt said Uncle Ryatt has been talking incessantly about it. Have you ever heard of the Ghosts? I bet you'll be their commander soon." She holds my gaze like she's trying to gauge my reaction to... something. I just can't tell what it is. What a strange woman. She blinks, shrugging, and snatches her phone off the bed. "Anyway, welcome to Maatua."

She rises, but I sit up, pulling the sheets up to my chest. I'm wearing new clothes. A black tank top and what I think are shorts, but I haven't looked. "Where's Ryan?"

"I don't know. I'll find him for you, though."

"So he's here?"

"Yeah, 'course." She gives me an odd look. "Where else would he be? You're his mate."

"And he's okay?" Something shifts in my chest. My heart lurches as the memory of my out-of-body experience rushes toward the forefront of my mind. I try to shove back the image of Ryan screaming as he cradled my limp, lifeless body. It's replaced by his trembling hands as he held that bloody piece of fabric to the gaping wound in my neck, unable to even look down at me as I slowly died again, that time in his arms.

Guilt washes over me like the waves crashing onto the nearby beach. My expression crumbles as tears start to singe my lower lashes.

Misty's hand on my leg drags me back to reality. "Remember how I said you were a badass? I meant it. It's probably the nicest thing I've ever said to anyone in my life, so you should be honored, and also, Ryan is so *sensitive*." I gape at her. Now she's grinning. "He's been moping around for the last three days with that stupid bow in his hands acting like his world is ending because his mate, who just saved an entire territory from deformed, undead *zombie-wolves*, was taking a much deserved rest. So, I'll go get him, and he can be your problem again."

My jaw hangs open as she flutters out of the room, flipping her sheet of pure-gold hair over a dainty, freckled shoulder.

But an identical, albeit older, version of Misty passes her in the doorway leading to the rest of–well, wherever I am–and stops short of the bed holding a tray of vials. The woman turns to look after Misty, mumbling something to herself before righting her expression and giving me a dazzling smile.

"I'm sorry for whatever she said to you. I'm Isla."

I look from Isla to the door where her twin, younger by fifty years at least, just disappeared. "Oh."

She clicks her tongue apologetically. "You must be exhausted. It's going to take a little while to get back into your body again. The amount of magic it took to heal you was extraordinary. You're going to feel a little woozy for a while." She walks over to me, setting the tray down on a bedside table, and proceeds to check my vitals. Her small hands warm my skin as she inspects my neck and chest. She checks my pulse, smiling to herself as she looks into my eyes with a light that makes me want to blink repeatedly. "Good as new. Ryan will be so happy–"

"Can I see him?"

"Of course. He's on a walk with Sarah right now, but I let him know you were waking up, so he's probably sprinting back to the house as we speak."

As if on cue, a door slams somewhere in the depths of the house, followed by heavy, rapid footsteps. Ryan appears, bracing himself on the doorframe with his head lowered, his eyes on the ground.

He's so tense. I can see his muscles straining under his white T-shirt. His hair is ruffled and skin flushed from the sun as his knuckles go white.

Why won't he look at me?

"Ryan, honey, make sure she takes these," Isla says as she gathers a few things off the tray. She looks down at me with a knowing smile, and into my mind her voice whispers, *'He's had a hard time with all of this.'*

I watch her walk toward him. She extends a few vials of medicine, and he takes them but keeps his eyes on the floor while allowing her to pass him. He closes his eyes, whispering something under his breath, before stepping into the room and closing the door behind him.

His back to me, I hear him turning the vials against each other, the glass clicking together.

"Misty said you have my bow," I say weakly, and he goes rigid.

49
THE GILDED BOW

Ryan

I CAN'T SCRUB THE IMAGE OF AVIVA DEAD IN MY ARMS OUT OF MY HEAD. It's been several days since the battle, since the moment I put her in my uncle's arms and turned back to the ravaged scene, not knowing whether or not she survived the journey all the way to Maatua.

Three days. It was three entire days before Sydney arrived in Silverhide with news about my mate. I'd just arrived back at my territory, exhausted and in tatters, when he clapped a hand on my shoulder and used his powers to spirit us to Moonrise, then to Veiled Valley, then to Maatua. He's not as strong as Ryatt. Jumping took a toll on us both, and when we finally arrived at my grandparents' beach house, I collapsed before I even made it up their driveway.

Everything since the battle is a blur. Navvan is just... gone. The few survivors were mostly women and children who'd left the village and sought shelter in a nearby cave system. Those fifty or so people are in Silverhide now, recovering. Assimilating to a new home, new support systems.

And I'm here, in a beach house, walking up and down the driveway in the hot summer sun, trying to get my mind right.

Sydney and Sarah are here with their boys, having stopped by to visit our grandparents before returning to their home in Crescent Falls. Mom and Dad are still in Moonrise but are supposed to be here tomorrow. Sarah ties up her sneakers, squinting at me through the glare of the sun. "You don't have to go with me."

"I need to. I need to get out of here for a second." I haven't been able to leave the house since I arrived yesterday morning. I've been sitting in a chair in Aviva's bedroom looking down at my hands, imaging her blood there, imaging her there, looking up at me sightless, no longer breathing.

By some miracle, she'd pulled through. She came back to life long enough for us to get her to safety where she could get help. My grandmother's tears worked on her almost immediately, but she hasn't woken up yet.

"Has Isla given you an update yet?" Sarah asks timidly.

I pause at the top of the driveway a few feet from where she's sitting on the front steps. "Same as before."

"So she's sleeping?"

"I wouldn't call it sleep, Sarah."

Sarah stops me with a hand on my arm. "She's going to be okay. She'll wake up."

"And what will she be like when she does? How do we go back from this? I finally found my mate. I got the second chance I didn't deserve, and I've spent the last several weeks reckoning with the–the gift I was given and I... nearly lost her." I'm not sure why I'm even talking. I can't help myself, not around Sarah. "I should have stopped her from the beginning."

"Stopped her from what? Being who she is? She's a warrior, Ryan. The best. Ryatt...." She licks her lips and levels me with a look. "Ryatt and Evander have been in talks, according to Sydney, about sending their Ghost army to the Deadlands to train with *Aviva*. She saved hundreds, if not thousands, of innocent lives during that battle. She's tough as nails, okay? She's going to pull through. You have nothing to feel guilty for–"

"She's my wife," I rush out, closing my eyes as we stand in the center of the road, barely having passed through the security gate. "I'm her Alpha. When she got hurt, I couldn't do anything but sit there and try to slow the bleeding for what ended up being… hours…."

"Ryan," Sarah places her hands on my shoulders. "We've all been through this in some way, shape, or form. Your mate is alive and safe. She's whole, and she'll wake up. And when she does, you're going to take her home and start living your life again. You deserve that."

What I want to say is that so much is up in the air right now. We don't know why Hardan turned the rogues on us, creating his own army. We don't know why he turned on his own pack, and we never will, because he's dead. We don't know where the *Book of Whispers* is.

And now there's a gold-plated bow and quiver sitting in the corner of the bedroom where my wife is sleeping that just… appeared in her hands after I thought I'd lost her, like she'd been given back to me but with strings attached.

Aviva is a warrior, and she works for the Goddess now. That's clear to me, at least.

That has to mean she's going to have to use it soon, and I'm full of dread at the idea.

'Where are you?' Grandma's soft voice drifts through my head. *'She's awake and asking for you.'*

Sarah and I look at each other. Sarah heard Isla's voice through the mind-link as well. I turn back to the house, unsure if I heard her correctly.

"Go," Sarah says, giving me a shove.

I trip, catch myself, and then I'm sprinting back through the gate, up the driveway, hopping up onto the porch and darting inside.

I nearly trample my little sister in my haste to reach Aviva's room. "Hey!" she shrieks, swatting me as I rush past her.

I reach the bedroom at the end of a long hallway on the first floor and brace my hands on the doorframe, my head lowered. All I want is to see her sitting up in bed, smiling at me with that ruffled, sleepy grin she gives me every morning. All I want is to run my fingers through her curls as she leans into my touch.

But if she's awake and changed? Or awake just enough to feel pain instead of a dreamy, drugged bliss?

I'm not going to be able to handle it.

"Make sure she takes these," Grandma says, handing me three vials of medicine, one of which is her tears.

I drop my arm to allow her to pass, then I step into the room, turning for the door and closing it gently. I feel the breeze drifting in from the patio door and the open windows, carrying Aviva's scent. It's different. There's something new there that hadn't been there before.

"Misty said you have my bow."

My heart skips a beat. Slowly, I turn from the door and look down at her. She's sitting against the pillows, the strap of her tank top sliding off one shoulder as she adjusts her position to sit completely upright. Her hair is curling like mad and falling loose over her shoulders, and her eyes are… clear. Clear, and bright, the color of my favorite whiskey.

I take a breath, close my eyes, and open them again. She's still here, smiling at me.

I crush her flat against the bed, the vials of medicine forgotten and cracked on the floorboards.

"I can't breathe!" She gasps but laughs as I roll over and pull her against me, taking her face in my hands. "Hi."

"You idiot," I rasp, then I'm kissing her harder than I ever have, parting her lips with my tongue and tasting her. My mate. Her mark on my neck burns with satisfaction and relief as her scent and touch works through my body, untangling knots of stress and anxiety that've been festering for days.

"I'm sorry," she says, but I shake my head.

"I knew you were going to go after those rogues. Your eyes were glowing, Aviva, and I couldn't stop you."

"I had to."

"I know you did." I brush her hair away from her face. "Goddess, I love you. I thought I lost you."

"I–" she licks her lips and looks up at me with a strange expression on her face. "Do you believe in angels, Ryan?"

"Maybe. Why?"

"They tried to take me away, and I refused. I wasn't done here. I wasn't done with you. So I came back and… I held on as long as I could. You handed me to Ryatt, and that's my last memory until waking up a few minutes ago."

"You were severely injured." The words fall out of me, broken by emotion I've been trying to keep tamped down. "I don't have healing powers that I could have shared with you. I had to send you away. I didn't want to, but I was going to lose you if you stayed in the Deadlands."

She grips my hand. I pull her closer so we're flush against each other. "My sisters?"

"They're alive."

"Jacob and Andrew?"

"Yes," I whisper into her hair, tears blurring my vision. "They made it. Mercy and Jacob marked each other. I just took Andrew home to Freya."

"What day is it?"

I tell her, and she sighs heavily, a few tears sliding down her cheeks. "She turns twenty-one in two days. Do you think we'll be home in time to see them find out they're mates?"

"I think Andrew already knows," I tell her, closing my eyes as my body sinks against hers, relaxing for the first time in days.

But I tell her everything else. The casualties, the investigation in Navvan, the missing book. Eventually we untangle, and I walk to the corner of the room where I'd lazily discarded a sweatshirt over the huge bow leaning against the wall. Aviva sits straight up as I carry it over to her, biting my lip as I hand it to her.

"Firestone made," I say, watching her hands grip it. "Ella confirmed it."

"This is the Gilded Bow, isn't it?"

I nod. "I don't think it could be anything else."

"Where did you find it?"

"You said angels were trying to take you away. I think you brought it back with you."

Our eyes meet in the hazy midday sunlight. "What does this mean?"

"We don't know yet." War. Chaos. Battles so epic I can't form them in my mind. I don't voice these worries. But Ryatt's warning still echoes in my head.

The battle of Navvan all but confirmed his worries that something was amiss. This was just the beginning.

But I'm tired, and so is she.

I get under the sheets with her and mold my body against hers, holding her as close as possible. Images of her from the battle rage through my mind but in a new light now that this is our outcome. "You were incredible out there. Everyone agrees that you won that battle for us."

"You went over the side of a cliff with Hardan. You won the war."

"The rogues would have overrun the tribal lands. You saw what they were able to do to Navvan, even with warriors there to try to keep them out. You gave Endova and Teshka a chance. I... I spoke to your father, and the patriarch of Teshka."

She curls into me, burying her face in the crook of my shoulder. "About what?"

"Silverhide formally got an invitation to the harvest festival two months from now. You're going to be honored there."

She sits up and looks down at me, narrowing her eyes. "I am?"

"The patriarch of Teshka mentioned something about initiating you into some... round table, of sorts. I didn't really understand."

"The Firestone witches used to have knights," she says, her eyes still narrowed. "But that practice has been reduced to legend."

"Well, my aunt will be there to see us get married officially, anyway. I guess she's going to give you a medal or something."

She swats me playfully, but I can feel the nervous energy pouring off her. "I just killed a couple of rogues. That's nothing new for me."

"You killed over five dozen before the battle even began."

Her cheeks go a little pink. I sit up facing her, smoothing my hand over her cheek. I pull her in for a kiss and linger there, my lips brushing across hers.

"I want to go home," she whispers against my mouth.

"We will. Ryatt will be here tomorrow. We'll leave then."

"Then what?"

"Then we… settle in. Finally."

She rests her forehead against mine, closing her eyes. I should let her rest so she's strong enough to travel. So, I reluctantly untangle myself from the sheets and pick up the cracked vials, directing her to take the carefully measured doses that thankfully haven't leaked onto the floor, and she's asleep before I even leave the room, walking across the patio and out onto the beach.

I sit in the sand and watch the tide roll out. A shadow passes over me, and then Misty is sitting on my left side, her hair bunched on the top of her head and held in place by a huge claw clip.

We silently watch the waves for several minutes before she says, "Do you feel at home in the Deadlands?"

I ponder the question for a moment. "I do. Now I do."

"Because of Aviva?"

I nod, looking over at my sister, noticing for the first time the lines around her mouth from… frowning. I've never seen Misty stressed out before, but now?

"I heard that Mom and Dad want you to come back to Crescent Falls," I say.

"I'm not."

"I know."

She looks at me, searching my face, my expression. "Did you ever feel like you were being pulled toward something that was just out of reach? Did you feel like that when you lived in Crescent Falls? Did it change when you moved to Eastonia?"

"Are you asking if I found myself in the Deadlands?"

"I guess… yeah, I guess that's what I'm asking."

"I think I was always supposed to end up there."

She turns back toward the waves, her glacier blue eyes narrowed in thought.

"Is everything all right?" I ask, noticing the strange tension causing her shoulders to tighten.

"Something's coming, isn't it?"

Now I'm looking out at the water, at the peaceful, untouched turquoise of this absolute paradise.

"Yeah."

"I feel it," she murmurs to herself, turning to look at me with her lips parted like she's going to continue, but Grandma calls out from the deck, telling us lunch is ready.

50

TATTOOED

TWO MONTHS LATER…

Ryan

THE HARVEST FESTIVAL HAS BEEN HELD AT THE FESTIVAL GROUNDS between Endova, Teshka, and Navvan for centuries. When we arrived two days ago, leaving only a few people behind in Silverhide to make sure the animals are tended to in our absence, the wide, open space had been nothing but rolling plains.

Now, it's a city of canvas tents and twinkling lights, the air spiced with smoke and the smells of meals being cooked at each fire. Songs mingle as I walk through the festival with Aviva on my arm. I'm wearing a normal outfit. Well, not normal, actually. Mom forced me into a suit and tie with the Crescent Falls royal banner and all of my metals from my years as a warrior draped over my shoulders. Aviva is wearing that white, fur-lined dress again and a pair of new sheep-skin boots Freya and Mercy made for her, but inside of freshwater clam shells and pearls decorated her hair, her curls are woven into a tiara my mom gave her.

Sapphires twinkle in a white gold setting as we pass another fire, another row of tents. Children dart between us, squealing as their mother's shout after them.

"What are we supposed to be doing again?" I ask, looking down at my wife.

She frowns playfully, nudging me with her hip. "Getting married."

"Again? How many times are you going to put me through this?"

She rolls her eyes and scowls. "It's your own damn fault for killing that hellhound during the spring hunt. That was the deal, remember? Whoever made a clean kill first got the final decision, and you decided to marry me."

"Oh, yeah," I tease, "that does sound vaguely familiar."

She chuckles lightly as we cut through another row of tents, following a path toward a row of even larger tents that rest at the base of a hill.

The hill is the only rise for miles, and on top, an ancient stone circle sits in the glare of the full moon, which is nearly at its apex. The moon is an incredible burnt gold color tonight and just… massive. The largest moon I've ever seen in my life.

The harvest moon, of course, hence the name of the festival.

"What's on the agenda tonight? Are they cutting our arms off this time?"

"Misty told me you were dropped on your head as a baby, and I believe her," she quips, glaring at me, her eyes full of moonlight. "And no, we're not being flayed open this time. But…"

She turns us into a tent where Freya and Andrew are taking up most of the snug space. Freya is standing over Andrew with a supportive hand on his shoulder while he sits on the ground, pale and flushed, with his eyes closed as a gnarled old woman pokes a needle into his ring finger over and over again.

"He's a bit squeamish," Freya says apologetically. She flexes her hand, giving us a glimpse of the tattoo on her ring finger.

"What is it?" I ask, more than curious about the strange symbol she'll wear on her skin in place of a wedding ring.

"A hammer and a knitting needle," she says proudly. "For his forge, and my skills with textiles, of course."

I glance at Aviva. "Do we get to choose?"

Aviva shakes her head with a sly smile and motions to the absolutely ancient woman currently torturing my friend. "She's a seer. She decides on the tattoo."

Something stirs in my chest reminiscent of unease. I wonder what the symbol for our union will be but then notice that the third couple getting officially married tonight isn't in the tent with us. "Where's Jacob and Mercy?"

Aviva turns to Freya, but Andrew murmurs, "They went first, got here early to get it over with." He grimaces as the old woman pauses to inspect her work and then continues with fervor, much to his dismay. "Goddess, I hate needles."

Freya grips his shoulder in solidarity. "They got two crescent moons, crossed."

Aviva tilts her head from side to side. "That's fitting for them."

"How so?" I ask, but neither woman is listening to me. Two more couples crowd the tent, and now it's a party, even though Andrew looks like he's about to throw up or faint. Finally, he's released, and Aviva is motioned forward. She sits cross legged on a rug and extends her hand to the woman, who takes it and examines the scar running across her palm.

"So many fated mates this season," the old crone says in a gravelly voice as she examines Aviva's palm. "What an interesting change of pace."

I watch with bated breath as she rights Aviva's hand and wets a fresh tattoo needle with black ink.

Aviva sits perfectly still, barely breathing, as the needle hovers, but then the woman stops. "Interesting."

"What's interesting?" I ask, looking from Aviva to the Seer.

She begins to make little marks across Aviva's ring finger. Four long, arched lines. Talons.

My heart races as the Seer works quickly, drawing an arrow through the talons. Aviva's skin turns pink, but if she's in pain, she doesn't show it. Around the original marks, she sketches a circle, like the full moon.

Wordlessly, the woman motions me over to sit beside Aviva. My mate watches as the same marks are made on my skin.

"A beast and his hero," the seer whispers to herself. "The gods are rejoicing in your union tonight."

A chill whispers up my spine as her milky eyes meet mine. She's probably completely blind yet makes such beautiful tattoos. Still, I can feel my heart rate skyrocketing as Aviva stands and extends her hand to me. "Ready?"

I'm not sure what I'm ready for, but I am. In my eyes, we're already married. We have been for months now, but there's something special about this festival, something that hums through the air as we walk side by side toward the hill where a crowd has started to gather.

"There's thirteen couples getting married tonight," Freya explains when we reach her and Andrew. I spot Jacob and Mercy making their way toward us, following an excited Lora and Shoshannah, who skip with their lanterns as the moon starts to creep toward the center of the night sky.

"Thirteen might be a new record," Aviva replies, stepping closer to me as the crowd swells, everyone clambering for a view of the stone circle. Some groups are sitting on the side of the hill while others stay near the tents where food and drink are being shared.

I look over the top of what looks like hundreds of heads and spot my mom, dad, Sydney, and Sarah cutting through the crowd, nodding and smiling at surprised onlookers who didn't expect a group of royals to show up.

But a hush runs through the sea of people as figures appear in the stone circle.

Jerrod and the patriarch of Teshka, their priestesses, and... someone else.

The couples are called forward. I take Aviva's hand and led her up the hill. There's a chill in the air brought on by the changing of the seasons. From the top of the hill, I can see the distant forests washed in gold instead of green. Soon, we'll face another winter in Silverhide, but we are much more prepared this time. In the darkest days of winter, I can happily imagine myself tucked in my house with Aviva, watching the snowfall. I can imagine a future together where we're happy, and safe.

She knits her fingers in mine as we stand before the patriarchs, flanked on either side by Jacob, Mercy, Freya and Andrew.

But my eyes land on Kenna, who's standing between her parents on the far side of the circle, her eyes glowing silver and her shadows dancing around her in a show of her strength.

To my surprise, Maeve is on her hip, and squeals when she picks Aviva face out of the line of couple.

Aviva takes a deep breath and smiles at her while the priestesses rattle off some speech in the old tongue. Each couple is blessed, showing the priestesses our tattoos, as moonlight bathes us in gold. There's an electric feeling in the air as the moon drenches the circle, and when I look at my aunt and uncle again, I notice they're watching our every move.

Ella, dressed in a dark red cloak and dress, steps forward. She looks down the line of couples, looking less like my aunt and more like the Firestone Queen these people worship like one of their own gods.

Her eyes land on mine, and she gives me a glimpse of a smile, a wink, then looks down at Aviva.

"What you have done for your people...it was an extraordinary sacrifice that hasn't gone unnoticed. The old gods and our Goddess thank you, Aviva, Luna of Silverhide, for your service to my crown and kingdom." Ella, who bows to no one, drops to a knee in front of my wife.

A hush falls over the crowd at the base of the hill. I look down the line of couples, noticing the confusion on their faces. But then Jacob steps forward and drops a knee. Andrew follows suit, followed by Freya and the rest of the couples. Aviva is blood red as she watches, her hand gripping my fingers so tightly they're turning white.

Mercy is the only one standing. Her watery smiles reaches her green eyes as she nods at Aviva and kneels, her expression shining with pride.

Aviva whips around as the crowd below kneels, falling to their knees in a wave that rushes toward the city of tents. I spot my parents and brother kneeling and it does something to me. My heart lurches as I turn to my mate, caressing her cheek. "Aviva," I whisper as she turns from the crowd to look up at me in awe. "I love you."

"I love you," she echoes, her voice cracking over the words.

And then I kneel, brushing my lips over her knuckles, just as the moon fully illuminates the clearing.

Ella steps toward us, Ryatt by her side. He reaches into his jacket pocket and hands something to Ella–a necklace. Ella turns to a shocked Aviva and motions for her to turn to the crowd as she places the necklace on her neck. It's a moonstone...I think. It's not milky white or translucent. It's red...a soft crimson that shines to life when it touches Aviva's skin. Aviva jerks, surprised by the feeling I can sense down the bond.

"You are our commander. The leader of the Firestone army, from this day forward."

Aviva gapes up at Ella, who's roughly a foot taller than her by my estimation. But Ella's serious, queenly expression breaks just for us. She squeezes our joined hands as I rise and says, "Congratulations, you two. We'll see you for the Solstice? Right?"

"Yeah, Aunt Ella," I croak, but the words are stolen by a rush of applause coming from the crowd.

Ella hugs us, and then Uncle Ryatt is clapping me on the shoulder. But he leans in, and instead of offering congratulations, he says, "I need you both in Moonrise for a meeting soon, once your harvest is over."

With that, I watch them walk away.

Soon, we're overrun by excited family and friends of the new couples married under the harvest moon. Mom kisses me on each cheek before throwing herself on Aviva, going on and on about she's thrilled there's another red-head in the family, and how cute our future children are going to be, and how excited she is to be able to spread a week with us in Silverhide after the festival.

Dad hugs me for the first time in what might have been years, and I lean into it. They leave our side to go talk to Ryatt and Ella.

"I want to see the tattoos!" Sarah beams as she releases us from a hug, taking our hands. Sydney examines the tattoos with his mate. "Did it hurt?"

"No," I reply under my breath. It's a lie. It hurt like hell.

"He's lying, trying to be tough." Aviva grins up at me with mischief in her eyes and suddenly the only thing I care about, the only thing I want, is to go back to our tent and make love to her until morning, and then take her home.

"Sarah has a tramp stamp," Sydney says unprompted, his cheeks going red.

"I do not! He's drunk, don't listen to a word he says!" She howls with laughter and swats her mate on the chest.

"The Deadlands makes great—wine," he hiccups, laughing. "Terrible whiskey, though."

I laugh and smile as my family gathers around us again, feeling like…like everything is fine, for the first time in years.

I take Aviva's hand, and she looks up at me, smiling knowingly. "What do you want to do now?"

"Let's go home."

5 1

EPILOGUE

Aviva

THE FIRST FLAKES OF SNOW FALL FROM THE SKY AS I WATCH RYAN trying to herd everyone in position. Bundled against the cold in a wool coat Freya and I worked tirelessly on for the last three weeks, I step to the side, finding myself in the center of the crowd standing in the middle of the village of Silverhide. I watch my mate and his Beta, James, nudge families together and run back and forth toward a tripod where Ryan's camera rests, facing us, to gauge whether all one-hundred and fifty people are in view of the lens.

Ryan stands behind the camera with his hands up, his hair dusted with snow. "Okay. Nobody move!"

A few excited giggles whisper through the front of the crowd where the numerous children are arranged. I glance around, watching as James joins Dahlia's side, their baby on her hip. The baby girl finally has a name. Cosette, named after a friend of Dahlia, but they call her Cossie for short. Other babies coo and choke on soft cries throughout the crowd. All five women who were expected to have babies on Silverhide territory this summer had successful labors. I'd assisted a few, which had been healing in a way I hadn't expected. Now, after the battle of Navvan, several new families have joined our pack. Mostly women and children whose fathers and brothers were lost when Hardan took over, but a few of the warriors from Navvan were able to get their families out in time, and now they're here, living in cottages scattered across the farm lands and inner village.

I smile as I catch the eyes of one woman in particular. She lost her Navvan husband and has two young toddlers with her, but found her mate here, in Silverhide, within minutes of crossing the territories boundary.

The summer after the war was a rich, bountiful season in so many ways.

"Seriously, do not move!" Ryan rasps from the tripod, adjusting the setting on his camera.

"We're freezing, Alpha. Hurry up!" Andrew's voice echoes directly behind me where he's standing with his arm roped around Freya's shoulder. I glance to my right, finding Jacob and Mercy. He's nuzzling her neck, and she's blushing like mad, but the happiness in her eyes makes my heart melt.

Standing on my toes, I spot Lora and Shoshannah, who're staying with our pack for the winter. They'll return to Endova in the spring and currently live with Jacob and Mercy, but I see them every day.

Shoshannah is already participating in warrior training. I run my fingers over the moonstone necklace, wondering if one day she'll have a necklace like this, too.

Ryan presses a button on the camera and sprints toward us. "Ten seconds! Okay? No one blink. I'm not doing this a second time. Three pictures back to back!"

A mumble of understanding passes through the crowd as they part to allow him to rush to the center, taking his position beside me, his Luna.

"Ready?" he asks, panting, his hand sliding across my back to rest on my hip.

"Eight, nine–" James shouts, and then a flash blinds everyone.

Several choruses of, "I blinked!" are shouted over the crowd, followed by laughs.

Ryan huffs a breath, counting to three before another flash lights the air in the center of the village. Lifted giggles break out through the crowd again.

"One more," he says under his breath.

"You haven't smiled," I whisper to him.

"This is an impossible task."

"Just smile once–for me." I take his free hand in mine.

"I'm going to lift you up so we can get your belly in the picture," Andrew says behind us. Freya squeals, telling him to stop.

They have a baby on the way, a baby that'll be making its arrival this spring, within a few days of Mercy and Jacob's baby.

And ours.

But Ryan doesn't know that yet.

"Smile," I whisper, resting his hand over my belly and covering it with my own.

He looks down at me in confusion. I smile up at him with a pleading look in my eyes. We've been trying unsuccessfully for months. I just found out. I haven't told anyone yet.

"Aviva?" he says, his voice wobbling over my name. "Are you–are we–"

"Yes," I whisper, tears blurring my vision just as the flash goes off for a third and final time.

While the rest of the crowd laughs and sighs in relief that this photoshoot is over, Ryan leans down, brushing his lips over mine before curling his body around me, kissing me deeply, a tear sliding down his cheek.

I reach up and cup his cheek, laughing as the snow falls around us. He rests his forehead against mine and laughs, pulling me close so I'm crushed to him.

"I love you so much," he says into my hair.

I wrap my fingers into his jacket, looking over his shoulder at the two white wolves watching us from afar. They turn and disappear into puffs of mist in the snow, carried away by a phantom breeze.

* * *

"I don't want you handling any of these chemicals anymore," Ryan says with his back to me. He's wearing the poorly knitted sweater I made for him that he refuses to let me unweave and start anew. It was my first attempt, in my defense. The navy blue wool brings out the blue in his stormy, dark eyes as he turns to look at me over his shoulder, hanging the three prints of our pack up to dry. He looks at me with so much love in his eyes that my body responds, my skin warming, and tingles ghost down my spine.

He looks me up and down, giving me his signature cocky smile. "The pictures turned out terrible."

"You knew that was going to happen. Nobody in Silverhide takes anything seriously. It's a pack trait, something their Alpha must have ingrained in them."

He arches a brow. I smile, leaning on the doorframe. Our bedroom is mere steps away. Our bed. Our warm quilts. What do I have to do to get him there, preferably without clothes on?

His eyes drop from my face to my chest. It's warm in our house with the fire raging in the living room, so I'm in a tank top, and his gaze makes my skin tingle and nipples harden under the fabric. His pupils expand as he slowly looks up at me again. "Go get in bed."

I turn and pad into the bedroom, my heart rate skyrocketing as I hear him close the door to his darkroom and follow after me. It's dark in here, too, the light off, and through the window I see the snow piling thick, casting the village and fields beyond in white. In the darkness, he comes up behind me, pulling me against him with a hand splayed over my stomach.

His mouth finds my neck, kissing bruises onto my skin as I close my eyes and sink into his firm, heated touch.

He pushes me onto the bed where I watch him pull the terrible sweater off his frame and toss it in a corner. The dim, silver, snowy light plays over his broad muscles as he walks to me. My mate. My husband. The love of my life.

The father of my child.

It's gentle and easy. We know each other now after months together. He knows where to kiss me, where to touch me, like my body is second nature to him and his to me. He doesn't knot me this time. There's no need for that now. This is just for us. A celebration, a reminder of peace, of a warm, happy home and a pack that's thriving with us at helm.

Afterward, I lie beside him, running a finger around the tattooed moon on his ring finger. We haven't questioned what the symbols mean yet. We haven't talked about the necklace. We returned to Silverhide after the festival and acted like nothing had happened this summer. I've been grateful for it, honestly. If I'm ever called to be a warrior again, I will go, but for now, this is all that matters.

"Next spring I'll start on adding two more rooms to the house." He draws lazy circles on my lower back, which has been aching for weeks. I haven't been sick yet, thankfully, but based on how Freya and Mercy are faring, I know it's coming.

"What will the second room be for?"

"If we have twins," he sighs, shaking his head. "I'm a twin, remember? We could end up with two pretty easily."

I rest my hand on my still flat stomach. "I think it's just her in there."

"Her?" His touch halts on my spine. "How do you know?"

"I just feel it. It's strange, but I just know that it's a *her*, and she's here with us. Tiny. Just a flicker of who she'll be, but she's there, and she's safe and warm and really likes… chocolate."

He chuckles. "I was wondering why you'd been spending so much time with Mrs. Craw in the kitchen. She makes the meanest chocolate muffins."

I lick my lips at the thought, suddenly starving. "Are you disappointed?"

"About what?" He sounds sleepy as his fingers pick up their lazy exploration of my spine.

"That I think she's a girl?"

"Oh, Aviva." He rolls over from his back to his side to face me, pulling me close. "No. I'm not upset at all."

"But you're an Alpha. She won't be your heir–"

"What are you talking about? Of course, she will be." He runs his fingers through my hair. "She will be an Alpha, like her father. She'll rule Silverhide, and one day, the Deadlands will be hers as well as Alpha King–Alpha Queen. She'll be sweet and beautiful–like me–too."

I wrinkle my nose at him, but he smiles, chuckling. He continues, "She'll be headstrong and wild like her mother. She'll be a fearsome warrior. She'll be brave, like you. Beautiful, like you. And we'll love her."

"We'll love her," I echo, closing my eyes. He rests his chin on the top of my head as my heartbeat begins to slow and sleep creeps through my body, dragging me under.

But I wake in the middle of the darkest night I can imagine to Ryan sitting up, still as a statue.

"What's wrong?" I whisper into the snowy darkness.

Ryan looks around then slides out of bed, dressed in nothing but boxers as he pulls on a pair of pants and his discarded sweater. I follow, of course, not liking the tension I feel pouring off him through our bond.

I pull a robe over my nightdress and slip into my sherpa lined slippers at the front door, following him outside where he stands on the porch and looks up. A flash of black darker than the cloudy, socked-in night sky splits the air in two.

Ryan doesn't look back at me as he heads down the steps with me following close behind him, unease tightening my chest to the point it's hard to breathe.

Ryatt is walking toward us dressed in black armor–the kind with scales made of impenetrable leather. His face is cast in shadow and set in a serious, vengeful expression.

"What are you doing here?" Ryan asks with an edge to his voice.

There's only one reason Ryatt would show up unannounced in Ryan's territory.

Something's wrong.

I pull my robe tighter around my middle to fight the cold creeping over my skin, and it's not from the bitter late fall air, no.

Ryatt's eyes sweep over Ryan's face. "Alpha King Jaxon of Tarsian is dead."

Ryan and I both jolt to full awareness.

Ryatt doesn't give us a chance to react. "His son, Cole, has proclaimed himself the Alpha King."

"Well, he's the heir," Ryan says slowly, but we can both tell, based on Ryatt's expression, that there's something sinister about this.

"He killed his own father," Ryatt says like someone took a rake to his vocal cords. "Ryan–"

"Why are you here?" Ryan repeats, his hands curling into fists. "What happened?"

It's the middle of the night. Ryatt is dressed in armor. And now, he's looking right at me.

"Tarsian is at war. The Alphas loyal to King Jaxon are revolting against Cole. Cole has an army. How, we don't know, but..." Ryatt's expression shifts from serious to pained. "The University was attacked a few hours ago."

My heart stops. I grope for Ryan's arm and squeeze.

"Misty's been taken," Ryatt breathes.

MISTY'S STORY BEGINNS

Misty

TWO WHITE WOLVES IN A CLEARING.

Their bodies made of mist and aether, standing side by side.

Mates. A marvel of second chances and extraordinary fate.

Two white wolves turn toward the sunrise knowing what they must leave behind; what he sacrificed for those he loved and her refusal to let him go into death alone.

Two white wolves stand over their earthly bodies. He, battered and still.

She, going into death with eyes open, cupping her mate's face between her graceful hands, her eyes locked on his at the moment of her dying breath.

Their last words had been simple. I love you.

They always had.

They'd promised this instant in stolen moments, in private corners, when there was nothing but the stars to light their way.

I will not stay here without you.

I will not leave you behind.

And so, it was.

Two white wolves face the sunrise.

. . .

I PEEL MY CHEEK FROM THE PAGES OF THE MASSIVE BOOK SPRAWLED across my desk, blinking into the soft glow of the sun pouring through the window. The tan stone walls and crappy wood furniture come into view, replacing another vision of dense forests and moonlit plains. "Shit," I whisper, running my hand over my face, then through my hair as I blink down at the book. What had I been doing? Oh, right. Studying for an upcoming exam about the Rosetta people.

I lean back in my creaky chair and look down at the page, reading out loud, "The Rosetta people thrived in Eastonia three to four thousand years before the first Firestone witches appeared and we're believed to have been the first worshippers of the Moon Goddess who gifted them with the power to shift into creatures of the night." Creatures of the night. Owls, foxes, the works. I rub my tired eyes and close the book.

I didn't really need to study for this test. It's one of those early fall semester things to make sure me, and my fellow archeology students entering their senior year at the ancient University of Tarsian, considered the first university like... ever... in our world, haven't totally fallen behind over summer break.

I'm a straight A student. My professors and fellow students think I'm a know-it-all, which I've always taken as a compliment. Nothing about this program has challenged me so far, and I don't expect it to. I'm exactly where I need to be, surrounded by books and intellects who can challenge every theory and point of view I have.

I tuck the book in my backpack, deciding to go across campus to the library to find something bigger, more interesting, knowing the librarians are already sick of my presence in their domain, but outside of my dorm room, I spend most of my time in the library. It's six levels of books—some more modern, including copies shipped from Crescent Falls covering subjects like modern medicine, engineering, and energy, but my interest has always been in the ancient tomes locked away in the three lower levels, deep underground.

The air carries a salty breeze that reminds me of Maatua as I toss my backpack on my bed and strip out of the pajamas I'd hadn't bothered taking off when I woke up a few hours ago and immediately hit the books. I pull on a pair of black athletic shorts and a gray tank top to beat the heat during my walk across campus but tuck a sweatshirt in my bag. It gets rather chilly in the library.

I'm just turning to the mirror to try to brush out the tangles in my hair when Georgia, my roommate and best friend, rushes inside our room.

She nearly knocks her head on the sloping stone ceiling in her haste to get inside and slams the door shut, her eyes wild with excitement.

"Did someone die?" I laugh, pulling my hair into a ponytail as she fights for breath.

Georgia dumps her bag on the floor and pulls a black envelope out of the pocket of her jean shorts.

I gape at her. My heart bounces, then stops. "Shut up. Is that what I think it is?"

"It was in our mailbox," Georgia pants, her tightly curled black hair bouncing off her shoulders as she nods. Georgia is gorgeous, and the moment I saw her, I decided we were going to be friends. That was the same day my dad reluctantly dropped me off at Tarsian University two years ago, a massive campus in the heart of the second largest city in Tarsian, Serpentia, on the southern coast of Tarsian. Georgia has dark skin and large, expressive brown eyes. She's fit and sharp tongued, just like me. When we were freshmen, we haggled with the room directors to let us kick our old roommates to the curb so we could room together, and we've been together like this ever since.

She's from the Roguelands, but her mother is from Crescent Falls, one of those curious wolves who came to Eastonia in search of adventure after the veil was lifted and found her mate instead. There's a lot of students from families like that here. Students come from all over to attend this prestigious university, which specializes in the natural sciences, art, and history.

Within the alabaster walls of what used to be a grand fortress during Firestone times, the campus is a hotbed of activity. The academics are superb, sure.

But so are the parties.

"Did you see who delivered it!?" I snatch the envelope from her and rip it open.

"I didn't." She steps up behind me to read the words over my shoulder. There's only a few things handwritten in neat, black ink.

"Tonight, 9:00 PM, the Bell Tower?" I say, turning to face her. "The Bell Tower? What kind of party can be had in the Bell Tower? It's tiny!"

She shrugs, buzzing with nervous energy. "This has to be from the Arcane Umbrae, right? Every rumor we've heard, there's always a black envelope mentioned."

I point to the letterhead. In red wax, a snake is twisted in a figure eight, eating its own tail. "This is from Arcane Umbrae, all right." I'd recognize the symbol anywhere. It's dotted all over Serpentia, carved into the ancient flagstone side streets, carved into doors in random inns and bars. The Order of Arcane Umbrae has been around for centuries and began at this very university, according to legend. It's a heavily guarded secret, so much so that no one knows who's a part of it, or what it's about, or what secrets they've been chosen to guard. But occasionally, they threw parties, always in a different location, and I've spoken to a few people that have gone, and they were too nervous to give me any details about what happens during those exclusive, secret events.

As a historian, and a know-it-all, I've been dying to get this letter. I can die happy now. My life's work has been fulfilled.

"These came with it," Georgia whispers as she reaches for her bag, pulling out two black masks.

"Creepy," I whisper, smirking. "I do love a masked ball."

"We need dresses, stat."

"Shopping?" I ask excitedly, and she nods, and then we're squealing and jumping up and down as we throw away any plans we might have had to be good students and study for our upcoming exams.

An hour later, I'm roving the racks in a boutique with a massive pair of sunglasses on my face to hide the fact we stopped for lunch and shared a bottle of wine to celebrate our good luck. Wine goes straight to my head, and I feel a slight headache forming right behind my left eye as Georgia holds up a short black dress for me to examine that I can tell came from Moonrise. "I like it. Try it on."

"You need something, too."

I wave my hand in dismissal. Georgia has no idea that I already have a dress picked out for this very moment. I bought it two years ago after I first heard the rumors of the Order of Arcane Umbrae in anticipation of getting my invite, which never came. Until now.

I choose a few dresses to try on but settle on a pair of shoes instead. As we walk to the next store to check out wares shipped in from Veiled Valley, Georgia asks, "So, do you think Nate had anything to do with this? He's part of the order, isn't he?"

"I believe so," I reply with a shrug. "Even if he is, he can't tell me." I bite my tongue to stop myself from admitting I rummage through his things every time I stay over at the apartment he shares with two roommates across town. Nate pops up in my mind. Tall and lean, he has a runner's body, which makes sense because he runs long distance for TU's track team. Dark brown hair, brown eyes, handsome and… well rounded. I enjoy his company. I believe we might be mates, which is an exciting thought. I'd be, like, the first person in my family to find their mate in a normal way instead of a life-threatening twist of fate.

He's twenty-two already, so he knows we're mates, but my guess is that he's keeping it a secret until my upcoming birthday this winter so he can propose when I feel the bond for the first time and then tell me all his dirty Order secrets.

That's not the reason I'm dating him… of course. I love him. I really do.

"Should you, like, tell him you got the invite?" she asks, looping her arm in mine as we walk across the narrow, cobblestone street toward another row of shops built from bright, alabaster stone with red, pitched roofs.

"No, I think I'll surprise him. If he's actually part of the order, of course. If not, I'll tell him all about it tomorrow!"

We laugh together, both daydreaming about what the night has in store for us, when a quartet of black wolves blocks our progress down the street. I drag Georgia to a halt, a chill snaking down my spine as a group of men steps through a door, surrounding the man in the center of the group.

His head is down as he ducks out of the shop. The hot, tropical sun illuminates his short, sandy blond hair and tan skin.

Georgia grips my forearm, startled, then lowers her head.

"What are you doing?" I hiss.

"That's Prince Cole," she hisses back under her breath.

Instead of bowing my head right away, I narrow my eyes at the man and his entourage. He's dressed in all black–a fine fitting suit that shows off the promise of a very broad, muscular build. He's clean shaven, handsome in a polished way that screams royalty and privilege.

His wolves and guards, I assume, pass us by. I bow my head ever so slightly, but keep my eyes on him out of sheer curiosity.

The Alpha King of Tarsian lives far away, in Oasia. What is his son doing here?

The group passes us, and just as I'm starting to lift my head, Prince Cole looks right at me.

Stunning gray eyes hold mine for a fraction of a second before he looks away. My chest tightens. I've forgotten how to breathe.

"I wonder what brought him to town?" Georgia rushes out, tugging me away, but I'm still watching the group walk down the street.

"There's unrest in Oasia. Maybe he's here trying to find new investors for his father's superhighway."

Georgia clicks her tongue. "Still bitter about that, huh?"

I take a deep breath, watching the group turn down a street. The prince stops in his tracks and turns to look right at me again.

I straighten my shoulders, narrowing my eyes at him. I swear, even from this distance, I see him smirking as he disappears from view.

"I'm not bitter. I'm just… peeved that busting through the desert to build a highway, when no one here even has cars, was more important than preserving an archeological dig site." In fact, I'd been torn from that dig site after weeks spent waist deep in sand at the location of what we believed to be an ancient temple, buried for millennia under hundreds of feet of sand. Now, it's likely gone, paved over.

Fury simmers in my blood.

"Come on, we need to get ready. We need to eat something. I've heard these parties are ragers, Misty. Do you want to be on your deathbed with a hangover tomorrow?"

She tugs me forward, walking in the opposite direction of the group of guards and their precious prince.

As we head back to campus, enjoying the warm, fall heat, a voice in my head warns me not to go to the party.

I ignore the voice–like usual.

Thank you for reading! While you're waiting for book 11, please check out my new romantic suspense novel, The Boy Who Died.

ALSO BY BELLA MOONDRAGON

The Alpha King's Breeder series:

Bought by the Alpha: The Alpha King's Breeder Book 1

Loved by the Alpha: The Alpha King's Breeder Book 2

Lost by the Alpha: The Alpha King's Breeder Book 3

Luna of the Alpha: The Alpha King's Breeder Book 4

Legacy of the Alpha: The Alpha Kings's Breeder Book 5

Daughter of the Alpha: The Alpha King's Breeder Book 6

Descendants of the Alpha: The Alpha King's Breeder Book 7

Shadow of the Alpha: The Alpha King's Breeder Book 8

Son of the Alpha: The Alpha King's Breeder Book 9

The Luna's Vampire Prince series:

The Culling

The Kingdom

The Conquered

Pregnant With Four Alphas' Babies

Chosen As the Breeder

Mated to Four Alphas

Threats Against the Breeder

At War for the Breeder

The Stolen Breeder

Four Alphas, Four Babies

Becoming the Luna Queen

Descendants of the Breeder

Desired by the Devil series

Whispers of the Devil

Banter of the Devil

The Mafia Kings series

Indebted to the Mafia King

<u>Loved by the Mafia King</u>

Claimed by the Mafia King (releases 11/15/2024)

Writing as B. Moon

The Boy Who Died

Sign up for Bella's newsletter here.

Follow Bella on Facebook here.